LOVE HACK

SERIES BOX SET

ALLYSON LINDT

ACELETTE PRESS

This book is a work of fiction.

While reference might be made to actual historical events or existing locations, the names, characters, places and incidents are either the product of the author's imagination or are used fictitiously, and any resemblance to actual persons, living or dead, business establishments, events, or locales is entirely coincidental.

Manufactured in the United States of America
Acelette Press

HIS HACKER

ONE

Jared's fingers twitched toward the slew of jumbled shot glasses on the shelf in front of him. He shouldn't be browsing the gift shop of the hotel he was staying in; he should be on the same conference call as his best friend and business associate, helping to wrap up the biggest sale they'd had in their sights in months. He could have listened in. Just this once. Kept himself on mute and not said anything.

Compulsion won out, and he turned back to the shelf of shot glasses. His fingers flew across the rims and, within seconds, the entire section was a series of straight, neat lines.

He exhaled loudly. Okay, so maybe he couldn't have listened quietly on the phone and kept his mouth shut.

And none of this junk would make a good souvenir for his sister. She'd asked for something simple, but everyone brought back tiny trinkets from Las Vegas. He was halfway to the gift shop exit when a tucked-away display caught his attention. The digital photo frames were tacky as hell, trimmed with gaudy, gold Greek temples, and was that supposed to be a crown of leaves? Alyssia's entire desk was lined with photos. It was perfect.

Great. A line at the checkout. His toes tapped a tuneless beat inside his shoes as he waited for his turn to pay. At least waiting would give him something else to think about for a couple of seconds longer.

He couldn't help checking his watch as he stepped from the store. He'd killed six minutes and fifty-four seconds.

Tate, Vivian, and he would be heading to dinner as soon as the call was done. His associates were staying in the same hotel. But until then, Jared's schedule was open. *Time to sequester myself in my room and get some work done.* He'd get back to the proposal sitting in his briefcase for new call center hardware. Answer the emails with red exclamation points on them that had come in during his flight.

His gaze tripped around the lobby as he pulled out his phone and unlocked it. People came and went. The couple checking in, she with silver hair cropped short, he in jeans and a T-shirt and probably thirty years younger, spent more time gazing at each other than looking at anyone else. Even across the room their adoration was almost tangible.

Too bad it won't last. People never took the time to figure out their own oddities before they hooked up with another person. But over the years, he'd assembled a solid algorithm of what did and didn't work for him in a personal relationship.

He didn't expect perfection from a significant other, but there was no reason the relationship couldn't be flawless. The math was there to support it, as long as the variables were right. In a way it was harsh, but it hadn't let him down yet.

A twinge of envy echoed in his chest as he pulled his attention away from the loving couple, aka pending heartbreak. His eyes grew wide when his gaze landed on the woman whose black hair—complete with a Kool-Aid red streak down one side—just brushed her jaw.

Back to your hotel room. Work awaits. But the woman had his attention, and his feet refused to move. Even from this distance, she screamed *chaos* in a way that made his fingers twitch with the need to bring order. And at the same time, he couldn't stop staring.

Her hot pink T-shirt draped off one shoulder, exposing a strap of the black tank top underneath, and her messenger bag hugged her body enough to highlight perky breasts and round hips. Her lips moved as her gaze traveled the tablet in her hands. She glanced up occasionally when she swiped the screen, and then went back to whatever had her so engrossed.

Beautiful. The thought caught him off guard. It was true, her face was attractive and her bag enhanced every seductive curve, but something else had captivated him. He studied her a little longer as she shuffled at half-speed toward an unknown destination. It was the intensity she read her tablet with. Her gaze and focus were enthralling.

Being able to pay attention was an important quality in any individual. Not that he was keeping track. Even if his thoughts were taunting him with images of stripping her shirt off and exploring her bare skin. He had way too much work to do this trip to deal with something like base lust.

He turned toward the elevator.

He exhaled as he stepped into a waiting car. *Don't think about the call. You've got other work to do. Like making sure this sale and the next aren't repeats of those in the past.*

His eyes grew wide when the woman with the tablet stepped through the closing doors, only looking up long enough to push a number on the control panel. The elevator sealed them off from the rest of the world, and she continued to stare at the device in her hands.

What's she reading that's so fascinating? He inched a step closer and peered over her shoulder. The faint scent of citrus teased him and kicked his pulse up a notch. His mouth twisted in ambivalence when he saw what had her attention. "You know none of that's accurate, right?"

He hid his wince. This was why he didn't talk to anyone on sales calls except the technical people.

She spun, eyes almost as dark as the eyeliner rimming them taking a moment to focus on his face. Her confusion vanished in a smirk.

"Which bit of it?" Between words, she clacked something against her teeth. A barbell—she had her tongue pierced. There was absolutely nothing logical about the accessory. But knowing as much didn't stop the blood from draining from his head and racing toward his lower extremities. She traced the metal ball along the back of her teeth, gaze never leaving his face.

His thoughts teased him with images of what it would be like to feel the piercing in other places, and his cock twitched in response. *Down, boy. Don't go there.* "The entire article." She hadn't balked at his comment. Might as well push the subject.

She glanced at the device in her hands, as if she'd forgotten it was there, and then back at him.

Completely captivating gaze.

"I think you're being a bit extreme." She tapped her nails on the edge of the frame, attention locked on him. "You can't tell me things like gateways, the NSA, and the deep web don't exist."

A shimmer of appreciation pinged inside him. She was reading tech and had been absorbed by it. *Sexy.* He couldn't think of a better word for it. Except it didn't make the information any more correct.

"I'm not saying they don't exist. Just not in that capacity. It's a sensationalist article meant to strike an irrational fear into people." He knew better than to unleash his unfiltered thoughts on the general public, but something about the challenge in her expression told him she didn't mind. It wasn't as though he was trying to extend the conversation. Or maybe he was just a little.

The car came to a stop, and the door slid open on what he assumed was her floor. Attention never leaving his face, she reached behind her and pressed the *Door Open* button. "That's the point."

He needed to cut this conversation short. Too bad his mouth didn't agree. "To read something that's wrong?"

She dropped her tablet into her messenger bag, eyes never leaving his for more than a few seconds. "Someone obviously thinks it's true. Which means there's value in being able to plainly state why it's not possible, and knowing if it actually is."

"But that's why computers are fantastic. Only so many possibilities exist, and the things they mention in the article—" he nodded at her tablet, "—aren't on the list."

"Not yet, anyway. I love this place, you know?"

The circuits in his head tripped and stumbled, trying to keep up with the conversation. Time to regain control. "I'm not seeing the connection to the *Wired* article."

"No connection. It's my first time here, so I'm still awestruck. It's amazing, right? All the lights, the people, the energy."

Now he had enough information to switch tracks and fall back into the discussion. "It's fixed odds, careless dreams, and when it's light outside, really dirty."

What was wrong with him? Besides the fact he couldn't get a handle on this woman and his fantasy was still running rampant, having now stripped her down to her panties. Did she taste like the faint lemon and plum drifting off her? *None of those thoughts are logical. Get a grip.*

"Once again, that's the point." Enthusiasm shone in her eyes as she talked. "It's a chance to experience things that aren't a part of everyday life. For instance, how many of those couples downstairs will only spend the one night together and then never see each other again?" She ducked her head as the question trailed off, but not before he saw the red flush her cheeks. "Sorry. I get carried away. Guys like you probably have more important things on their minds."

The alarm on the door protested at being held open so long. A part of his brain said the sound was another hint it was time to cut things short. *Soon.*

"Guys like me?" One thing he never did was one-night stands. But just then, studying each move and gesture and fighting a raging hard-on at the thought of trailing his fingers over her bare skin, he wondered if she was on to something.

She met his gaze again. "Jared Tippins, Director of Information Technology for Skriddie Bust Media, and world-renowned network security genius."

An uncomfortable chill crept through him, and he shook it off. She could have recited that off his business card, it was so eerily succinct and accurate. Except the bit about being a security genius. That was implied. Was he supposed to know her? Great, he was fantasizing about screwing a prospective client or something. But he would have remembered her. "We haven't met."

"Not really." She extended the hand not holding the elevator open. "I'm Mikki."

Which didn't clear anything up, but did give a name to his out-of-control thoughts. The strain against his jeans had already passed uncomfortable. When her warm, smooth palm nestled in his, it only got worse.

Something hummed in his jeans' pocket. He dragged himself out of his own head, forcing away the arousal and trying to shake off the disorienting cobwebs left by the fantasy.

She nodded at his waist, playful smirk dancing on her lips, and leaned in close enough to whisper, "You're vibrating."

The heat brushing his skin, her teasing voice, and those full lips... He was seconds from suggesting they take this back to her room so he could add some reality to the fantasy. Except, even if she wasn't everything chaotic and unpredictable, his work phone was buzzing. No one was texting him this late unless it was critical.

"Duty calls." He gave her an apologetic smile.

"Enjoy work." She laughed lightly and spun on her toe. "See you around," she called over her shoulder.

It took the last of his willpower to drag his gaze from her ass before the elevator doors cut off his view. It wasn't the round shape, or the hint of wiggle—though both were incredible. It was the bounce in her step. *Right. Work. Back to it.*

His creeping good mood sank with the extra gravity of the rising elevator when he saw the text from Tate. He rubbed his forehead to chase away the tension, but a headache still threatened at the simple note. *Dial in. Now.*

That was a bad sign. Jared reached his floor, headed toward his room, and pulled up the info in his calendar. He was already calling before he slid the keycard in the lock. Tate wanted him there to finalize details; that was all. *If only I believed it.*

Jared swiped in the call pin and dropped into the chair in front of the desk in his room—alone. Regret murmured in his thoughts. *How can I be so disappointed about letting someone I just met run off?*

The line clicked into a conversation already in progress, and it took a few seconds for his ears to adjust to the speaker's heavy accent. It was why the call was happening after business hours. Skriddie specialized in electronic security for retail stores, and this potential client was overseas, building sites for a wide variety of companies. That was what made the sale so big—they had dozens of customer sites that would need to be verified, tested, and put through the wringer. All of them worth millions, and most of them high-profile.

As an independent third party, Skriddie would be responsible for certifying that each site, and all the customer information contained there, was safe from hackers.

Tate cut through a pause in the dialogue. "I think someone just joined the call."

"Good evening, or morning, everyone. This is Jared Tippins, director of technology for Skriddie Bust Media." He kept his tone light and friendly, despite the anxious march dancing through every limb. "I'm sorry I'm late." Which was ridiculous, since he wasn't originally invited, but professionalism was what it was. Easy enough to remember, now that the blood wasn't rushing away from his brain.

"Glad you could join us." It was unlikely anyone on the call had heard the tension in Tate's greeting, but after almost three decades of friendship, Jared knew how bad a sign it was. "We just have some questions for you before we finalize everything—"

"*If* we finalize anything," someone corrected him.

Jared snarled silently at the receiver, glad no one on the phone could see him. He swallowed his retort and kept his mouth shut, waiting for more details.

"Right, of course." Tate's chuckle sounded like it had been strained through a cheese grater. "Jared, we have their head developer with us, so feel free to get as technical as you need to address their concerns."

Which, Jared knew from experience, didn't mean he could get technical at all. He'd have to walk a fine line between letting the developers know he was knowledgeable, and not boring anyone else listening in.

And then the questions began. Five minutes in, Jared's grasp on not getting too in depth slipped. After ten minutes, he tossed all filters by the roadside as he was assaulted with some of the most obscure, low-level questions he'd ever encountered. Ranging from things that hadn't been an issue since the internet was born, to little-known, cutting-edge techniques he knew almost no one had dared implement yet.

He handled it all, the entire time curious about where the third degree had come from and confident he answered every concern with zero error margin.

"Jared." He recognized the voice at this point as their developer. "Do you test for all these possible holes in your own network?"

Jared choked down a sarcastic laugh. Did he monitor his own systems for weaknesses no one had heard of in a decade, or wouldn't be familiar with for at least six more months? "Of course we do. We conduct internal audits on a regular basis, and my staff is encouraged to keep current on any and all new developments in the technology industry."

The muscles in his neck tightened, and the beginning of an ache throbbed behind his temples. This was too much like the other two lost sales they'd been sure they'd had in the bag. Both contracts lost to NetSafe Systems. He clenched and unclenched his free hand. And Jared was almost convinced NSS was behind whatever was leading to these lines of questions.

At first he and his colleagues at Skriddie tried to convince themselves it was just sour grapes, that they were pissed off NSS was owning their pitches so much better. But the pattern was too familiar. Every time Skriddie competed with the other company for a client, the question of internal network security came up.

But at least that meant Jared could anticipate the next question and could head off the concern before anyone asked. His network was perfect, and he was certain of that. Time to restore some confidence. "We have copies of those internal and independent system audits. We, of course, would never expect you to put your faith in someone who doesn't hold themselves to the same security standards as their clients. I'll send them to the group as soon as this call is finished."

"We'd appreciate that, thank you." That would be one of their executives.

"Fantastic." The dash of stress still flavored Tate's reply. "So if no one has further questions, we can have the contract ready for you tonight and schedule a kickoff meeting for early next week."

"I think we'd like to hold off on that," another of their managers said. "We still have significant concerns and need time to discuss our options internally while we conduct due diligence."

"Of course." Tate's tone was too cheerful. "Let us know if we can answer any more questions at all. We're here for you."

Jared muted his phone and kept silent as they exchanged pleasantries and wrapped up. *Due diligence my ass. There's nothing to see.* The moment he disconnected, he let out the roar of frustration that had been building in his chest for several minutes. It echoed harmlessly off the surrounding walls.

The pattern was exactly the same as the last two times. That wouldn't stop him from sending off the information he'd promised. But experience told him it wasn't going to matter.

Email sent, he dialed Tate and started talking as soon as the line clicked on. "We're fucked. You know that, right?"

"Intimately." The phony professionalism had vanished from Tate's voice. "You with V?"

Vivian, their counterpart from operations, was still in her room working. "No."

"So she doesn't know yet. Lucky her." Tate's sigh clattered over the receiver. "I say we grab a taxi and find a local place where we can get so drunk we forget this happened until tomorrow morning when NSS rubs our noses in it."

"We can't." Jared didn't know where Tate had gotten the notion taking the night off was a good idea. "We have to track this down."

"You've vetted this rumor five billion times already." Tate sounded exhausted. "Staying up all night for the five billion and first time looking for something that doesn't exist won't do you any good."

"You want answers as much as I do." Jared let the irritation leak into his retort. "If the rumors are still out there, we've missed something."

"What are you going to check that you haven't yet?"

"I'll figure that out when I get there." Finding answers was just as important to his friend. Then again, Tate had a point. They didn't know where to look next. He could drag this conversation out for the next half hour, or concede, and search for solutions while he tried to unwind. If he was going to yield, he was doing it on his terms.

"All right." Jared relented. "I'll ping Viv and then get a recommendation from the concierge."

"That was too easy. We're *not* doing karaoke."

Jared smiled at the phone. Music was his one outlet. People said it was an artistic medium, but he knew better. A good, solid song followed the same methodology as a well-written software program. There was a math to it. Only so many right answers and a series of patterns that made it pleasant and functional.

Tate was welcome to get wasted. But Jared needed a new angle to approach this problem from, and this was how he wanted to let his mind wander. "Yeah, we are."

"Pfft. Then V and I are picking your songs."

"Fine with me. Meet us in the lobby in five." Jared dialed Vivian the moment the call disconnected.

Maybe he should have chased down miss hot-pink T-shirt Mikki, who had the gorgeous eyes. At least then he'd have some satisfaction to go along with the feeling he'd just been fucked.

TWO

Mikki tossed the who's-who packet from her trade show registration back onto her hotel mattress, the page still flipped open to the page with his picture on it. Jared Tippins. As far as she was concerned, one of the greatest minds in computing, and absolutely hot at the same time.

She left her room—and her dusty clothes from setting up their booth in the exhibit hall—behind her and made her way toward the elevators. She'd gotten the peasant blouse, corset, and leather skirt she wore now at a consignment store. They made her feel seductive and bold, and she was going to find a place with loud music and lots of energy to enjoy the feeling.

Not that she'd needed the extra confidence earlier. Had she really asked him about one-night stands? The reminder flushed her skin. It was true she'd not only come out of her shell, but left it completely in the dust since Payton, but this was a new level of bold, even for outgoing her. For a moment she'd thought Jared was considering her offer, but she must have read him wrong, for as quickly as he'd brushed her off for a phone call. Guys like that had busy schedules to keep. They didn't do random hookups.

Not that she ever had before. After she'd broken up with her jerk wad ex-boyfriend, she'd become that kind of adventurous when it came to any man who wasn't him. She'd even considered the possibility a couple of times. But she'd never actually found a guy who inspired her to pursue the idea. Turned out, in her fantasy dreamland, Jared Tippins was the perfect guy to figure out how that kind of thing worked.

Outside the hotel, she grabbed the next cab in line. Speaking of firsts… "I'm looking for a club."

The cabbie met her eyes in the rearview mirror. "A specific one, or you want me to just drop you off somewhere?" His accent was heavy, his R's vanishing into the words surrounding them. He reminded her of her history teacher when they'd lived in New Jersey.

"Karaoke. The newer the equipment, the better." She could have checked online before she walked out the door, but that wasn't any fun. She'd never done something like singing in front of a room of strangers before, but it sounded fun.

"I know the perfect place." He navigated the packed streets with ease while he chatted at her. "Just dropped another group off there. They've got the latest and greatest technology. They even let people text in to get their names on the karaoke jockey's list."

Her phone buzzed in her purse. "Speaking of texting." She grabbed the device, her good mood wrinkling when she read the message from her boss, Hayden. *How'd booth setup go?*

Time to report to her keeper. It was one of the few things she'd didn't like about her job. Hayden was an okay boss, but he wasn't much on delegation. His constant need to know what all his people were up to reminded her too much of Payton. Which meant she knew how to handle him, but it still didn't make it any more pleasant to deal with. On top of that, she didn't think it was a good sign she could compare her current boss to an ex-boyfriend who'd almost torn her down completely.

Hayden always wanted to know what his people were up to when it was work related. She'd flown into Las Vegas early because she was involved with setting up their booth, so it technically meant her entire trip was work related.

She sent back a quick, *Like clockwork.*

Seconds later, another message buzzed in. *You set for your demo tomorrow morning?*

She wasn't so irresponsible she forgot what she was supposed to be doing. It was probably a good thing irritation didn't carry in text messages. She replied, *I've got it under control.*

Her recently acquired appreciation for the spontaneous meant she tried not to let much faze her. Getting hung up on the details and people's opinions had almost destroyed her once. But there was no reason to snark herself out of a good job and decent paycheck if she didn't have to.

When her phone stayed silent for longer than a few seconds, she decided she must be off the hook and tucked it away again.

After paying the cabbie, she made her way inside a club that was all neon, chrome, and incredible sound. Music blared in the background, accompanied by decent karaoke vocals, with the clang of glasses on backup.

She loved it already. She had her choice of tables, so she picked one close to the stage, ordered a drink, and settled in to decide what to sing.

Her thoughts kept drifting back to the encounter in the hotel. It was a shame Jared had to cut things short. She was such a fan girl sometimes. Normal women swooned over actors and fictional characters. She'd had to go and be odd—again—and get all wobbly about some tech guy. Not that she thought it was a bad thing. Okay, so she was a complete dork, still lingering on one simple encounter in an elevator. They'd barely exchanged words. It wasn't like he'd propositioned her.

A flat rendition of a country song she couldn't name filled the bar. She definitely wasn't singing something like that. She wanted loud, with a lot of guitar and hopefully some good orchestration.

Too bad mister tall-dark-and-smoldering wasn't the kind of nickname that rolled off the tongue. Fantasy teased her thoughts— though she could think of a couple of things she'd like to try with Jared that involved tongues. *Jared Tippins. What would it be like to spend a few hours with him?* Not just the getting naked, but picking his brain after about where he got his ideas, if it was weird being one of *the* names in the industry, and if programmers really did do it with their fingers.

But even without him, she was going to enjoy her free night before she went back to playing professional. A wolf-whistle echoed through the room, adding to the hum of her excitement. Her gaze darted around, the sound of more whistles and clapping finally drawing her eye to a group just a few tables away.

Because she'd jumped ahead a grade when she was in high school—not that she'd ever attended any school longer than six months, thanks to her dad's work—and had spent most of her time studying even through college, she'd never had any close friends or understood that kind of camaraderie. A ping of longing echoed in her chest. It looked like fun, though. Too bad friendship wasn't one of those things she could just try, and then file away if it didn't work out.

Two of them—a guy and a woman—were cheering a third man on as he walked toward the stage. Recognition tickled Mikki's thoughts. *No way. It's him.*

Jared. Yup, he was still hot in person. Nerds weren't supposed to be good looking. Most of the Fortune 500 names were faces who blended into a crowd. But this guy…tasty.

"Next up is J." The KJ's voice rang over the speakers. "Who, according to the schedule, needs to stop dragging his friends around when they just want to drink until they forget their woes."

Jared fired a smirk at his friends. "You know you love it."

Mikki dropped back into her seat. This would be worth watching just for the view. Jared's brown hair was cut short on the sides and spiked on top, his shoulders did his T-shirt justice, and no man's ass should look so good in a pair of jeans. And here she'd thought she'd have to relegate her swooning to the trade show.

She leaned back. Time to enjoy the sights while she decided what to sing. Maybe he'd inspire her.

The first strains of something familiar filled the bar, and the whistles and claps from the other table died down, replaced with a quiet snicker. She knew that song. "Private Parts," Halestorm and James Michael. Gorgeous, haunting duet.

"You want me to sing her parts, too?" Jared stepped away from the microphone and toward the edge of the stage.

"You said we could pick," the guy with him taunted.

Inspiration stuck, and she knew exactly what she was going to sing. And in the process, she could spend a little more time appreciating the view all up close and personal-like. Mikki was on her feet and walking toward the stage. Her heart hammered against her ribcage, and her fingertips twitched in anticipation—not at the idea of being on stage, but that she was going to do so next to *him*. "I'll sing her parts."

His blue eyes grew wide, but appreciation lingered behind his shock. His voice was low, meant only for her ears. "Are you following me?"

"Not yet." She gave him what she hoped was a teasing smile, took the spot next to him by the mic, and slid into her part just as the female vocals kicked in.

His mouth twitched, and he picked up the next line without hesitation.

She sang her parts with only the occasional glance at the prompter. It was one of her favorite songs, and he carried the sad baritone with zero hesitation, sending chills through her.

As the music progressed, easing into the crossover and refrain, she lost herself in the lyrics and his voice. He was good. Maybe not professional quality, but neither was she, and at least he could keep up.

He stepped closer, never quite touching her as he traced a finger inches from her cheeks and sang about not blaming anyone, just trying to figure things out. Her nipples tightened at the intensity in his voice, and her skin hummed with anticipation each time he drew close but never quite made contact. It was easy to fall into the seductive pantomime. She let her hooded gaze rake over him while she slid into the chorus about getting naked but not undressing his heart.

The song ended, and as the last strains faded away, she found herself held captive by his gaze. Such clear blue eyes, she couldn't look away. He stood close enough the faint spice of his aftershave tickled her senses, and his heat brushed her skin. Every impulse in her screamed to lean in and kiss him. Just a taste. He tilted his head closer, and her breath hitched. Maybe tonight was her chance to live out any fan girl's fantasy—a random, no-strings tumble with her idol. She could imagine losing herself in him, at least for another hour or two.

A chorus of catcalls rocketed through the room, shattering her thoughts and the bubble around them. He stepped back, a smile drifting in to replace the intensity that had been on his face moments earlier, but not quite reaching his eyes. "Thanks for rescuing me."

Her body still tingled, pleading for more. Taking things further wasn't the plan, though. She forced her smile to stay in place, despite the voice in her head begging to find out what he could do besides sing, and put more space between them. "It was my pleasure."

"I'm going to have to repay you somehow."

She had a couple of ideas about what she'd like as remuneration. Even when he was pretending to be humble, he was sexy, in that sharp, too-serious-for-his-own-good kind of way. Images danced through her thoughts, teasing her with what it might have been like to end the song with a kiss. To feel those long fingers at the back of her neck, or gliding even lower. Heat and desire flooded her, and she tucked the notions aside before they could grow graphic and rampant.

And apparently he'd said something to her. She shook her distractions away. "I'm sorry, what?"

He rested a hand at the small of her back, and gestured toward the edge of the stage with his free arm. "I think they're waiting for us to leave so they can cue up the next song."

"Right, of course." Embarrassment joined the warmth flowing through her. She was tempted to lean into him and enjoy his touch a little longer. They reached the main floor too soon, but he didn't pull away. Instead he steered her away from her table, and toward the bar. He didn't break the contact until she was seated.

"Before you vanish into the crowds again, can I buy you a drink?"

So, so tempting. Despite the things she was willing to play fast and loose with, she knew she was a lightweight when it came to drinking. And if she was going to enjoy this opportunity, she was going to stay in full control of her senses. "I have to work in the morning."

"So you're going to nibble on chips the rest of the night without anything at all? Coke, water, nothing?" His expression never shifted, the pleasant but infuriatingly neutral smile staying etched in place. He slid onto the stool next to her, and his arm brushed hers when he rested it on the bar top. Had his face just twitched? Or was she imagining that he'd just bitten the inside of his cheek?

Maybe she wasn't the only one who thought there was an almost tangible cord between them. After all, he hadn't made his excuses and left yet. "Diet Coke, wedge of lime."

He grabbed the bartender's attention and ordered two. She fumbled for something flirty to say. Normally it wasn't a problem. She didn't tend to care what people thought of her, so whatever came out of her mouth came out. This was different, though. She idolized this man. She sipped her drink while a variety of witty openers—or maybe they weren't so witty and that was why she was hesitating—flitted through her thoughts.

"Well, ladies and gentlemen." The KJ's voice blended with the closing strains of a falsetto version of "Made in the USA" they'd just been subjected to. "Apparently our sexiest couple of the evening wants to do an encore performance for us."

Mikki was still processing the words when Jared's, "They wouldn't," cut into her thoughts. "Nope, they did." There was no irritation in his tone, and amusement danced on his face.

Her mouth drew into an O, and then a small laugh slipped out. "They mean us?"

He held up his phone with a text message on the screen from someone named "T." *You're up again.*

His friends must have set them up for another round. Boldness spurred by lust spiked through her. She hopped to her feet, intertwined her fingers with his, and tugged him back toward the stage. "We can't let our fans down."

He raised an eyebrow, and for a moment it looked like he might argue. Her pulse skipped when he fell into step beside her instead. "All right. But after this song is finished, I pick the next one, and you'd better keep up."

A new energy surged inside at the suggestion they'd be spending at least two more songs together. Her lips hummed in anticipation. "Me?" No way was she passing up that opportunity. She stepped in front of him on the stage. "Is that a challenge?"

He winked and took his spot next to her as the opening strands of "Close My Eyes Forever" by Lita Ford and Ozzy Osborne filled the room. "Take it however you'd like. Just keep making me look good."

True to his word, when they finished, he stopped by the KJ's booth and lined them up for another song. Because it was a weeknight, the bar was mostly empty. So twenty minutes later, they were on stage again. She lost track of time as they stepped in every few songs and picked new duets each time, alternating who got to choose. His taste ran softer than hers, and he seemed to prefer the classics from the eighties, but he didn't have any trouble falling into the tracks she picked.

It had to have been hours later when "This Mess We're In"—PJ Harvey and Thom Yorke—filled the room. He stood close, like he had every song, gaze locked on hers, never once glancing at the prompter, as he sang about looking each other in the eye directly, meeting on a Wednesday, and the mess they were in.

She pressed into him, sliding along his frame with lyrics of dreaming of making love and impossible dreams. Her nipples tightened each time he drew near.

His fingers glided up her spine as they moved into the last chorus, with her speaking the words and him singing about never changing or meeting again. The feather-light touch dragged her longing to the surface, and her skin tingled, begging to feel more of him. Each word sank deeper into her soul, drawing her into the moment as if she were living it.

The surreal, seductive feeling lingered as the last strains of the music faded from the speakers, not disrupted by the applause filling the room. She stood toe to toe with him, gaze locked on his, her breathing heavy and face hot. This time she didn't fumble when he led her from the stage. He steered her out of the main flow of traffic, waving off the KJ to indicate they were done.

"I need to stop for the night." He navigated them toward the bar again.

"If you're getting tired." She winced at the raw rasp in her voice.

His hand rested at the base of her neck, and her breath caught at the spark that ran though her. His thumb traced up her throat so lightly she wondered if she was just imagining it. His voice was low, and a current of something she couldn't identify lined his teasing. "Thanks. My voice is a little worn out."

She nodded at the empty table behind him where his friends had been sitting at the beginning of the night. "I think you were abandoned."

He pulled his phone from his pocket and with a few swipes, showed her the screen. It was another message from T. *Bailing. Tables are calling my name.*

"Did you see that come in?" That meant no one was waiting on him now. And the message had a time stamp of almost two hours ago. So had he intentionally given them some alone time? The realization heated her further.

He shrugged and pocketed the device. "I was having fun."

"You've got a nice voice." Why had she said that? Of all the witty, flirty, intelligent things she could have come up with, a weak nicety passed her lips instead. The fact that his hand still rested on her neck must be short-circuiting her thoughts.

He tilted closer, stopping when his head was just inches from hers. "I was going to say something similar." He was near enough the faint spice of his aftershave filled her head again. "You've got incredible vocal cords." He dipped his head, hot breath brushing her ear.

The haze of the song still enveloped her. His nearness pushed a wave of want through her, and the suggestion in his very movement clenched in her belly and traveled lower. His breath on her skin enhanced her already rampant fantasies.

"I've got other skills besides singing." Instead of the seductive innuendo she'd intended, her voice came out as a shy whisper, and she hid a cringe.

"I bet."

She realized she was leaning into him and didn't pull away. Hesitation thrummed through her at what she was about to do, but this was one of those moments she couldn't let get away from her. A random, foolish, completely tempting, once-in-a-lifetime chance. "Do you ever think about the lyrics when you sing along?"

His brows rose, question dancing in his expression. "Sometimes…"

She tried to be subtle about taking a deep breath. It had been ages since she'd worried this much about the words coming out of her mouth. She forced a wash of courage through her veins and let the question roll. "It makes me wonder what it would be like to make love while the sun sets over the city."

She'd managed to ask without her voice cracking. Slick need ached between her thighs. A tiny nagging in the back of her head pointed out this might not be her best idea ever. Something about being neighbors at the tradeshow, and working for competing companies.

Which was laugh-worthy. There was no way she wanted to walk away from a chance like this.

A frown crossed his face, and her gut sank. "I'm from out of town."

That doesn't sound like a no. And his hands still rested at her waist. "We met in a hotel. So am I."

"I don't do things like this." His words didn't match his actions. His eyes stayed locked on hers, and his palm slid toward her back, drawing her closer.

"Duets in karaoke bars?" She let her growing hope keep her question light. Even his low, smooth tone made her think he was more interested than his words indicated.

His breathing quickened. "One-night stands."

"Me neither." She risked stepping closer, and her pulse threatened to race away when his thumbs pressed into her hips, holding her captive. "But I figure sometimes you have to make an exception."

His fingers stroked small circles along her back. "I don't make exceptions, either."

Then she wasn't the only one this was a night of firsts for. The idea sent tingles from her fingers, through her entire body, and down to her toes. She dipped her head in. He smelled incredible up close, like musk and fresh rain. She let herself fall into the scent as she whispered, "That's why it's called an exception. Because you don't normally do it."

His lips moved along her neck, never touching her, but making her blood roar in response. "You make a good case. And I'll admit, you're absolutely intoxicating."

No one had ever described her like that before. Something between a giggle and a sigh bubbled up inside, and she swallowed it back. *Don't lose it now.* "So what's stopping you from sating the curiosity?"

His mouth twisted into a hungry smile that stole the last of her reason. "Nothing, apparently."

THREE

Jared brushed his lips over hers, and she leaned into the kiss without hesitation. The ordered part of his brain twitched that he couldn't get a solid read on this woman. In the few short hours they'd known each other, she'd been demure, confident, sarcastic, and removed. No one had that many variables so close to the surface. On top of that, she'd never stopped being sexy. Her black hair with a red streak, the off-the-shoulder shirt and corset combination highlighting the curves underneath, and the skirt ending a few inches above her knees drove his imagination wild.

And the way her tongue darted into his mouth completely disassembled his thoughts. His blood pressure increased another notch when a smooth metal ball rolled along the inside of his mouth. The fabric of her corset teased his fingertips, and the intoxicating scent of lemon and plum still drifted from her. His mouth watered at the thought of running his tongue up the long curve of her neck. Seeing if her skin felt more like silk or the suede tempting his palms.

He didn't have time for this. He had pressing problems to solve, and her *what the hell* attitude was as disconcerting as it was contagious. Except, for the first time in he couldn't remember how long, this moment was the only thing he wanted to focus on.

He dropped into a nearby stool and tugged her closer. She slid between his legs without hesitation, fingertips digging into his chest and soft gasps tearing from her throat. He glided his hands down her back and rested them on her ass. She pushed even closer, brushing his cock through his jeans. Jesus, he wanted more.

He trailed his nose up her neck, inhaling the sharp scent making every one of his senses sing. It took the last of his restraint, and the intense knowledge they were in a public place, not to push her skirt out of the way, bend her over the bar, and slide inside her. What was wrong with him? Tempted to misbehave just because he was a little turned on?

No way was he walking away now. Every gasp and moan whispering from her stole more of his reason. She was different—unrestrained didn't begin to describe her—and his senses begged for more than just a taste. He grazed his teeth along her ear, nipping at her lobe. "I should warn you now, if we keep going I won't want to stop. Hell, I already don't want to stop."

Her tiny laugh ended with a sigh when he traced up her collarbone with his tongue. The faint salt of perspiration mingled with the velvet of her skin. Another tick in her favor—his bluntness didn't seem to faze her. He needed to get some of these clothes out of the way. She rubbed against him, her response quiet. "I'm not letting you strip me down in the middle of a bar."

If he asked nicely, would she? He couldn't hold back his smirk as inspiration struck. "We could go back to my room."

"Or we could sneak off into one of the practice rooms they have."

Her breathy suggestion glitched his thoughts, but reason wriggled its way in. "You think they're not going to know exactly why we're going back there?"

She stepped back as far as was possible without breaking the contact between them, and her lower lip jutted out. "Does it matter?"

He wanted to kiss that pout away, then run his lips lower along her collarbone and dip between the curve of her breasts. Fuck propriety. At least for the next hour or so. He waved the bartender over and dropped a bill on the counter. "We want one of the sound rooms to warm up in."

He received an electronic key card and a raised eyebrow in return, but no comment. He tugged Mikki away from the main stage. As they passed the bathroom, something occurred to him. *Convenient.* He pressed her against the wall, using the dark corner to block them mostly from view. He ran his hand up the back of her leg, pushing up the hem of her skirt.

"And you were worried about what people would say," she teased as she squirmed under his touch.

He tangled his fingers in her hair and crushed his lips to hers. When he broke the kiss, he pressed his forehead to hers. "Fifteen seconds. I'll be right back."

Pink flooded her cheeks. "I'll give you twenty and then I'm leaving."

He chuckled at the joking threat, ducked into the bathroom, and returned twelve seconds later—he'd counted—with protection.

"You've thought of everything."

He nudged her toward the sound room. "Not everything, but I've got a head full of starting places to pick and choose from."

The room was barely big enough for a bench and table mounted to the wall, a microphone, a screen in another wall, and a computer keyboard to let people make their play selections.

Is this place as clean as it looks? How many other people have had this same idea?

Her pelvis ground against his cock and shoved the nagging questions aside. He'd never been with a woman who was this kind of bold. His imagination was already careening out of control with the filthy things he wanted to do to her. He could overlook invisible germs. The space was small, but it was all they needed.

He twirled her so her back was to him and pulled her close again. Her warm figure pressed into him cranked his internal temperature several notches. He undid the hooks on the front of her corset and kissed along the back of her neck. The heady scent of citrus sang to his senses and filled him with a longing to feel every inch of her at once.

He tugged the bottom of her shirt out of her skirt. Every time her ass shifted, the friction made him harder. It was going to be difficult to be patient with her. He rested his palms on her bare stomach. Her skin was smoother than the silky texture he'd imagined. Warm and eager beneath his touch.

Her every sound tugged at his gut every time he touched her someplace new, making him want to hear more. He moved one hand higher, fingers brushing the bottom of her breast through her bra. His head swam at the thought of what was hiding under her skirt. He kissed the edge of her ear. "Are your panties the same black lace as your bra?"

To her credit, she didn't ask how he knew. So, somewhere around the third or fourth song, she'd consciously undone the top two hooks on her corset, exposing a hint of lace as she'd traced her finger along the neckline of her blouse. Instead she pushed into him again. "I guess you'll just have to find out for yourself."

The attitude made his blood scream. He needed to be buried inside her. But first things first. He shoved her bra up, and she whimpered when the elastic brushed her nipple, followed closely by his fingers. He tweaked the hard nub between his fingers, tugging and pinching in response to her panting.

That sound was intoxicating. He moved his other hand to her other breast, squeezing both mounds. She ground into him in rhythm to his massaging, her gasps growing more punctuated with each movement. Was her frantic grinding enough to get him off? It was tempting to find out, but her pleasure came first. Always.

He couldn't help but smirk when his hands fell away and she let out a whimper of disappointment. It melted into a gasp seconds later as he trailed his fingers down her back. Friction built between his palms and her thighs when he pushed up the hem of her skirt. The slick leather was a sharp contrast to her warm skin beneath. He couldn't believe he was doing this. It was true, he wasn't new to the idea of a one-night stand, but they were all but in public, and there were no ground rules around the encounter.

He didn't want to walk away though. She was different from the women he dated. He didn't know anything about her besides her name, and that she had a fascination with incorrect tech articles. She had stepped onto the stage with such abandon. Hadn't caved under his attention, but made the most delicious noises as she yielded to his touch.

She pressed into him with more force when he dipped his fingers under the thin elastic holding up her panties. He glided down her slit, moisture coating his fingers before he even slipped between her folds. A groan tore from his chest. "You're so wet already."

She arched her back, head resting on his shoulder. His teeth sank into her bare shoulder, each twist of her body sending an exquisitely painful dagger of want through him. A loud gasp echoed through the room when he brushed a swollen nub between her legs. She rocked against his hand as he traced circles around her clit, growing tighter each with pass until she was bucking under his attention, breath coming in short bursts.

Her back went rigid, and she pressed hard into his hand as a final, soft cry tore from her throat, and a shudder racked her body when she came.

She wobbled, still panting. He laid a line of soft kisses along her neck, and then down her spine through her shirt. Hooking his thumbs into the elastic of her panties, he dragged them down her legs. "They are black. Lucky me."

She let out a small laugh as she stepped out of the lingerie. "Glad I didn't disappoint." And there was her attitude. It made him as hard as the thought of burying himself inside her did. She spun to face him and plucked the panties from his hand, a teasing gleam in her eyes. She stepped close enough to rub her entire frame against him. Her hand slid along his waist, and she stuffed the lingerie in his pocket. "In case the memory of tonight isn't enough of a souvenir for you."

What made someone so tantalizingly bold? No, he didn't need to know, as long as she didn't stop. He tangled his fingers in her hair again, barely able to grasp the short strands. He pressed his forehead to hers, not able to keep the hunger from his voice. "Trust me, the memories are already enough to keep me company for a while. But when you walk out of here, at least I'll know it's without anything on under your skirt, the cool air brushing your skin, reminding you why you're so wet."

"Good thing I packed extra." She tilted her head and nipped at his bottom lip before kissing him.

A twinge pinged deep inside at the reminder this was only a one-time thing.

He shoved the thoughts aside, more interested in the moment. His tongue danced with hers, the smooth metal of her barbell stroking him as he guided her the short distance to the table behind her. Hands on her hips, he lifted her to sit on the edge.

She never broke the kiss when he shoved his knee between her thighs and forced her legs apart. Her skirt crept higher up her hips as he stepped closer. His chest was tight from the shallow breaths he drew. The hammering of his pulse in his ears blocked out every sound not associated with her, and his tongue wanted another taste of her. Of that silver ball that teased him as effectively as her words did.

Her fingers trailed down his stomach, and she only fumbled with his belt and button for a moment before opening his pants. He growled when her cool fingers wrapped around his warm shaft, freeing it. He nudged forward, and she scooted back, breaking away from him. Teasing eyes met his, and her hand slipped into his pocket. She plucked out a condom. He'd been getting to that, but at least she wasn't completely careless. Apparently, she could get sexier.

Seconds later she had it unwrapped. He groaned at the light sensation as she rolled the rubber onto his cock. The moment she was done, he dug his fingers into her hips and thrust forward. Her cry mingled with his when he pushed inside her.

"You're so tight." He spoke through clenched teeth. "So slick."

Her knees hooked on his hips, and she yanked him closer, nails gliding down his back.

The buildup had already drawn him close to the edge, and he wasn't going to last much longer buried inside her. She grabbed his wrist and pulled his hand up. He took the hint, finding her breast and stroking his thumb across the rigid peak. He kissed along her neck, the soft scent of her shampoo stealing his oxygen.

She matched his pace as he slammed into her depths. God, she was incredible. Her breathing grew shallow again, and this time he knew she was close to orgasm. The thought was enough to draw his own arousal to a peak. She didn't slow down as she climaxed, milking his cock and squeezing him until he burst. Endorphins raced through him, stealing the rest of his reason and plunging him completely into the moment. He grunted when he came, biting her shoulder and not stopping until he was spent.

She rested her forehead on his chest, breathing heavy, her laugh warm through his shirt. "I've never been the lucky lady to come to the rescue of a helpless businessman in a karaoke bar before."

"Honestly, I prefer to be the hero." He pulled out of her.

"I'm not saying I mind being swept away by a knight in shining armor." She nudged him back with her body as she jumped from the table. Pleasure rushed through him at the teasing contact. She straightened her skirt and clothing while he stripped off the condom, wrapped it in a tissue he kept in the small pack in his wallet, tossed it in the trashcan in the corner, and did up his jeans.

"I had a lot of fun tonight. All of it. Thank you." She stepped up to him again, rose on her toes, and brushed her lips over his. "But I have to get back before I turn into a pumpkin."

The kiss stole his thoughts. He could take her back to the hotel. See if she was interested in round two. He'd be up for it by the time they got there, if he could keep his hands to himself on the ride.

But that was a bad idea. Reason was returning. This was a one-night thing, and he had meetings in the morning. No need to prolong the inevitable, beyond making sure she got back safe. "Do you want to share a cab?"

She hesitated for a moment, brow furrowed, and then shook her head. For the first time that night, she looked like she was actually hesitating. Great, now he'd made things awkward. He should have established some ground rules.

"Thank you, but no. I've got things covered," she said.

He shoved his whispering disappointment aside and instead loosely grasped her wrist, tugged her close, and rested his other hand on the small of her back. He kissed her deeply, searing the sensation into his head.

A gasp slipped from her throat when they broke apart, and the corner of her mouth tugged up. "Good night."

He sank back onto the bench after she was gone, mixed emotions coursing through him. He focused on the pleasant ones. She'd even made him forget about work and that damn phone call for a few hours. Maybe he'd have to let Tate and Vivian pick his songs more often.

FOUR

Mikki's tiny smile—the one that had lingered even in a sleep that graced her with sensual dreams—couldn't be convinced to leave. This morning, when logic tried to horn its way in and remind her everything about the last night had been completely irrational, she'd smiled wider. And had she really given him her panties? Her own boldness made her grin in retrospect. So worth it!

Growing up, she'd always been the shy, quiet, nerdy girl. The way they moved around, combined with her younger age in school, had only helped keep her in her shell. Even through college she'd kept to herself. *Yawn.*

After graduation, she'd met Payton. The name made her thoughts snarl in irritation. The things he'd said to her. To other people about her. Her gut clenched at the half-formed memories, and she shoved them aside.

It didn't matter. He was in the past, and the poor decision to date him had led to her choice to experience life after they broke up. It had taken some time to get comfortable with stepping out of her shell, but she'd faked it until she made it. Her personal mission statement had become live first, think later, and never say "if only."

The night before had been the perfect addition to her memories.

Sexy guy who just happened to be an idol of hers, tons of fun, and wow…some sizzling mental souvenirs. The only regret she had—and she didn't usually do regrets—was that she hadn't been more up front about who she was. She'd assumed he knew, but maybe she should have made sure.

She smoothed out the polo shirt with her company logo on it, grabbed her exhibitor's badge for the trade show and her purse, and left her hotel room behind her. Time to see more of Vegas, even if a lot of her view would be from the confines of a trade show booth.

It was her first time in the city of lights and though she was there for business, she was going to take every free chance she could to at least see the part of the strip their hotel and the convention center were on. When she'd wandered the shops the day before at Caesar's Palace, she'd spotted the perfect place for breakfast. Now it could also provide a few more minutes for her to drift in the memories of last night. She and Jared had had undeniable chemistry on stage, and he was bandwidth-choking hot.

Her body flushed at the memories. She'd probably never do something like that again, which was all the more reason to relish the images seared in her mind.

The cafe looked like most she'd seen in her life—treats under glass, the smell of coffee in the air, and eclectic furniture. But it was nestled in the middle of a hotel and that made it awesome as far as she was concerned.

"Michaela." The staccato word cut through all the noise, like Styrofoam on Styrofoam. She hated her real name, and she only knew one person who refused to call her anything else. He insisted it was professional. *Playtime's over. Bossman's in town.*

She pasted on a smile and turned toward Hayden. He was attractive and as clean cut as she'd ever seen a person. Close-cropped, dark blond hair, broad shoulders, and doing a decent job of hiding he was almost forty. And his suit ensured he'd blend in with all the retail store owners they were about to mingle with—beige, pressed, and plain.

He was the senior vice president of the team she worked for. She couldn't imagine wanting to climb that high on the corporate ladder. *Boring.* His father owned NetSafe Systems, a company built on creating everything digital one could imagine for retail stores. Websites, shopping carts, point of sale software. Their group offered ethical hacks to companies with website security concerns.

Her job specifically—and the best job ever, in her opinion—was to try from every angle possible to break into a company's website or network, and then tell them how to keep people like her from doing it again.

Which was the only reason she was okay with being reminded regularly to put on a polite face for the public. This was her dream job, and NSS was one of the two top firms in the country. Jared's was the other. Okay, so it wasn't *his* company, but still… Heat shimmered through her as more memories and fantasies teased her.

She would have liked a few more minutes alone with her thoughts, but she couldn't completely brush off her boss. Especially on a business trip. She grabbed her food and crossed the short distance to the table he'd secured.

"I hope you weren't too bored last night," he asked as he toed out a spare chair for her.

She dropped into the wooden seat. Sometimes it felt like he asked too many questions, but most of the time she was pretty sure he was just making small talk. Not that the details of her night before mattered in the grand scope of work. She hadn't missed anything, and she was awake and alert this morning. Besides, the question reminded her things had ended much better than she'd expected. "I kept myself occupied."

More memories flashed through her head. Jared's hands on her legs, roughly shoving her skirt up. Heat flooded her skin and she tucked the pleasant thoughts aside before she could fall into them.

"Glad to hear it."

He riffled through the laptop bag resting next to his leg and pulled out a magazine. A whisper of relief flitted through her. Small talk was fine most days, but this morning she had other things on her mind.

All her other thoughts evaporated when she saw his reading material. Staring back at her from the cover were Jared and his two friends from the bar, the headline proclaiming them the corporate dream team that was Skriddie Bust Media.

She couldn't pull her attention from the photo. The three had made their company a name. Vivian Graf was director of operations, Tate Foster was director of sales, and Jared Tippins rounded out the trio as director of technology. Her cheeks warmed, and a pleasant tingle crept through her. She'd really hooked up with *him*.

"Hey." Hayden had set down the magazine and was staring at her. "Earth to Michaela. Did you just check out?"

"I'm good." She swallowed, not able to push away the distracting fantasies tripping through her thoughts.

She'd heard stories in college—and after—of the legend that was Jared. A decade ago, he'd been her age—twenty-three, when he'd built one of the biggest, baddest-ass security systems corporate America had ever seen. He'd been some kind of genius savant back in his day, before he'd traded it all for a suit and an impressive title.

Hayden looked between her and the picture, and his eyebrows rose. "I'll do you a favor right now, not as your boss, but as a friend. He's not your type, Michaela. Trust me. He likes his women with a digital voice and a square shell."

A cloud drifted across the vivid images painted across her thoughts. There was that. According to Hayden, Jared was the industry's version of a monk—more interested in machines than dating. In fact, those were frequently the exact words Hayden used to describe him. Except, that didn't mesh with the man she'd met the night before. "You're exaggerating."

He set the magazine down and locked a steady gaze on her. "It doesn't matter if I am or not. I'll remind you once because I'd hate to see you destroy your career before it even starts—keep your distance from these guys."

She had a list of things that irritated Hayden, but she hadn't ever expected to have to add "Don't sleep with Jared Tippins" to it. She tried to be subtle about inhaling deeply. It didn't get rid of the memories, but it did mute her body's reaction. She wouldn't blurt out she'd already crossed that line, but couldn't hide all of her irritation at his *professional* advice. "I'm pretty sure my contract doesn't delve into who I can and can't talk to."

"Does conflict of interest mean anything to you?"

Oh. That. Hayden had made it clear what he thought of corporate espionage, or any violation, real or perceived, of the non-disclosure agreement all employees signed. In fact, he'd spelled it out for her during the later stages of her interview. After he'd fired the guy who'd made hacking the Skriddie systems network a part of her technology test even though the interviewer told her she was still on NSS systems.

Hayden had reiterated his, and the company's, zero tolerance policy about the ethics of spying on the competition. He also drove home that Skriddie would demand her head when they found, unless he smoothed things over first. She'd committed a serious transgression in breaching their security. All for a job.

She turned her attention to her breakfast, keeping her tone casual. "You want a dictionary definition of each word?"

"You kill me sometimes, you know? Slay me dead." He pointed at the magazine cover. "Look, I'm not trying to be a wet blanket. This is standard stuff." Concern edged his kind tone. "They were furious when I told them what you did, and steering clear of them is going to make your life less stressful. I just want you to avoid any unpleasant situations."

She frowned at the reminder she might have pissed off someone at Skriddie and gave her full attention to her food. Six months, and she'd almost managed to put the entire thing out of her mind. Hoped the situation might just evaporate. Talk about a buzzkill. "I get it. Thanks."

"Are you ready for the panel this morning?"

Good. A neutral topic. Dull as hell, but neutral. "I'm set." She redirected her thoughts to work-related subjects. "I pulled anything that could be considered interesting—sorry, *proprietary*—from the slides."

An unpleasant thought joined Hayden's warning. If Jared had known who she was last night, would he have had a different reaction to her? What if he was still angry about what she'd done?

Professional people didn't hold grudges like that, right? He was way too mature to do something like resent her just because she'd found a teeny, tiny…okay, fairly significant hole in their security when she wasn't even supposed to be on their network. Besides, at least she'd found it before someone else. And Hayden had made sure they knew about it. There should be some forgiveness for that, right?

Still, conflict of interest. Not that it was Hayden's—or anyone else's—business who she did or didn't sleep with.

Images and sensations teased back in response to her mental question. Jared's breath on her skin, his teeth digging into her shoulder, his hands gripping her hips. No regrets. She just had to keep it quiet.

FIVE

Jared's sneakers thwapped against the rubber of the treadmill, the sound filling the hotel gym with a rhythmic pulse. The beat echoed in his skull and with images of the night before. He'd had enough impulsiveness to last him the next year, but it had been worth it.

The sensations from the bar still teased him. Her heady scent, the rainbow of sounds she'd made, and the carefree attitude always dancing behind her eyes.

"Ever stop to wonder why you're the only person in here at seven a.m.?" Tate's jab shattered Jared's rambling thoughts.

"Nope. Never even considered it." He couldn't help the tiny smile that slipped out. He owed Tate a thank you for ditching him the night before. Or maybe "giving him some room" was a more appropriate way to put it. He continued running—no reason to interrupt his daily routine—but did set the speed slower so he could talk and jog at the same time.

"Of course not." Tate used a nearby wall for support and took a long swallow from his oversized coffee. "Then you'd have to admit your routine is boring and predictable."

"Predictable and consistent," Jared corrected him. "Unlike, oh, say, abandoning your buddy in a bar after you suggested we drink all night."

Tate snorted. "Right. Because you're so torn up about that."

Jared couldn't suppress his grin. The expression had to be a dead giveaway about what happened. "If you'd rather have hit up the tables, you should have said so before we left."

"I have to do something to make sure they give me the room again next trip."

Jared doubted that. For as much money as Tate dropped on high-roller tables every time they were in town, he was pretty sure the guy had a lifetime's worth of comp in the luxury suites. Once upon a time, the way Tate went through his father's money had been a sore spot between them. Now that Jared had his own cash— even though he still couldn't justify twenty-five hundred dollars a hand for poker—it didn't faze him the same way. "So really, you should be thanking me."

Tate laughed. "I don't think so. And for the record, if I'd known you'd get that kind of response, I'd have gone up there myself. Next time, you're forcing me onto stage and playing wingman."

"I've never stopped you in the past."

"Whatever. Speaking of your velvet-voiced siren, did she spill anything good? It would serve Hayden right after the bullshit he's already pulling today. I ran into him in the lobby, and he spent fifteen minutes trying to get me to slip up and tell him who we were in negotiations with."

Spill anything good? Serve Hayden right? Wait, what? The circuits in Jared's head collided with each other and he stumbled. He stepped on the edges of the treadmill before confusion could become a full-blown face plant, and shut the device off. She'd definitely said and done things that would stick in his head for a long time. But the tension rolling under his skin told him that wasn't what Tate meant, and shouldn't have anything to do with one of the senior vice presidents at NSS. "I'm missing a key point of reference, aren't I?"

Tate grimaced and set his coffee aside. "You don't know."

Obviously not. "Know what?"

"Vivian told me. I think she would have told you too, but figured you'd find out directly from the source. You and your karaoke partner seemed to be getting on just fine without us."

For the most part, he was used to Tate's tendency to not get directly to the point. He didn't appreciate it, but he accepted it. Just now, he needed to have details sooner rather than later. His brain was already erroring out from lack of information. "Tell me."

"She's Michaela Elford."

So that was what Mikki was short for. Why did her full name sound familiar? From Tate's expression, it was clear Jared should know it.

Tate continued, "She's the new prodigy Hayden hired. The one he stole from V six months ago."

Right. The weird interview that had pissed Viv off for weeks after. Apparently Michaela—Mikki?—had been just as impressive in her resume as in person when Vivian had interviewed her, and had seemed like she was ready to all but sign. Then, out of nowhere, she'd sent Vivian a very polite and apologetic *thanks but no thanks* letter. Something along the lines of, "I hope you're not too angry with me. I think we can all agree the best place for me is with NetSafe Systems."

Viv had tried to reach her a handful of times after, but Mikki hadn't returned her calls.

Yup, that was exactly where he'd heard her name. He never should have misfiled information that important. *Fuck.* Jared stepped off the treadmill. "Got it. And no, it didn't come up."

"Maybe she didn't recognize you."

Except she had. Alarms clanged in the back of Jared's thoughts. Suspecting anything was off about the situation was ridiculous. The encounter in the elevator had been random chance, and she couldn't have known they were heading out to get wasted and sing bad music. His paranoia might be a rampant bastard sometimes, but there was no way this was like Karen.

But Mikki working for the competition dragged up unpleasant memories he hadn't expected to deal with on this trip. Especially if she was associated with NSS.

Karen had taught him years ago getting involved with anyone in that company was a dangerous path to follow. Good thing he and Mikki knew last night was a one-time thing. The thought didn't take the edge off the realization she'd kept something as significant from him as working for the competition.

"Speaking of, if you want to see your karaoke partner on stage in a more professional fashion, she's running an NSS panel in the morning breakout sessions." Tate took another sip of coffee, grimaced, and tossed the cup in a nearby trashcan.

Jared cringed as coffee splashed in the waste bucket. So messy. Despite his irritation at being deceived, his pulse kicked up at the thought of hearing that playful voice again. He beat the reaction back with the rest of the morning's conversation. "I was planning on it anyway."

He was going to see if there were any hints about the direction NSS was taking their security offerings. And hopefully uncover a detail or two as to what he was missing in these rumors that his company wasn't worth its own press releases. Not that he expected there to be any usable information—providing as little information as possible was status quo for these demos—but there was always a chance. And he could almost convince himself Mikki wasn't adding another layer of incentive.

Tate's brow furrowed, and he studied Jared for a minute. "I was joking. Vivian's already attending. You can skip it if you want."

Jared shrugged. "Hayden's been bragging they've got something that can put us in the dirt. I'd like to form my own opinion."

He didn't want to be excited, or intrigued, or anything besides nonplussed about the thought of seeing the playful siren again, but he couldn't swallow his growing arousal. Every inch of him hummed, his pulse racing in a way he knew wasn't related to his abbreviated jog.

"Almost forgot." Tate plucked Jared's phone from the top of his gym bag. "Check your mail."

Jared glanced between him and the device. "Just tell me what I'm looking for. You know I have about fifty unread messages." His own verbal reminder set his mental compulsion on edge. He always forced himself not to check before his morning workout. Otherwise he'd be stuck in email hell before he had a chance to wake up. But he'd have to catch up on those before the morning breakout sessions.

"That's it? How late were you up last night?" Tate shook his head. "Anyway. Peacock announced his retirement."

That was almost enough to pull Jared back to the now. Larry Peacock was chief operations officer for Skriddie, and rumors of his retirement had been circulating for a while.

Jared wanted the job, and he knew he was one of the people being considered. The kinds of changes he could make in a position like that... Excitement tingled in his limbs, and he drummed his fingers against his leg. One of the reasons he loved his work was because there was always something new to learn—another way to make things perfect. And a step up the ladder would give him even more access to exactly that. "Any other news?"

Tate tossed the phone back on the bag. "Nah. But I'm sure you'll hear before either of us anyway."

JARED SLIPPED into the conference room with a just a few minutes to spare. Vivian already stood near the back, despite the empty chairs lining the last couple of rows. She gave him a tight-lipped smile and nodded him over.

"I didn't expect to see you here." Her voice was low amid the chatter of the trickling in crowd.

"I had to sate my curiosity." He kept his tone as cool as possible and tried to convince his rampant imagination to chill as well.

"If everyone wants to have a seat, we'll get started in a minute or two." A familiar voice sliced into Jared's thoughts, and his head snapped toward the stage.

Before his brain finished processing what the sound meant, his body reacted. Want tugged his cock to life and tempted him with memories of the night before. Even in her company's basic trade show uniform, she still made his blood run hot. *Not good.* He needed to bring that under control.

Vivian looked between him and the podium, eyebrows rising. "Tell me you didn't share more than a mic with her."

Fuck. Why did she have to know him so well? When she'd been brought into the company a few years back and dropped into a high-ranking position, he'd resented her. This person didn't know their business, especially not something as critical as day-to-day operations.

Since then, he and she had become solid friends. She understood things no one else did. And she had an odd—sometimes refreshing, occasionally irritating—way of looking into his head and helping him sort out his malfunctions when he wasn't thinking straight.

He couldn't pull his eyes away from Mikki as he talked to Viv. Maybe he could redirect the conversation. "Speaking of, did it occur to you to tell me who she was?"

"When would I have done that?" She dropped into a nearby seat. "While you were singing round after round of cheesy love songs? Besides, I figured she'd tell you."

He took the spot next to her, attention still fixed up front. "It didn't come up." Would the knowledge would have stopped him? Of course it would have. He needed to stop that line of thinking now. If he abandoned the logic and reason he used to keep his life in line, he'd surrender the grip that order had on his sanity.

"Weird. But it was just a couple of duets. Given this entire week is about networking, the two of you were going to meet anyway, and it's not like you screwed, right?"

"Hmm?" He'd heard the question clearly, but the sick clenching in his gut didn't know how to respond.

"You're pulling my leg. You did not do something that random. She's an incredible talent, and I have nothing but respect for her. But she's a decade younger than you."

"You make me sound ancient. We're both consenting adults."

Vivian brushed a nonexistent strand of hair from her forehead. "Not that it matters, as long as she knows it was only one night."

"Of course she does."

"Did I ever tell you she gushed about you in her interview? Some kind of minor hero worship."

Vivian had never told him that. And he wasn't pleased to hear it. *Or maybe I am just a little.* "Doesn't sound familiar, or relevant."

"Right." She crossed her legs at the knee. "Since you're here, tell me if you think she's got the skills everyone says she does. I still want her."

That made two of them. Fuck, he needed to stop that. Of course Vivian was still trying to recruit this talent. She'd never been a good loser, especially when it came to Hayden. "Sure. I need you to give me something in return, though."

"What's up?"

Mikki's eyes met his, holding him captive. The corners of her mouth twitched, and then she looked away. The teasing half smile of her not-quite acknowledgement made his pulse quicken and refreshed the page file of his mind with pleasant memories.

"I need to talk to her, strictly business, and I need someone to run interference."

"Absolutely."

SIX

Mikki paced next to the image projected on the wall behind her. It took every ounce of her concentration not to yawn at her own presentation. Fortunately the talking itself took minimal thought. Every time she touched on what the company could do technologically, she had to swallow back the details, and that made the entire thing duller and more bullshit-filled than an end user license agreement.

Even if she were allowed to talk outside the company about the specifics of her job, these people didn't want to hear what really made the technology work. They wanted glitter and bows and reassurances their information was safe from big, bad hackers. They didn't care if it happened because of a tear in the space-time continuum, as long as it happened.

She'd seen Jared and Vivian hovering in the back of the room, but resisted the urge to stare, turning her attention away from them instead. That was a distraction she didn't need. Or at least, she was telling herself she wasn't distracted. Her heart hammered in her throat, she'd stumbled over more memorized lines than she'd nailed, and she'd emptied more glasses of ice water than she cared to admit, to dissuade herself from the rampant fantasies taunting her.

She needed to keep cool; they were. They would only be there to see what they could glean from the competition. And possibly see if she was using what she knew against them. Not that she ever would. Besides, they'd have corrected any security holes the moment Hayden told them there was an issue with their network security. And where had the sudden train of worry come from?

She rolled the question around in her head. It was because she cared what they thought. That was new. Or rather, an old feeling she thought she'd rid herself of. Before she'd set out to prove Payton wrong, it had been an intricate part of who she was to not make waves. After all, the nerdy girl two years younger than most of her class was safer going unnoticed.

But after his cruel words back then… She needed to remember why others' opinions didn't matter, or risk being that kind of vulnerable again. Yet she couldn't help hoping Jared and Vivian would be impressed with what she had to say.

As she wound up her presentation, relief trickled through her, and her zombiefied state ebbed. Next time, she was staying at home and Hayden was showing the slides. Traveling on the company dime wasn't worth it if this was what she had to put up with.

She almost laughed at the thought. *Who am I kidding? It totally is.* First time in Vegas, she already had memories to show for it, and she only had to surrender a few hours to boredom in exchange. She still had nearly three days left in town, the last day as authority-free as the first, and she was going to take advantage of her time here.

The room didn't empty immediately, as she'd thought it would. Some people lingered in corners, heads bowed together. Others waited to talk to her. She wouldn't have minded setting everything else aside and spending hours just chatting with people and answering their questions, but it didn't seem like anyone wanted real answers, just more pretty special effects. She used the excuse of needing to pack up her laptop and projector to give vague replies to vague questions. The room had come with its own computer technology, but since she was there representing a tech company, she'd brought their higher resolution equipment.

She'd expected to have to argue to get the budget for it, but

Hayden had agreed appearances were important. Despite her reluctance to chat, she wasn't in a rush to get back, so making sure everything was securely packed away was a good excuse to drag her feet.

She shook hands with a couple of people in suits, accepted the compliments, and exchanged business cards. The entire time she was intently aware of Jared and Vivian hovering in the back of the room. Would it be worse or better if it was just him? What could they get up to if everyone else left? An unpleasant voice reminded her of Hayden's warning from that morning. Stupid propriety.

And then almost everyone else was gone. Vivian stood near the back door, but her attention was directed outside the room. Mikki's heart hammered a beat on her ribs when Jared approached.

"Let me guess." His familiar voice called to the pleasant half of her warring thoughts. "You're not the one who writes all the pretty words that take forever to say nothing."

She cursed her racing pulse. It was because he'd startled her was all. *It has nothing to do with the chills his voice sends down my spine.* "I wrote it myself, if that's what you're implying. I'm not just a pretty face."

"I wouldn't dare assume anything of the sort." He stood less than a foot away. Slacks and a suit coat had replaced the jeans and T-shirt from last night, and he looked incredible. He leaned against the podium, shoulders tilted toward her. He wore the same flat, difficult-to-read expression he'd had on when they'd first met last night. His gaze flickered over her before he met her eyes, and a hint of a smile threatened his face. "You know, when they talk about the NSS prodigy, they leave out the bit about you being really good at sounding like you're saying everything when you're not really saying anything."

She blinked and shook her head at the double talk. *Insult or compliment?* "Only when it's required of me."

"I mean it in the best way possible. I was impressed. And sympathetic, if it helps."

Warmth flooded her face, and she couldn't ignore the pleased note springing though her.

He opened his mouth and then snapped it shut again, brow furrowing for a moment. He took a deep breath. "I don't have any idea how to do this other than being direct, so please don't take it the wrong way."

"I'll do my best not to?" Wow, this was awkward. Maybe she should have considered the morning after before now. Still, she was tired of a morning of vagaries. Actually hearing someone speak his mind would be a nice change.

"Last night was incredible." A current of confidence and heat ran through his words. "But I didn't know who you were."

Okay, she could do this. They'd set things right and life would move on. "I told you."

"You told me your first name."

Right. Embarrassment flooded her. So he really hadn't recognized her name. She couldn't believe she'd assumed something like that. Just because she knew who he was didn't mean she'd ever registered on his radar professionally. The realization kicked stones in her gut. At least that meant he didn't hold her hack against her, right? "I'm sorry."

He studied her for a moment, brows furrowed. "I should have poked for more information."

She couldn't help herself and let the teasing slip out. "I think you did an incredible job poking."

The corner of his mouth tugged up, but the smile vanished before it could form completely.

Don't be pleased he smiled. You're not trying to impress him. Nah, I totally am. She nodded toward the door, and Vivian. "Does she know…?"

This time his smile bled in and stayed. "She knows how to keep quiet, if you're worried."

He glanced around him before locking his gaze on her again, and stepped closer. She should put more space between them, except his heady scent, and the response her body had to the crisp smell, made reason evaporate. He wasn't touching her, but he was close enough she felt his heat.

He tilted his head toward hers, and the growing tingle in her belly stretched through her, hardening her nipples. Damn her body for betraying her need to put this behind her. His breath was hot on her ear when he spoke. "I still had an amazing time last night, don't doubt that. Even if it was just one time, and even though we can't do it again, I'm glad you gave me the souvenir."

Every inch of her screamed to lean in. To grab one last kiss, or something more. To add to the taunting fantasy dancing in her thoughts. She shoved it all aside and replaced the distance between them. The cool air rushing around her didn't soothe her roaring blood. She kept her smile casual. Apparently, picking his brain wouldn't be an option right now.

She needed to bring her body under control and regain her rational ability to speak, before they could have a decent conversation. She would fan girl after he was gone and she was alone, and then tell her brain to start doing more than just swooning when he was around. Maybe next time they ran into each other, she could actually talk to him.

She shouldered her laptop and took another step back. "Me too."

They exchanged generic goodbyes, and she reined in the impulse to make the conversation any more than it already was. After he was gone, she packed up the rest of her stuff.

"Mikki." A pleasant female voice cut through her rambling thoughts as she left the room.

She whirled to face Vivian. Given the time they'd spent together when she'd interviewed with Skriddie Bust—they'd hung out after hours, seen the town, all as part of the recruitment speech—this conversation should be casual and normal. But Vivian knew. Maybe everything, since she'd seen them singing together last night, and it looked like she'd been running interference while Jared talked to Mikki. *Does she think less of me? Is that even possible?* Based on what Hayden had told her, Vivian's opinion of her was no longer measurable anyway. She hoped her tone sounded even and calm. "Good to see you again."

Vivian's smile grew, never appearing anything but genuine. Every hair was perfectly in place, and her suit looked like it cost more than everything Mikki had packed. "You never told me you're so impressive on stage."

Is she talking about last night, or today? "It's not really the kind of thing that comes up in casual conversation."

"I guess not. I'll let you get back to work soon. I just wanted to let you know it was a great presentation. I'm just sorry you weren't giving it for us."

A trickle of surprise nudged Mikki's senses, surging around every time Hayden had warned her that Skriddie was disappointed in her actions. On several occasions, he'd told her Vivian made no secret of the fact she was glad she hadn't hired Mikki after all. What were the words he'd used? That Vivian couldn't have someone working for her who didn't know the difference between ethics and a challenge. "I'm sor—"

"Don't." Vivian waved her off. "You did what was right for you. But you should know, I still want you on our team, so if you ever change your mind…"

Mikki shifted her weight from one foot to the other. *She's kidding, right?* She started to say she was happy where she was, but the words died before they reached her lips. *Odd.* "I didn't think the job was still available."

Vivian furrowed her brows. "Why wouldn't it be?"

"You know… What I did."

"It's in the past now, right? We're all adults. We can handle it." Vivian adjusted her purse and glanced at her phone. "I'm sorry, I have an appointment. You still have my card?"

At least no one there was still mad about her hack. A guilt Mikki didn't know she was carrying slipped away. They exchanged handshakes and said their goodbyes. As soon as the other woman was gone, Mikki sank into a nearby chair. Her head was whirling even more than before. The two contrasting conversations had her thoughts in a jumble. She wasn't cut out for this casual sex thing, so why was she willing to do it again if it meant another night with him?

Bad road to go down. She needed to get back to work. She forced her feet one in front of the other toward the exhibit hall.

The next hour in the NSS booth dragged like dial-up. People came and went, but most of them only stopped for the free stress-relief balls with the company logo on them. She couldn't ignore her tingle of disappointment at the distinct lack of Jared's familiar face in the Skriddie booth.

"Michaela." Hayden stepped into an empty spot next to her, smile wide and warm. "Great job this morning. Everyone's talking about the impression you left, and we've pulled in a couple of significant leads."

"Thanks." The compliment warmed her, and she couldn't help but grin. It was true, sometimes he fell into the repetitive, micromanager role, but it was times like this she remembered he really did recognize and appreciate her skills.

"So." He puffed out his cheeks and exhaled slowly. "Something's come up this afternoon, and I need you to step in a second time."

Her mind whirred, trying to process the words. "For…?"

"There's that panel on shopping cart security. I can't make it, so you're up."

Epic. That meant no script, shoot-from-the-hip answers, on a topic she loved to discuss when she was given free rein. "Awesome. Absolutely. I'm there." She couldn't keep the excitement from her voice.

He gave a small laugh and shook his head. "Glad to hear it. Just do me a tiny favor."

"Of course."

"There will be five of you on the panel, including a representative from Skriddie. My only request is you steer clear of them outside of the discussion. No reason to bring up bad blood here, right?"

Something ticked in the back of her head. That was the second time today he'd mentioned avoiding them. He seemed more fixated on the issue than anyone at Skriddie, and considering he wasn't the one whose network had been hacked, that seemed odd.

Maybe he's just looking out for me. Except, she couldn't make herself believe it. For a brief moment, she considered telling him Vivian had assured her it was all done and in the past. Instead, she just turned a smile on him. "Of course not. I'll behave."

"Go grab some lunch." He nodded toward the exhibit hall doors. "Panel's at two-thirty. Take it easy until then."

"Right, sure." As she wandered away, she couldn't help the doubt gnawing at her thoughts. Vivian had been genuine. Sure, there were some things Mikki didn't know, but she thought she could at least tell when someone was being phony. But apparently either Vivian or Hayden had lied to her. A million prickles crawled under her skin at the idea Hayden knew more about the situation than he was saying. She just wished she had a focus for her misgivings, rather than just a suspicion.

SEVEN

Jared snarled at empty air and jammed his phone back in his slacks pocket. He didn't need any more info from Tate to know what had happened. After the call last night, he'd expected to lose the overseas contract, but the news still infuriated him.

The first time it had happened, almost six months ago, it had been a fluke. Sometimes they lost sales. It wasn't a big deal. He'd personally dug into the rumors. Scoured every inch of the network himself to make sure they were unfounded, and moved on. Reluctantly, but he'd done enough investigation to put his mind at ease.

The second time, two months ago, at least they'd been ready to answer the concerns about their own internal security. But their responses hadn't been enough, and since they weren't accustomed to clients giving such specific reasons for going with another company, he had been suspicious.

He'd dived back into the rumors. Even going so far as to spend an entire week personally checking every password and the security settings for every employee.

Money? Sure, sometimes someone balked at their pricing. But

that usually happened early on in the process. Personality clash? Again, it came up. Just not often.

But to be minutes away from signing a contract and be told, "We heard a rumor you don't even have it together internally," and for it to have happened three times now…

It didn't feel right to Jared. Especially since it had never been an issue before.

The flaws weren't in his network, he was certain of that, which meant he needed answers. Since they'd lost to NSS each time, he could only think of one place to look. Even if he couldn't leverage a new contract to make him look better for promotion, if he could tie a tourniquet around the issue before it got worse, that would still work in his favor. He made his way through the convention center crowds, cutting a straight line for the exhibit hall.

His determined footsteps slowed as he neared his destination. Mikki was at the edge of the NSS booth, back to him, tugging her messenger bag over her head. Each movement elongated her curves, and his chest tightened. He drew in a shallow breath, unable to drag his gaze away. *She'd be the perfect way to get rid of some of this tension.*

Too bad it wasn't an option. He'd been right to put an end to things before they started. She whirled toward him, and as her gaze met hers, joy dancing in her dark eyes, he realized he was still staring.

He let his smile grow and failed to completely suppress images of pinning her to the wall and trailing his lips along her collarbone. *You have work to do, remember?* "Is Hayden around?"

The corner of her mouth drooped, a half-frown flitting in. She nodded behind her. "Right there, can't miss him."

Jared might argue he could miss a lot when he was enthralled with someone else. Except missing details was counter-intuitive to everything he believed. His mind balked at the fact he'd missed one as obvious as the full-grown man just a few feet away. He still couldn't tear his gaze from Mikki. Professionalism warred with lust. Right. Promotion and reputation on the line. "Thanks. See you around?"

The only word he could think of for her expression was impish. "I'm hoping."

It took the last of his restraint to end the conversation there, but he still couldn't help watching her walk away.

After she was absorbed by the crowds, he forced his attention back to the task at hand. He caught Hayden's eye long enough to let the other man know he was waiting, and then meandered around the booth. NSS had a more diverse product line than Skriddie. They also built websites and point of sale software, so they had a bit more to show off.

"Stealing company secrets?" Hayden asked with a laugh.

Jared tried to make his chuckle sound genuine, but was pretty sure he failed when the stilted laugh choked from his throat. He hated this game. If tossing passive aggressive insults were his thing, he'd considering firing back a, "Learning from the best." He'd rather not dive into that kind of pettiness. He didn't have to rein in his thoughts, either. This wasn't a prospective client. "We both know you don't keep the important stuff on display."

"So true. Speaking of, I don't suppose you're working with anyone new."

Jared gritted his teeth. He should have expected the question—Hayden was eternally looking for one of them to drop names about prospects—but today it carried a new cloud of irritation. "You know I won't tell you that."

"Had to try." Hayden winked. "What can I do for you?"

"Congratulations on your newest security client." Jared kept his posture casual and his attention on Hayden's face. He was surprised when the other man looked away and rested his hands in his pockets.

"Thanks." Hayden finally met his gaze again. "I need to get going."

Jared had expected…well, he wasn't sure what. Gloating, at least. Not whatever this was. Especially since he hadn't asked the hard question yet. "Sure. I was hoping you could tell me one thing first."

"As long as it's quick." Hayden took a step back.

So odd. If Tate were here, the conversation would probably go much differently. There would be deflection, and niceties, and a slow, subtle lead-in to the actual topic. Still, Jared had expected at least a little smugness about the lost client before he launched into the direct question. "They asked some things that seemed to come straight out of left field. Do you know anything about that?"

Hayden waved a hand. "Don't know how I could. But I'll tell you this, if the infamous Jared Tippins can't fix all his internal security leaks, I don't know how we could hope to if we had a problem."

Jared couldn't keep his shock from his face. He hadn't even mentioned what cost them the deal.

"I really need to jet." Hayden was already turning away. "We'll catch up soon."

Jared didn't need to stop him. The conversation had been enlightening enough as it was. Hayden's behavior was too off-the-charts guilty, especially for a man who smooth talked his way through almost everything.

Something was going on, and Hayden wasn't going to say anymore. Without solid answers, Jared would just have to cover as many bases as he could. He needed to get his own internal team on things, reaffirm internal operations were solid, and then put a plan in place to tie off the flow of bad press before it got worse.

He already had his phone out as he headed in the direction of the hotel, sending texts to Tate and Vivian to join him as soon as possible, and another back to the office to get the internal investigation started.

Five minute later, he'd secured a large booth in the back corner of a restaurant built to look like an old English pub. The setting hadn't been as important to him as the fact that it was mostly empty.

He flipped his tablet open and started making lists. Writing notes. Getting every thought written down, regardless of how small it seemed.

By the time Tate and Vivian joined him, a plate of cheese fries sat untouched in the middle of the table, and he had a rough plan mocked up. He'd sifted through everything they'd already heard from lost clients—including the details of last night's call—and had his top person investigating back at the home office.

"What's up?" Vivian grabbed a fry, nibbled, and then grimaced and set it aside. "Cold."

"Order more." Jared wasn't eating. He spun his tablet toward his colleagues, pointing to different sections of his notes as he talked. "We need to stop this before it gets worse. Distribute talking points to anyone who's client facing, remind people about internal procedures. I'll email you both. We need to start this sooner rather than later."

Tate pulled his attention from the waitress after sending her away with a smile. "Is this overkill?"

Jared frowned. "You tell me. Do you want another sale like last night's?"

Tate exhaled loudly. "Then is this enough?"

That was the problem. The one question Jared couldn't stop asking, regardless of steps on a page. It should be plenty. And Tate was right. Under normal circumstances, it would be overkill. But obviously they were missing something, and they needed to make sure the situation didn't get worse.

* * *

Mikki crossed her legs at the ankles and kicked them beneath her chair. Fortunately, the drape covering the front of the table she sat at should hide the movement from the room full of people. She sat on a raised stage, along with five other people—one a moderator standing at the podium separating the two tables.

Jared was on the other side, and she was doing her best to pretend he was just another person. Her racing pulse and vivid imagination disagreed, but she beat them back with moderate success. She needed full control of her sensibilities for this conversation.

Someone in the crowd asked an opened-ended question, directed at anyone. Mikki's answer rose to tip of her tongue but stuck there. She wasn't sure she liked this new internal filter that cared what people thought, even if that person was Jared Tippins. Everyone else was exchanging looks, but no one seemed to want to delve into a response.

Before she could force out her thoughts, Jared leaned forward, and in some of the most measured words she'd ever heard, handed out a nicely wrapped answer about internet security and industry standardization.

He was sexy, but not very outside the box as far as she could tell. Was this the man she'd been taught had revolutionized network security? A tiny snort slipped from her throat before she could stop it. Heat flooded her cheeks when several pairs of eyes swiveled in her direction.

Like most the people in the room, Jared locked his gaze on hers. His voice was smooth and confident. "I think Ms. Elford has a different opinion."

She shook her head. "I'm fine." It didn't matter if she disagreed with him or not. It wasn't even because she hadn't stopped thinking about him for more than a couple of minutes at a time all day. If she pretended hard enough, it didn't even have to do with what he thought about her. This all centered around how much respect she had for the legend. If he said something was the case, he either knew more than she did about the subject, or would figure it out on his own later.

"Please." There was no condescension in his tone. Only confidence and curiosity. "If you've got a different opinion, I'd like to hear it."

Great. Now he'd backed her into a corner. Either way, she'd lose. She forced herself to look him in the eye, took a deep breath, and let the words flow. "That's the problem with industry standards. They only matter to the people who are using them, and just because you've standardized something doesn't mean everyone is complying."

He shifted in his chair, turning more toward her, and rested his arms on the table. "It's true, but offering standardization up front gives people a certain level of expectation. They know they're getting specific services and that they can take that technology elsewhere if they need to expand or add on new components."

He didn't see it. The surprised realization sparked a new kind of confidence. She recognized the feeling inside—it was the same one she'd had six months ago when she'd breached the security on his network. The knowledge that for as much as this individual knew, he wasn't perfect. She felt surer of her response this time. "Which is great, I agree. Standardization makes business run smoother."

He smiled, nodded, and turned away.

"Except." She spit out the single word and once again felt every head swivel in her direction. *Having their attention is a good thing. Remember that. You don't care if they don't like what you have to say, as long as you state your point clearly.* She had this right. "When it comes to security."

Jared raised an eyebrow.

She leaned one arm on the table, directing her statements at him. "Some bored chaos hacker stumbles on your website and decides they want to leave a little 'I was here' note. Or even worse, they want access to your customer database. They're not thinking, 'Oh, I need to use industry standards to break in.'"

"But why are they doing it in the first place?" Jared countered. "Why are they even there? That scenario doesn't make any sense."

"Chaos hacker. The explanation is in the name. They don't need a reason besides boredom. But if you'd prefer, let's make it more personal." She barely registered the hush in the room. Something in the back of her mind told her it was significant, but she was too focused on the debate. On making her point.

"Are we talking vengeful ex kind of personal?" Jared's attention was all on her now, never wavering. "Because it's true, that happens, but things like a girlfriend stealing your administrative password are a little harder to code for." He turned his attention back to the room. "Not that measures can't be put in place. Once again, industry standards dictate things like IP checking for logins. Trusted computer settings. There's an intensive list of things that prevent the up-close and personal violation from becoming an issue."

Vengeful ex. She hadn't even thought about that. Something to add to her ever-growing list of possible loopholes she tucked away for work. "I'm not talking about the trusted friend, loved one, or family member. Though there are things to be concerned about there, too." But that was a different conversation. "Everyone has beliefs, right? Something at their very core that they hold true?" She couldn't help her satisfaction when he shrugged in agreement. "With today's instant access to all things news—whether it's really news or not—more and more people's beliefs go on trial on social media every day.

"Suddenly, regardless of what you think or believe, someone decides they disagree with you, and they take it out on your business's online presence. Graffiti on the website, maybe? Or again, stolen customer information. Names, phone numbers, addresses. Do you think they really stop and ask themselves, 'does this website follow industry standards?' and then steer clear if the answer is yes?"

Jared's mouth drew into a thin line, and he half rose from his chair. "But you're painting the rare scenario. Standardization and certification statistics show those things impact less than one percent of online businesses. These are companies who are paid to verify things work the way the rules say. Time and again, research has proven the chaos hacker is the boogey man in an executive's closet. It doesn't happen to the everyday user. Statistically it doesn't even register on the radar."

"But that's what we sell." The words slipped out without her considering them. "Peace of mind. You're not buying security because it happens all the time. You're buying because you don't ever want to be the person who said, 'That'll never happen to me.' And then it does."

The corner of his mouth twitched up. It looked like he wanted to reply when the moderator cut in. "Thank you, Ms. Elford. Very enlightening. But I think we've gotten off topic. Next question?"

She turned her attention back to the audience, but not before she saw a hint of a smile whisper across Jared's face. Had she impressed him? She liked the thought of that.

The rest of the panel passed without incident. After, she

lingered, shaking hands and accepting business cards, along with a smattering of, "Great insight. We'll be in touch."

Part of her wanted to wait for Jared to extract himself from the small pocket of people around him. For professional reasons, of course. So far he'd had some very specific opinions on what did and didn't work in this business, and she wanted to know how a brain like that crossed the line into innovative.

And maybe she was lingering just a little because every time she looked at him, new images flashed through her mind. Of his lips gliding up her throat. Or his hands on her hips. Or his mouth swallowing her cries in a hungry kiss.

Her skin tingled, reacting to the simple caress of her shirt against her body. She pushed the onslaught of fantasy aside. Too bad she had to get back to work. She made her way toward the exit, still toying with fantasies around the familiar voice fading in the background.

"Michaela." The sharp word cut into her thoughts, and she spun toward Hayden. He stood on the other side of the hallway, face stretched into a grin. "A minute?"

She crossed the short distance, taking a cue from the fact he'd picked an out-of-the-way spot and keeping her voice low. "What's up?"

"I caught the end of your performance in there. Absolutely brilliant. Want to run the rest of the show?"

"I—" How was she supposed to answer a question like that? It was tempting, but only if it came with the great view again. "I think tech's more my thing. I didn't say anything you wouldn't have."

His expression shifted, corners of his mouth tugging down. "Except you did the one thing I really need you to not do."

She replayed the panel in her head, focusing on the bits that weren't blurred together. Nope, nothing stood out as "bad." "Which was?"

"Making waves with Skriddie."

"Oh." *This again?* What had he expected? So much for him giving her more excuses to stare at Jared. When she rolled his words around in her thoughts, his request dragged back her nagging question from earlier. Why was he so fixated on this? "You know it was a panel discussion, right?"

He jammed his hands in his pockets. "Just… Please. You're fantastic at what you do, so I let you do things your way. I only have this one request."

She bit back a snort at how his idea of doing things her own way contrasted with the tight leash he kept on everything, but she couldn't suppress her next question. "You're really kind to worry about my wellbeing. Especially since you already have me on staff, and technically I'm just a grunt. Are all bosses this concerned about how the competition views their employees?"

His jaw clenched. "No. Most of them are assholes. I know you're new to jobs like this, but I'll remind you again, making waves in an industry is never a good idea. You're talented. I'd hate to see you throw your future away because your ego is bigger than your sense."

She forced a smile onto her face, despite the welt his words left on her thoughts. "Of course. My mistake." She wasn't sure which bothered her more. The insult, or the thinly veiled threat about the future of her career.

EIGHT

Jared scanned the dining room, gaze flitting from face to face. Compared to the impromptu brainstorming session at lunch and the intriguing debate with Mikki, the rest of his day had dragged in a way he wasn't used to.

He didn't have time for a business dinner tonight. He should be going hands-on with the network again. Getting to the bottom of these rumors. Except he didn't have any leads beyond what he'd already checked. Any and all digging had come up clean.

So he was taking this chance to learn what people were talking about. Where the concerns were, and if there were any new rumors that might point him in a specific direction.

If only he could focus on the whispers around him. His attention kept drifting back to one face in particular. The way her black hair framed her face, and how her oversized, button-down shirt hinted at her curves without revealing anything. Then there was the fact he couldn't stop thinking about pushing up her knee-length skirt…

A sharp elbow dug into his ribs, dragging his attention back to his own dinner table. Vivian's voice faded in. "I'm sure it's all up to spec, but our tech brain can give you any details you want."

He smiled at whomever they were talking to—the owner of a small website making polite conversation. The man had indicated when he'd made himself at home at their table an hour ago he had no need of Skriddie's services. He'd spent the rest of the time trying to convince them to sign up for the same multi-level marketing company he sold candles for.

"Sure." Candle guy's smile was thin. "I'm just hearing rumors you've got some holes in your security. I wonder, if a big player like Skriddie can't keep their secrets hush-hush, what chance do I have?"

Something tickled the back of Jared's memory. *You're most vulnerable where you'd least expect to look.* Mikki's words from the presentation this morning. She didn't know about this, did she? His nerves protested the idea she might be involved, but he couldn't shake the nagging thought.

He dragged his attention back to the conversation, nodding and smiling as was appropriate, and grateful when it was over.

"What's up with you, space case?" Vivian hissed in his ear as candle guy turned to someone else at the large table.

Besides non-stop thoughts of stripping Mikki out of whatever she was wearing? A fantasy he really needed to stow until they were back home. This was exactly why kept his attention on work, and order, and making sure everything in his universe lined up the way it was supposed to. Which Mikki didn't. She didn't fit into any of his plans or logic. "Do you think NSS really knows something?"

Vivian pushed her salad aside. "I knew you were thinking about her. I just didn't think you were still dwelling on what she said. It was a sales pitch."

"A very convincing one." When Mikki had said in her presentation NSS had something that could trump the competition, he knew she was hyping things up, and probably not of her own accord. At the same time, something in her body language said she believed it, at least to some extent. Mikki slipped out a side door, and he pushed back from the table before he realized what he was doing. "I'm done for the night. I'm going to get some work done."

Viv and Tate wouldn't argue. They'd both expected him to step out early anyway. He moved into the hallway and surveyed his surroundings. Now where had she gone?

Something caught his attention, a flash of electric blue like the shoes and shirt she was wearing, and he chased after her.

"Mikki," he called as he rounded the corner.

She paused, and the smattering of people still in the convention center milled around her. Her back stiffened, and she turned to face him. "Hey."

Don't stare. He forced himself to make eye contact. "Do you have a minute?"

She glanced around her, over his shoulder, pretty much everywhere. "Sure."

She almost looked like she expected someone to jump out of the shadows at any minute. He stepped closer. His questions were strictly business, but he still didn't need anyone else eavesdropping. What was off about her posture? "Are you all right?"

She didn't keep her attention on him for long. Every few seconds her gaze darted around again. "I'm fine. What's up?"

He caught sight of a small alcove behind her. He'd noticed spaces like it around the convention center. The spots were set aside to help people keep their phone calls or other conversations more private. As long as it was empty, they wouldn't have an audience. He nodded toward the hidden spot. "Away from prying eyes?"

She let out a tiny breath, and her expression relaxed. "Good idea."

Was she terrified of being seen with him? That didn't fit. Nothing in the last twenty-four hours aligned with that. But the moment they were out of sight, her posture eased further.

"What's up?" she asked again.

He leaned against a nearby wall. It was tempting to stand closer, just enough to dive into the heady scent of energy and citrus she radiated, but he hadn't tracked her down to get up close and personal. "Can I ask you something?"

She tilted her head to the side and leaned closer. Her voice dropped until he felt as much as heard the words brushing his cheek. "They don't match tonight."

Match…? She means her bra and panties. His eyes grew wide and he straightened, surprised when she met his gaze. "I wasn't…"

She blinked back, a tiny smile slipping out.

There was the woman he'd sung with. He resisted the urge to trace a finger along her bottom lip. "You should do more of that. You're beautiful when you smile." *Not where I want this conversation to go. Focus on the facts. What does she know? How much can you get from her about her presentation? The verifiable info.*

Pink flooded her cheeks and she ducked her head. "You didn't pull me aside to flirt, I'm sorry."

He did need to keep things on track, or risk the conversation sliding into territory he couldn't have it in—like what color was her underwear if it didn't match?

He was better off just asking his question. "Do you really know what we're up to? And do you really have something better?"

She crossed her legs at the ankles and used the wall to support her, putting a few more inches between them. "It's a demo. It was made to sell products." Which was what he'd expected. There was no reason to put her on stage just to taunt Skriddie. Still, he wasn't surprised when she continued. "But."

Lust and fantasies of stripping her down aside, he wanted to know what came next. "I knew it."

She laughed, and the carefree note tickled his senses. Damn it, he wished he could ignore his response to her. "It's all the same old stuff. Things you already know," she said.

Something about the casual assurance, as if this were shared knowledge between them, triggered another wave of warning bells in his head, but he couldn't place the source. "Placate me."

She shrugged and fiddled with the edge of her shirt. "It's all about the remote machines, right? The ones no one realizes are connected directly to the servers. The machines they wouldn't expect to have access to their deepest, most important information. They're a risk for anyone, because no one thinks to check them thoroughly. All it takes is one person giving someone a password who doesn't deserve it 'just this once' and you're compromised. It happens three times, and if you don't catch it, you're screwed."

Three times was an awfully specific number. *What's hiding under her explanation?* He scooted closer, irrationally pleased when his hand brushed hers and she didn't pull away. "They got lucky hiring you, didn't they? There's no one there who recognizes how much you know. Or have they just hidden their appreciation of your skill that well?"

"I'm not the best they have, and they gave me a chance."

She wouldn't look at him. Every few seconds, she wove the hem of her shirt through her fingers and then released it again. She glanced behind her, and then gave him most of her attention again.

"Am I holding you up?" he asked.

She finally met his gaze again. "Do you work all the time? Like, twenty-four seven all business and professional and company first?"

If he'd guessed a hundred times what she might ask next, that wouldn't have been anywhere on the list. "I do what's required of me."

Her lips twisted, and she ran her tongue along her teeth, metal ball clacking. "What was different about last night?"

Everything. The question loosed a floodgate of memories, rushing across his skin. He couldn't hold them back. *Not good.* "Last night was out of character for me. A one-time thing and such."

Her brow furrowed. "So you wouldn't do it again? It's not professional."

He was missing something; he had to be. When he set the rapid-fire questions aside and studied her face, he didn't see any irritation or malice there. In fact, the same challenge as the night before stared back. He didn't know what she was looking for, and trying to make sense of it simultaneously excited and infuriated his brain. "I wouldn't rule out the possibility, but I don't spend a lot of time doing things like that."

"Things like what?" She clucked her tongue along the roof of her mouth. "Having fun, or being impulsive?"

Great, now she was twisting his words. "I can be impulsive. When I've got time."

She rolled her eyes. "Checking your calendar isn't being impulsive. You need to look up the definition of the word. Before last night, when was the last time you did something out of the blue, without second-guessing yourself? Without planning, without having a step-by-step list of possible outcomes, consequences, and stumbling blocks?"

The question flipped a switch in his head, taunting him. How did she make perfectly reasonable behavior sound so unreasonable? He searched her face, not sure what he was looking for. Then he let instinct take the wheel. He rested his hand at the back of her neck and kissed her.

She leaned in to the gesture, full lips crushing into his, almost imperceptible gasps drifting from her throat. Every sound goaded his pulse, and his lower extremities stirred in response. Jesus, she tasted good.

He let her go but didn't pull back. "Just now."

Her cheeks turned pink, and she smirked. "And was it as horrible as you thought it would be?"

Did she have any idea she was fucking with his head, or was she just talking as things occurred to her? "No. It was pretty incredible." Another flash of inspiration struck, sending electricity through his veins. The idea heightened the heat of her standing so close and brought every nerve ending to life. His gut tightened with the swelling potential. If he was going to do this, it would be under his terms. "Help me be impulsive again tonight."

Her breathing quickened, and her pupils dilated. "What did you have in mind?"

He pulled the spare room key from his wallet, slipped it into her hand, and gave her his room number. "Meet me upstairs. We can play things by ear from there."

"You're on."

He shouldn't be doing this. Going a second time with anyone he wasn't dating, but especially her, was a bad, horrible, terrible idea. Too bad his aching cock disagreed.

Please don't let him run into anyone between here and the elevator. Not just because he desperately wanted another round with this gorgeous, brilliant woman, but because he was so hard it hurt, and he didn't know if he could hide his erection if he had to stop and make small talk.

NINE

Mikki's heart threatened to tear from her ribcage. She hadn't started the night out meaning to goad Jared, but opportunity had struck, and the inspiration was too tempting to ignore. And if he was offering another chance, there was no way she was turning him down. A hint of hesitation—if this became a habit it would be harder to walk away from—mingled with her excitement, both spreading under her skin and making her squirm in anticipation.

She counted off the room numbers to keep from sprinting down the hallway. No reason to make herself breathless before things even started. And then she was there, in front of Jared's room. The door swung open before she could slide the key into the slot, and his confident grin sent another layer of tingles through her.

He grasped her fingers between his and tugged her inside. His arms wrapped around her waist from behind, and he pulled her back into him as the door clicked shut. Comfort and desire flooded her frame when his solid chest pressed into her spine.

Everywhere he touched, the textures of her clothing caressed her skin. The anticipation had made her hypersensitive. The shift of fabric against her arms, her back, and her stomach sent shudders of want through her. *I can't believe I'm doing this.* For the second time in less than twenty-four hours, even. She needed to feel his skin on hers, not muted by too many layers of decency. She tilted her head back to rest on his shoulder, exposing her neck.

He took the hint, kisses so light along her skin she wondered if she actually felt them. The hard length digging into her tailbone, though, she definitely felt that. His hands glided forward and under the hem of her shirt, palms resting on her bare stomach. How could such a simple gesture short-circuit so many of her thoughts?

"There's something alluring—" his voice vibrated through her skin, "—about every curve and slope of your figure, and the thought of revealing it all inch by inch."

His touch called to the compliment wrapped inside his words. She closed her eyes so she could focus on each sensation.

He made quick work of the buttons on her shirt, breaking contact with her long enough to rake it down her arms and toss it aside. It landed near the bed, but he stayed behind her, hands returning to dance along her ribs.

Cool air brushed her mostly bare chest, and a new thrill rushed through her. Sex with Payton had been getting naked in the dark, crawling under the covers, and a couple of minutes of grinding before he rolled over and fell asleep. She'd been interested in more, but his passive belittling had kept her from asking. Even worse had been finding out after the fact that he blamed the boredom on her lack of impulse.

Last night had been a rush—sex in a public place. But something about now sent a new kind of euphoria racing through her veins. She was standing topless in an almost-stranger's room, about to let him do whatever he wanted to her. She forced herself to swallow.

His thumbs trailed up her sides, voice low, a commanding current running through it. He brushed the bottom of her breasts, and she gasped in surprise. "Watching you all day, and only having a hint from last night of what's hidden under your clothes, has been driving me insane." His hands continued up, fingers brushing her throat before gliding down her spine. "You know what my one consolation is?"

Each time he leaned in, she caught a hint of the rain-and-after-shave scent whispering from him. She shook her head, not trusting herself to speak. The only thing she knew was how wet she was from his attentions. Memories of his fingers bringing her to orgasm teased her, mingling with the thoughts of what it felt like to be spread open when he'd pushed inside her. She had only been in his room a few moments, and already the way he was drawing out the moment was a more delicious torture than she'd ever imagined.

He unsnapped her bra, and the fabric fell away. He drew the straps down her arms, letting the cups drag across her already rock-hard nipples before he tossed the lingerie on top of her other clothing. Everywhere his hands moved, his long, talented fingers danced along her skin. "My only consolation is finally getting to see."

Oxygen stole from her head when he grazed her shoulder with his teeth, leaving her light-headed and wanting more. "You can see it all if you want."

"Oh, I want." The seductive baritone of his voice hummed through every inch of her, adding flames to her desire. He unbuttoned her skirt and slid the zipper down, a tooth at a time.

She pressed back into him, grinding into the erection tempting her. The buttons of his shirt were cool against her bare back, and the cotton teased the hyper-sensitive skin. He inhaled sharply. His fingers dug into her hips. Her belly clenched in response as desire pulsed through her legs.

He pushed on her skirt. It dropped to the floor, pooling around her ankles. He traced a line along the elastic of her string bikini panties. "Black bra and red lacy bottoms? So not only do you not match, but you're trying to obliterate my thoughts before I even get you naked? Fucking sexy."

"You've figured out my master plan." she teased.

"I doubt such a thing exists, but I have more important things to focus on." He moved his hands back up her chest, cupped her breasts, and sucked on the soft flesh between her neck and shoulder.

She gasped, and her knees wobbled at the combination of light pain and exquisite pleasure. He pulled her closer, fingers rolling her nipples, gently at first before he pinched both.

The need between her legs screamed for attention. She ground her butt against him as he massaged and sucked relentlessly. She was vaguely aware of the soft cries tearing from her throat and mingling with his hungry groans.

One of his hands moved away from the pink nub it had been lavishing, but before she could wonder why or feel disappointed, he brushed the crotch of her panties.

"Jesus, you're soaked." He rubbed through the lace, pushing the fabric against her slit.

She was too lost in the multiple sensations to reply. She covered his hands with hers, partly to help her stay upright and partly to make sure he kept going. The only thing she could manage was, "Harder."

He obliged, going straight for her clit, pressing back when she ground into his hand. Was she crying out? She didn't know, and she didn't care. Every single touch was pushing her closer to the edge. She tossed her head back further as she came, waves of ecstasy pouring through her. He eased off as she struggled to catch her breath, but he didn't stop kissing along the back of her neck.

"Better than just okay?" His warm breath teased her skin.

"Better than chocolate." She managed to find her footing enough to spin and face him. She made a point of studying him. "But I don't want to make a habit of this."

His brows rose in response.

He thinks I mean the sex. Which she should, but she didn't. She worked her fingers into the knot of his tie, loosening it. "I don't mind being naked in front of you." Understatement of the decade. That thought alone was enough to make her even wetter. "But you can't stay mostly dressed all the time."

She kicked her shoes and skirt into the rapidly growing pile and tossed his tie on top of it all. He hissed when her nails trailed down his chest, undoing each button in her way.

She dropped her hands to his waist, only fumbling with the belt for a moment before undoing the buckle, then sliding his zipper down. She grasped his shaft, and his growl filled her head. His hot skin seared her cool palm. She worked him free as she dropped to her knees in front of him.

Her tongue flicked over the bulbous head in front of her, licking a drop from the tip. The salty taste flooded her tongue. His fingers tangled in her hair. She took the hint and wrapped her lips around him, taking his length into her mouth and sliding down.

He rocked against her face, grip tightening as his breathing grew shallow. "Jesus." His voice was strained. "That metal ball on my cock. You're killing me."

He caught her wrists, grip tight, and pulled her to her feet. His gaze locked on hers, eyes dark and holding her captive. He pulled her nearer, lips hovering close enough to her ear for his breath to tantalize her skin. "I'd draw this moment out all night if I could." A hard edge lined his voice. "But I can't stop thinking about how good it feels to be inside you, and I know how wet you are, and I don't want anything else right now."

Each new word sent another pang of want through her. He pushed her backward until her calves collided with the bed. One more nudge, and she was sitting on the mattress looking up at him.

He rested a hand on the back of her neck and his thumb brushed her windpipe. "Don't move."

Her anticipation spiked again when he stood and stepped back. He stood just out of reach as he tossed his shirt and undershirt aside. When he paused, she stopped breathing for a moment. *What's he up to?*

He bent to fumble with one of his bags and a moment later produced a condom.

Prepared. Again. Did that mean the evening with her was just another plan, and she'd only been the right person at the right time? She pushed the doubt aside and dove into the direct question instead. "So, Mister Impulse-is-horrible-and-scary. Do you have that because you were planning on getting lucky this trip?"

"I have it because it never hurts to be prepared." Every inch of his body molded to her. "And possibly because hope compelled me to pick up an extra last night."

The idea sent a new flush of heat through her and tapped a seductive rhythm in her veins.

Within seconds, he'd shed the rest of his clothes and wrapped himself in the rubber. She reached for him. He gave her a wicked smile, grabbed her wrists again, and pulled them above her head as he nudged her onto her back. He bent over her and crushed his lips to hers hard enough their teeth collided. She struggled under his grip, not to break free, but to get closer to his touch.

While his tongue danced with hers, hungry and demanding, his free hand dropped back to her waist. He broke away long enough to tear her panties away and discard them. The friction heightened her want.

He nudged her knee with his. "Scoot back."

"Yes, sir." She gave him a teasing smile and relocated to the center of the bed.

He pushed her thighs apart with his knee and moved between them. Lowering his head, he drew his tongue across her nipple and sucked it into his mouth. She gasped and arched her back when he nibbled the hard flesh. He never let up his attentions on the nub as his cock nudged her opening. He pushed inside her, driving in his thick length all at once. His movements were slow at first, drawing out almost to the tip before plunging inside her again. She wanted more. She wanted things fast and hard like the night before. Her hips bucked against him to speed things up.

He sat straight up, driving deeper into her. "If you keep that up, I won't last."

"Isn't that the point?" Her question melted into another moan as he placed his hands on the back of her knees and pressed them toward her chest. The position put him deeper inside her than she'd ever been penetrated and slammed into a spot that made her groan louder with every thrust.

And then he picked up the pace. As he pounded, she felt climax claw its way through her again, and her hands dug into the blankets, looking for something to grab tight. A scream tore from her throat when she came, and she clenched tight around him, focused on every sensation at the same time.

His breathing grew more punctuated, and his thrusts reached a frantic pace. Never breaking the rhythm, he dropped her legs suddenly, rested his hands on either side of her head, and locked his gaze on hers. "You…feel…incredible," he managed between short breaths. His grunts became staccato and frantic as he peaked. Even after his groans reached their apex, then faded, he continued to pound inside her. Her head floated back to reality, gaze locked on his, as his pace slowed to a stop.

He hovered a little longer, both of them searching for their breaths. She couldn't look away. Her heart squeezed at the raw lust staring back. What was it about him that had her so captivated? The impulse to curl up in his arms and stay there for hours flooded her, gnawing at a longing she knew wasn't appropriate. It wasn't just the sex. The thought hit her hard, and she couldn't shake it. There was a deeper connection she couldn't place. Damn it. How was any guy ever going to stack up to this once they went their separate ways?

TEN

Jared rolled onto his back, struggling to catch his breath. Mikki lay close enough the heat of her skin brushed his, teasing his thoughts with possibilities and memories. Condom disposed of, he pushed onto his side, propped himself up on one elbow, and rested his hand on her stomach. "You were right. Just this once, being impulsive was worth it."

A gentle smile played on her lips—he liked that look. It was natural and carefree. If he wasn't careful, he could start to miss it when it wasn't around. She scooted closer until her side pressed against his chest. "Just this once, huh? Last night was a disappointment after all?"

He traced light lines along her skin, memorizing each silken dip and curve. "Okay, maybe it paid off twice." He made sure teasing was evident in his tone.

She tilted her head up long enough to kiss him before dropping back again. "I hope all this nasty impulsiveness didn't take you away from anything important."

Christ, after feeling that steel ball roll along the head of his cock, he wondered what they could get up to that actually fit the word "nasty." Just the thought of it was enough to make his pulse race.

"I'd say I got quite a bit more out of the evening than I hoped to. Besides, I'm not the only one who snuck out early."

She studied him for a moment, amusement still dancing on her lips. "But you had a plan, didn't you?"

He was still trying to figure out how she thought, but he was getting a better idea. It seemed to fall along the lines of the more random, the better. "And you didn't?"

She chewed on her bottom lip. "Believe it or not, I had a destination in mind. But I suspect this was better."

"You just suspect?" Pride bristled to the forefront of his thoughts, prodding him to remove any of her doubt. He glided his hand up her stomach and along her ribcage between her breasts. "What can I do to make it certain?"

She laughed and intertwined her fingers with his. "It's not that. You were incredible. This is incredible. I can't believe…" She jolted upright, taking his hand with her. "Anyway. There's still time. You should go with me."

Uh… "Where?" He couldn't peel his gaze from her as she tugged on her bra, and then pulled her top on. She fastened buttons starting from the bottom. Watching her hide her curves was almost as seductive revealing them. She left the top few buttons open, just enough to tease.

She gave her panties a sad glance before shaking her head and shoving them into a side pocket on her purse. She finished dressing and dropped back onto the edge of the bed. "Outside."

He raised an eyebrow. "I can see how you might not want to get tied down by details."

She stuck her tongue out at him. "I've never seen the strip before. I'm going to see the casinos, be a tourist, everything fun and non-professional that Hayden would lecture me for hours on end if he knew I was doing on his time."

Jared was pretty sure they could check one thing off that list already. "The strip. Like The Thunder from Down Under?"

Her eyes grew wide. "Should I ask why you know that?"

He smiled at the lilt in her voice. "It's nothing scandalous. Viv has been talking about it."

"Mmm." She sank back into him and rested her cheek against his. "So I'm not keeping you from checking out the male strippers yourself?"

The quiet banter was pleasant, lulling him into a comfortable spot he didn't mentally get to rest in very often. "Nah. I don't want those poor men feeling inadequate."

"Too bad. I think you'd look good up there with them."

He nipped her earlobe with his teeth. "I don't need to advertise. I win people over with my personality."

"You're so arrogant." Her entire body went limp, her weight pressing into him. "But I still buy it. That's how you suckered me."

Her familiar scent filled his head as he nuzzled her neck. He couldn't help the serious tone creeping into his voice. "If I thought for a moment you were easily suckered, I wouldn't be interested."

"So brains really are sexy?"

He dipped under the bottom of her shirt, palm resting flat on her stomach. "*Your* brains are sexy, just like the rest of you. I just want to know how to keep seeing more."

Great, now he was taking a light-hearted conversation and turning it intense in just a few swapped words. He wasn't even sure what he meant. More after the show? No, that wasn't possible. More of the fascinating mind behind this sexy creature? That was certainly alluring. And just more of her in general. He scrambled to slide things back to neutral territory. "So you're really ducking out on me to hit up the card tables?"

"I was *really* hoping you'd go with me."

He needed to tell her no. If he was going to have another sleepless night, it should be spent catching up on work, making sure all his ducks were in a row everywhere, not meandering through Las Vegas, gawking at the sights. He had plans to implement and a promotion to secure. Part of him roared in protest even as he forced the words out. "I can't. I'm sorry."

Her back stiffened, and she pulled away. He beat back his disappointment. It wasn't like he could keep her wrapped up in his arms all night. He needed to get dressed. To move past this infatuation.

The smile she gave him didn't reach her eyes. "You're sure? I might get in trouble wandering the streets alone."

He swallowed hard but couldn't choke back his regret. He grabbed his own clothes. "I'm sure. Is it a mistake to ask if you have a starting destination in mind?" Why was he still making small talk?

Her brows furrowed, and her mouth twisted in a frown. "A mistake? No." She stepped back when he reached for her hands. "Presumptuous? Yes. Probably Circus Circus."

He shoved his hand in his pocket to hide the fingers that wouldn't stop twitching, and to keep them from tugging her back to him. "Sounds like fun. Enjoy yourself."

***

Mikki walked straight past the line of cabs. Her insides were twisted in sick knots, and she didn't even know why. Sure, the brush-off had stung a little. But it wasn't like she and Jared could just abandon the rest of the world because they'd had a little fun together. She had her life, he had his, and she needed to let him get back to important things.

A lump swelled in her chest at her own implication that she wasn't important to him. But why would she be? They didn't know anything about each other.

She stepped out of the flow of foot traffic, leaned her back against the concrete of the building, and tried to bring her racing thoughts under control. Maybe playing fast and loose was catching up to her. Was it possible living for the moment had its drawbacks? No, she refused to believe that. She'd learned to step out of her shell, she'd taught herself lust was lust and shouldn't bleed into the rest of life, and she could force herself to remember Jared Tippins was just a fling.

Several minutes and breaths later, she had managed to smooth the wrinkles in her thoughts. It wasn't a big deal. She inhaled a few more breaths of exhaust and heat-laden air and pushed away from the wall. At least she'd gotten out for the night. She could still see the sights.

Going out alone was something she'd learned so long ago; it was a part of her. Growing up around people who didn't share her interests had taught her early on that if she wanted to have fun, she had to be willing to leave everyone else to their own devices.

Circus Circus still sounded like a good starting spot. The thought tugged some positivity back to the surface. Her step lightened as she headed toward the bright lights and garish carousel top. She stepped through a side door indicating it led to the casino and stopped as joy rushed inside her. It wasn't the same as Cesar's. There was something brighter about it. Less…adult.

She smiled and picked her way across the floor. The slot machines were vibrant and eye-catching—cartoon characters, gems, some digital and some mechanical, spinning in relentless circles. But if she wanted to play video games, she had her phone.

She came to a stop at the edge of the pit of card tables. Her hands twitched at her sides. That could be fun.

"You don't strike me as a poker person." Jared's smooth voice flowed over her skin.

Her heart kicked against her ribs, both from being startled and the sudden sensation of him standing so close. His warmth caressed her back, and the intoxicating scent of his cologne made her lightheaded. Her smile grew, and she faced him. "Are you following me?"

"If I say yes, does that make things better or worse?"

Good question. The heat and excitement rushing through her hoped the answer was yes. But since she'd just told herself they needed to tone things back less than ten minutes ago, not to mention the less-than-sweet brush-off in his hotel room, she needed to ignore her rampant hormones. Then again, they were surrounded by people. That would make it difficult to get into too much trouble. Probably. "If you say no, you have to convince me it's a coincidence you're here."

"Not quite a coincidence." His eyes never left hers, as if he was searching for something. "It turns out I can't do my work until I have someone on site in the morning, so I thought I'd take a walk. I was hoping you wouldn't be too hard to find. I'm sorry I blew you off."

She wanted to push the apology, and the events leading up to it, aside. Act like it was no big deal he'd sought her out. But the rhythm of her pulse tearing through her veins wouldn't let her ignore how happy she was to see him. "I'm glad you changed your mind." There, that sounded casual, right? If so, it defied every giddy bubble flitting through her.

He gifted her with one of those rare, genuine smiles she hadn't seen him use anywhere else. "Me too."

Silence sank between them, filled with the clatter of bells and chimes in the background. She shifted her weight from one foot to the other. If she stayed here, she was going to do things she shouldn't. Flirt, be impulsive, hope for another sleepless night. She didn't know what bothered her more—that he might think less of her for being so flighty, or that she cared. Maybe she should see the town another night.

He locked his gaze on her, eyes searching hers. "I was wondering something, but I don't know how you'll take it, and I don't want to spoil the mood."

Not what she expected. Was it about the sex? Oh jeez, they weren't going to have an "it didn't mean anything" conversation, were they? The subtle lead-in didn't really seem to be his thing. "I pretty much expect the conversation to go south when you start things off like that."

"No reason to hold back then. Why did you sign with NSS?"

She felt like the air had been sucked from her lungs. Her eyes grew wide and she looked away. Her gaze flitted around the casino before finally landing on him again, but she didn't look him in the eye. She should be over this. However, the reminders from Hayden in the last twenty-four hours had her paranoid. Jared already knew she'd taken the NSS offer because of Vivian's reaction to her hack. Was he just trying to trip her up? "I was under the impression Vivian's offer wasn't on the table anymore."

He frowned, but seconds later the expression melted into

neutrality. "Why would you—" He shook his head. "What would we have had to do differently to secure your talent?"

She twisted the edge of her shirt around her fingers. This was too much like the conversation with Vivian. Her racing pulse and thoughts had shifted away from how close he stood.

Hayden had told them what she did—everything she knew—six months ago. Hadn't he? She couldn't fathom why he'd keep something so important from them, competition or not. But Hayden seemed far more fixated on the entire thing than either Jared or Vivian. Maybe they'd gotten past their anger? None of it made any sense. What was she supposed to say? She struggled for an answer that wouldn't turn into a rambling, incoherent ball of thoughts that didn't quite make sense to her.

His brow furrowed. The seconds dragged on between them, his attention never leaving her. Finally he said, "As long as you're happy there."

Of course she was. Wasn't she? For the second time in the last twenty-four hours, she questioned her own certainty. And it honestly had nothing to do with Jared. Though, she was going to be daydreaming for a long time about the different ways he made her moan. "I guess."

He shook his head, the creases around his eyes and on his forehead taking a moment to fade. He nodded at the pit behind her. "Were you going to play?"

This was neutral. This she could do. "I've never played at tables. I've played Texas hold 'em online. I've played at parties."

"So I'll show you." He reached for her, then dropped his hand at the last moment.

Disappointment tickled her senses. She kept her voice low, embarrassed at what she was about to admit. "Not poker."

"You just said you knew how to play."

She stepped closer, watching the floor instead of him, chewing on the inside of her cheek. "But I always lose. I'm really bad at reading people." *Like Hayden?* She didn't obliterate the thought but tucked it aside to let her secondary processors deal with it. "I always bluff at the wrong time."

"So no cards? You're just observing?"

She still wanted to play. And maybe if Jared was here, he could teach her a couple of things. Besides, if she didn't ask, she'd never do it. "I didn't say that. I was thinking blackjack. But...I don't know what I'm supposed to do at the tables."

"You have to pick one first."

She already knew the one she wanted. The signs said it was a five-dollar table, and the dealer was only using a single deck, which meant she could count cards. She crossed the short distance, relieved when he followed her. She hesitated a few feet back, her voice a whisper. "What now?"

He nudged her forward, breaking contact again quickly after. "You take an empty seat, you buy into the game, and you'll be dealt in." He nodded at the dealer. "She's a little new."

The woman behind the table gave her a warm smile and explained the basics.

Mikki dropped her hand by her side, a pleasant rush greeting her when she brushed Jared's fingers. It spread through her when he gave her a gentle squeeze before letting go.

She'd picked blackjack, and this table, because she'd be playing against the dealer, not the other players. There was no bluffing; it was all about the odds. And she knew how to read the odds.

Her confidence grew as the clock ticked away, and she won more hands than she lost. It wasn't supposed to be this easy. Warmth flowed through her from the spot along her spine where Jared's arm rested, occasionally making contact.

She pulled in more chips and was about to buy into the next game when his hand rested on the small of her back. "Cash out." His low voice sent tingles running through her, but the abrupt words filled her with a doubt she couldn't place. He almost sounded irritated, or upset. God, now what had she done?

Mikki couldn't help her frown that he wanted her to end the game, but waved off the dealer and gathered her chips. She slipped from the chair. At least Jared's hand never fell away; that was pleasant.

"What was that about?" She wanted to know as they made their way to the cashier.

He nodded back toward the table she'd been playing at. "The two gentlemen as wide as you are tall, standing at the edge of the pit?"

Right, she'd seen them step up fifteen or twenty minutes ago. They looked like they were enjoying the game. "What about them?"

He waited for her to get her cash and tuck it away in her wallet. Hand still on her back, he steered her away from the casino floor. His voice was so low she had to strain to hear it. "You count cards."

He noticed. She smirked. "I didn't think I could, but turns out it's easy."

He sighed and nodded at the burly guys again. "They won't usually throw you out, but they'll ask you not to play at the blackjack tables anymore."

He sounded irritated, or annoyed. She bristled in response. "I just wanted to see if I could do it. I wasn't trying to break the house or anything."

He relaxed. "It's not technically against the rules, but they don't like it. I didn't want it to ruin your night."

She flushed at the consideration. "That might have spoiled my mood a little bit. Two big burly guys telling me I had to stop. You deliver the message a lot better."

"We're here; we can still do other things." A hint of levity returned to his voice.

Like walk around being adult and responsible, and not taking risks, and not pissing off management, and not being alone together. It all sounded like less fun than the boredom centers of her brain could handle. "I didn't really have anything else in mind."

He tugged her fingers. "Isn't that status quo for you?"

The light teasing flitted through her veins. "As long as I'm not keeping you from anything…"

He nudged her further into the casino. "I'm here because I want to be, not because anyone made me. This is your show, you pick."

Go back to her hotel. That was what she needed to pick. *Screw responsible decisions.* She wasn't ready to walk away from Jared, even if he was just trying to keep her out of trouble. But at the same time, she didn't have any idea what else to do.

It was true the city looked like it never slept…sort of. She could still go gamble her heart out if she wanted, but none of the attractions were open this late. While it was interesting to wander around looking at the closed shops and all the overpriced trinkets she was sure were ninety-nine percent for show, the hands-off experience wasn't quite the same.

A familiar flash of lights surrounding a glass box caught her attention. Her cheeks warmed at the unintentional squeal that escaped her throat. She grabbed his hand and dragged him toward the claw machine. "I love these things."

She glanced up at him, surprised by the expression staring back. His brows were arched and his lips drawn in a thin line.

"What?" she asked.

He shrugged, and his face relaxed. "Nothing. It's just…you

know these things are a waste of money, right? The five or ten bucks you spend to win one toy would pay for everything in there?"

Wow, he was really no fun sometimes. She got his concern about the bouncers—or whatever they were—and the blackjack table, but this was different. She twisted her lips in mock irritation. "First of all, that's not the point. Second, you're just jealous because you don't know how to do it right."

"Really?" The corner of his mouth twitched with unformed amusement. "Tell me what I'm missing, then."

She scanned the interior of the machine while she talked, looking for a viable target. "It's not about winning, it's about the challenge."

"Still not getting it." He shoved his hands in his pockets and rocked on his heels.

"Then you don't have to play." She plucked her wallet from her purse and rifled through the bills and coins. Disappointment that she didn't have the right change settled inside. She tucked it all away again. She shouldn't be wasting his time with childish games anyway. The thought jarred her. Why was she letting him dictate her schedule? "Never mind."

He wrapped a loose hand around her arm before she could turn away. Even through her shirt, the contact sent a scorching jolt of want through her. "I'm not trying to talk you out of it."

She shrugged. "No quarters or ones."

He produced a leather tri-fold from his back pocket, extracted a one-dollar bill, and slid it the machine. "Two attempts."

She should probably be more contained, but she couldn't help her giddy rush. She kissed him on the cheek, lingering long enough to memorize the scruff of his five o'clock shadow on her lips, and then turned back to the claw machine. "Watch and learn."

She'd located a white bear on top of the stack, as close to the middle as anything and not buried under any of the other toys. The mantra repeated in her head as she drove the claw, *stick up, nudge nudge, stick right, nudge nudge, click the button...* The mechanical arm dropped, clasped around the bear's head, and lifted. Her elation was short lived when the stuffed toy slipped away and plummeted back to the mountain below.

"One more try." Jared's arm, shoulder to wrist, rested against her back, his warm breath caressing her neck. Her body swayed, temped to lean into him. The lingering musk of his cologne drilled into her thoughts. "Make it good."

Ten seconds later—according to the timer on the machine—the bear dropped into the slot.

"Sometimes though, winning makes the trying that much sweeter." She bent at the waist to retrieve it and handed it to Jared. "For you."

He held the furry toy up by the ear, examining it from every angle with a critical eye. "I don't think I need it."

She looped her hand into his arm. *What am I doing?* He hadn't pulled away, so he didn't mind, did he? *But it just feels right.* Instead of continuing to second-guess her actions, she went with it and led him back into the thinning crowds. "It's a gift. It doesn't have to be practical."

He untangled himself from her grip and seconds later rested his hand on her hip, holding her close as they walked. He continued to examine the toy in his other hand. "But what is it?"

"It's a teddy bear."

"What kind of teddy bear wears a beret, a black leather apron, and nothing else?"

"A BDSM bear." She flushed as soon as the words passed her lips. *I wouldn't mind him tying me up for a while.*

He paused in the middle of the walkway and spun her to face him. The sparse foot traffic cut a path around them He stood toe to toe with her, blue eyes searching her face. "A bondage bear, really?"

"What? An apron, nothing on underneath, that's sexy." Her skin heated, and she couldn't pull her gaze from his. He was still studying her. "What?"

"You know what's sexy?" He smiled, dipped his head, and traced his lips along the edge of her ear.

That was an intoxicating sensation. Too many things were easy with him. A pleasant chill raced through her, and she slid along his frame him with a, "Hmm?"

He dropped his empty hand to her hip. "Watching you lose yourself in whatever you're doing, seeing how genuine your joy is, and…" He trailed a finger down to her ass. "Knowing you're not wearing anything under your skirt."

Her breath hitched, and any witty response she might have had died in the back of her throat. Fun to intense in a millisecond. She couldn't code for response times that fast. Not that she was complaining. "I think you're trying to change the subject."

He stepped back, intertwined his fingers in hers again, and tugged her into step beside him, a serious note sliding into his voice. "You're right, I'm sorry. We're talking about the bear, aren't we? Is she into spanking, or does she prefer being tied up?"

He was one of the only people she'd ever met who didn't seem to recoil at how blunt she was, and was just as outspoken on top of that. Something about that was so damn appealing. "First of all, who said it was a she? And second, it's hard to tell by just looking. I have a feeling *he's* open to exploration. He just doesn't know it yet."

He half glanced in her direction, brows raised, before turning away again. "You're still talking about the bear, right?"

"Of course I am." Was she? She hadn't meant to imply anything with her statement, but now the idea was there—the implication this might be about the two of them—it made her curious whether or not her unwitting observation was correct. She drifted closer as they wandered, resting some of her weight against his arm. Heat flowed between them and taunted her with promises of something she knew wasn't hers.

As they wandered farther from the casino, the chatter and bells faded into the background. The half-lit, mall-like environment closed in around them. If she stretched her imagination just a few inches, it was easy to believe there was no world outside this place of fake pillars and painted-on skies.

"Have you rescued a lot of these poor, unexplored souls from claw machines?" His voice dropped in volume, adding to the surreal feeling of pleasant isolation.

The only issue she saw with their journey was eventually they'd run out of walkway. A soft glow broke the dim lighting ahead. Espresso. Perfect. She leaned into him enough to change their trajectory and memorized the sensation of her head on his shoulder. "Not as many as you might think. The odds on those things can be fixed. The claws made to not consistently grab as tightly. Typically only about in ten quarters wins, regardless of how good someone is."

"Now we really are talking about the bear. If you know the odds, why do you still play? You were pretty diligent about securing your odds at the blackjack table."

She scanned the menu on the small cart and reached for her wallet. For someone so bright, he sure had a hard time with some concepts. "Because with the blackjack I wanted to see if I could do it, not because of the need to win. Once again, it's not about the outcome, it's about how you get there."

"Journey versus destination. Right." He rested a hand on her arm. "Which is why you're drinking, what, caramel mocha with extra whipped cream at almost midnight?"

"Americano, skim milk. It's way too late for that much sugar." She knew it sounded ridiculous. She'd been told so on several occasions and didn't care. The caffeine didn't keep her awake, and she enjoyed the flavor.

"Of course. Let me get this." He stepped up to the cashier before she could protest.

A moment later, he returned with a paper cup, steam escaping from the top, and a bottle of water. He handed her the coffee, rested his hand on her back, and guided her to a table half in the shadows.

He held her chair out for her. She'd never had someone do that before. It heated her inside almost as much as the brush of his fingers along the back of her hand as he took the seat next to her.

She held up the drink. "Thank you for this."

He gave her a look she couldn't interpret, brows furrowed and a question in his eyes, before his expression shifted to something more neutral. "It's not quite as grand a gesture as rescuing me from singing a duet alone, but it's a start."

The reminder tickled her amusement and brought back a flood of warmth from the shared time on stage. "Another thing I'm glad I did. I got at least as much out of the evening as you. You don't actually owe me anything."

"I do." He leaned forward, water ignored, and focused on her. "It's a nice philosophy, but as life goes on, you'll find it gets harder to ignore the final outcome in favor of living in the now."

Some of her euphoria squished out around the implication she was too young to know better. Payton had drilled that point home over and over again—that she didn't have enough life experience to have an opinion on anything if she disagreed with him. "I'm not naïve just because I'm not as old as you. Some of us learned early on not to let life break us."

He leaned back, eyes wide. "I'm not broken."

She tried to swallow back her indignation. Things had been fun and lighthearted just seconds ago, and now she'd let something get to her. Problem was, it stung too much to ignore. Did he really think she was a child? "And I'm not stupid."

TWELVE

Irritation raced through Jared. How had this all gone downhill in an instant? She hadn't had a problem with him speaking his mind up to this point. In fact, he appreciated that she was well-versed in the art of blunt when she wanted to get her point across, and now he was just trying to decompile her logic so he could figure out what language it was in.

A retort tried to force itself past his lips. Something about not knowing enough to know she knew nothing. However, not only was that cliché, it wasn't true. He had no doubt she knew quite a bit. He just needed more information to help him understand. Besides, the flush of her drawn lips, her narrowed eyes, all exposed his desire to make this right.

He held up a hand in surrender. "I didn't mean anything like that."

She rubbed her face. An irritated tone that hadn't been there before lined her voice. "Sorry. Some things hit me harder than others."

The revelation, not just that she had vulnerabilities, but that part of him had thought otherwise, barreled through his head. Suddenly, making her feel better and figuring out how to protect her, seemed as important as the answer to any other riddle. It was an odd sensation. Except, he didn't know how to approach the situation any other way but directly. "Why?"

She leaned back in her chair, deep frown lines crossing her forehead.

That hadn't been the right thing to ask. "I want to know." He poured all his sincerity into his reassurance. "Tell me what I said."

She looked him in the eye, her playfulness replaced with the soft edges of hurt. "Most of my life, I've been younger than the people around me. And then there was—" She clenched her jaw and dragged in a deep breath. "Do you know how tiresome it is constantly hearing how I must not be as smart as them just because I haven't lived as long?"

He didn't miss the unfinished thought, but filed it away for future reference. There were things he didn't like talking about either. The chink in her shell made his heart clench. So she wasn't all fun and games after all. "I wasn't saying—"

"But you did." She took a long swallow of coffee. "That's exactly what you said."

He wanted to wrap her up and patch this wound that had painted a scowl on her features and ruined her smile. But that didn't make any sense. There was no mathematical calculation for fixing emotions. "It's not what I meant." The logical part of his mind said he didn't owe her an apology. However, he very much wanted to make this better. "I just wondered, why is the *now* so important?"

She dropped her gaze to her hands, fiddling with the corrugated edges of the cardboard sleeve on her cup and shredding off tiny bits of brown paper. "Then you should have said that."

"I'm sorry."

She looked back up, lines fading from her expression. "I spent my entire school career shooting for tomorrow. When I graduated high school, things would be better, I just had to make it through. And then it was the same in college. I kept my head down; I did my work, because when it was all finished it would be worth it." She licked her lips. "Except I woke up one day and realized tomorrow never gets here. If I don't enjoy what I've got now, there's no point in pushing for more of the same in the future."

Her logic was painfully simple. Too bad life was too intricate to just toss all cares aside for happiness. "Sometimes you have to miss out on the right now to experience what comes next. If you take everything as it happens, instead of considering the bigger picture, you're going to miss out on just as much."

She pushed her coffee aside. "Unless you spend so much time weighing your decisions and overanalyzing the world around you that you miss your window of opportunity."

"Then you wait for the next opportunity." He'd never come across any situation he felt like he was missing out by giving it his full consideration. Except, if he'd stopped to be rational when it came to Mikki...he'd be back in his hotel room pretending there was anything work-related he could accomplish tonight. The idea he might have passed up time with her in favor of being reasonable pushed past the debate and ached in his chest.

She slid her hand across the table and under his. Her soft skin teased the pads of his fingers and made his pulse race. She clacked the barbell on her tongue along the back of her teeth before replying. "I'm not trying to convert you. I'm just answering your question."

He exhaled slowly to force the circuits in his brain to catch up with the broad shifts in mood. "Is that why you have the piercing?"

Her hand stopped moving under his, and her jaw clenched. She shook her head. "A different story for a different time."

Twice in so many minutes he'd summoned her frown without having any idea he was even pushing her buttons. "So impulsiveness doesn't always work out?"

Her laugh sounded forced. "I'm not as interesting as you think. What about you? I can't be the only one whose past still haunts me, despite my best efforts."

The question, combined with the aching desire to make her smile again, knocked something loose in Jared's head. Karen. The betrayal, the lies, the reason he personally never got involved with people who could be considered competitors.

The jumble clawed at his thoughts and powered through the pleasant shell the night had wrapped them in. They were all notions he didn't need in his head right now. He scratched at his mind until he could gather up all the doubt and file it away. Mikki wasn't Karen, and even if the two did have something in common, he and Mikki weren't a couple. This wouldn't be a copy of what happened before. "You're right. Sometimes the past is best left in the past."

Her somber expression vanished. She ducked her head and peered up at him through her eyelashes. "If we're not lingering on what happened then, and we don't have any way of knowing what waits for us tomorrow, it looks like the only choice we've got is to live in the now."

A laugh slipped out before he could stop it. "I walked right into that."

"The timing definitely worked in my favor." She shrugged and scooted her chair closer until her knee brushed his. A shock of warmth raced through him. "But I promise it was far more coincidence than a setup."

As with the night before, it amazed him how this woman could make him forget the rest of the world, including the problems at work. It was too bad their time together didn't actually make the world stop, but this was far better than pacing in his hotel room because he couldn't troubleshoot.

"A more neutral question, then," he said. "Why did you get into this line of work?"

Her playful expression had returned full-force, and her eyes almost seemed to glow at the words. She tilted closer, the intoxicating scent of lemon and plum filling his nostrils, and excitement lined her voice. "I love figuring out how things work. Pulling the pieces apart, deciphering why someone did something, and reassembling it all into this nice, pretty package that just makes sense. You know?"

Hearing her unique twist on what he thought was an everyday necessity was one of the sexiest things he'd heard her say yet. He dipped in, grazed her throat with his teeth, nipped a line up to her lips, and stole a kiss. "I know exactly what you mean."

MIKKI LEANED into Jared as they walked through the hotel lobby. His arm wrapped behind her back, and his hand rested on her hip. A tiny voice in her head whispered a reminder that this wasn't going to last. She was getting too attached for a couple-day fling.

Which was silly. She wasn't attached. Or maybe just a little. But what was the point in doing something like this if she didn't enjoy it?

It was late enough that the only people still awake were in the casino, and the desk clerk, who looked like he was falling asleep on his feet. Mikki and Jared had hopped from one topic to the next without much pause. Whether it was the latest in technology, or stupid things they'd done to cram for deadlines both in school and at work.

She didn't know if she'd enjoyed a conversation that much in… well…ever.

"The tongue piercing was because of a guy." She winced as soon as the words were out. Why had she just said that? That annoying, tiny voice squeaked it was because this was a good way to put distance between them. Or maybe it was just too easy to be honest with him. She didn't want to hold anything back.

He glanced at her as they stepped into an elevator. "Did he ask you to? Do you regret it?"

She might have tried to brush the comment off, but stubbornness forced out a response. "I don't do regrets. And no, he didn't ask. Not in so many words."

"How do you hint at something like that?" He pulled his arm away to push the buttons for their floors and shoved his hand back in his pocket after.

Disappointment ached in her limbs at the loss of contact. She should probably get used to it now. Which also meant plowing ahead with her story. "My first real boyfriend was a guy I dated after college." It felt odd saying these things out loud, especially to Jared, but at the same time it felt safe. "He broke up with me because I wasn't *wild* enough." And too immature, and boring in bed, and too focused on work, and, and, and…

Jared half turned and studied her face. "I can't even imagine."

"Yeah, well, I decided to prove him wrong. I did everything I'd ever heard him mention he thought was *hot*. Pierced my tongue, started wearing the clothes I wanted instead of what I thought other people wanted, stopped holding back." She stared up in to his eyes. Jared hadn't looked away yet. In fact, was that a tiny smile playing on his face? "Except it turned out I liked it. A lot more than I liked him. I told him no when he asked for a second chance, and never looked back."

He brushed a strand of hair off her forehead. The gentle gesture raced through every inch of her, humming along her skin. His voice was low and firm. "Don't misunderstand. You're gorgeous. But the way you think—the way your mind works—is at least half of your sex appeal. I want you regardless."

Heat flooded her cheeks, warmth clenched in her chest, and for a rare moment, she found herself without a response. The elevator saved her, and at the same time flooded her with disappointment, when the doors slid open. She nodded behind him. "Your floor."

Never looking away from her, he stuck a foot back to block the door and hold it open. "Come back to my room."

Tell him no. Cut this off now. Don't make walking away hurt even more at the end of this trip. "Don't you need your sleep?" Not quite what she meant to say, but at least it wasn't a yes.

He kissed her, and the feather-light touch sent tingles of want from her lips to clench in her belly. He rested a hand at the base of her neck and said, "I'm not sleeping tonight anyway. I might as well enjoy as much of your company as I can before…" He gave a tiny shake of his head, as if trying to toss a thought aside. "Before the sun rises."

She needed to argue. But the desire to spend a few more minutes, maybe hours, with him won out. "I'd love to."

Moments later, his hotel door latched shut behind them, and Jared rested his hands on her hips. Her nipples strained against fabric when he trailed up the back of her neck, lips humming along her skin with each word. "It's true, thinking about the fact you've got nothing on under your skirt has made me hard all night." He nudged her toward the center of the room, the heat of his chest on her back never letting up. "But talking to you, seeing your mind at work, that's making it impossible to keep my hands to myself."

"I'd be disappointed to hear otherwise." She leaned back into him. Everywhere they connected, she felt the pulse of need flow between them.

Hands on her hips, he guided her toward the desk in the corner instead of the bed, pausing long enough for him to toe the chair aside before he pushed her closer.

"It's too bad I ran out of condoms earlier." His fingers dug into her flesh as he raked them up her sides, and she moaned at the hungry contact. "I guess I'll just have to improvise." His hand traced up her throat and he tilted her head back. His teeth grazed her shoulder and then her neck. His words rumbled through her skin. "Bend over."

His hand dipped under her shirt and up her spine, lightly pushing her forward. Slick warmth grew between her legs when he nudged them apart with his foot. One hand moved to her stomach and then higher, cupping her breast. The other found the edge of her skirt and pushed it up past her hips. The rough friction spiked through her, and she inhaled sharply. She rested her weight on her wrists, grinding her ass into the hard length pressing back. The air kissed her wet arousal, and she squirmed in anticipation.

"Jesus, you make it tough to behave." He rolled the hard nub of her nipple between his fingers.

"Behaving is boring…" Her words melted into a moan when he dipped between her folds and sought out her clit.

"Good thing we don't have to find out if that's true." He bumped her sex, a finger on either side, stroking fast and hard.

She dropped her weight onto her forearms and arched her back. The combination of sensations left her dizzy. She pressed into his hand, wanting more.

He pulled back from the swollen button between her legs and

sought her opening. She cried out when he shoved two fingers inside her.

"You get so wet when you're turned on." His voice was lined with gravel. "There were so many times in the casino, knowing you didn't have any panties on, I wanted to pin you against the wall and see how far we could get without getting caught."

The images his words summoned sent a new spike of desire through her. "It's too bad you didn't," she managed between gasps.

He pulled out of her and focused his attention on her clit again, this time grinding the button hard and fast. "Then I'll have to make sure this makes up for it."

She couldn't find the air to reply with more than a series of moans. He'd hit the right spot, and the pressure had her right at the brink, but wasn't pushing her over.

"Come for me, Mikki." His breathless prompt drilled into her head, coaxing and heightening her pleasure further. "I want to hear you scream again."

She was so close. Without anything to grab on to, she clenched her hands, nails digging onto her palms.

He nudged his fingers just a fraction against her clit and hit the right spot. Orgasm spilled through her, tearing a cry from her chest.

She rested her forehead on the cool varnish of the desk, waiting for her legs to steady out before standing. An unfamiliar but amazing feeling flowed through her. Everywhere he touched drew her to life more. Every word seduced her thoughts and senses. She was spent, but filled with an aching need to curl up in his arms instead. The rush of emotion made something squeak inside her. A fear she had fallen too far.

His fingers slipped out of her, and seconds later his lips brushed her cheek. "You're incredible."

She hadn't thought her face could be any warmer, but she was wrong. The compliment flooded her. She managed to find her footing and force herself upright. He wrapped his hand around hers and turned her to face him. She let longing blanket her fear. Dove into his touch instead of lingering on how much it was going to hurt when she couldn't have him anymore. He cupped her cheek and kissed her gently. The gesture defied everything about the way he'd just made her come, but at the same time it felt right, and fluttered along her skin.

He brushed his lips over hers. "Don't leave yet."

The simple request latched on to every hope she'd tried to suppress all evening. At least she wasn't the only one wanting to make the most of this temporary connection. Temporary—the word made her ribs ache. She shoved the longing aside. She had him now, and this was more about living in the now than anything she'd ever done. Right? "I'm not dressed for sleeping over."

He unbuttoned the first button on her shirt, and then continued his way down. "Fortunately, there's no dress code."

"Lucky me."

His palms caressed her skin when he pushed the top off her shoulders and down her arms. He draped the garment on the back of the chair, and seconds later her bra joined it.

Embarrassment and pleasure flitted through her when his gaze lingered on her naked chest, eyes tracing every line. It was an attention she wanted to bask in, and though the sensation was new, it was welcome.

"Let me return the favor." She mimicked his previous movements as she stripped off his shirt. His bare chest was muscled, but not overly defined. That wasn't fair. How did some executive geek look so good shirtless? Not that she was complaining. She traced down his sternum and along his ribs, memorizing the sensation on her fingertips.

She dropped lower, to his waistband. The trail of hair running from his navel and disappearing under his boxers tickled her touch. She didn't have to do much to push his slacks and boxers to the ground, since they were already undone. She brushed his rigid cock, and he groaned. The skin of his shaft was warm and smooth against her palm as she stroked. He leaned his head back, eyes closed. Every sound that tore from his throat spurred guided her movements.

He wrapped a hand around her wrist and pulled her away. "I didn't do that so you'd have to reciprocate."

Her shoulders slumped, and a whisper of doubt flitted into her thoughts. *Maybe he's not feeing the same emotional connection.* Stupid brain. "I want to."

He rested his hand on the back of her neck and kissed her gently, only lingering for a moment before pulling away. "We've got to sleep sometime."

Which made sense. But she couldn't ignore the tiny question repeating in her mind. *Is he holding back?*

He trailed his nose along the curve of her neck. "I just don't want you to think you have to." His hot breath on her skin chased away the sting of his no. "If that makes sense."

She nodded.

His wicked smile returned, and he made quick work of her skirt button and zipper before pushing it to the ground. He led her toward the bed. She couldn't help but enjoy the view, his gorgeous, chiseled ass, when he pulled back the comforter. He nodded at the mattress. She climbed between the sheets, and seconds later, he pressed into her back, arm draped over her waist. He kissed along the back of her neck. Neither of them spoke for several minutes.

They'd learned so much about each other in the last few hours, but she still wanted to know more. Her gaze drifted around the room, flitting past generic luggage, a black laptop, and a router that could be any model on the market. None of it had any personality.

Her eyes landed on something odd in the corner, on top of a suitcase. She squinted, trying to make out the letters in the dim light spilling in under the door. And then it hit her. A novelty picture frame. Nothing in their brief time together would have made her think he'd know what the point of something like that was. "Do you take a lot of pictures?" she asked.

His thumb traced lazy circles along her hip, and drowsiness lined his voice. "Not really. Are you offering to be a subject?"

The notion flooded her with a series of muddled emotion. Heat flared through her at the thought of being his private peep show and mixed with more aching at the reminder they didn't have the kind of relationship that allowed them to make plans like that. Not that she needed to plan anything out. She nodded toward the box. "Are you going to put the pictures in that?"

Behind her, the mattress shifted. He raised his head into view, kissed her shoulder, and the flopped back down. "It's for my sister."

Right. Because he had a life and family outside this bubble of pleasant euphoria. The simple statement was a reminder how much they still didn't know about each other. "Are the two of you close?"

"I love and adore Alyssia."

Mikki couldn't help her smile at the sincerity in the simple statement, even though he couldn't see it. "Are you one of those overprotective brothers who thinks his younger sister is pure and innocent, and you'll hurt anyone who dares suggest otherwise?"

His chuckle rumbled through her. "To hear her say it, I am. I'm just a normal kind of brother though. Not that I mind the questions, but conversations about my sister rank pretty far on the opposite end of the scale from sexy pillow talk."

"I always wanted a brother like that. Or any kind of sibling, really." She pushed back into him.

"Once upon a time, I would have told you it wasn't that great, but really it is. Her, Tate, and Viv, they're pretty much the sanity in my life."

"You're lucky." She swallowed back the sting his words dragged up. Both that he had friends like that in his life, and that she wasn't on the list.

"What about you? Family? Girlfriend you're squealing about me with?"

She wanted to smile at his words, but her sadness had sunk too deep. "Dad's a government contractor." *Mom walked out before I was old enough to remember her, and we never heard from her again.* "We moved a lot growing up, so I didn't really make any close friends." She couldn't completely keep the ache from her voice.

"I'll share mine. You'd love Alyssia."

The simple statement warmed her as much as his touch. Until her brain kicked on and reminded her he wasn't part of her future. Not like that. She bit back the creeping sadness and concentrated on his embrace instead. Silence settled in the room again. Behind her, his breathing slowed into a quiet rhythm. Her eyes began to droop.

"This is almost perfect." His drowsy voice drifted to her ears.

It really was. She was opening her mouth to reply when he said, "Now we just need to figure out how you guys are stealing our clients, and I'll be set."

Her eyes jerked open. "What?"

He didn't respond. The steady rise and fall of his chest against her back told her he had probably drifted off. Something about his question wouldn't let her do the same. Why did that single thought make her stomach lurch and her skin crawl? Not even the warmth of being wrapped in his arms could chase away the chill his drowsy statement had covered her in.

THIRTEEN

The bed shifted under Jared, nudging him awake. He forced his eyes open when the warm body next to him pulled away. The night before teased his half-conscious mind, and a nagging reminder wormed its way into his thoughts; a voice whispering how completely she'd almost made him lose control.

She'd drawn out a side of him he thought he'd reined in long ago. The side that should know better than to say what was on his mind and wanted nothing more than to growl dirty words into her porcelain skin. He'd even considered sex without protection.

At least he'd pulled back before they'd gone too far. Stopped her from doing whatever her version of "returning the favor" might have been. He'd kept things from being about anything more than just immediate pleasure. Right?

Something tickled the back of his thoughts, reminding him he'd all but offered to introduce her to his sister. Maybe he'd lost a little more control than he'd intended to.

What was wrong with him? He watched Mikki climb out of bed and pluck her clothes from the floor.

"It's five a.m. You've only been asleep for a couple of hours," he said

She jumped and turned to face him, giving him a fantastic view of her naked figure. "We both have places to be today."

He pushed up on one elbow, smothering the disappointment swelling inside. She had a good point, and he didn't have an argument. It wasn't like they could lock themselves away for the rest of the week. Or that he'd ever see her again outside of trade shows. "Right."

Still, he couldn't just let her walk out. He sat up and scooted forward on the bed until he was sitting on the edge. He tugged her between his legs and pressed his lips to her stomach. The sound that tore from her throat was somewhere between a sigh and a moan. He continued the line of kisses as he stood, tracing up her sternum, her throat, and finally her mouth. She molded into him, palms hot on his chest.

It was too soon when she stepped out of his grasp, dark gaze not meeting his. "I have to go. Last night was good." She shook her head. "No, that's not true. It was amazing."

He sank back to the mattress, silent and watching while she dressed. She gave him one last weak smile before she left. The moment the door swung shut behind her, he flopped back onto the bed, stare directed up but thoughts turned inward.

"Fuck." His soft curse echoed in the quiet room. The ache in his chest defied every denial he tried to feed himself that this was all over. He couldn't do this. He couldn't fall for her. It didn't matter how much she was everything intoxicating, she was also everything completely wrong for him.

He wasn't going to throw away his career or sense of order for a fling. This job was important, and she worked for the competition. On top of that, he'd already let himself be distracted too much this trip. He needed to remember where his priorities lay. His personal rules and boundaries existed for a reason, and she was so far from falling into the ordered pattern he required that he couldn't begin to rationalize making it work.

He didn't have to be downstairs for a couple more hours; he should get some more sleep. As seven a.m. rolled around, he hadn't done anything but stare at the clock.

He was due to meet with a potential client soon. He rubbed his face. Time to put the night behind him, except maybe the memories, and hope he could down enough coffee between now and then to make it through things without yawning.

He got ready for the morning and made his way to the lobby. For as little sleep as he'd gotten the night before, his eyelids should have been drooping. *So why do I feel like I couldn't sit still if I needed to?* He hadn't even touched the coffee yet. He stepped off the elevator and out of the flow of traffic. This tension needed to be under control, whatever the source. He closed his eyes and took a few calming breaths.

Nervous energy still coursed through him, itching under his skin. *This meeting isn't going to go well.* The thought came out of nowhere. That was ridiculous. He was just jaded because of the string of bad luck they'd been having with new clients. They'd still signed people. It hadn't been a complete dry spell. Worrying about where the next contract came from was Tate's department. The sleep deprivation was attacking him from a different angle than he was used to.

Still, despite the lack of rest—remembering Mikki's gasps when she was turned on, the scent of citrus on her skin, her bare body under his, actually having someone who was interesting to talk to and didn't make him filter his thoughts—he'd do last night again in a heartbeat.

Half an hour later, he made his way to the back of the exhibitors' hall, near the row of rooms set up for private conferences. Tate was already waiting with an older gentleman, who glanced at his watch the moment Jared made eye contact.

And I'm five minutes early. Time to wrangle this in before it spirals out of control. He extended his hand as he drew closer. "Mr. Rosen. I'm sorry to keep you waiting."

Rosen glanced at his watch again before returning the handshake. "No worries at all. Some of us aren't as busy as others. Call me Adam."

Jared's pleasant expression never cracked. If there was ever a time to not be blunt, it was now. He nodded at Tate. "Speaking of, I know Tate has other things to take care of."

Tate's attention stayed on the client the whole time. "And I'm off to it. Adam's in good hands."

A snort of laughter barked from Rosen's throat.

Jared held the door open, ignoring the implication he wasn't capable of handling this conversation, and gestured for the older man to join him in a more private setting. Adam Rosen worked for Lenoronto—one of the largest umbrella corporations for retail websites in the country. Tate had been negotiating with him for months, pitted against NSS and whatever secrets they were hiding. The reminder of Mikki almost knocked Jared's thoughts offline, but this wasn't the time or place. Contracts and promotions were on the line.

He took his seat across from Adam, leaned forward in the leather plush, and rested his elbows on his knees, hands clasped. "Are you enjoying the trip?"

Adam checked his phone and then pocketed it again. "I wish they'd stop holding these things in places like this. An excuse for drunken foolishness. I'm petitioning the board to move it to Miami next year. We'll keep the warmth and lose the distractions."

Right, because Miami was such a dull place. Jared never flinched. "I look forward to the outcome."

Adam let out a long exhale. "Look, I'll be honest. When Tate told me he could hook me up with someone technical, I thought I'd be talking to one of your people who's actually close to the action. No offense, but how long has it been since you did any actual security work?"

The first few times someone had asked that question, Jared had gotten defensive. He'd learned since, the best way to prove he still knew his shit was to prove it rather than argue. "It's true; I'm not as involved in the day-to-day tech as I used to be. But we like to let the real talent do their jobs, and any questions you have I can't answer, I'll take back to them and get you an in-depth response within a few hours."

That had never happened. He didn't take questions back to his people, but it made the conversation flow more smoothly. As Adam launched into a series of concerns, Jared responded to each without hesitation. He'd heard them all before—it was a fairly standard list.

"So tell me about these holes in your own security," Adam said. "What are you doing to address them?"

For the first time since sitting down, a sick pit settled in Jared's gut. He nudged it aside. He had this as well as he had anything, and the answer was right there. Especially after the extra hours he'd put in yesterday making sure his network was still tight.

It didn't matter that he hadn't been able to do more work last night; he'd still covered all his bases. He just hadn't expected to use the reassurance again so soon. "We don't have any internal holes. We undergo both internal and independent audits on a regular basis, and those results are available to anyone who'd like to see them. As a company who places so much importance on security, we're always aware of the risk—the badge of honor, if you will—for a hacker to poke holes in our walls. If a situation like that were to arise, and it hasn't in years, we'd have the weaknesses patched within hours."

Adam's lips drew into a thin line and he stared back, green eyes unblinking. A heavy silence hung between them before he finally spoke. "I guess what I heard can't be true then."

An alarm clanged in the back of Jared's head. This was the same conversation he'd already heard three times in the last six months. So why was it tugging up new memories he couldn't quite grasp? "You're in contract negotiations. I'm sure a lot of things were implied that aren't necessarily true."

Rosen laughed. "Fair enough. Then I guess there's nothing to the rumors some of your outlying departments have made your entire network vulnerable."

The simple phrasing kicked the right pebble in Jared's head, and the conversation from the night before avalanched back. The words were almost identical to what Mikki had told him. It was a coincidence, right? "Absolutely no truth to those at all." He kept his uncertainty from his voice.

Was this the basis of the rumors they'd been hearing in every missed sales opportunity for the past six months? Ever since… No, there was no way. "Our networks are secure; you have my word."

Adam stood, his expression flat. "Of course. I know your certifications support that, to the point I know something like a Trojan would be spotted in an instant. You understand, of course, this is just due diligence."

Fuck. That's new. "Of course. And I can assure you there's nothing to worry about when it comes to Skriddie and the standards we hold ourselves to." A Trojan virus was the digital equivalent of its namesake. Once it was on the network, it provided someone outside access to the inside. That was so many steps beyond—and a much larger threat—than just a couple whispers they might have security holes.

Call the office. Isolate every server. Go into full lockdown until we know this is just a malicious rumor. Jared's thoughts raced with next steps, but he forced himself to stay in the conversation. "Can I answer any other questions for you?"

"No." Adam stepped away, ignoring the offer of Jared's extended hand. "I think I've got the information I need. Thank you for your time."

Jared sank back into his seat the moment Adam was gone and dropped his face into his hands. Shit. How would a Trojan even make it onto their systems? The server should have caught it. The virus software would have stopped it. There were so many check points along the way where it should have been obliterated. He was dialing the office before his thoughts finished forming. *Dewson can hole up in the data center. Tate needs to know I'm skipping the courtesy suites.* To-do items continued to stack on the list in his head while the phone rang.

At least he knew one thing—the rumors had begun six months ago, while Mikki was still interviewing with both companies. So even if there was anything to what Rosen had said, she couldn't have done it. Her odd questions and statements about why she'd signed with NSS instead, those weren't related at all. Were they? A new nagging doubt joined his mounting concern.

Not that it mattered if she was involved—it wasn't like he was attached. Fuck, who was he kidding? He was so hooked on her it ached to think about parting ways. How had she done that to him in just a few short days?

If she meant so much to him, why didn't everything he felt for her and knew about her reassure him? He was just being paranoid. Businesses went through slumps. Still, he couldn't take a chance on this. He snarled at the receiver when he went to voice mail after several rings. "Dewson. I don't care what you're working on. You have a new critical priority. Cancel your plans for the night. I promise I'll make it up to you. We need a deeper scan than you've ever done, yesterday. From the top down, servers, every department, any device that's ever even touched our network. Call me for details."

He dropped his phone into the coffee table in front of him. It would be okay. He'd work with his staff, they'd secure an all clear, and he could set everyone's minds at ease. His network wasn't flawed. There was no way something so severe had made it in. And once he proved it, all would be right with the world again.

FOURTEEN

JARED ROLLED HIS NECK TO TRY AND LOOSEN THE TIGHT CORDS running from his shoulder blades to the base of his skull. His eyes never left his laptop screen. The hotel desk wasn't an ideal workspace, but his room was private. At least he didn't have to rely on the free, unsecured Wi-Fi. A hotspot he'd rigged himself sat next to his computer, signal lights flickering and blinking as he worked.

"Peachtree servers next," he directed the comment at his phone, which sat next to the entire setup, with the speaker on.

A knock echoed through the room, and Jared's train of thought snapped.

He growled at the empty air. "Do not disturb means do not disturb. Hang on, Dewson." He crossed the few short steps to the door, shoved down some of his irritation when he saw Viv through the peephole, and let her in. He gave her a brief nod and gave his attention to the phone. "Dewson, rinse and repeat on that entire stack. I'll call you back in ten."

"Got it." The disembodied voice sounded tinny and distant coming from his phone. Jared glanced at the device long enough to see the call had been disconnected and turned back to Vivian. Her gown hugged every curve enough to show it off, without ever looking anything but professional, and the emerald made her eyes flash.

He offered her a weak smile. "You look great. Are you turning heads on purpose, or is that something you dug out of the back of your closet?"

The dress was new. He didn't have to hear her response to confirm it. She wouldn't do things any other way.

She tugged on the sleeve of his T-shirt. "It's not nearly high fashion as what you're wearing. I drew the short straw, so I get to come nag you to join us in the courtesy suites."

"Not happening." His fingers twitched toward his phone. "We're not done."

She pursed her lips and trailed a fingernail down his arm. Once upon a time, the gesture would have been seductive. These days that moment was in the past, and he never questioned she knew it as well as he did. "You're ninety-nine-point-nine percent sure they're rumors." There was no question in her voice. "The odds Hayden's behind the gossip are so high, you couldn't even find someone in this town to bet against it."

He exhaled loudly. "But we're not at one-hundred percent." He pushed aside the part of his brain that agreed with her. Walking away for the night meant asking his people to do something he wasn't willing to do. Making them work while he went out and had fun. And there was no part of him at all worried that if he ran into Mikki downstairs, it would be even harder to say goodbye tomorrow.

Her lips drew into a thin line. "How much worse do you think we look when you miss rubbing shoulders with the industry tonight because you're chasing a rabbit down a hole that doesn't exist? Executives smile and shake hands. Their people do the grunt work."

A laugh slipped out, despite the tension permeating every inch of his body. "You're good. If you didn't wear that dress so well, I might have mistaken you for Tate." He knew his friends well enough to realize even though Vivian had been sent to bring him downstairs, it wasn't her idea.

She leaned her weight on the corner of the dresser the TV sat on. "I'll tell him I made a valiant effort."

He gave her a grateful smile. "Say I'm wrapping up negotiations with India, or have him make something up. You know no one will miss me."

"I suspect *someone* will. Speaking of, if you need an extra set of eyes, I can put a contract in front of some new talent. Sounds like decent revenge for rumors like this, right? Steal Hayden's prize out from under his nose at a trade show?"

Jared didn't have to ask who she was talking about. His pulse quickened at the idea of getting into a different kind of hands-on work with Mikki. Actually seeing what she was capable of in front of a computer. *Don't linger on this.* "She's already turned you down once."

She pushed upright again, and her gaze drifted to the ground. "When was the last time you checked your email?"

His teeth clenched before he could process how on-edge her question put him. "I shut it off hours ago so I could work. Why?"

She pulled her phone from the small bag hanging from her wrist, made a couple of swipes to the screen, and handed it to him.

Hesitation told him not to reach for it. That was ridiculous. If she thought it was important, he'd rather know now than later. He exhaled slowly as he read the company-wide announcement from Sterling Foster, and all the strength drained from his legs.

They'd named a new chief operations officer. Gone outside the company for the guy. The email even said they felt the external insight would be more beneficial to them than pulling from internal talent.

He forced a smile onto his face and handed Viv's phone back. All his work… That job was supposed to be his. He couldn't keep the strain from his voice. "Good to know."

Her expression softened. "I'm sorry."

He couldn't even grasp enough of his thoughts to figure out how he felt. "No big deal. It's not like anyone actually promised me the position."

"As long as you're all right."

"Absolutely." He wasn't. Not that he knew what he was, but he was pretty sure it wasn't all right. He nodded at his computer. "I need to get back to work. Make my excuses downstairs?"

"Of course." Sympathy lined her smile, and he was grateful she didn't push the issue.

MIKKI STEPPED out of one heel and dropped her foot to the floor so she could take the weight off her other leg. The shoes were killing her. She scanned the faces in the Skriddie courtesy suite. *He's not here.* She couldn't ignore her disappointment.

Vivian was. The other woman stood at the far end of the room, smiling and laughing with a small group of people. Vivian's heels were even more severe than Mikki's, making her taller than several of the men around her. *How does anyone do professional that gracefully?*

Mikki had struggled with whether or not to dress up tonight. Looking now at what everyone else in the room wore, she was glad she'd gone with the simple suit she'd brought. Maybe she should have toned back the camisole, though, and found something boring and off-white in one of the shops.

It was true, Jared had played along with her last night. Gone along with her silly games. But she needed to prove she could be responsible too, and her bright red lace top in a sea of whites and grays couldn't be supporting that image.

"What are you drinking, my dear?" A warm voice dragged her attention away from searching for Jared.

She slipped her shoe back on and turned toward the bartender. Shock and recognition raced through her. She'd never been introduced to Tate, but even if he hadn't been the third Musketeer at the karaoke bar, his picture made more industry papers than anyone else at Skriddie. The face of sales for Skriddie Bust Media. And the best friend of the guy she wasn't supposed to be falling for. "I, um…" She glanced around her. "Are you allowed to be back there?"

He winked and grabbed something from under the portable bar. "I am as long as no one complains." He extended his hand. "We haven't been formally introduced, but you're the name on everyone's tongue. I'm Tate." His grip was warm and firm without being too tight.

His smile was so genuine, she couldn't help but smile back. "I know."

He grabbed a bottle off the shelves behind him. "You look like a 7 and 7 girl. Yes? No?"

She shrugged. To be honest, she hadn't done a lot of drinking in her life, and since she knew she was a lightweight, it was taking her some time to figure out what she liked.

She hadn't planned on drinking tonight, but Hayden had specifically sought her out and asked her to be on her best behavior. The request had gnawed at her. The implication she'd acted anything but professionally in public up to this point devoured her sense of decorum and wrapped it in spite.

It was true, she was travelling on the company dime, and this was a business function. She didn't have a problem with that. What was stuck in her brain was his comment. His assurance he was just telling her as a friend and his implication that she didn't know better without the warning. She was getting sick of it. *One drink won't hurt anyone.* "Possibly."

Tate handed her a glass with pale amber liquid in it and a swizzle stick. "Mostly sweet, just a little kick. I think you'll like it."

"Thanks." She wasn't sure what else to say to him. What kind of conversation did one strike up with the guy whose best friend she was sleeping with? The man who helped run the company she'd hacked as much to prove her skills to herself as anyone else? Her gaze drifted back to Vivian. Then again, none of them seemed to mind that she'd done either one.

"Did you lose someone?" Tate asked.

She stared at him again, heat flooding her cheeks that she'd been so obvious. She tried to joke it off. "Not that I'm aware of?"

He laughed. "You keep searching the room. You're not obligated to sit here and talk to me."

She tried to hide her embarrassment by taking a long drink.

Sweet rushed across her tongue, followed seconds later by a smooth burn. "It's not that, I promise."

"I'm teasing. If I might be so bold as to guess, he's working. We probably won't see him tonight." He slid her a cocktail napkin.

"Like, actual work?" That sounded so much more appealing than pretending for appearance's sake. "I mean, who is?"

Out of the corner of her eye, she saw Tate lean forward and rest his forearms on the bar. "The person you're not looking for."

How much has Jared told them? Had she been a conquest to brag about? The thought clenched in her gut. She swallowed more of her drink. "Let's say I was looking for someone specific. How'd he get lucky enough to get out of the evening? Is that a perk of having a nice title?"

Tate's brow furrowed and he studied her for a moment. "Perk. Right. Are you enjoying the show?"

Small talk. Yay. She turned her full attention to Tate. He was kind of cute when she thought about it. Blond hair, blue eyes, broad shoulders, and a smirk that said he was probably plotting something devious. Still, if he were Jared, the conversation would be about anything but the menial. The idea filled her with the temptation to walk away now and go find Jared. *Down girl.* "Are they all like this?"

"More or less."

A yawn swelled in Mikki's lungs, and she knocked back the rest of her drink to hide it. The liquor didn't burn as much going down this time. She slid him the glass. "Having to make nice with a bunch of people who may or may not like you doesn't really sound like the best way to spend work time."

Why had she said that? Her head swam when she tried to pull up an answer. It was that damn insecurity rearing its head again. That voice that cared what people thought of her. The one that always sounded like Payton. She squashed it as best she could.

He filled her glass again. "I'm sure it works that way for some people. You, on the other hand, probably don't have anything to worry about."

The compliment mingled with her drink and warmed her from the inside out. But the vague gnawing in her gut didn't believe it.

"Honestly, before I got here, I didn't think any of you liked me." She winced at the honest words. Blunt was one thing, but spilling her guts and letting her vulnerabilities show was completely another. "I mean, not that you're not all nice people, but after what I did…" She snapped her mouth shut. Babbling wasn't making anything better.

He studied her, brows knit together, before smiling and topping off her drink again. "We're all grown-ups here. There's no reason to let the personal bleed into the professional."

The words whirred in her brain, taking longer to find purchase than she would have liked. Did he think she was talking about her relationship—correction, non-relationship with Jared? A portion of her mind begged her to ask him directly, but some of the words stuck in her throat.

It was that damn bit of her caring what he'd think again that was keeping her from specifically asking how they'd dealt with her hack. "I mean what I did during my job interview with NSS. I thought—that is, Hayden said—I just… I thought it might be an unforgiveable sin kind of thing."

He poured her another drink and leaned forward, forearms resting on the bar. "Signing with the competition? Some of us aren't fond of Hayden personally—" he looked around him before locking his attention on her again, "—Not me if anyone asks, but there's some tension. And I know V was disappointed, she has nothing but praise for your talent. But your life, your choice. No one blames you for that."

Reality seeped into her veins, and her insides felt like they were about to liquefy. "I don't mean signing with NSS. I mean what led up to it."

He raised an eyebrow. "The need for more employees?"

She tried to keep her posture casual, despite the growing turmoil in her gut. He didn't know. It was true, Vivian might not have told him, but something like that would be conversation fodder, right? Especially with Jared's best friends? "Sorry. I'm just babbling."

Tate smiled. "No worries. I promise there are no hard feelings about any of it. Not that I'm aware of. Business is business, right? It's not like you're plotting to take us down."

"Oh, God." *They don't know what I did.* The realization crashed around her, and she almost emptied the content of her stomach. *Hayden was supposed to tell them, and they have no idea.*

"Are you all right?"

"No." Acid churned inside, bubbling up in her throat. "I'm so sorry. I need to talk to Jared. Where is he?"

"His room, probably."

"Thank you. And I'm so, so sorry." *Shit, what have I done?*

She stepped into the cool of the hallway, needing the air to clear her thoughts. Except it didn't help. The room spun around her. She hadn't had that much to drink, had she? Maybe she shouldn't have skipped dinner.

She wobbled, and the carpet danced to life beneath her. This wasn't good. Stepping out of her heels, she bent at the waist to grab them. Her head threatened to float away when she straightened again.

There were too many people. She headed away from the crowds. The people faded into the background as she found a spot away from the suites. She leaned into a nearby wall, gulping deep breaths and trying to make the room stop spinning.

This was bad. This was so bad. She needed to tell Jared what she'd done. Her gut lurched. And then brace herself to never see him again.

FIFTEEN

Jared raked his fingers through his hair and leaned back in the chair. The frame creaked, but held. He blinked to restore the moisture to his eyes. *Finally.* He'd been through everything with Dewson. Made sure every last bit of hardware and software was checked. He could say with one hundred percent certainty his network was clean.

With the immediate problem cleared, his thoughts were free to ramble. To drift to the sexy brunette who was probably downstairs right now, mingling with his colleagues. His chest deflated, almost collapsing in on itself, as he exhaled. An unreachable ache throbbed beneath his ribs. It had been less than twenty-four hours since he'd seen her. How did he already miss her?

A quiet knock startled him out of his musings. He glanced at the clock. The suites would still be in full swing, with everyone taking advantage of the free booze. It wouldn't be Tate or Vivian.

He peered through the peephole, eyes growing wide and gut clenching. His senses flared to life, a million prickles of desire dancing over his skin. Mikki stood in the hallway, gaze directed at the floor and shoes dangling from her fingers. *So gorgeous.*

He yanked the door open, and her head flew up, eyes wide. He shouldn't stare but couldn't help himself. The way her suit hugged her hips, the not-quite-sheer of her lace top enhancing her breasts, and the flush on her face. Except something was off in her expression. He forced words past his lips. "Not that I'm complaining. I'm glad you're here. But are you okay?"

The pink on her cheeks grew, and the corners of her eyes tugged down. "I need to talk to you."

Not quite the answer he'd been looking for, but nothing in his mind was prepared to turn her away. He liked the talking. And what it could lead to, but he'd take the just talking if it was her. "Of course." He stepped aside and latched the door behind her.

She hovered in the middle of the room, staring at her feet. Alarms sounded in his head. Something was obviously wrong, but what? A million possibilities ticked through his head, each discarded before it could become a full thought.

"I'm so sorry. I didn't know." She whirled to face him and stumbled.

"Careful." He wrapped an arm around her waist to help steady her. Even through layers of clothing, her heat threatened to sear him, and his pulse spun up another processor in response. Images taunted him of pressing her against the wall, sliding his hands under her shirt, and tasting every inch of her.

He mentally shook the temptation away, but his body didn't stop reacting. Now was definitely not the time.

She fumbled a few times before finally extracting herself from his arms. "I have to tell you something."

The wash of alcohol on her breath hit him, and he cringed inwardly. She was drunk. At least now he knew what was wrong. It didn't erase his fantasy, but it did squelch any desire to act on it. "You look like you need to lie down."

The corner of her mouth tugged up, and a high-pitched giggle slipped out. "Are you propositioning me?"

Any other night but tonight. He shook his head and held out his arm. "Come on. I'll take you back to your room."

She stepped back and wobbled on her feet again. "Does rescuing the fair maiden ever get you in trouble?"

His brain's reaction to her slurred words battled with his body's response to wanting her closer. "Sometimes."

Even if she weren't so drunk she could barely stand, this had to end now. It was already tearing a hole in his chest to admit they'd never see each other again after this week. The further he got away from her now, the better.

She lunged forward suddenly, fingers digging into his shirt and face buried in his chest. "I didn't realize. I thought you knew."

Knew what? Did she regret what they'd done? A screaming in the back of his head told him to look deeper, but he didn't dare. She wasn't making sense, and any drunken confession wouldn't do either of them any good.

"Come on. You need to sleep this off." He tried to point her toward the door.

She turned wide eyes on him. Smudged eyeliner rimmed her red gaze. "You haven't even heard what I have to say, and you're already throwing me out. I swear I didn't know."

Her head tilted up gave him an incredible view of her entire outfit. Jesus, the top really was almost sheer. Right, she was drunk. Fuck. He pressed his lips to her forehead, and then stepped back. "I'm not throwing you out."

"I don't want you to hate me." She grasped his wrists.

Her palms on his bare skin flooded him with desire, and the impulse to strip all their clothes out of the way rushed through him. He couldn't bring himself to break her grip. She pulled him closer and interlocked her fingers behind his head, hands resting at the base of his neck. A low groan tore from his chest when she pressed her lips to his. Soft, full, and hungry.

His hands slid to the small of her back, holding her captive. Her tongue darted into his mouth, the smooth ball at the tip teasing him and tempting his thoughts. She tasted like Seagram's and 7 Up. He'd never thought that flavor combination could be intoxicating again. Seemed like a good excuse to replace the old memories with new ones. Her body molded to his. Her yielding curves send daggers of want through every inch of his frame. It took more restraint than he knew he had to keep from inching her shirt up, then yanking it over her head.

She moved her hands to his waist and pushed up his T-shirt. He was as hard as a rock, and his cock ached to be free every time her hip rubbed it through his jeans. How was it possible to want someone this much, even though he had a list of reasons it could devastate his life? Or at least, his career and sanity.

He was about point-two-five seconds from lifting her onto the bed and removing her clothes in ways that would ensure she could never wear any of them again.

He summoned the last of his self-control, dragging it past every sensual, aching inch of arousal, and wrapped his hand around her wrist. A painful chill rushed in around him when he broke all other contact between them. "I don't hate you, and I'm not throwing you out. Tell me what's wrong."

She turned her dark gaze on him, lower lip jutting out. "Promise not to get mad?"

He closed his eyes and took a deep breath. He needed answers now. "Talk to me."

Her pout melted into a quivering chin.

"Oh, shit." He clenched and unclenched his left hand. "Don't cry, please?"

She sank onto the edge of the bed, and tears streamed down her cheeks. Her shoulders shook, but she didn't make a sound.

He couldn't ignore the pain echoing inside. "Mikki. Talk to me?"

"I'm… I'm so… I'm sorry." She forced out between sobs. "I didn't mean to. Please don't be mad. I'm so sorry."

What was she apologizing for? Being drunk? That didn't tie into the carefree image she projected normally. He moved onto the mattress next to her and wrapped a tentative arm around her shoulder. "You didn't do anything wrong."

She turned into him and buried her face in his shoulder. And then the body-wracking sobs began. Her tears soaked into his shirt and skin as she cried, and he didn't care. All he could think about was how he couldn't take pain this from her, whatever it was. He trailed his fingers through her hair. "It's going to be okay."

She shook her head. "It's not. I can't undo this."

He pulled her to him, holding her tighter. Between him and his friends, they could talk or buy their way out of almost anything. But he had no idea what this was or how to make it better. He'd forgotten what it was like to feel so impotent, and he didn't like the reminder.

Each sob tore away another shred of his soul, but slowly she calmed down, until all that was left was a few sniffles.

She finally pulled away and dragged the back of her hand across her cheeks. Why wouldn't she look at him?

He held her at arm's length so he could look her in the eye. Even red-eyed, with tear stained cheeks, she was gorgeous. And breaking his heart. "Don't move." He grabbed a glass off the tray near the TV, filled it with water, and handed it to her. "Drink."

She drained the water and set the glass on the floor next to him.

She looked miserable, and he wanted to fix it. To wrap her up and protect her and make her feel better. But she wasn't telling him anything.

He gripped her fingers lightly and traced the back of her knuckles. "Doing better?"

She gave him a weak smile. "Not really. But I'm not thirsty anymore."

He kissed her fingertips one at a time. "Whatever this is—Hayden, something else at work—there's always an answer."

"Hayden." She let out a bitter laugh. "I used to think he was a swell guy. Or at least an okay person."

Had she been fired? Something else? At least the conversation was moving forward. Jared just wished the progress had come with more answers. "What did Hayden do?"

She dragged in a deep, shuddering breath, and looked him in the eye. "You have some gaping, horrible holes in the security on your network."

The words stole the air from his lungs, and he sank back, ass resting on his heels. Of the billions of things he expected her to say, that was nowhere on the list. He knew people were talking about it, but he hadn't expected to hear it from her. Dread crept through him, and he tried to push it aside. "No. I don't."

Was that hope in her eyes? "So you do know? Did you fix it?"

No. Nonononononono. This wasn't Karen. It couldn't be. "There's nothing to fix."

"Shit." The word slipped past her lips and hung between them. "I thought you knew. When I told Hayden, he swore he'd shared the information."

The cryptic circle of random words was compiling into something recognizable in Jared's mind, and the output made every inch of him ache with betrayal and fury. It wasn't true. He was going to make her spell it out, whatever this was. "Thought I knew what?"

"In my interview with NSS, they told me I had to prove my skills. Gave me an IP address and told me it was an internal site. Told me to find the holes in the security. Except it wasn't internal, it was the Skriddie network. And your network has holes."

Every thought in Jared's head crumbled. She was leaving things out. Little details most people wouldn't notice. Not only had she done this, and then kept it from him, she was still hoping he wouldn't notice how deep the deception ran. Hurt mingled with anger. "So, you still poked around, even though you knew it wasn't an NSS network."

She bit the inside of her cheek not meeting his gaze. "I didn't realize it at first."

"Bullshit." He spit the word out, not able to completely hide his agony in the venom. "You knew exactly what you were doing. You dug in first and didn't stop until you'd had your fun."

"I'm sorry." Her voice cracked.

"I don't care." He stood and backed away. "You need to leave."

Her chin quivered. *Please, don't let her cry again.* His splintered psyche didn't know how it would handle that.

Instead, she brushed past him without another word. Seconds later, the door latched shut between them.

He collapsed onto the bed and dropped his face into his hands as two hundred and fifty-six shades of confusion pixelated his thoughts.

Morning. Maybe if she lay there just a little longer, Mikki could pretend this entire non-relationship hadn't completely outlived its license. Pain echoed in her temples, taunting her with reminders of too much alcohol and everything else from the night before.

She rolled onto her side and pulled her knees to her chest. Why had she trusted Hayden? Because he'd never given her a reason not to. Except the entirety of how her job interview went.

She was so stupid, and now she'd lost the trust of a wonderful man. Betrayed someone she adored, respected, and cared about.

The words hit her hard, carried on the furious look Jared had given her last night when he'd asked her to leave.

Pain throbbed behind her temples. She hadn't been thinking straight. Hadn't said everything she needed to.

She forced herself to sit up, and her skull screamed in protest. As soon as she found some aspirin, and maybe brushed the horrible taste out of her mouth, she'd find Jared and make sure he knew everything. Not because she deserved to be forgiven, but because he deserved the full story.

SIXTEEN

Mikki's gut hadn't stopped churning all morning. *First hangover, on top of all this. At least I went all out.* It was going to be hard enough getting Jared out of her system. In addition, she had to deal with the professional aspect of things. The fact that no one had ever told Skriddie what she'd done; they hadn't been warned about their own security leaks.

It took her remaining willpower to force one foot in front of the other to lead her into the exhibitor's hall. People meandered from spot to spot, stopping in aisles, chatting, going about their everyday business. Relief and disappointment warred in her veins when she didn't see any familiar faces at the Skriddie booth. She'd find Jared. But she was going to do something else in the meantime.

Hayden looked up from his phone as she approached. "Hey, Michaela."

Irritation surged inside. He was behind this. So was she. She'd have to take some of the blame herself, but the promises he'd made, and the guilt he'd poured on her for things that had never even happened. Telling her for months that Vivian hated her. And the fact he'd still never learned to call her by the name she preferred.

For the first time that morning, she smiled. But she didn't feel any joy. She tried to keep her voice even. "Do you have a minute?"

His brow furrowed. "Actually, I was going to ask you the same thing. Let's go somewhere quieter."

The tone in his voice dragged up her past insecurities and guilt. She wouldn't let him brush this aside again. As long as she could keep her fragmented thoughts in line, she could do this. She fell into step half a pace back as he wove his way toward the private conference rooms at the back of the exhibit hall, and gestured for her to step into their company's spot.

She hovered at the edge of the room. Where to start? She should just lay it all out there, or at least most of it. No reason to get into what she'd done with Jared. They were done. But the rest of it, holding back wouldn't do her any good.

He dropped into one of the overstuffed chairs and nodded at the other. "Sit down. You're making me nervous."

Good. The admission gave her a touch of satisfaction. Even if he was just talking for the sake of being polite. She perched on the edge of the seat, knees together and legs tucked to the side. Begin with what had happened in the interview. That made the most sense.

He held out her cell phone. "I found this in the booth yesterday afternoon. You should keep a closer eye on it."

"Thanks." She grabbed the device and stuffed it in her purse. No, that wasn't right. She'd had it last night, before the party, hadn't she? Another lie to add to the stack. Why did he have her phone?

Something else nagged in her head. How much could she say to Hayden without losing her job? Was it worth trying to save? Skriddie wasn't going to hire her. Even if there had been a chance before, there wasn't now. Still, she couldn't let that fear keep her from speaking her mind. Not now.

"Why didn't you tell them?" The question slipped past her lips before she could formulate what came next.

His mask slipped, and his lips drew into a thin line. "I'm sorry, I'm confused."

She wasn't going to be vague like she'd been last night with

Jared. Her thoughts were clear now, though she was still struggling to keep her hangover from making her head implode, and she was going to be direct with Hayden. "After my interview. You agreed with me Skriddie needed to know about their security holes. You said you'd make sure it was taken care of. Why, six months down the line, don't they know? Why didn't you tell them?"

He crossed the room and paused, hand on the doorknob, kind mask back in place. "Why didn't you?" He pulled the door open. "You're due on the floor in ten minutes, and we need this room for client meetings."

"I did tell them." She let the words fall out and take mountains of weight with them.

His eyes narrowed and he let the door swing shut again. "I thought you were smarter than that."

The words burrowed under her skin, and she sat straighter. "Excuse me?"

"This isn't a matter of us versus them. This is about your entire career, hon. Who do you think is going to hire you when word gets out you do shit like this for kicks?"

"But I didn't…" The protest died in her throat. In a way, that was exactly what she'd done. "They deserved to know. They needed to know. *You'd* want to know."

Hayden's irritation vanished behind a smile that made her blood run cold, and he stood. "If this comes back to bite us in the ass, it's all on you. And I can make that happen."

Acid churned in her gut as the door swung shut behind him. She was going to be ill. What had she done?

Her morning passed in a haze of self-doubt and ill-conceived resolutions, which were discarded before they could fully form. At least today was the last day of the show. She'd track down Jared as soon as she could, explain herself, and then stick around with the tech staff tomorrow to tear things down. Fortunately, most of the suits were flying out that night or early in the morning. So she wouldn't have to see the disdain on his face after she finished explaining herself. She wouldn't have to deal with Hayden, either. At least until the weekend was over.

And when the trip was finished, she would go back home, lock herself in her empty apartment, and be alone long enough to sort out her thoughts.

Instead of soothing her, the realization stung her eyelids with unshed tears. She angrily pushed the unexpected grief aside, along with the clouds of confusion. Where could she find Jared?

JARED TAPPED a finger on the edge of his coffee cup, mentally counting off each tick. Ten. *I should have known better.* Eleven. *Every single fucking step of the way.* Twelve. *I should have seen it coming.*

Tate and Vivian were in sales meetings, and Jared was grateful. Normally he'd bend Viv's ear. She was the one person who could screw his head back on straight when he let his thoughts get too fragmented. They'd been nothing but since Mikki told him the truth last night.

But Viv wasn't an objective ear this time. She still wanted to hire Mikki, and even after their brief conversation this morning, her response had been, *"You shouldn't have gotten attached. But this means she's got the skills, right?"*

And he hated that a bit of him saw exactly where she was coming from.

"Excuse me." Mikki's familiar voice cut through Jared's swelling frustration. A part of his brain sprung to life, flooding him with the compulsion to wrap her up, accept whatever she had to say, and just leave it behind them. He wasn't going to make that mistake again. Even if she hadn't used him for the information the way Karen had, she'd still had her fun at his expense, and the company's.

"Can we talk?" Her gaze never left his face.

He didn't want to look in her eye. There were too many reminders, both good and bad, of the last few days. But he wasn't going to turn away. He nodded to the chair next to him. "I'm listening."

Her gaze flickered toward the empty seat before landing back on him. "I'll stand, thanks." Her expression was impassive, but by her side, she rubbed her thumb and forefinger together. "I don't remember what I told you last night, but I wanted to make sure you knew I meant it, and you heard all of it, once I was more coherent."

He wasn't going to be sucked into her apology, despite the frown lines in her forehead and the waver in her eyes. It was bad enough she'd lied to him. Tricked him. Threatened his livelihood and held the ability to destroy his friends' careers and his own. And she was still taunting him.

"We're not repeating this. You've told me plenty." He couldn't keep the hurt from his anger. Since she'd confessed last night, he'd rolled every inch of her story around in his head. She was still leaving out details. "It's bullshit you didn't know you were on our network. You recognized it and did what you did anyway. Even if you never meant any harm. And then you told someone what you'd found. Someone who wasn't us."

Her firm stance faltered, and her voice was barely a whisper. "I did it for the challenge."

Challenge, he understood. Digital breaking and entering? That was a violation he didn't get. "I don't think I heard you right."

She looked Jared in the eye again, as if he was the only other person in the room. "I did it for the challenge. You're a name. You're *the* name. You were on our college curriculum. Jobs, Gates, Zuckerberg, and Jared Tippins. You revolutionized network security. You were a minor deity to my graduating class, and you aren't even some old, stuffy dude. I knew there was no way I could find holes in something you built. So yeah, I knew what I was doing, and I couldn't believe I actually pulled it off."

He didn't miss the underlying awe in her confession. He wasn't going to linger on it. It was too difficult to focus on with a new, furious voice asking if he'd ever been anything more to her than a legend. Not only had she violated his work, but she'd used him like a groupie would her favorite actor. "And then instead of telling us, maybe calling up Vivian, you gave that information to the one company who would love to see us go down like the Titanic."

"I wanted to tell you. I told Hayden. I said you needed to know. He promised me it would be a lot less damaging to me if it came from him. That he'd handle it, he'd smooth things over, and you'd be fine. He told me if I went to you, I risked destroying my career before it started, which he hated the thought of me doing. I didn't have any idea no one had ever told you until none of you were nearly as cold as Hayden said you'd be. And even then, I thought it was just in the past.

"Except the pieces didn't add up. I realized you didn't know. That's why I told you as soon as I found out. And I can give you all the details. What holes I discovered. How I uncovered them. I swear I never did anything with information except try and make sure it got back to you, but I can help you fix it."

Jared's pride surged in on his hurt. He'd already fixed anything that was there. He'd been through that fucking system so many times in the past six months, he had no doubt it was solid. Especially after listening to her every time she'd talked about what kinds of unseen holes could be in networks. He'd taken every hint from anything she'd said and applied it. The last thing he needed was her help, or anything that meant spending more time with her.

He couldn't meet her hopeful eyes. He pushed back from the table, focusing on the irritation coursing through him. "I'm done here."

He put as much distance between himself and the coffee shop as quickly as he could. At least the show was wrapping up for the day, so he didn't have to meet with, or pretend to be civil to anyone else. He was starting to regret that the three of them were sticking around through the weekend just to enjoy Vegas.

He ignored Mikki's weak protest behind him as he wove through the crowds. The night before and this morning ran in a non-terminating loop in his head.

He walked without purpose, letting his feet pick the direction.

How had he missed so much? The signs about his nonexistent chances at promotion. Getting hooked on a woman who'd lied to him, used him, and betrayed him. Buying into the delusion that she had the right idea about work and life.

And still a part of his mind reminded him she didn't have to track him down last night or today. Whispered she'd seemed to be as into him as he was into her.

The words sank under his annoyance. *Into her.* The thought hit him harder than he expected, and a sharp pang ticked in his chest. Was he actually falling for her? The revelation tumbled in on top of the question, and he ground to a stop in the middle of the foot traffic. How fucking stupid was he?

"Watch it asshole." Someone jostled him from behind, and then someone else.

He shook his head to clear his thoughts, but it didn't work. She was flighty and impulsive and unpredictable. She was too young, worked for the competition, and wore sheer red lace to business dinners. Oh, and she thought breaking and entering was fun.

He stepped aside in the Skriddie booth and gave Tate a weak smile. Apparently the sales meetings had finished.

Tate joined him, dropping his voice so only Jared could hear. "V tells me you were Karened."

Great. Now my past is a verb. A growl rolled through Jared. This wasn't a conversation he wanted to have anywhere, but especially not in public. Still, the answer rose to his tongue. "She didn't tell you that. She doesn't think the two are the same at all."

He wasn't sure how he knew that, or why he said it. They were similar enough that it didn't matter. And why was he delving into this? He'd already made up his mind.

"She didn't use those exact words. She didn't use many at all." Tate and Viv frequently didn't see eye to eye, so Jared wasn't surprised the conversation had been brief.

"She probably told the story better than I would have," Jared said.

"For what it's worth, I'm sorry it came to this." Tate kept his voice low. "You know what I say about business and pleasure, but I'm still sorry."

Jared wouldn't mind going the rest of the day without one of his friends pointing out how they thought the physical part of this mess had been stupid. He knew that, and it hurt a lot less to focus on the ethical issues he had with the entire thing. Still, he couldn't take his frustrations out on them.

He could make his excuses and walk away long enough to get his head on straight, though. "Yeah, thanks. I need…" What? The words died in his throat, assaulted by an avalanche of conflicted thoughts. He shook the jumble away. "I need to get some work done."

"Sure." Tate shrugged. Jared turned away. Tate's next question made him pause. "Would you have done it?"

Jared bit back a sigh. He didn't want to delve into this. "Done what?"

"Say you're up for the job of a lifetime, at least so far in your career. You can't get your foot in the door because you're young and inexperienced on paper, but you've found a place that looks promising. They say prove your skill, and you realize you're on a Microsoft network."

Jared clenched his jaw, not liking where the question was going.

"Do you really walk away and not touch it? Even if you don't work with the company after, because ethics. Do you really keep your fingers by your sides and not even test your skill?"

"I thought you were on my side." Jared didn't like the immature sound of his own response, but it was better than letting himself admit what his answer was to the question.

"I am," Tate replied. "The last thing I want is to see you devastated like last time. And not just because you're a superior ass when you're heartbroken."

"Thanks." Jared spat the word out. He wasn't heartbroken. Furious. Betrayed. Pissed off beyond belief. But not heartbroken. He strode away without another word, not sure what else to say.

The longer he wandered, the more his friends' words gnawed at him. Their logic mingled with Mikki's apology. It was true, both had warned him away from her in their own way. But neither seemed to think it was reasonable to hold her transgression against her.

He couldn't let it go, though. This wasn't the kind of thing he could just forgive. That realization warred with the bits of him that adored Mikki. It had been a fling, a stupid decision, and something he needed to put in the past now.

If it had really been just a fling, his chest wouldn't ache this much. He wouldn't keep coming back to how much it hurt that she'd betrayed him, even if she hadn't done it intentionally.

And he wouldn't be itching to talk to her again. To see if this could actually be made right. Stupid, fucking, irrational attachment. Goddammit, why did he have to want her in his life so badly?

SEVENTEEN

MIKKI COULDN'T BELIEVE SHE'D STARTED TO FALL AT ALL, LET ALONE so hard it was going to leave bruises on her psyche. A stupid fucking hookup, apparently wrapped in a tremendous lie of her own making, and she'd sunk into it.

For the last four hours, she'd replayed her apologies in her head. Or at least the bits from last night she remembered. It had been the perfect background music to packing up the NSS booth and private conference room. Replaying Jared's disdain. Looping his dismissal.

She tossed a wound-up network cable against the wall, where it clattered harmlessly into the box below. Yup, it was the perfect series of thoughts to keep her company.

She didn't blame him for being furious. She would be too. It didn't matter how much she'd tried to tell herself their opinions were inconsequential. For the first time since she'd entered the industry, she'd met people she respected, and now she'd destroyed any ties with them.

She was stuck in a job with a shitty, lying, asshole boss, who'd made it clear he wasn't giving her references anywhere else. She'd destroyed her personal and professional lives just like that. *Poof.*

Maybe Payton had been right. She was awfully stupid for someone so smart.

"Do you have a minute?"

She jumped at Jared's question, pulse screaming into overdrive, only partly because she was startled. *Calm down.* He probably wanted details about her hack after all. He'd want to fix his network, not their relationship. She had a feeling there was no fixing them, even on a friendship level, let alone more. She faced him, unable to think enough to know how she should look or react.

He was lounged against the door frame, watching her, expression flat and guarded. "Is now a good time?"

She might as well get whatever this was over with. She nodded.

"In private?"

She nodded again. Where the hell was her voice?

He kicked the doorstop out of the way and stepped inside before the door swung shut. "Are you flying out tonight?"

"No." She managed to force the single word past her lips but couldn't hide her cringe at how weak it sounded. She swallowed. "Later tomorrow. I'm part of the cleanup crew."

He bounced on his toes, still hovering near the door. "That's nice."

What did he want? Was he hoping for more of an apology? Was this his way of digging in the knife? She certainly deserved it. But nothing in their short time together convinced her he was like that. "You?"

"We're here all weekend. Probably to see more of the sights and ignore work for a few days."

"Awesome." She couldn't play this game. Whatever he was up to, she wouldn't let it devour her. It needed to be out in the open. "What can I do for you?"

A tremor ran through his laugh. "That's a loaded question."

Was he nervous? That didn't feel right. She shrugged, not sure how to respond.

He took a few steps but still kept his distance. "The other night you asked me about my past. You spilled your guts, I shrugged you off."

She had no idea where he was going with a line like that, but it was better than his barely controlled disgust, so she let him talk.

"That shit people say when they talk about what I did all those years ago. The stuff I assume you learned in school. I'm not some great, genius mastermind. Don't get me wrong—" he looked at her, the corner of his mouth tugging up for the briefest moment before the smile vanished, "—it was impressive, groundbreaking shit. I knew what I was doing."

A tiny laugh slipped from her throat, driven by too much mounting tension, and she swallowed it back. "I don't doubt it for a second."

He gazed past her, at something she assumed wasn't there, and then shook his head. The focus returned to his eyes. "I didn't do it to get my name in textbooks, or even to impress anyone. I did it out of spite. There was a woman—Karen—who was like no one I've met before or since."

Mikki's gut clenched at the implication there was someone in the past she'd never measure up to, and she bit the inside of her cheek. Not that it should matter. She and Jared were so finished they'd never really started. The reassurance didn't stop her heart from aching.

"She used to tell me everything I wanted to hear." The clouded expression returned to his eyes, as if he'd stepped out of the room and into another place. "About work, and life, and all of it."

Did he want someone like that? Mikki recoiled at the thought. Half their relationship had been about her challenging everything he said. But the idea of coddling anyone's ego left a sour taste in her mouth. "I see."

"It was horrible," Jared said. "I didn't believe so at the time, but I hated it. I didn't have to think when she was around. Or grow, or change. I just had to be. But all I knew then was I had someone who adored and worshipped me. I was in love, and I was going to propose, and we were going to live happily ever after."

A stone sank in her gut at the word "love." He'd felt that for someone once. Obviously not someone he was with anymore, but the knowledge still dug deep. *I adore and worship you.* She swallowed the retort before it could spill out. *Probably not the right thing to say.*

He met her gaze, jaw clenched. "Except she didn't mean any of it. I mean, maybe she did once upon a time, but I have a hard time believing it. She..." He drew in a shuddering breath, and then exhaled slowly. "She worked for NetSafe Systems, of all companies, who at the time was in a completely different industry than we were. About three weeks before we were set to launch a new offering I'd been lead on, they released something almost identical. Not just similar. Not as in, okay, there's an industry need for this, and we both thought of it. Their early demos had my wording on them. They approached our clients before we did. She was operating off everything she'd taken from my computer.

"I didn't come up with this 'amazing revolutionary code' because I was some genius kid looking to make his mark on the world. I did it to spite her. To prove she hadn't beaten me, and to save my career at the same time."

Mikki's insides twisted in on themselves. He'd been comparing her to an ex-girlfriend in pretty much every way imaginable, and now she was guilty of a similar betrayal. Except, she wasn't. Defiance surged inside. Even if he thought the worst of her—a concept she wasn't happy with—she wasn't going to be lumped into the same category as this other woman.

"I'm sorry." She struggled to find her voice, but once she grasped the words they spilled out. "I'm sorry someone screwed you over. I'm sorry no one told you what I did, including me." She breathed deep and let momentum carry her. "But I didn't steal anything from you. I never set out to hurt you. It's true, I was a little naïve and reckless about the entire situation—"

"A little?"

She glared at him. "But I never did any of it for money, or vindictively. And my attraction for you now isn't based on what you did back then, or work. Yeah, I idolized you. But turns out, you're not some god on a pedestal. You're a regular, normal, sexy, intelligent..." She ducked her head at his raised brows and her voice dropped. "You know what I mean."

"I've learned not to take that for granted." His voice carried no emotion. "Trying to assume what you mean, that is. It's one of the things I adore about you."

She risked a glance up, eyes growing wide when she saw the intensity in his gaze.

His impassive expression yielded to a soft smile. "I know we just met a couple of days ago, but I'm struggling with how dull my life is going to seem if I never see you again."

The words clicked in her brain, returning a syntax error. She examined them again, and a gentle warmth nudged aside the knot that had moved into her gut. "Really?"

"What makes that so hard to believe? You're intelligent, fun, unconventional." His gaze raked over her. "And sexy as fuck."

The words pushed aside more of her stress, but not her reservations. "But what about what you said this morning? What about what I did?"

"We're not okay." Those three words hurt more than any others he'd said. "This isn't the kind of thing that just gets shrugged off, even if you are all about living for the moment. But I know I'd be missing out if I walked away now."

Her breath hitched at the honesty, and her pulse quickened. "I can't argue with that."

He crossed the remaining space between them.

He raised his hand to the side of her head and tugged the short braid she'd pulled her red streak into. "I guess my point is, I don't want us to be over yet."

The confession was vague, but she wasn't about a detailed plan anyway, and the words pushed aside the tension that had haunted her all day. "Yeah, me too."

His lips moved against the top of her head, and his voice held a raw edge. "How much of your time can I steal before you fly out tomorrow?"

All of it. Hayden could rot in hell for all she cared. But she wasn't quite impulsive enough to stick someone else with her to-do list. Animosity toward her boss aside, no one else needed to be cleaning up her messes today. "I'm almost done here. Another couple of hours tops."

"Will you let me make a plan this time? Buy you dinner, learn about you, pretend we're normal people?"

"Lose the pretending-to-be-normal thing, and I guess. Just this once. Pick me up at my room at seven?"

He kissed her hard, holding her tight for a moment before releasing her. "I'll be there."

EIGHTEEN

JARED'S PHONE BUZZED IN HIS POCKET. HE SHOULD HAVE GIVEN Mikki his number. He couldn't help his smile at the thought. Great, he was acting like a crushing teenager. Which, when he thought about it, wasn't as much of an issue as it should have been.

He pulled up the text from Dewson, and his gut turned in on itself. *We're infected.*

Maybe it wasn't a big deal. Sometimes someone clicked something in an email, and it was always isolated immediately. It had been almost twenty-four hours since he'd asked Dewson to look into the rumors Rosen had mentioned. This couldn't be related. He sent back a reply. *How bad?*

Trojan. Database array.

Shit. His mind was already whirring ahead several steps, even while he executed each thing that needed to be done now. *Are we clean now?*

Probably. Need a second set of eyes.

A directory of names ticked through his head. Who could check Dewson's work? His staff was small, but they were all good at what they did. No, he'd do this one himself. Another question slammed into the forefront of his thoughts, pushing all his lists and plotting to the side.

It died at the tip of his tongue. Something told him he didn't want to know the answer, but that was ridiculous. It wasn't like it mattered. Still, he had to force his fingers to type it out. *Do we know where it came from?*

Jared had stepped aside from the flow of traffic and had all his attention focused on his phone. The seconds ticked away, and his hands twitched. How long did it take to type out a name, or a "no"?

When his phone finally vibrated, he jumped. Tension ached in his temples. *You.*

A bitter laugh slipped from his throat. If his promotion hadn't already been shot, it would have been now.

More digging uncovered that the message had his name on it, and someone in IT had opened it and clicked the link, but after having Dewson forward the appropriate information along— message headers and such—he knew it hadn't come from his computer or phone.

But it was an amazing imitation. Who knew how to do something like that? Jared pushed aside the nagging in the back of his head. It was an old scar. Resurfacing insecurities. Mikki may have been at the root of the original problem, but just finding out he didn't know about that simple indiscretion had torn her up. Hadn't it? There was no way she was doing something actually vindictive.

He told Dewson he'd take care of the rest—double-checking to make sure the virus was gone, figuring out what systems had been breached, and uncovering out how someone had tricked their network into believing the email was from him.

He took a deep breath and corralled the rambling bullshit to the back of his thoughts. If they were home, he'd take point on something this serious and his people would back him up. But he wasn't trusting it to anyone except himself and his friends. Tate and Vivian could keep up under his direction, despite their different career paths. Between the three of them, they would make this right.

Within minutes, they were waiting for him in a quiet corner of the hotel lobby. He gave them the lowdown as quickly as possible.

Vivian's brow creased with concern. "You're okay, right?"

Besides stressed, concerned, and a little wounded that this had happened under his watch, it was all status quo. "Why wouldn't I be?"

She wouldn't meet his gaze.

Tate cleared his throat, and Jared's head swung in that direction.

Tate shrugged. "This kind of violation isn't exactly easy to pull off, is it?"

"You know it's not."

Tate glanced at Vivian, but she was still fiddling with her purse. He looked back at Jared. "So who would love to see us fall? Who has someone working for them who knows how to do something like this?"

He was asking if Mikki was behind this. Jared wanted to snap at him for the assumption. What he hated even more was that part of him was asking the same question, even though she'd just finished apologizing.

He stashed the doubt. "If someone on Hayden's side did this, we'll shut them down. First, we have to make sure we're clean, we have to make sure this won't happen again, and we have to do it now. Where can we set up?"

Tate's face twitched with a bitter smile. "I've got the high roller suite. A lot more room to spread out."

"Good call." Jared glanced at Vivian. "Grab your laptop. Track down the concierge and see where we can find a couple of clean ones as well. Out of the box. Nearest Fry's, Walmart, whatever. I'll grab the secure hotspot."

"Right. I'll meet you both upstairs as soon as I can." Vivian turned away even as she spoke.

A hollow ache throbbed under Jared's ribcage. It wasn't true. This was bad luck, and it had nothing to do with Mikki. Except it did. Even if it didn't come directly from her, her carelessness, combined with a scary knack for the obtuse, could have made this happen. He shoved the thoughts aside. Wallowing could wait.

"Can we get Legal on the phone?" he asked as he and Tate made their way to the elevators.

"Can you prove NetSys is behind this? Like undeniable, some-one's-grandpa-could-understand-it proof?"

Jared clenched his teeth. They both knew proof was almost impossible. Some hackers signed their names, but not usually those involved in corporate espionage. Besides, right now it all pointed back to Jared anyway. Unless they could pinpoint where the infected message had actually come from, there was no point in doing anything besides plugging the hole as quickly as possible.

Mikki set her phone on the counter in the bathroom and cranked the volume. It wasn't as good as having it attached to the docking station she had back home, but the echo of the tiles gave her enough to sing along with. She wiped the steam from the mirror. Happy eyes and cheeks flushed with the heat of her shower stared back. She'd finished clearing up their display in the exhibit hall early and rushed back to her room, giddy with fantasies of the night ahead of her. She'd tried to take her time in the shower so she wouldn't have to wait long. Her clock told her she still had more than an hour until Jared would be there, though.

Blow-drying her hair only took up fifteen minutes. She stared at her luggage. Now, what to wear? After examining and discarding every piece of clothing she'd packed, she sank onto the bed. Maybe she should have thought of that earlier. Stopped by one of the casino shops and picked up something sexy. She absentmindedly twirled the belt of her robe around her finger, sliding the red satin back and forth.

She looked down at the kimono-style robe. Then stood and spun, examining herself from every angle in the mirror above the desk. The thought of opening the door for him dressed in nothing but the robe sent a rush of excitement through her. She needed to calm down a little. He'd mentioned dinner and conversation. And as much as she loved the memories of what he could do to her body, she was looking forward to some more in-depth getting to know each other as well.

Her imagination wanted something else. She perched on the edge of her bed, legs crossed.

The minutes passed, and the clock rolled past seven. Something twinged inside as the time hit five minutes late, and then ten. He was just tied up, right? She knew how busy he was. Something had snagged his attention. He couldn't let her know because he was on the phone or in a meeting.

And didn't have her number. The thought rolled through her head, taunting her. But trailing behind came another, much better one. She did have his. She'd snagged business cards from pretty much every booth at the show, and his was in the stack.

Seconds later, she dug his card out and had his number in her phone. Her thumbs hesitated above the screen. Would she seem needy if she sent him a message? He was probably on his way up now. Right? She glanced at the clock. Twenty minutes late. No, this would be okay. She sent him a quick text. *It's Mikki. Just making sure everything's okay.*

Another half an hour ticked by, and nothing. Sick dread nudged her senses. He'd said they weren't completely okay but had still forgiven her. Had he changed his mind? Had the few hours apart given him a new perspective on how badly she'd fucked up?

She was overreacting. There was nothing wrong. Sometimes life happened. She set him another quick note. *You all right? Where are you?*

Which was okay, right? They hadn't exactly defined their relationship this afternoon, but she assumed when he said he wanted to see more of her, he'd meant it.

Except an hour after she sent the message, and still had no response, she wasn't so sure. She clicked on the TV and cycled through the channels two times before she realized she had no idea what she'd just seen on any of them. Another hour passed. He wasn't coming. Whatever was going on, he wasn't going to show up.

She set her phone on the nightstand and lay on her stomach on the bed. Crime drama. That should take her mind off things. Classic, straightforward whodunit with a smattering of interrogation and court room drama. The victim had been killed by his business partner, who had been sleeping with the victim's wife, and embezzling from their company.

Mikki clicked the channel to something with cartoons instead. The inanities and three nights of almost no sleep combined with her wounded disappointment and pulled her eyelids shut.

A loud hum tore through the room, jarring her awake. She stared around her room, blinking away the sleep. What the hell? She turned toward the nightstand. A sad giggle escaped. It was just her phone vibrating against the solid surface.

She grabbed the device, not able to suppress her hope. It was Jared. It had to be. He had a good excuse. Her gut sank when she read the message. It was definitely him, all right.

His note just said, *Cleaning up your mess. A Trojan, really?*

She clicked the words around in her head, looking for a meaning. She knew what they meant, but how did it relate to her? Realization crashed in around her, and she sank to the floor. Someone had exploited what she'd found. It was the most plausible reason she could think of for why he'd be blaming her. Someone who'd known all the details of what she'd uncovered and had access to her phone less than twenty-four hours ago.

Her hands were shaking as she pulled up her phone's email history. There it was, sitting in a file that was deleted but still hiding on her phone, with Jared's email information spoofed as headers. Whoever had used her phone to do this hadn't even bothered to cover his tracks.

She pulled up Hayden's number, her raging fury making it difficult to even think. He'd still be on his flight, but he always checked his messages as soon as he landed. She didn't try to keep her voice steady. It took enough effort to keep a string of profanities and cruel names from flying to her lips. "It's Mikki. I know it'll be late when you get in, but I thought you'd like to know sooner rather than later. I quit."

All his warnings about her finding other work faded into the back of her mind. This was unacceptable. It bordered on illegal. She couldn't draw a paycheck from these people even if it did mean finding another job would be a struggle.

She pulled herself into the easy chair next to the bed and turned her attention back to the TV. *Cleaning up your mess.* Jared's text echoed in her thoughts. She hadn't meant to cause a mess. It was never supposed to be like this. This was more than the simplicity of her wanting to know if she was better than the legendary Jared Tippins; it impacted an entire company. The livelihood of thousands of people.

She needed to find Jared and make things right. It didn't matter that sleep tugged at her senses. Rest could wait until this entire thing was straightened out.

She pulled on some clothes, grabbed her phone and her room key, and headed straight for the elevator. Hopefully Jared would be in his room. She had to help him make this right.

She pounded as loud as she dared without drawing attention from the neighbors and staff. Her gut sank further when there was no answer. Now what?

When her phone vibrated against her hip, it jarred her from the edge of panic. She didn't check the display, hitting answer on autopilot while her brain whirred for solutions on where to look for Jared next. "Hello?" Her voice cracked, and she winced.

"Everything all right?" Hayden's cheerful tone sharpened the edge of her exhaustion.

Any restraint she'd used earlier was lost in the haze of exhaustion and frustration. Time to be blunt. "No, it's not. Things have moved past bad and straight into fucked up."

His chuckle drifted over the phone line and sent ice dragging up her spine. "Then maybe you should have been more selective about how you landed your job." His tone was steel. "I've tried to put this politely, and I've tried to hint. You're smart. I figured you got what I was implying. The signing bonus was to help soothe your conscience. The fact you've kept quiet for six months implies you didn't want to be found out. That you fucked their director of technology and still didn't say anything indicates you're getting off on the entire thing. If you quit now, you'll never work tech again. Not just in this industry, but in any. Just like the guy who interviewed you. And your resignation is accepted, by the way."

The line clicked off, and Mikki stared at the device in her hands. Rage, fear, and nausea all rolled inside. She didn't know how she was going to make this better, but if it was the equivalent of spitting in Hayden's face and helped Jared out at the same time, she'd sacrifice a lot to make it happen.

NINETEEN

Jared stared at the laptop in front of him, and tried to blink some moisture back into his eyes. Vivian's phone sat in the middle of the table, speaker on and cable running back to her machine to keep it charged. The clack of keys filled the room. Occasionally Dewson would report something, or one of them would snap out a question or command, but for the most part, they kept their heads down.

When he'd gotten Mikki's first text several hours ago, the rest of his doubt had been obliterated. The message headers matched. The email—the one pretending to be him—had come from her phone.

He didn't want to believe it. It devoured every thread of his consciousness not already dedicated to fixing the problem at hand. He'd really fallen for it again. Not in a million years would he have ever guessed...

Then again, that seemed to be his curse. It really was true—what his parents had between each other, the love he'd grown up around—that was the shit of fairy tales.

He hadn't been able to tell his friends the newest information. Vivian at least thought highly of her. They could deal with that after. The only thing he didn't understand was the shitty job she'd done covering her tracks. Six months ago, he hadn't seen a trace anyone had been on his network. This had her name stamped on it. Literally. Was she mocking him? He didn't want to believe it, but he also couldn't ignore the possibility.

He raked his fingers through his hair. He needed to focus on work. Where was the hole that had allowed the Trojan onto their network? What was he missing? Maybe Rosen had been right; he'd been out of the tech for too long. At least the network was clean, as far as they could tell. That was killing him, too. Not only could they not find the holes in their network, they didn't even know if they'd completely removed the immediate threat.

"Next steps?" The exhaustion in Tate's voice reflected the weary atmosphere of the entire room. It was barely eleven, but they'd been at this for hours, only breaking long enough to down another can of Red Bull or cup of coffee. For about thirty seconds, he'd considered using the former to make the latter. Fortunately, he wasn't that exhausted. Yet.

Would Mikki do something like make coffee with Red Bull? He hated himself the moment the thought passed through his head. He'd managed to keep from thinking her name all night, and now there it was, flooding back in and taunting him. Maybe that was what he needed to do. Think like her.

Sexy, alluring, deceptive… He pushed the string of words aside. *Later. Wallow later.* Impulsive, fickle, and fleeting. There was the mindset he needed. He closed his eyes and breathed deeply—one… two…three times, trying to push away all the indoctrination he'd picked up over the years. If he was just some person, someone who had the skill and intelligence, but not the corporate experience, where would he poke around for holes?

Her words echoed in his head. *Remote computers. Machines you wouldn't ever expect to have access to your deepest, most important information.* He focused on the room again, gaze pausing on Tate. "Check the virtual machines quality assurance uses. You're looking at database users. Accounts with no passwords, admin access, shit like that." He turned to Vivian. "Same thing; focus group VM's. Dewson."

The drowsy "Yeah?" echoed off the glass coffee table.

"Every fucking administrative assistant we have. Ours. Reception. All of them."

That was it. It had to be. Hope surged inside as he dove into his own work, searching and scanning the same things he'd ordered everyone else to do.

Except an hour later, no one had anything. It was all tight and secure. He flopped his head back against the couch, letting a frustrated grunt escape. "Fuck."

A knock echoed through the room. Jared shot a questioning glance at Tate.

His friend shrugged and nodded at the tray on the table. "Room service was already here, and even if it wasn't the middle of the night, I told the front desk to give us some quiet—including housekeeping."

Vivian sighed and stood. "Staring at each other isn't going to answer the 'who' question, and we're obviously at a standstill, so an interruption won't hurt." She pressed her eye to the peephole and muttered, "Well then. Didn't expect that."

Jared's gut sank, rage twisting with betrayal. He didn't have to ask who it was.

"We're kind of busy for a booty call." Tate's comment barely reached Jared's ears through the scream of his thoughts.

What the hell was she doing there? Rubbing it in? The latch clicked, and the hinges squeaked. He didn't want to look, but he couldn't help it. There was Mikki, standing in the doorway. Even across the room he could see the circles under eyes. Her shoulders were hunched. She shifted her weight from one foot to the other, gaze darting everywhere. Every time she reached him, she skipped past, never making eye contact. "I want to help."

Vivian opened the door wider.

Jared's protest stuck in his throat. He should be ordering her to leave. Ignoring everything she said. But that tiny little voice in the back of his head refused to accept all the facts at face value. Mikki stepped into the room, and the door swung shut behind her.

Vivian nodded at Jared before she turned away. "It's his show, it's not my call."

Apparently it was her call, at least on some level. He fixed his most damning glare on Vivian, who shrugged it off and settled back onto the couch across from him. Maybe he should have told them there was evidence to back up their suspicions of where this had come from.

A heavy silence descended on the room, filling Jared's lungs until he thought it might suffocate him. He forced himself to breathe but still couldn't look at her. "How did you find the room?"

"It's um…luck?"

"We have work to do." Jared couldn't keep his exhaustion from his voice. "You hacked another computer so you could come tell us you're sorry for hacking ours?"

He finally forced himself to look at Mikki. Even being as furious with her as he was, she still spoke to parts of him which were desperately infatuated with her.

Her shoulders straightened, though she continued to shift from foot to foot. "People talk. You know that, right? Hayden. I mean, apparently not about the significant things like corporate espionage and ethical violations, but he does talk. I've never figured out if he hates you three or wants to blow you."

Vivian snorted, and one corner of Mikki's mouth twitched, but her expression didn't shift. "Which is how I know one of you is a high roller. They only have so many of those rooms, at least the really nice ones, in this hotel. And logic dictates it's more likely the one with the Red Bull on the tray outside the door than the empty champagne bottle."

Jared's brows rose. She was more observant than she gave herself credit for. Not that it mattered at this point.

"You still have to have a card to get up to this floor," Tate countered.

Her gaze faltered, but only for a moment. "If you step onto an elevator someone else calls, and look like you know where you're going, no one questions whether or not you belong up here."

Jared rubbed his eyes. The contacts would have to come out soon. Fortunately, he had a spare set of glasses in his laptop case. "Why are you here?"

"I told you. I want to help."

He was on his feet in an instant, crossing the room in a few short strides and stopping less than foot away from her. Her eyes grew wide, but she didn't move. He couldn't keep the anger and irritation out of his voice. "I'm pretty sure that's how this started. You wanted to help someone."

Her chin quivered, but she regained her composure quickly. "I can tell you everything they know. I can tell you more than they know. I can show you all three weak spots, and where I assume another two exist."

Her confidence, the quiet but firm voice, and the fact part of him still couldn't hate her, made something inside Jared snap. He didn't try and hide it when he spoke. "Is this fun for you? Is that why you did it? And now you're here to hold it over our heads? I didn't peg you as a sadist. Did you plant the Trojan yesterday for challenge too? To prove you could do it?"

Her face went blank, the color vanished from her cheeks, and even as she shook her head, her eyes never left his. "You don't think that little of my skill, do you? Thirty seconds after you mentioned a virus, I found what I assume is the same thing you did. That someone else used my phone to set us both up. I'm reckless, but I'm not stupid." She licked her lips and bit the inside of her cheek. "And I quit by the way. About the moment I realized what had happened. Told Hayden he could shove his job."

Fuck. If he hadn't believed her before, that really drove her point home. It didn't make the situation any less stressful, or alleviate his anger. He just needed a new focus for it. "So what are we missing? We've been through every inch of the blade array, and there's nothing."

"The holes aren't in your data center." She was standing straight now, defiance flashing in her eyes. It was the same sense of challenge he'd seen the night they met. Had it really been less than seventy-two hours?

Disappointment rushed through him. He turned away and headed back to his spot on the couch. "I kind of figured. We've checked everywhere."

"You'll need someone on site. Is anyone on call?"

"Dewson, you still with us?" He'd been hollowed out. The pain was vanishing. The anger. The exhaustion. He didn't feel anything.

"Present. Barely."

"Listen to the lady," he told Dewson. He couldn't believe he was turning this over to her. "Do what she says."

Mikki had followed him and stood a few feet back from the circle of furniture. "You have a handful of machines—probably marketing or accounting, since they're full of profit-loss projections. That's your first weakness."

This was useless. Now she was just mocking him. At least before she'd arrived, they'd been spinning their wheels in useful directions. "Marketing doesn't have access to the data center."

Her jaw clenched. "Number two, you have a server, probably call-center based, with no admin password."

Jared bit back a snarl. "Call center operates on its own domain. It doesn't touch us."

"And then there's the Exchange server."

This was bullshit. There was no way their email was an issue. "If you're not really here to hel—"

"Stuff your ego back in your pants." Her nostrils flared and her eyes narrowed. "I'm sorry. For everything, the stuff I did on purpose, the stuff I chose to ignore, the stuff I never saw coming. But I'm not here because I like you glaring at me. All of you. I want to make it better. If you don't want to know what I know, I can leave."

He locked his gaze on hers, half scowling, half searching for answers he knew he wouldn't find. An eerie silence settled into the room. He nodded to an empty chair, jaw clenched. He wanted to ignore her, except every one of the things she'd mentioned could be a real problem. It was what he'd been searching for, just in a different place. Fuck. "Do what she says."

TWENTY

Jared rolled his neck and stretched his arms above his head. Muscles protested and joints argued as he tried to force out the kinks of falling asleep on the hotel room couch. At least the silence was pleasant. A glance at his phone told him it was almost nine. Later than he'd slept in years. Then again, they hadn't pulled an all-nighter since…

The Karen incident, right. His creeping good mood vanished under a wash of too many emotions to identify. He let his attention trip around the room while he tried to work the knots from his arms. The suite was a wreck. Cups, cans, and picked-at snack platters littered the coffee table.

His heart sank when he looked further. On the opposite couch, Vivian had fallen asleep mostly sitting up, and Mikki was curled up next to her, head in her lap.

They'd fixed it. Plugged every hole and set measures in place to prevent a series of new ones. He was confident in that. Too bad he wasn't as confident about anything else. He pulled his gaze from the sleeping brunette. The last thing he needed was one more memory seared into his thoughts of another mistake.

But there was one thing he had to admit. It was the one thing he had Mikki to thank for, even if everything else was a wreck. She'd reminded him why he did this. That he'd gotten into this line of work for the challenge, for the way he worked with his friends, and because it pushed his limits mentally, and he loved it.

There would be other promotions. He'd already dedicated a portion of his brain to figuring out how to get Skriddie to add a CTO position to their list of executives, but until then and even after, he wasn't going to lose track of his roots again. What made him love his work.

He wandered to the sink in the kitchenette, grabbed a glass, and downed the lukewarm tap water in a single swallow. It wasn't the most exquisite drink ever, but it did help his throat loosen up. He splashed his face and reached blindly for a towel. He raised an eyebrow when one landed in his hand, and dried his face off enough to open his eyes.

Tate sat on the counter next to him, staring at something in the living room. His voice was low when he spoke. "You know how many guys would give their right nut to wake up to that?"

"Because they haven't had to." Jared didn't have to turn to see he was talking about the two sleeping women, and honestly, the last thing he wanted to do was see Mikki any more than he had to. Second to last was having this conversation.

"Ouch." Tate blew a strand of blond off his forehead. "She saved us."

Jared shook his head. Warm fuzzies aside, he was still struggling with what Mikki had done. Even if she hadn't done it maliciously, she still wasn't innocent. "She almost ruined us."

"Yeah, but—"

"I'm going back to my room to shower." Jared tossed the hand towel at Tate and pushed away from the counter, spinning back toward the living room. He managed to hide his shock when he saw Vivian was awake and sitting on a stool at the breakfast bar. Mikki was upright now, too. Still on the couch. Legs drawn to her chest.

"He's got a point," Vivian said. "She didn't have to track us down. Yet here she is."

Jared looked back and forth between his friends. And to the

sunlight streaming through the window. And the doors at the far end of the room. Anywhere but the dark eyes watching him from Mikki's expressionless face.

Vivian leaned forward, but her voice was distinct enough to carry through the entire room. "I can have an offer letter ready by ten on Monday."

Mikki's jaw dropped, and she stared at Vivian. Her voice was tiny in the large room. "For me? Why would you—"

"Whoa." Jared shook his head. "How did we go from 'oh fuck, we're screwed' to 'come work for us?'?"

Vivian's brows rose. "Have you heard anything I've said for the last two days?"

"Really, she hasn't shut up about it." Tate tossed the towel back at him and moved to stand near the balcony. His gaze was directed outside, but it was clear from the angle of his body he was still part of the conversation.

Jared couldn't believe what he was hearing. "A person can't just make a mistake like that and hope it all goes away with an apology and a bit of hard work."

"Not that you'd know from experience." Sarcasm dripped from Vivian's every word. "You'd never make a mistake like that. And then spin your entire career off it. What is it they say about you? That you're a demi-god on college campuses?"

"Deity," Tate offered.

Jared didn't need this. "Why the fuck are we having this conversation while she's still here?" Guilt followed the almost-yell. Better question, why did he feel so bad for snapping? It had nothing to do with the fact that as much as he was trying to ignore Mikki, his gaze kept drifting back to her. The sorrow and apology in her dark eyes. That his friends were making more sense than him. And it had nothing to do with how much of an ass he was being.

"Because it's rude to talk about someone behind their back," Vivian offered.

Jared ground his teeth, trying to maintain his composure while he spoke. He finally forced his gaze to stay on Mikki. To keep his stare hard and demand the rest of him feel the same coldness. "It's nice you helped make it better. We all appreciate last night." He let the ice from his tone flow through his veins. "But sometimes after the fact isn't enough. This wasn't an apologize-and-forget-it mistake. A lot of people might have found themselves out of work."

It was only a slight exaggeration. If someone had exploited the virus before they'd obliterated it, or if someone more malicious than Hayden—he shuddered at the thought—had known about the security holes, it could have cost the company millions.

"You can't live life one minute to the next, hoping it will all work out." Each word tasted bitter on his tongue, but it was true. "Sometimes being impulsive has terrible consequences you have to live with. And I don't know how Vivian, or anyone, could trust a job—especially in security—to someone who doesn't know the difference between ethics and a challenge."

Vivian's tone was sharp. "That's not—"

"He's completely right." Mikki finally spoke. She uncurled herself from the couch pulled her stare from Jared. "You should be all set now. I have a plane to catch in a little while."

The moment the door clicked shut behind her, Tate tossed the towel back at him, full force. It fluttered to the floor before it reached its destination.

"You're an ass." Vivian pushed away from the counter. "I'm going back to my room to clean up. Do we need to get early flights out of here?"

So he could head home and spend the rest of the weekend alone with his thoughts? Even hanging out with pissed-off friends was a better option. "We can stay the weekend. We're in the clear."

"Wow, I wonder how that happened. No, wait, I don't. I was there. Are you sure you were?" Tate turned toward the bedroom. "I'm going back to bed for a few hours." He paused halfway to the door. "I know you think that stupid fucking logic of yours is going to save you from yourself."

Great, the lecture was taking on a new tier. That was what Jared needed—to hear Tate talk about how love wasn't a business negotiation. "I'm going now."

Tate faced him again. "She's nothing like Karen. Mikki's her own person. I can't fathom she's ever catered to your ego just to make you happy, and I'd never bet on her to back down if she knew she was right. Oh, and there's her honesty. The list goes on. In fact, the only thing they have in common is they worked for the same company. You and Mikki, the two of you have sparks. Sorry to sound cliché, but every time you're together, they're bright, they're electric, and you feed each other." And with that, he vanished into his room and the door swung shut behind him.

"You think you're the only person suffering here?" Vivian asked. She stood near the door, arms crossed, glare fixed on him.

"Really?" He couldn't hide the disbelief in his voice. "That's the problem, isn't it? Everyone suffers for this. She almost destroyed lives."

"Melodramatic much? And I meant her."

"You're taking the sympathy a bit too far, Viv. And it's not melodramatic. She could have collapsed the entire fucking company because she wanted to see what she was capable of."

She gave him a smile he knew from experience was laced with condescension. "Do you really still blame her for the Trojan?"

His thoughts ground to a halt, tripping over the sudden shift in conversation. He'd completely forgotten. One more thing to be furious about. "Even if she didn't plant it, she's not innocent."

"You know those assholes look for every chance they can find to make us look bad." She had a point. Hayden didn't have to be technical if Mikki had laid out every detail for him, hoping it would help someone tell Skriddie how to fix the problem. He knew enough to manage a technical team. That was all the knowledge it would take.

"Do you really think she'd leave fingerprints, and then come groveling for forgiveness?" Vivian asked.

It didn't matter that all the pieces pointed to Hayden. He couldn't forgive this, and he wouldn't be suckered again. He fixed a cold smile on her. "But she didn't ask for forgiveness, did she? She showed up hours after the fact, flaunting the fact she'd found something we couldn't. You do understand how that kind of ego works, right?"

She studied him, disgust and disappointment heavy in her frown. "Apparently not. But I can tell you've got a solid grasp on it."

She thought he was describing himself? Jared obliterated the part of himself agreeing with her disdain. Squashed the voice into oblivion pointing out he was the one being irrational by refusing to yield. He grabbed his laptop and walked out of the room without another word. It didn't matter how much he wanted to convince himself otherwise, what Mikki had done was unforgivable.

It had to be.

MIKKI DIDN'T BLAME Jared for his reaction. He had every right to be furious. At least she'd finally corrected her original mistake. His friends were wrong though, in comparing her actions to any he'd taken in the past. She wasn't trying to spin it into some sort of career-changing move. She'd just wanted to make things right.

She pushed into her room. Everything inside her ached with sorrow and regret. And a little bit from the position she'd slept in. She stripped off her clothes, cranked the shower on, and stepped under the stream. The water heated as it beat into her skin. It didn't dredge away her exhaustion, or anything else.

Her thoughts fumbled for focus as she toweled off and dressed. The bed beckoned her, but she had to be on a plane in just a few hours, and there was no reason for her to stick around. She'd grab the biggest cup of espresso hopped-up coffee she could find and snag a cab to the airport.

Her phone buzzed. She snagged it off the nightstand to press *ignore* and saw Hayden's name on the screen.

Her ambivalence and self-pity evaporated in a rush of angry heat, and she clicked *answer.* Her frustration had just found an outlet. "Hello."

"Michaela." Hayden was the kind, friendly person she remembered. "You were pretty stressed last night. I just called to make sure you were all right."

But she'd seen his true face, and she was tired of filtering her thoughts. "You mean last night when I quit and like the asshole you are, you threatened my entire career? Or are you thinking of a different conversation?"

His nervous chuckle was hollow over the line. "It was late, I was tired and jet lagged. That's behind us, right?"

"Oh yeah, completely." She let her irritation flow into her responses. "So behind us, it'll never be an issue again."

"Glad to hear it—"

"Because I just finished typing up my resignation and it will be on HR's fax machine in about twenty minutes."

"Excuse me?" And just like that, Hayden's smooth talking vanished.

"No, I won't." She held her free hand out in front of her, palm down, as she talked. She should be shaking from all the anger and adrenaline pumping through her, but all she felt was a growing calm.

"You'll go down for this." A low threat ran through his words.

"Too late." She let the words flow as they popped into her head. Impulsiveness had already ripped so much away from her, why not let it rain down chaos a little longer? "I'll destroy my corporate card before I walk out of the hotel, and drop my laptop with security on Monday. I expect they'll have the contents of my desk waiting for me by then."

"Where are you going to go? Skriddie's not going to have you. You're not getting a reference from me. So…you're planning to go back to call center life? That's not going to pay the bills."

"It's better than working for someone who thinks healthy competition is planting a virus on another company's network." It was true, Skriddie wouldn't have her. Jared had made that clear, and he was right. Not that she needed the reminder. She wasn't giving up a job opportunity because of a guy. It was because it was the right thing to do. Even though missing Jared was tearing her up more than the damage to her career. "If I burn, I have ways to take you down with me. You shouldn't have used my phone."

"Mik—"

She was done. As she hung up, the adrenaline took its toll. It plummeted into her gut, snatching away her breath and leaving her ill. She sank onto the mattress, staring at the wall. In less than a week, she'd gone from being a growing name in her field and falling in love to being heartbroken and unemployed. Even worse was she didn't know which devoured her more—her career being dead or the realization she'd actually been falling for Jared.

TWENTY-ONE

JARED TOSSED HIS LAPTOP ON THE HOTEL BED. IT SANK INTO THE smooth comforter, wrinkling the only order in the room. He dropped onto the mattress next to it, gaze drifting around what had been his temporary home. Memories seemed to leak from every corner, hiding in the shadows, taunting and urging him to remember. But he couldn't.

Living the last few days had already created too much of a mess. Clothes draped on chairs, nothing on hangers or in the "dry clean back home" side of his garment bag. He hadn't even stuck to his morning run. On the surface it wasn't a wreck. However, he knew how it normally looked, though, and it was all out of place. He wanted to be bothered by the disarray, but he was more bothered that most of him didn't feel it was significant. At least not on this scale.

Jesus, could he be more melodramatic? He'd dealt with this before. He knew how to move on. The idea was so overwhelmingly unappealing it almost made him retch. He only wanted one thing right now, and she wasn't here.

No, he couldn't do this. He wouldn't linger on her face, her laughter, her gorgeous body and the way it fit perfectly against him, the way her brain whirled so fast it was a rush to keep up. He wasn't going to think about any of those things.

He forced himself to stand. A semblance of order would help him compartmentalize his thoughts. He moved his misplaced clothes into their proper places. He plucked a shirt off the top of his garment bag, and his chest almost collapsed on itself. A teddy bear stared back, black eyes blank and accusing, taunting him in nothing but an apron and a beret. He grabbed the bear to fling it across the room, and a pair of black, lace panties tore loose from its arm and drifted to the ground.

Mikki was everything that could destroy him. She'd almost done it once. She was flighty, impulsive, and prone to do things like hack the competition's network just because she could. He tugged the apron down on the bear and set it back on top of his luggage. He knew all those things at his core. So why did it feel like he was being ripped apart at the thought of never seeing her again?

Suddenly the air around him felt too heavy. He needed to get out of there. Being alone with his thoughts was going to crush him. He'd text Vivian and see if she wanted to do anything while they waited on Tate.

And listen to them lecture me some more. Fuck that. He'd surround himself with strangers instead. See if he could live their emotions through osmosis, or some stupid bullshit, instead of having to deal with the parts of him whispering she'd suffered through this as much as he had.

He showered as quickly as he could, hating the way the beat of the water drew his own thoughts back to the surface. He pulled on slacks, a shirt, and a suit jacket, and headed toward the elevators. When he reached the lobby, he couldn't find enough concentration to even figure out where he was going. Breakfast was a good start. Somewhere with lots of people. Loud people.

As he let his gaze drift around the lobby, deja vu coursed through him. Had it really been less than four days since he first saw the distracted woman wandering across the lobby, oblivious to the world?

Great, now his imagination was taunting him. No. He narrowed his gaze. It was really her heading toward the business center. Time for breakfast. But he couldn't convince his feet to move in the other direction. She was only inside for a few moments before she emerged again. Her gaze stayed on the ground as she headed toward the front door, duffel bag and laptop slung over her shoulder, trailing a rolling suitcase behind her.

Let her leave. The two of us are done. Fuck it, he was an ass sometimes. His feet were carrying him toward the exits before the automated door finished swinging shut behind her. She was halfway to the cab line. This mental argument was stupid. He'd admitted yesterday he wanted to work through things with her. Nothing had changed except more of the truth was in the open now. Things that hadn't been her fault any more than his. He forced himself to speak. "Mikki."

A doorman had a taxi at the curb, waiting for her. "Miss?"

She didn't turn to face Jared, but she didn't move toward the waiting car, either.

She couldn't leave. The single thought pushed aside all of Jared's hurt and confusion. He needed her. Everything Tate had said was true. Vivian was right. Logic be damned, he was going to be miserable without this woman, and she'd been as betrayed as he had. "Please?"

The seconds ticked away in slow motion. She finally shook her head at the doorman and stepped aside so the next person in line could have the waiting ride.

She turned to face Jared, jaw set and eyes hard.

He forced the words out. "Hear me out."

She shrugged her bags off her shoulder, let them drop in a controlled fall, and grasped the straps in her hand. She bumped her laptop with her leg each time her foot bounced. "There's not really anything left to cover. I told you everything I know."

It took him a moment to process the words. She meant about the security holes. He shook his head. "I know. And I'm grateful. So much more than I could ever say. But I meant about us. Can we go somewhere? I'll buy you coffee, or breakfast, or a day pass at Adventure Land. Just hear me out?"

"I have a flight to catch."

He deserved the brush-off. He closed the distance between them, but suppressed the urge to kiss her until neither of them could breathe. "Give me five minutes. You should still be able to catch your plane."

She crossed her arms, gaze locked on him, lips drawn into a thin line. And then her chin quivered. She swallowed, took a deep breath. "I have a little time."

Fuck, now what was he supposed to say? Every thought assaulted him at once, forcing his mouth open before he could process. "I need—"

Her "I can't—" overlapped him.

He choked back the words. "You go first."

She caught her bottom lip between her teeth, and her brow furrowed. The cold mask slipped away, and worry fell in to take its place. "I'm so sorry. I really am. If I had to do it all again, the whole hacking thing, the jobs, all of it, I'd do it differently. Except maybe you. Do you have any idea how much it hurts to realize that? How selfish it feels? To admit I'd still suffer through never seeing you again just so I'd have the memories?" She shook her head. "But that's the awesome thing about hindsight, right? It never happens before the fact."

He knew exactly how she felt, but he didn't dare interrupt. A sharp silence settled between them.

She stared at him. "That was it. I'm done."

He measured his words. "Thank you for everything you did last night. You saved us, and I don't have any idea how hard it must have been to track us down just to help."

She tugged her bags back onto her shoulder, eyes glistening. "Yeah, of course. Is that all?"

Maybe it was time to take a page from her book and stop over-thinking everything. "No, it's not. It's not even close to everything." He didn't pause to consider the words as they spilled out. He let whatever came to mind have its day. "I know it's only been a few days. I know because I won't stop reminding myself. Years of cutting myself off from anyone and everyone except my closest friends, and you come along and bam, I'm hooked. I can't stop thinking about you. Not just how sexy you are, but the way you make me think, the fun we have together, that you challenge everything I believe."

He reached for her, and traced a finger along her jaw, relief flooding him when she didn't pull away. Apparently his brain wasn't done talking. "I'm falling for you, hard and fast and uncontrollably. I don't want you to walk away. I can't think of anything I want more right at this moment than to keep you in my life. Somehow."

She ducked her head, staring at the ground for a moment before meeting his gaze again. A tiny smile threatened her face. "That makes it easier."

His eyebrows rose. "Oh?"

"Telling you I'm falling for you is a lot easier than hoping the pint of ice cream calling my name can make me forget."

A laugh of relief rushed through his lungs. "It depends on what flavor it was."

She shrugged. "Whatever was on sale." She dropped her bags to the ground again, nudged them aside so they no longer rested between them, and stepped forward. Rising on her toes, she brushed her lips over his before pulling away again. "But I like losing myself in you better."

"You know that was really corny, right?" he teased.

She stuck her tongue out at him. "Because a heartfelt confession of love right before I fly into the sunset is so original."

He tunneled his hands into her short locks and tugged her close. His lips crushed hers, and everything negative evaporated. She kissed him back, hard and hungry, and caught his bottom lip between her teeth as she broke away. She flashed him the mischievous smirk that made his blood run hot. "Maybe there's a reason it's all so cliché."

"Give me a day." He traced his hand down her arm, then tangled his fingers with hers. "I'll get you a flight out tomorrow. At least we'll have twenty-four hours to figure out what happens next."

"I already checked out." She nodded at her luggage.

He waved a busboy to them, slipped him a twenty, nodded at

her bags and gave him his room number. "But wait a couple of hours," he told the busboy.

She pressed closer, body molding into Jared's, still gripping his hand tight. "I'm not going back to your room. You promised me breakfast."

He kissed her again, head swimming from the euphoria flooding his veins. "We'll order in." He moved his mouth to her ear and traced the lines with his tongue before whispering, "We have a problem we need to work through first."

Her brow creased, and concern leaked into her voice. "Oh?"

He nipped her earlobe, and then trailed his mouth down her neck. Her gasp filled his head with helium. He traced a line back up her throat and kissed her on the nose. "You're wearing too many clothes."

She shifted her weight, and her entire frame rubbed against him. "I can't argue with logic like that."

He slid his hand into her back pocket and steered her toward the hotel. It felt right when she leaned into him with a contented sigh. He didn't register anything except her warmth, and the faint citrus he associated with her, on the short path to the elevator.

A tiny wave of disappointment crashed over him when the car was packed. She slid in front of him as it rose. The shift of her body was almost imperceptible, but he was suddenly intensely aware of her ass pressing into him, grinding just enough to tease him but not enough for anyone to see her moving. His pulse kicked up another notch.

The moment the doors slid open on his floor, he nudged her out, and his hands slid to her waist, under the hem of her T-shirt. He dipped his head, voice low as he guided her toward his room. "You're horrible."

She broke away and turned, her grin spreading as she studied him, gaze lingering on his crotch. "I thought your slacks were looser. Oops."

Fuck, she had him wandering the halls like a teenager who couldn't control a hard-on, and all he could do was smirk like an idiot in response. It seemed like an eternity before they finally reached his room. He fumbled with the lock before finally getting the door open and pushing her inside.

She squealed when he backed her against the bed. She fell back with a laugh, sitting on the edge and staring up at him. Eyes never leaving his, she traced the bulge below his waist. His cock threatened to burst from the teasing contact and strained to get closer to her touch.

"I don't think I'm the only one wearing too many clothes."

She unbuckled his belt and slid down his zipper. He clenched his toes inside his shoes. She wrapped her warm fingers around his shaft and freed it from its prison, and a low groan tore from his chest.

He almost came at the sensation of her lips wrapped around him. The smooth ball in her tongue glided along his length, teasing him further. She looked up at him, lips circling his shaft, tongue wet and warm on his skin. She caressed his sac. He closed his eyes and leaned his head back. Her other hand pumped him in rhythm with her sucking. His balls tightened, and he almost squirmed in agony when he forced himself to break away.

She looked at him, hurt dancing in her eyes.

"You're going to make me come," he managed.

Her playful expression returned. "That's the point."

Yeah, it really was. He hated himself for stopping her, but he knew it was going to be worth it. "Not yet."

TWENTY-TWO

The hunger in Jared's voice stole Mikki's breath.

Part of her still struggled to believe this was actually happening, but the rest of her had locked the doubt aside and was diving in headfirst. He studied her for a moment, before he lowered his mouth to the hollow at the base of her throat. He trailed his tongue along her collarbone and up her neck.

While his mouth worked the soft skin along her shoulder, one hand glided under her shirt and up her back. Seconds later, the clasp on her bra snapped free, and the restraint tumbled loose. He tugged the undergarment and her shirt over her head, and cupped her breasts in both hands. She gasped and squirmed, the dampness between her legs growing when he lowered his head and drew a nipple into his mouth.

She leaned her weight back on her wrists, arching her back to get closer to his touch. Her sex ached, wet with need, as he relentlessly nibbled, alternating between the twin nubs on her chest.

He nudged her shoulders, and she fell back onto the mattress without protest. When his lips trailed down her stomach, she lifted her hips off the bed out of instinct. The smooth fabric of the comforter caressed her bare back. Each new texture on a different bit of sensitive skin melted together, making her head swim. He traced a single finger under her waistband, half tickling, and half taunting before finally undoing her jeans. He slid the remainder of her clothes to the ground.

She struggled for breath as the air kissed her bare skin. "How is it," she managed to say, "regardless of my attempts at the contrary —" she moaned when his lips brushed the edge of her calf, "—I'm always the one naked first."

He kissed the edge of her knee. She felt more than heard his response, as his lips vibrated over her skin. "You're complaining?"

His mouth reached the inside of her thigh, and want spread between her legs. Her muscles clenched in anticipation. She managed a breathy "No."

His tongue trailed along her skin and along her lower lips. "Good." The single word carried on a deep growl, drilling into her thoughts.

She gasped and tangled her fingers in his hair when he dove between her folds. She couldn't find any intelligible words any more. When his mouth wrapped around her clit, a new spike of pleasure jolted through her. She squeezed her eyes shut, and stars danced behind the lids. "Oh, fuck."

"Soon enough." His words bounced against her swollen sex. "Jesus, you taste amazing."

He licked and sucked, and she held him close as she drew toward the edge of climax. Just as she was about to peak, he shoved two fingers inside her. Her entire body reacted, her back arching, driving her into his touch. He pumped, fingers hooked up to hit just the right spot, never letting up anywhere, until a shudder raked her frame and she climaxed.

She pulled away from his touch, every inch of her hyper-sensitive. Slowly she opened her eyes. Her nerve endings felt raw and aware. The caress of the air conditioner, the gentle brush of his lips on her skin, the satin-like fabric on her back, it all danced in and out of her awareness.

She struggled to catch her breath, unable to turn her head or pull her gaze from the ceiling. Seconds later, the mattress next to her shifted, and his bare flesh pressed against her side, cock digging into her hip.

He appeared above her, propped up on one elbow, and brushed a loose strand of hair off her face. "Now, we can do it your way." The gravel in his voice sparked her desire.

The scent she loved—rain and faint cologne—filled her head. She tilted her head up to kiss him. Her tongue dove into his mouth, the salty, bitter taste of her on his lips. She raised her hands to his shoulders and in a single gesture shoved him onto his back and straddled him. "You don't give up control very often, do you?"

His gaze lingered on her naked form, searing her skin. He shook his head. "Not really."

She hovered above him. His skin was hot between her knees, and if she lowered herself just an inch or two, the swollen head between her legs would nudge her opening. "I can live with that." She rested her hands on either side of his head, leaned forward, and kissed him lightly before saying, "Most of the time."

His hands found her hips, thumbs digging in and lighting her desire. As she straightened, he thrust up. She moaned and sank onto his shaft. He tried to set the pace, hard and fast, but she rocked slowly instead. His groans rolled through the room, echoing in her chest.

One of his hands trailed down her leg and along the inside of her thigh. She whimpered when his thumb pressed into her still-tender clit. She didn't know if she should pull away or let him keep going. His hips slammed into her, and she didn't resist the increased tempo this time. Each time he thrust, he bumped her aching sex as well, and she felt another orgasm build inside. She gasped as she came, and he didn't let up, still pounding furiously. Her head swam, and every inch of her body sang with pleasure.

A long series of punctuated grunts rose from his chest, and she knew he was close. He gripped her hips tight as he came, the frantic pace slowly fading off into nothing.

She leaned forward, head resting on his chest. His heart hammered against her cheek as she struggled to catch her breath. Comfort enveloped her when he rested his palms on her back, holding her in place. They lay there for a few moments, until she thought she might be able to speak again. She rolled to one side and curled up next to him instead, head on his shoulder and hand on his chest.

"You still want breakfast?" His question was quiet even in the still room.

She shook her head, her vocal cords feeling as wobbly as her legs. "I think something else filled me up."

He chuckled and tugged her closer. "So what are you doing instead of eating?"

***

"Falling asleep on my boyfriend. I don't know if you know this, but I didn't sleep much last night, and screwing you takes a lot of energy." Mikki's words were warm and soothing against Jared's skin.

He was intimately and pleasantly familiar with it. Boyfriend, he liked the sound of that. "Sounds like a solid plan. And now you don't have to sneak out in an hour or two before anyone knows you're missing."

She stiffened in his arms.

He shouldn't have brought up her lack of job. Even if he respected her completely for the decision, she didn't need to deal with the stress of being unemployed right now. "I can help, you know. I have contacts."

"How would that look?" There was no bitterness in her voice. Only calm. "For me to use the guy I'm fucking for a reference."

He knew she didn't mean the words harshly, but they still stung. "Is that all I am?"

"Definitely not." She kissed along his side before leaning into him again. "But you know what I'm saying."

He hated it, but he did. "Your skills speak for themselves. You'll be fine, regardless of whatever threats were hurled when you resigned."

"I guess."

He ached to erase the hesitation in her voice, but he didn't know how. "I'm here in whatever capacity you need, I promise. Even if it's just to ravage you so you forget your troubles for a few hours."

That drew a laugh. She sat up and turned so she was facing him. The sheets fell away, and he couldn't help but let his gaze trace her breasts and waist.

She looked down, and then back at him, mouth twisted in amusement. She tilted off the bed for a second and came back up with something in her hand. She tugged her T-shirt on. "Now are you listening?"

She was too much fun. He nodded. "I was listening before."

"Right." Her pursed lips faded into a smile. "Since we already ruined the pillow talk, I need to know something. About the future."

He pushed himself upright. "You're talking about making plans?"

She ducked her head, suddenly intently focused on the stark white of the comforter. "No. I mean, yes, but it doesn't have to be concrete or anything, just kind of a loose idea, and—"

"Stop." He placed a finger under her chin and raised her face so he could look her in the eye. "I'm teasing. Tell me."

She let out a tiny sigh, and the corners of her eyes tugged down, marring her smile. "We live several states apart. All this talk about lov—falling for each other, and still seeing each other, the details don't quite add up. I mean, okay, so I'm a bit transient, especially if I don't find a new job before my rent's due again, but you're a busy guy. You're not going to have time to drop by whenever, and I can't afford to travel like that."

He wrapped his fingers around hers. He hated to admit, he hadn't thought that far. All of his focus had been on not losing her now. "I'll make time. And you *will* find a new job. If you're interested in Atlanta…there are a lot of good companies out there." He didn't even know what he was trying to say. Something was stuck in the back of his head, but he couldn't reach it. "I'll visit on weekends until we can make it work. I promise. Okay?"

She nodded, but creases still lined her forehead. "Okay."

He pulled her back toward him and lay down again, tugging her back to his chest. He wrapped an arm around her stomach. "You've been running full throttle all week. Get some sleep. When you're rested, you'll be able to think better."

She nodded and pressed back into him. He held her tight until her breathing grew steady. The sound lulled away his tension and dragged his eyelids shut. They'd both think clearer once they'd slept.

A FAMILIAR CHIME echoed through Jared's thoughts, jarring him into consciousness. The first thing he registered was the warm weight in his arms and her mumbles of protest.

He kissed her cheek as he sat up. "Phone. Go back to sleep."

He could get used to this. Waking up next to her. Fuck, who was he kidding? He was already used to it. What was he going to do when she was gone tomorrow?

The clock on the nightstand said it was three, and the light peeking through the curtains confirmed yes, they'd slept into the afternoon.

He grabbed his phone and swiped *Answer.* "Yeah?"

"You still pissy and vengeful?" Tate asked.

"Uh…" Jared had to fumble through his memories to figure out what the question was linked to. That morning, arguing in Tate's room, seemed like an eternity ago. His entire world had shifted since then, and his friends had no idea. "No, I'm so much better you wouldn't believe it."

"Right." Hesitation dragged out Tate's reply. "Or you started drinking early and without us."

Jared laughed. The sensation felt natural and light drifting from his chest. "No. I'm actually good. What's up?"

"V says you're ignoring her. We doing something or not? Dinner? Cards? Celebrate not losing our shirts last night?"

Or celebrate losing them this morning. He glanced at Mikki. She had rolled onto her back and was watching him, eyes half open, full lips twisted in unspoken question.

He dragged his attention back to the phone conversation.

"Yeah, dinner. We need to talk. Give me two hours. I'll meet you in the lobby."

"Two? Because you need to blow dry your stunning locks? Fine, but you text V, so she stops bugging me."

Jared said his goodbyes and sent Viv a quick message, assuring her he'd just been asleep and repeating the two-hour time frame. He set the phone aside and focused all his attention on the woman now sitting next across from him.

"You're okay with dinner, right?" Maybe he should have asked her first.

"With your friends?" Her expression had gone flat.

"Yes?"

She grinned. "Duh? Tate's kind of cute, have you ever noticed that?"

"No, I hadn't. And those rumors about college and experimentation aren't true."

"Too bad." She gave him an exaggerated pout. "I'd love to hear the stories. Why do we need the extra time?"

He shifted his weight and crawled toward her. He traced his lips up the side of her neck, inhaling her intoxicating scent. "I want to get to know you a little more first. Or a lot more. If I have to put you on a plane tomorrow, I want to learn as much as possible about you tonight."

TWENTY-THREE

Mikki drained half her orange juice in a single swallow. Embarrassment flooded her cheeks, when she realized all eyes were on her, and she ducked her head.

"Dehydrated?" Vivian teased.

Possibly. Dinner the night before had been a blast. Mikki knew for sure now why Jared, Tate, and Vivian were such close friends. At the same time, they hadn't left her out. Though for the fourth night in a row, she hadn't gotten much sleep. The sex had been amazing every other night. However, last night they'd only talked. Connecting with Jared, learning about where he'd grown up, hearing stories about his past, had been even more incredible. The sleepless night had been worth it.

"It's a desert, Viv." Jared grabbed Mikki's hand from where it rested on the bench between them and gave it a reassuring squeeze. "It's important to drink plenty of fluids."

"Good excuse." Tate wasn't paying attention to them. He'd been scoping out waitresses since they'd arrived. "Maybe it's more important not to deplete those fluids so quickly in this dry climate."

"No, I don't think that's the solution." Jared poked at his toast. "I'm almost certain of it."

Mikki's face flared red-hot. She was going to die of embarrassment, she knew it. It was one thing to let loose and experience life—she was still pretty happy with her decisions there—but she hadn't expected her impulses to be the focus of breakfast conversation. Especially since she hadn't indulged last night.

"Did you tell her yet?" The shift in Vivian's tone drew Mikki's attention.

"Nope." Jared suddenly seemed more interested in his food than the conversation. "I told you, I have nothing to do with this."

Her embarrassment skittered away, and Mikki gave her full attention to the woman across from her. "Tell me what?"

Vivian reached down, grabbed a manila folder from her briefcase, and handed it across the table. "Wait," she said before Mikki could open it.

A glimmer of hope flared inside Mikki, but she suppressed it. This wasn't the kind of thing she could afford to get her hopes up about.

"I should be allowed one more chance." Vivian's tone was serious and her expression neutral.

"Come on." Tate turned back to the table and looked at Mikki. "Please, for the love of all that's good, hear her out so she'll just shut up already. I swear, if I have to hear one more time—Ow." He rubbed his shin and glared at Vivian. "Kicking. Real mature."

Vivian gave him a casual shrug and nodded at the folder. "There are some ground rules. Things you have to keep in mind that don't really go in the contract, but are deal breakers."

Mikki's hope surged again. Contract? No. It couldn't be. She couldn't ignore the giddiness climbing inside, but she did manage to keep it from her voice. "Go on."

"First rule." Vivian ticked off on her finger. "I don't care what title the person you're screwing holds. You report to me, not him, so it earns you zero special treatment."

It really was what she thought. Mikki's fingers itched to open the folder. They were going to make her an offer. She glanced at Jared, then back at Vivian, not daring to interrupt.

"Which also means." Vivian ticked off another finger. "The two of you never work together, unless he needs you for collaboration."

"What else?" Mikki didn't care. She was ready to sign. This was her dream job. The one she would have taken in an instant if she'd been thinking six months ago.

"Nothing else." Vivian nodded at the folder again. "Take your time, think about it. Keep in mind the moving expense has to be repaid if you leave us within the next twelve months. Though honestly, that's just standard contract language. I'm not worried about it happening."

Mikki was surprised her hands stayed steady as she opened the folder. Skriddie letterhead sat inside, offering her a touch more salary-wise than she'd made at NSS, and more than enough to move cross-country. She looked at Jared. "You knew about this?"

His smile made her insides melt. "I guessed. Tate's right, she hasn't shut up about hiring you since she figured out it might still be an option. I fought it every step of the way."

"He begged me to take you on," Vivian countered. "Groveled at my feet and told me he knew I'd never find someone so talented again."

"You're both so full of shit." Tate reached across the table and flicked the folder. "They're going to insist you take your time. You're going to say you don't need to. They're going to say you really should. Tell them now you're serious when you say yes." He handed her a pen. "And let me enjoy my pancakes in peace?"

She took the pen without another word and signed on the appropriate line. She handed the pen back to Tate and the letter to Vivian. "I'm serious when I say yes."

"Good." Vivian tucked everything back into her briefcase. "It's about time."

"But I will need something from you." Mikki felt like dancing. She might still; she hadn't decided yet. She'd be living closer to Jared, and she'd be working for an actual respectable company. A tiny *Yay!* echoed in her thoughts. "The names of hotels near the office that will give me a corporate discount, so I have a place to crash until I find an apartment."

Vivian waved the comment aside and took a long sip of coffee. "Details will be in your email by the end of the day. You just tell me what you prefer, and we'll make the reservations."

Jared pulled her closer and prompted her to shift her position enough she was half leaning into him. He rested his forehead on the back of her head. His warm breath glided over her neck when he spoke. "And I'm hoping you'll leave a couple of weekends open for me. Or more than that."

Her smile grew and she leaned more of her weight against his chest. "I don't have any plans right now, so your chances are pretty good."

***

Six months later

Mikki leaned back into Jared, the overstuffed sofa enveloping them both, and he draped an arm over her shoulder. They were all in his—their, he'd correct her in an instant if he knew what she was thinking—condo. She'd only moved in a month or so ago, after their relationship had reached the point where she wasn't going home most nights anyway.

Vivian was tucked into one of the recliners, legs underneath her, sipping a margarita. Tate occupied a second chair, and Jared's younger sister, Alyssia, rattled through something in the kitchen. After moving to the new town, Mikki had quickly learned this was a typical weekend for all of them if they weren't traveling. Gathering at someone's house, bullshitting, and just unwinding.

She never would have guessed she'd get used to that kind of routine. Never would have seen this kind of camaraderie with a group of people in her future. But now that she had it, she didn't know if she could ever give it up. The one thing making tonight different was they were celebrating her birthday. She'd never had friends throw her a birthday party before. Turned out it was a lot of fun, especially the reminder they cared.

Empty and half-empty Chinese take-out boxes littered the coffee table in the middle of the living room. A box that had once contained cupcakes, but was now just filled with wrappers, sat to the side. She was impressed Jared hadn't moved to clean it up yet, but she knew the clutter wouldn't evade his need for order much longer.

Alyssia stopped at the edge of the living room, arms crossed, scowl marring her face. "I was sitting there."

Tate reclined in the easy chair, arms open. "There's still room."

A low growl rolled through Jared's chest, rumbling through Mikki's back, and she bit back her smile. The first time she'd seen Tate and Alyssia interact—flirt, really—she'd worried Jared might burst a blood vessel. Since then, she'd learned it was all part of who they were.

"No thanks." Alyssia didn't move. "I know where you've been."

"So do I." The menacing tone in Jared's voice might have held more threat if it wasn't so familiar.

Tate shrugged and stood. "Had to try." He gestured to the chair.

A smile twitched through Alyssia's irritation, and seconds later she dropped into the now empty spot. She snagged Tate's wrist before he could walk away, tugged, and let her hand drop.

He perched on the arm of the chair, a hint of smugness marring his expression.

Jared trailed his lips up Mikki's neck and ended with a soft nip on her earlobe and a whisper. "I'll be right back." He extracted himself from behind her, and she couldn't help the whisper of disappointment at losing his warmth, even temporarily.

Apparently the clutter's lifespan was even shorter than she'd thought.

Alyssia made exaggerated retching noises. "Could you not paw at each other tonight? Just for once?"

"Are you ten?" There was only light-hearted teasing in Tate's question.

Alyssia glared at his back. "I don't know, you tell me."

He glanced back at her, and his gaze traveled up and down her figure. "Nope. You're definitely not a little girl."

Mikki laughed at the antics. It had taken her a little while, but she'd finally figured out Tate flirted with everyone. And she adored spending time with Alyssia—the other woman was only a year older, and they had a lot of similar interests.

"For you." Jared handed Mikki a gift bag with a rainbow of tissue paper poking out of the top.

Her eyebrows rose. "I said no gifts."

He shrugged and kneeled in front of her. "I say otherwise."

She tugged out some of the tissue paper, and then some more, curiosity growing as quickly as the pile of colorful wrapping next to her. "Is there even anything in here?"

He nodded. "Almost there."

And then her fingers closed around something small and velvety. She pulled the box out, and her heart leaped into her throat before her brain finished telling her it was a jewelry box.

Jared covered her hands with his. "Mikki Elford. You're everything I need in my life to balance me out. You complement me, you make me think, and you keep me humble." He pulled her hand back with his, raising the lid of the box.

A small gold band stared back, with a diamond solitaire glinting at her from the middle of a cushion of satin.

"I can't imagine life without you. And I'll always love you for showing me that what we have can actually exist. Will you marry me?"

A giddy bubble rose in her chest, and a squeak pushed past her lips. She didn't have to hesitate to know the answer. "Yes. Absolutely, yes."

He slid the ring on her finger and rose enough to rest a hand on the back of her neck. He kissed her hard, tongue sliding into her mouth, dancing around hers, teasing the barbell piercing.

When they finally broke apart, he rested his forehead against hers. "I don't know what I would have done if you'd said no."

She gave a small laugh. "I love you dearly and completely. Why would I say no?"

He brushed his lips across her knuckles. "To surprise me?"

"There are some things even I consider too sacred to be random about." She tugged him to his feet, shifted enough for him to take his seat again, and leaned back into him.

Congratulations and teasing passed around the room, each new comment warming Mikki further. She couldn't imagine anything less with this wonderful man. She raised his fingers, kissing the tips one at a time.

He slid his hand under hers, extending her fingers until the light glinted off the diamond. His words were warm on her neck and meant only for her ears. "I really do love you."

She leaned farther into him, sinking into the familiar comfort. Yup, this was absolutely perfect. "I love you, too."

HIS INFATUATION

ONE

No one should be allowed to look that good in scrubs. The thought spilled into Tate's head when Alyssia walked into the office at her animal shelter, Great 'n' Small. He shook the words away, but not before trailing his gaze past her hips, up her narrow waist, and over the swell of her breasts, and landing on bright blue eyes and a face framed by long, dark hair.

That wasn't what he needed to be thinking about. Now, or ever really. He was here as a consultant, not to leer.

"Did I miss a memo?" Alyssia gave an exasperated huff. "When did it become acceptable for a guy to send a picture of his penis as a way to say 'I'm sorry, please take me back'?"

"Excuse me?" If he'd guessed a million times what she was frustrated about, dick pics wouldn't have been on the list. From Lys, he almost wasn't surprised by the blunt, ludicrous question. He'd known her for decades and very little was taboo between them anymore. This came pretty close, though.

She looked directly at him. "Sorry. But am I wrong to think this is creeptastic?" She held out her phone.

Apparently it wasn't a rhetorical question after all. He shook his head. "I'm going to take your word for it. And last time I checked it still wasn't acceptable. Care to fill in some blanks for me… Minus the visual aids?"

Her brow furrowed and she ducked her head. Her, "I suppose," was soft in the room, blending into the dogs barking in the background. "You know that guy I was talking to last week?"

"Not personally."

She stuck her tongue out. "You're funny."

He smirked. "Damn straight I am. So online distraction of the month…" He wasn't sure how he'd officially become the person she shared her dating woes with. It had started years ago. At first he participated just to make sure she wasn't hooking up with the wrong guys. She was his best friend's little sister, and looking out for her was status quo. He'd quickly realized though, that she could figure it out on her own, she just liked the sounding board.

She blew a strand of hair out of her face, sank into the chair across from him, and rested her arms on the desk. "I need to wrap my brain around how ludicrous this entire situation is first. And we have work to get done."

"If you're sure…"

She nodded. "What do you need from me?"

The conversation wasn't over, but she'd spill if and when she was ready. Besides, she was right about them being on a deadline. He was seated at her desk, using the computer to help set up a crowd-funding campaign for her animal shelter. She was one of twenty pilot groups for the application he was using to spin a new arm off his family's software company. "I've gone through the shelter's social media accounts. With the updated graphics, everything is in order. I'll write up the copy for the pledge page. You'll need to verify it. Then we just have the video left to shoot."

Normally, any computer-related favors would fall to his best friend and business associate, Jared. Or Jared's fiancée, Mikki. Both of them were scary brilliant programming geniuses.

However, this was more about sales and marketing, and proving this was a legitimate new market for them to enter. Once the crowd-funding site took off, he had several next steps, and then he'd be running the arm of the business himself. On top of that, he got to help Alyssia raise enough money for a down payment so she could buy the building her shelter was in. When it came to selling anything, Tate would rock the results like no one's business.

"Right. Video. Tomorrow night." She raked her fingers through her hair as she pulled it back, twisted it into a loose knot behind her head, and stuck a pen through it to hold it up.

Exposing her long, kissable neck—Tate mentally shook himself. Where the hell had that come from? Too long since he'd gotten laid or something.

"And recording the voice overs in office the day after—they finally confirmed your time slot." Every aspect of the project was part of an independent budget, to prove the idea was financially viable. Fortunately, he'd been able to contract most of the resources he needed from his parent company, Skriddie Bust Media. The art department was available for all the pilot groups. Marketing had a storyboard for each company's promo film. It was going to look as clean as possible out of the gate. Tate was making sure of it.

"It's just…" She fiddled with her watch. "I thought the guy was really into me. I mean, I know a lot of these men in online chat rooms are full of shit and just looking to get laid, but he actually seemed to be listening. Remembering what I said, talking to me. Interested in me and not just my boobs."

And they were back on that. "We could include those in the vid if you'd like. Draw in a new crowd." He wouldn't have made a joke like that with anyone else, but he hoped with her it would bring her out of her funk.

She looked at him, lips drawn in a thin line, expression flat. "My boobs?"

"Sure."

A smile slipped out. "You don't have to come up with excuses, you just have to ask."

Good, they were back to casual and fun. Except her teasing dragged up more mental images. Of stripping her top off, running his hands up her stomach, cupping her breasts. He needed to stop that. "But then I'd be like one of those guys online, right? I have to at least make an effort."

Her expression slipped, and her frown flew back in. "Which is where the problem started. He wanted to see me topless. I told him no. He wanted just a peek. Begged about five million times across twenty-four hours. And when I told him I was done talking to him, he sent me this—" she held up her phone, "—as a 'please forgive me' or something. I don't even know."

She sank further into her chair. "It's not like I was falling for him or anything, it was just nice… I'm about to get repetitive."

Maybe he could lighten the mood. He hated to see anyone bummed out, but especially her. He made sure to keep a teasing tone. "That's why real people are better than online people."

"Don't even start." Her mouth twisted in irritation. "The situation wouldn't have been any different if I'd met him in a bar."

He really did hate to see her like this. She deserved a guy who would give her happily ever after, not a jerk who just wanted dirty selfies. "I know, most men suck. But I promise, Lys, not all of them are bad."

Her mouth twisted in amused irritation. "What, like you?"

God, that would be a mistake. Even if he were interested—he forced himself to keep his eyes on the computer and not let them drag over her figure—she deserved better. "No. I'm an asshole. Guys not like me. Though, admittedly I've never sent anyone a picture of my junk."

"Junk. Is that the technical term?"

He liked seeing her smile. "You'd rather I called it Tate Jr.? Or George?"

"Touché. So, where do I meet this mystical man who likes me for my mind, isn't related to me, and isn't bound by some unwritten guy code not to touch me because I'm your best friend's baby sis?"

His mind stalled, and he processed her words again. Somehow, this had just become about him. "He's out there. You've got both body and mind covered when it comes to attractive, and if you were anyone else—"

"Really?" She stood so quickly it made his head spin. "If I weren't the person I am, with all the shared ties we have, you'd be interested? Or is that just lip service?"

It wasn't just lip service. Though he didn't see her as approachable, he still noticed she was equally intelligent and beautiful. Even now, he couldn't help but notice the flush in her full lips. The tinge of frustration on her cheeks. And it was all amplified by the back and forth fun of their conversation.

She moved around the desk, pushed her keyboard aside, and hopped up. She sat directly in front of him, just inches away. "Take that off the table. We're the only people in the room, right? And I know you wouldn't lie to me. If we didn't have that connection. If Jared weren't my brother, would you make a move?"

That escalated quickly. He swallowed, throat suddenly dry. Blood pounded in his ears, and his dick twitched at the thoughts of what he'd do to her if she weren't *her*. "If you were just some random woman in a bar, yes."

"Not quite what I asked, but let's go with it." She rested her stocking-covered toes near the inside of his thigh, close enough heat radiated through his slacks. "You know me as well as anyone, Tate. If there's more to me than a pair of tits, how come no one who gets to know me is interested in me *like that*? And how come no one wants to get to know me?"

His restraints were short circuiting tonight, for reasons he didn't understand. If she didn't pull her foot away in about two seconds, he might act on the impulse to find out if she tasted as good as she looked.

Except he wouldn't act on the desire. He mentally steeled himself. This was a moment of temporary insanity, on his part and hers. He'd ignore it, remind himself she was a client and his best friend's baby sister, and they could get back to work.

His cock twitched as her toes slid higher. Fuck.

***

ALYSSIA KNEW she was being a brat, yet she couldn't make herself stop. Tate was a convenient target, and she was asking more of him than was acceptable between friends. She needed to apologize. The problem was, now that she'd nudged the edges of this boundary—

this temptation that was him—she didn't want to stop. There was a reason she never pushed this line with him. What had gotten into her? Part of her brain whispered what a bad idea this was. That she needed to suck her up pride and just walk away, but the rest of her wasn't interested in backing down.

Her ego was already limping. It wasn't just him denying her now, or even that he had so long ago. It was all of it. It had been ages since she'd run into a guy who seemed to care there was a person inside her. Except Tate, and he treated her differently because of her brother. Tonight it all merged in her skull and was too much. So yeah, she was being pushy, and insecure, and bratty. And she was terrified if she stopped now—even if she backtracked and took a kinder route—she'd never find out what she needed to know. Was she only ever destined to attract, and be attracted to, the wrong guys?

Her toes slid higher on his thigh, and she paused when the landscape changed and she brushed his erection. He inhaled sharply through clenched teeth. Had she really made him hard just with a line of questions? The thought both terrified and excited her.

"The right guy is out there." His words were strained. Any of the humor that usually lined his voice was gone. "And you'll meet him, and you'll know when you do that he's different."

Of course. Just like eight years ago. Except this time, she was licking too many wounds to want to stop. His rejection back then, this bullshit online. It all jumbled into a mess, reminding her how much she normally held back around Tate, and that she'd never gotten over him. She draped her arms around his neck. "What if the right guy *is* you?"

Faster than she could blink, he grabbed her wrists, stood, and pinned her palms to the desk. He pushed her upright and slid between her legs at the same time, standing close enough heat radiated between them. Her pulse kicked into overdrive, and want slid through her. The intensity in his gaze made her mind stall.

He scraped his teeth up her neck, and she bit her tongue to hold back her whimper. Her pulse screamed for more, bringing every nerve ending to life. His warm breath on her skin was tantalizing and tempting, and she needed him to take this further. To feel his tongue explore her, his hands strip her bare. Every inch of his flesh against hers.

His whisper brushed her ear. "I promise I'm not."

"So everything you're saying is just lip service." Irritation tinged her desire, making it surge. He was so sure he knew what was best for her, and she was sick of that. She scooted closer, rubbing his erection each time she shifted her weight. He was definitely interested. What would it take to shatter his defenses?

"If we ever hooked up, it would be because you actually wanted me, not because you were hurt and wanted someone to take your frustrations out on."

That pushed another button of defiance. Heat—fury, desire, all of it mingled and seared her veins. She didn't know what to focus on, so she let it all course through her. "I do want you, and you know it."

He ducked his head closer without warning, still holding her hands captive, and crushed his mouth against hers. His groan mingled with hers when she ground against him. His tongue forced its way into her mouth. His insistent shaft pressed between her legs, making her go from damp to wet in an instant, and her nipples strained against her bra. So this was what it was like to feel sparks.

He broke away as quickly as he'd dived in, breaking all contact as he stepped back. Disappointment and longing surged inside her. His steady gaze locked on her face. "You deserve better than what I'm offering, even for just a night. Trust me."

"Goddammit, Tate." Her throat ached from just the few words. She hopped to her feet, bringing her closer to him again. She grasped at every strand of anger inside and used it to smother the overwhelming hurt making her joints ache. "I'm so tired of you telling me what I do and don't need. Do you maybe think I might know that better than you?"

She raised her hands to his shoulders to push him back, and he grabbed her wrists again, still looking her in the eye. Despite her irritation, his rough touch still spoke to the primal lust raging inside her.

"You might need to get off, but not with me. And I get as much say in the matter as you do. I can't stop you from keeping the fantasy, though."

Her face heated to red-hot. She broke free of his grasp and shoved him back. "You impossibly arrogant ass."

He opened his mouth, but a loud beep cut him off. Her heart beat against her ribcage in frustration and surprise. The tone of the speakerphone cut through the room, followed by her assistant, Sara's panicked voice. "Doctor, we need you out here."

Without thought, her fury and indignation were bundled up, shoved into a box in the back of her skull, and locked away tight, even killing her desire to tell Tate the conversation wasn't over. "On my way, what's up?"

"Mutt. Broken leg, fractured ribs, probably internal bleeding."

Alyssia's gut clenched. The stupid argument could wait. Her patient was more important. She pushed past Tate and out the door without stopping to see what he was up to. She'd care later, this was emergency time.

TWO

Tate shouldn't have kissed her. That was possibly the stupidest thing he'd done in ages. His cock still ached, straining against his slacks, and he'd been seconds from telling her yes. He'd never done that before. Only partly because Jared would kill him. Largely because she deserved better than a cheap one night stand. On top of it all, she was a client. He never mixed business with pleasure.

But the conversation was apparently over. She'd gone from stubborn to professional in a flash, face hardening, and him all but ignored. Thank God for small favors.

Then again, that was one reason she was so good at running the shelter. She knew where her priorities lay. She'd started volunteering there when she was still in high school. During college, she took on more administrative tasks, along with helping the doctors and nurses, which translated into great experience for veterinary school.

She'd officially become a doctor less than a year ago. When the owner had to sell three years ago, for personal reasons, Jared had loaned her the money to purchase the business itself. Well, technically Tate had loaned her the money through Jared, but she didn't know that. Tate tried to offer, but she refused to owe him. Now she was looking to expand the place and buy the property it sat on, which meant she needed another infusion of capital. Hence the crowdfunding campaign.

He followed her out of the office, staying a few feet back for his own sanity. Getting too close to that heady scent of soap would just screw with his head again. His footsteps slowed as he reached the front lobby of the clinic. The panicked woman near the front desk was probably just a little younger than his thirty-four, and she looked painfully familiar.

He scanned the face against a list in his head. Not a business associate. Not a one night stand, or a friend of a friend. Where did he know her from?

She looked up as soon as Alyssia drew close. Her words ran together. "He's hurt, I don't know how badly, but he won't come out of the car, and he just keeps whimpering, and you have to help him, please."

Alyssia rested a hand on her arm, tone kind but firm. "We will. Show me."

He'd let them get to work. Lys had everything under control. But he couldn't help following her to the SUV near the front door. And then it clicked in his head. The woman worked for a friend of his parents. Friend was a deceptive word. Her employer was sleeping with Tate's mother. The country club's dirty little secret that everyone knew. The woman was a housekeeper. She swung the back doors open, and a low growl echoed through the dark parking lot.

"Come on, boy." Alyssia's voice was low and soothing, as she crawled inside the vehicle. A loud series of barks reverberated, and she scrambled out backwards, face pinched.

"See?" Hysteria crept into the woman's voice. "I can't get him out. I don't want him to bite me again. He already did it once when I was putting him in there. She held up a hand wrapped in gauze.

"Tranquilizer?" Sara asked.

Alyssia shook her head. "Not until I can take a look at him."

While they were conferring, Tate pushed through the small group. His chest clenched. It was the neighbor's dog. Belonged to their teenage son. Even in the dim light, it was obvious he was in pain. Tate crawled toward him slowly, murmuring random reassurances in the softest voice he could. The dog whimpered, but didn't pull away or snap. It felt like it took ages to close the distance, but it was probably less than a minute. He cradled the mutt and backed out just as slowly, trying not to jar any injuries or startle the animal.

Three faces stared back in wide-eyed surprise. Alyssia recovered first. She didn't say anything, just nodded toward the clinic. He followed without question into one of the rooms. He set the dog on the table, gently stroking his head and whispering more incoherent reassurances while Alyssia examined the dog, and then hooked him to an IV.

"Okay." Her quiet voice sounded loud and abrupt, shattering the stillness but not the tension. "Thank you. I need you out now, though."

He nodded and extracted himself from the room. He let out a long breath when he was in the hallway. "Cait," he called to the pacing woman in the lobby. "What happened?"

She tugged on her blonde braid, not meeting his gaze. "Nothing. I got clumsy cleaning his dog run. Left…something out, and, um… he got hurt."

Tate wasn't even going to point out what a bad lie that was. He stared at her a minute longer, and her shoulders slumped. "I can't tell you. I need this job. You can't even tell them it was me who brought it in. Please."

It was times like this he had no idea how Alyssia did her job without surrendering everything fun and amazing about her personality. He jammed his fists in his pockets to hide his clenched fists. "Bryce Jr.?"

Her nod was so slight it was difficult to see.

He wasn't going to yell at her. He understood where she was coming from. But it took more restraint than he thought he had to suppress his anger. If he had a reserve of self-control, he was pretty sure he'd eaten through it twice over tonight. "She's not going to let the dog go tonight regardless. You might as well go home."

"No. I have to take him back."

"Not happening," Sara broke in from her spot at the computer. "Not with injuries like that."

"But what am I supposed to tell them?" Caitlin asked.

Tate sank into a nearby chair, his verbal filters failing fast. "A better lie than you told me."

ALYSSIA DIDN'T KNOW how many hours had passed. She'd splinted a broken leg, stitched up several cuts, and seen to the internal injuries before splinting most of the poor boy's frame. She was exhausted, but her patient should pull through.

Her stomach snarled. Maybe she should have taken Tate up on his offer for dinner instead of throwing herself at him like an idiot. Again. Apparently eight years was just enough time to forget the lessons of the past. Not that she would have had time to eat anyway.

She stepped into the waiting room, eyes taking a moment to adjust. They only kept half the lights on overnight. Sara looked up from behind the reception desk, and they exchanged smiles. No words were needed. They'd been working together long enough Sara would get it. The exhaustion, the stress, and the relief that the first bad part was over.

Alyssia halted in her tracks at what she saw next. Tate was seated in one of the plastic chairs, staring blankly at a magazine, not turning the pages.

"What are you still doing here?"

He jumped when she spoke, and whirled to face her. "Is the puppy okay?"

She wasn't going to acknowledge the adoration his question summoned. Especially since the dog was anything but a puppy. Tate's clothes were a wreck. Dark streaks—she assumed blood— smeared his shirt, tie, and slacks. In that brief second, any of her lingering frustration from earlier evaporated. "He'll be fine. Friend of yours?"

He gave a weak smile. "We've met. He lives near my folks."

Her stomach protested loudly, and her cheeks burned when he raised an eyebrow.

"No arguments this time." He tossed the fashion magazine aside and stood. "I'm buying you dinner."

"There's a 24-hour Mexican place around the corner," Sara offered. "I'm having two cheese enchiladas."

Tate looked between the two, pausing on Alyssia. "Chicken nachos, extra cheese?"

"It's okay. I'm fine." Alyssia didn't even believe herself. "I have cookies in my desk drawer."

Tate shook his head. "When you're not so tired, we'll work on what 'no arguments' means. I'll be back in fifteen minutes."

At least the place was drive thru, so no one would question why he was in blood-streaked clothes.

Alyssia leaned against a nearby wall for support when he vanished out the door. A glance at the clock told her it was almost midnight. She was going to need some serious coffee if she was going to make it through the rest of the night. She had her other doctors rotate night shifts. Of the four on staff, they rotated out the months and weekends they worked graveyards, and she didn't think it was fair to make them do what she wasn't willing, so she was part of that rotation. She was three weeks in, and she'd adjusted just fine, but days like today reminded her why she'd rather be asleep right now.

As if reading her mind, Sara nodded toward the kitchen. "He made a fresh pot of coffee just a little while ago."

Alyssia kicked away from her support and followed the aroma of consciousness.

"Have I mentioned yet today how sexy he is?" Sara's question followed her, carrying easily over the tile in the empty clinic.

Alyssia was too tired to roll her eyes. She didn't want to talk about Tate, because that meant thinking about him. And thinking about him meant regret, embarrassment, and a want she couldn't sate. "Not for at least six hours." She grabbed her mug from its spot near the sink, and filled it as full of coffee as she could. She followed that with generous helping of sugar and cream. Coffee threatened to escape as she stirred the mixture together. She took a long drink, not caring that it scalded her throat and tongue going down.

"Did the police say when they'd be by?" she asked as she wandered back into the lobby. She didn't have to ask if Sara had called. There was no question the dog's injuries were at least partially intentional, and that meant filing a report. Unfortunately, it didn't guarantee the felony conviction that should go along with the abuse, but it helped.

"I told them you'd be gone by seven. They said they'd be in before then."

The chairs called her name, but Alyssia couldn't sit down until she was a little more awake. "Did the girl leave a name?"

"No. But Tate really does know her and the dog. Called her Cait. She asked us not to mention her."

Alyssia rubbed her eyes as a new wave of exhaustion washed over her. That was never a good sign. Dread joined her jumbled thoughts as Tate's response about being friends with the dog floated back to mock her. Please, please, please let it not be someone powerful enough to do something like have the city change her zoning.

The front door chimed, and Sara hit the button to release the afterhours lock and let Tate in. The moment he stepped through the door, the scent of chilies and enchilada sauce nearly knocked Alyssia over. She was hungrier than she realized. She had to force herself to not tear into the food the moment he set the box in front of her. He leaned against the other side of the counter as she and Sara dug in.

"You're a heaven-sent demon," Sara told him.

"And not eating," Alyssia said once she realized it.

He shook his head. "Some of us have to sleep tonight, not tomorrow morning.

Right. She'd kept him up all night. "Thank you for everything. We're okay, now."

He still didn't move. His fingers twitched, and he stared at the wall behind her head.

Was he really making her do this? Why did he have to spoil the moment? "And earlier is in the past, right?"

"What?" He shook his head and finally looked at her. "Right. Earlier. Yeah. In the past." His brow furrowed. "The dog's name is Grim. He belongs to Thompson's kid."

Alyssia's appetite evaporated in an instant. He probably didn't have the power to get her zoning changed. Not directly anyway. But he did own a local TV network affiliate, which tended to be vocal about businesses he didn't like. He'd done editorial pieces on their place before, about how it was a waste of valuable retail space and community resources. Now she was about to potentially file criminal charges against his teenage son. She nibbled at her food, no longer tasting it. "Of course he does."

"He can't do anything other than huff and puff. I'll be back tomorrow night, we'll get your campaign up and running, and the one side of the business will never touch the other."

She ignored the reminder they would have made more headway tonight if she hadn't thrown a tantrum. The last thing she needed was to linger on the memory of the kiss. She was too busy trying to convince herself things really would be as easy as he said.

THREE

The moment the shelter door swung shut behind the police officer, Alyssia sank into a nearby waiting room chair. She leaned the back of her head against the wall, closed her eyes, and let the rising sun warm her face. Exhaustion rolled through every inch of her body. She was pretty sure last night had been the longest night of her life. Of course, just like the second longest night of her life, it had started with Tate, and her making a fool of herself.

She shouldn't go there. But she was too tired to hold back the unwelcome memory. Exhaustion seeped through her, dragging the memory with it. That night, eight years ago. She'd just barely turned eighteen, and her date to senior prom had canceled last minute.

When Tate found out, and asked if he could take her, she thought it was because he liked her. Teenage-her hoped he'd finally figured out she *like*-liked him, and he felt the same. She'd been in heaven the whole night. Some of her friends were dating college guys, but her, she got to show up with someone who was post-grad.

He'd been the perfect date. Sweet, attentive, a gentleman. Her friends insisted that meant he loved her. At eighteen years old, and crushing hard, that was exactly what she needed to hear.

She bit back a bitter laugh at the unwelcome rush of images and emotions. She'd thrown herself at him. Getting laid on prom night —all the movies told her that was a guarantee, and who better to lose her virginity to than the man of her dreams?

Turned out he was just that kind to everyone, and that he'd only asked her as a favor to her brother.

She sniffled and forced herself upright, shoving away the rest of the memory and the ache in her gut. Now she'd made the same mistake again.

But had she? He'd been interested, she knew it. The kind of reaction he'd had to her last night. Even before she touched him he'd been turned on.

"Ms. Tippins." A familiar voice burned away the last of her wandering thoughts, and she snapped back to the now.

Bryce Thompson. Sick dread made her insides lurch. She had a feeling he was about to become the bane of her existence. The older gentleman stood a few feet from her chair, not a single wrinkle or piece of fluff on his suit. His hands were clasped in front of him, and his dark eyes narrowed and locked on her.

"Good morning." She scrambled to her feet. Maybe this wouldn't be so bad. Sure, he'd made it clear in the past he thought her shelter was a waste of resources. That he was planning to tear the entire building to the ground to make room for retail property. On top of that, she'd just finished filling out a police report that directly involved his family.

Yeah, this was going to suck. She should have gone home as soon as she had the chance. It wouldn't have been fair to leave her staff with this burden, though.

His jaw-set expression never even twitched. "I understand you have my dog."

She could bend the truth a little. Tell him no, they didn't have anyone's dog until the animal was adopted into an actual caring family. Delaying the inevitable wouldn't make things better. "I understand the same thing."

"I'm here to retrieve him. How much do I owe you?" He pulled a checkbook from his jacket breast pocket.

This was too easy. He was being too calm. Alyssia's ill-ease grew, rolling through her and dragging more exhausted tension to the surface. "There's no charge. I can't—"

"No wonder you don't make any money here." The corner of his mouth pulled up in a sneer. "I'll take him and leave then."

Out of the corner of her eye, she saw one of the morning volunteers—the guy was as solid as a brick wall and almost as wide as he was tall, and normally a total sweetheart—step forward. She met his gaze, but didn't motion for him to stand back. Sweet disposition or not, his bulk was intimidating, and his presence made confronting Mr. Thompson that much less terrifying.

"You can't take him." She pushed the words out quickly, not talking over Thompson as effectively has he had with her, but still determined not to be interrupted again. "The new owners will pay whatever fees are associated with his care, and until then, he's not ready to be moved. He's still recovering, and will be for several more days."

"I see." He scribbled in his checkbook and tore the piece of paper out. "Then I'll be back when he can be moved."

"You can't take him home." Damn it, why wasn't he listening to her? Frustration crawled under her skin like a million ants, and she shoved her hands in her pockets to hide her clenching fists. She dragged up every ounce of forcefulness she had, and crammed it into her voice. "He belongs in a good home where he won't be hurt again."

He locked his gaze on hers, eyes hard and unyielding. "I'll be back in a few days."

He set the check on the counter, and was through the front door before she could say anything else.

A whole new wave of frustration crashed over her, mingling with everything else that had been the last twelve hours of her life, and sapping away her restraint. She had to bite the inside of her cheek to keep a string of profanities from spilling out. She grabbed the check off the counter, cringed at the four-figure amount he'd randomly chosen to write it for, a tore it into little tiny pieces.

It didn't solve anything, but the simple act made her feel a little better. A little.

———

"ALAN." Tate stood at the front of the conference room. He capped the dry erase marker and set it on the tray of the white board before turning to his administrative assistant. "Do you have this?"

Alan nodded, and Tate let his attention travel around the room, scanning the remaining faces. "Any other questions or concerns?"

He was met with a series of shaking heads and smiles. He was lucky he had a solid team on this project. Technically they were all on loan from Skriddie as contractors. The lines of the new business venture were blurred, but he was close to making the crowdfunding venture its own entity.

While it was nice to get back into the technical side of things, especially getting to meld it with the marketing he loved, he'd been working directly with sales so long that a good group made the transition easier.

He turned back to Alan. "Action items?"

His assistant ran through the list, and Tate made sure everyone was ready for their test users to launch by the end of the week. Tonight with Alyssia had to be all business. Not that it would be anything else. He still didn't know what had happened yesterday. His pulse twitched at the memories—the way she tasted, the tiny gasps she made when they kissed, and the combination of frustration and desire she'd managed to overload him with.

He tried to shake the thoughts away. The meeting wrapped up, and everyone headed back to their desks. Images of Alyssia still taunted him as he made his way to his office. Damn it, why was she getting in his head now? They'd dealt with this and moved on all those years ago. Or, at least, he thought they had. She'd barely been legal when he'd offered to be her last minute date for her senior prom. She'd looked gorgeous in that dress, no longer the little girl who tagged along with them as kids. And when she'd all but thrown herself at him—both too much and nothing like last night—he'd had to tell her no.

The rambling combination of fantasy and denial skidded from his mind when he pushed open his office door. Speaking of relationships that had jaded his reality. An older woman sat in the chair across from his desk, not looking up at the soft creak. She scrolled through her phone. He personally knew her hair wasn't that shade of auburn, but not because her hairdresser had made any mistakes hiding the gray.

He hid his sigh. "Are you here for business, or personal reasons?" Her answer would determine how he addressed her. He didn't like keeping his tone so formal, but years of having it drilled into his head didn't leave him much choice. There were no favorites in his mother's business world. Especially when it came to family. Though more and more their recent run-ins made him wonder if she was pushing things in the other direction. Discounting his ideas because of their relationship. He wasn't sure if she was doing it to prove there was no favoritism, or for some other reason, but each time they talked business, he became more convinced he wasn't imagining it.

She locked her phone and returned it to her purse, never turning to look at him. "Personal."

He wasn't sure if that was a relief or not. He gave her a light kiss on the cheek before moving around his desk and dropping into his chair. "It's lovely to see you, Mother."

"Of course." Her smile was as formal as his greeting. "How are things going, darling?" Her soft southern accent slipped in, adding a layer of artificial sugar to her words. He might not see it that way, except he knew the lilting drawl vanished the moment she was in a business meeting and felt like it would make her appear anything less than intelligent and businesslike.

"Fantastic. I've been drumming. Women think it's sexy as all get out. And I'm thinking of trading in the Bentley for an F-150." He cranked his own drawl a couple of notches, poured out the clichés she saw as being 'too hick' for people like them, and never let his

pleasant expression slip. "Y'all should stop by this weekend if you're free."

Her eye twitched and he knew he'd pushed the right buttons. Maybe he shouldn't have, but sometimes her sense of propriety rubbed him the wrong way.

Still, she kept smiling. "Sounds wonderful, darling. How's your little project coming along?"

He resisted the urge to snarl at the disdain in her question. She hadn't supported the idea for the crowd-funding offshoot. Had shot down his bids to rent the Skriddie's resources, saying that wasn't the industry they were in, and as COO of her husband's company, she had that kind of veto power. "I thought we weren't discussing business." His voice was flat.

"So right." Her eyes hardened, and her lips drew into a thin line. "How's Jared's baby sister doing? The one who follows you two everywhere, bless her little heart?"

That's where this was going. Please let him be wrong. Let this be something he couldn't even begin to guess at. "She hasn't done that for years."

"You're sure?"

"I'm positive. And she's fine." Wonderful, sexy, dangerously alluring. *Great, that's what I need to be thinking about right now. Not.*

"So you are on speaking terms with her. Are you personally handling her user experience for this little project of yours?"

His mother already knew all this. Frustration swelled inside. This wasn't the time to let his cool slip. "I wouldn't put it that way, but I am her contact. You're not here on business, remember?"

"Of course. Tell her to drop the charges against Bryce Jr., and give him back his dog."

She'd almost cut straight to the point. That was odd. "Why are you asking me?"

"You know her."

"Jared knows her. She's his younger sister. You're not in his office tossing passive aggressive formalities at him."

Her mouth pulled up at the corners, but her eyes were cold. "Mr. Tippins has work to do."

And Tate had the entire afternoon free? He clenched his teeth. "Why doesn't Mr. Thompson have this conversation with Alyssia himself?"

"He tried. She was unreasonable."

That almost made him smile. A hint of relief amid his mounting irritation. "I can't imagine."

"Talk to her." She stood. "Make this vanish."

"Or your boyfriend won't put out tonight?" Tate winced as soon as the words passed his lips. He'd let his guard slip for just a moment, and he shouldn't have done that. Just because everyone knew his parents had an open relationship, and his mother had spent as much time in Bryce Thompson's bed as she had her own in the last several years, didn't mean it was appropriate for anyone to talk about it. Oh well, too late to take it back. "Sorry. Gentleman caller."

Her eyes narrowed and she locked her gaze on his face for several seconds before turning away. "She won't like the alternative, and experience tells me that means you won't either."

The moment the door swung shut behind her, he clenched his hands into fists and dug his knuckles into his closed eyes. Stars danced against his eyelids. He took one deep breath and then another, struggling to find his composure again. He didn't even know where to start unraveling his fury. Had that conversation really just gone that way?

He took one more breath and tried to turn his attention back to work. It wasn't like his mother—or Bryce Thompson for that matter —was going to order a hit on Alyssia or anything so ludicrous. They were verbal bullies. His best bet was to make sure Lys got her site up and running as quickly as possible, funded her shelter expansions, and put this unfortunate coincidence behind her.

He slammed his fist into the arm of his chair. Why couldn't he believe it was going to be that simple?

FOUR

Tate glanced at his watch every few seconds as he crossed the short distance from the elevators to his car in the parking garage. Work had tied him up far longer than he'd planned, with 'just one more' phone call and email rolling in, one after another, until he had less than fifteen minutes to be at the shelter. Tate had given himself enough time to get there half an hour before the video guy who was shooting animal footage, and now he was worried it might not have been enough.

He'd sent Alyssia a text saying he might be late, but she hadn't responded. It was earlier than her overnight shift was scheduled to start, and for all he knew, she was still getting ready. Unbidden, images flashed through his thoughts of her in the shower. Tall, lean, with water cascading over her.

What was wrong with him? He dropped into his car, pulled onto the road, and turned on a local talk radio station. This time of night, they ran updates every ten minutes about the stock exchange, and he liked to hear the highlights.

Some of his tension slipped away as he navigated lighter than normal rush hour traffic. He might even make it with a few minutes to spare.

"Tonight on ABC News at seven…"

The pre-recorded commercial filtered into his thoughts, and blocked it out as standard chatter.

"You think you're taking your dog to the vet for a routine checkup, and suddenly the police are knocking on your door." The announcer's voice held a hint of threat, just enough to draw in listeners. Tate's brain froze, and then honed in on the words. "We'll tell you which local shelter may be up to no good."

Thompson's station. Please don't let this be about Lys's shelter. His gut clenched at the reminder of the scene he'd left behind the night before, and his mother's threat echoed in his head. The remaining time it took to reach his destination passed like cold molasses. Should he tell Alyssia she might want to check this story out? Keep what he'd heard to himself? She didn't need more stress, and there was no guarantee the news report was about her.

The moment he walked through the front door, Sara nodded toward Lys's office. "She said you could go right in."

He might have been worried to hear otherwise. He paused, hand on the doorknob, and spun back toward the waiting room. The TV they kept behind the counter was on, turned to the news, and a promo video for upcoming stories. Sure enough, the image on the screen was the front of the shelter. Shit. So much for figuring out whether or not he was going to tell her.

He pushed into her office, and knew immediately from the sound coming from her speakers that she was streaming the news.

She looked up from her monitor, forehead pinched, and jaw clenched. "We're so screwed."

His chest ached at the worry in her eyes. "It can't be that bad."

"No?" She raked shaky fingers through her hair. "The camera crews showed up about two hours after I told Thompson he couldn't have his dog back. I was already home asleep. The staff wouldn't tell them anything, because that's our policy. And now I see this on the commercials? How could that possibly be anything but bad?"

He forced a calm he didn't feel past his own concerns. "We'll watch; you'll deal. Life will go on."

She looked at him, eyes narrowed, and mouth flat. "That's not as placating as you may think."

———

ALYSSIA WASN'T GOING to snap at Tate. She had too many other things going on to deal with his brand of calm. He was trying to help, which was why she was biting her tongue, but sometimes he tried a little too hard. The streaming news shifted scenes, and her gut clenched. She crossed her arms. She was vaguely aware of Tate moving behind her, but her attention was focused on the news clip.

The lead-in to the story was almost the same as what she'd been hearing teased on commercials since she woke up. And then her world crumbled a little, and an insistent throb twitched behind her eye. The reporter was talking to Bryce Thompson Jr., his parents sitting next to him on the couch in a living room larger than her entire townhouse.

He frowned and sniffled as he explained how his dog had been struck in a hit and run. A growl slipped from her throat. The dog's injuries didn't coincide with that. He went on to say he hadn't known what to do. His parents were gone for the evening, but he was lucky a member of the staff was around. She took the dog in for treatment at an all-night animal hospital.

Alyssia's blood boiled hotter the longer she watched. The newsman talking about "and that's when the nightmare began." The camera and reporter trying to get into her clinic. The footage —only about three seconds compared to the truth on her own security cameras—made it look like Ricco had literally kicked them out on their asses the moment they'd walked in. "The shelter took his dog, and refuses to return the animal to its family. They declined our requests for comments. But as of now, they've kidnapped this poor child's best friend, and locked it away, cold and scared in some back room kennel."

She sank back in her chair, acid churning in her gut. A quiet, "Fuck," slipped past her lips and frustration stung her eyelids. Goddammit. What was she going to do?

She slowly became aware of Tate's hand resting on the back of her neck, his thumb kneading at the tight cord running from her shoulder to her skull. His quiet tone seeped into her thoughts. "Press release. Letter to the station. Contact Legal about slander."

His methodical list took the edge off her mounting fear and frustration, but didn't erase it. She nodded. "I should get on that." How could he sound so sure and calm right now? Everything inside her was screaming at her to do something. That this was bad. That the local news had just told the entire community that her shelter was essentially kidnapping dogs.

Nausea bubbled up again, and she swallowed it back. It didn't help. "I'll call the lawyer. And have Sara start on the press release. Someone needs to contact the station now. I should do that first. Can I counter before the ten o'clock news? We have security footage, we can show them that's not how this happened. This isn't right, we can't—"

"Stop." His voice was still low, but the single word stamped out her rambling. "Do the first two. Don't fly off in a frenzy and try and fight this war publicly. This is Thompson's TV station. Going into things half-cocked won't help."

"But he's verbally destroying the shelter." She wanted to scream. Was Tate trying to make this difficult? "He just told the entire town I'm a fucking puppy kidnapper. I have to tell them otherwise."

"Lys." Tate's gentle tone was still there but an edge lined the single syllable. "You should and you will, but not without a plan. Don't rush into this unprepared, okay?"

She ground her teeth at the condescension, but didn't have the words to argue. "Fine."

Her speaker phone buzzed, and Sara's tentative voice filled the room. "There's a camera guy here?"

Her already fractured thoughts shattered further. "They're back? What the hell? Can I go talk to them now? This is my chance, right? I can set things straight."

Her chair spun and she found herself face to face with Tate. He was half kneeling in front of her, gaze locked on hers, forehead wrinkled in concern. He rested a hand on her neck again, thumb stroking her cheek. She wanted to slap his arm away, but the shock of his touch raced through her and filled in the cracks in her thoughts with glue.

When he leaned in and kissed her, lips soft and tender, her entire world ground to a stop. Her tension was still there, struggling in the back of her mind to be heard, but she couldn't focus on it. Her attention was on the rough fingers against her skin, the tiny nips he laid along her bottom lip, the way his tongue swirled around hers.

She exhaled softly, when he broke away and rested his forehead against hers.

"Paying attention now?" The edge was gone from his voice. Was he breathless? No, she wasn't thinking straight. He was just trying to keep that infuriating calm demeanor.

She wanted to lean in for another kiss. Something more intense to chase the flutters through her veins like the night before. Instead, she nodded.

He bit his top lip for a moment, before continuing. "Good. It's Greg from the office. He's going to take video of the animals."

She swallowed, struggling with disappointment and relief, but she wasn't sure what the source of either feeling was. "Right."

"I'll hook him up with one of your volunteers. You start making phone calls about this news thing." He finally pulled away, and as he stood, she swore his hand was trembling.

"Right. Press release from Sara, and call Legal."

The moment the door closed behind him, the borders protecting her compartmentalized thoughts disintegrated. Had he really just kissed her? And why was she focused on that? Because it was an easier question that what the hell she was going to do about this possible media shitstorm. She took a few deep breaths. They had a plan, and she would follow it.

Her stomach lurched when she reached for her phone, and she pushed aside the nausea. She could do this.

Tate couldn't believe he'd kissed her. A single night of no sleep and a little stress and he was letting instinct and lust drive him? He was really off his game this week. Her taste still lingered on his lips. Stupid, stupid, stupid. But instinct had kicked in, and he'd needed to calm her down.

It was nothing more than a distraction to bring her nerves under control. Things were high stress right now. He obliterated his doubt, left the cameraman in capable hands, and pushed any tension or worry from his mind before he stepped back into Alyssia's office. He kicked the door shut behind him, only half aware he was locking it, when he registered the sight in front of him.

She was pacing and muttering to herself, not even looking up at the click of the latch. She raked trembling fingers through her hair, her feet slapping hard against the floor with each step. "I can't do this. It's not what I signed on for." Her tone grew louder and higher pitched with each word. "I can confront the abusive jackasses. I'm prepared for that. But to have to defend myself publicly, for something I didn't do, against a man who's never even wondered what it might be like to not have so many people responding to his every whim. I can't do—"

"Whoa." Tate stepped in front of her, palms on her cheeks, forcing her to look him in the eye. He couldn't watch this anymore. Her tension twisted every muscle in his body until he was sure something inside might snap if he didn't move, and her near-hysteria added a layer of something unfamiliar. If he had to name it, it was need. The need to wrap her up and protect her. The need to hold her and comfort her and let the rest of the world bounce off. The need to do something more than just gloss over things and move on.

"We'll figure it out." He kept his voice calm, despite the heat searing his palms and the nervous energy responding to her panic mingled with her soft scent. "You're not alone in this."

Her chin wrinkled, and she blinked several times. She drew in a shaky breath and then another. "It's not that easy."

He traced a thumb over her cheek. Her face was so soft against his calloused skin. Did this comfort her even half as much as it calmed him? "It's not easy at all. But it's also not unsolvable."

She covered his hand with hers, and licked her lips. A jolt of desire seared through him, ringing in his thoughts and tugging at his groin. He tried to will away his reaction. The last thing he should be doing was daydreaming about her. Even if she weren't floundering on the edge of a breaking point. She deserved—

She brushed her lips over his and all of his thoughts evaporated. Poof, gone. Her eyes searched his, wide and hopeful and terrified all at once. The kiss was so soft, rationally he wasn't sure he'd felt it. But the feather-light sensation and faint taste of bubblegum lingering on his skin snapped something inside. The tightly wound tension he'd struggled to contain broke free and shuttered open like a window shade.

He dragged one hand to the back of her head and tangled his fingers in her hair, gripping the closest thing he had to a lifeline and letting the strands bite into his palm. He couldn't ignore this. No one had that much control. He crushed his mouth to hers, years of repressed hunger roaring through him. Skin slid against teeth.

His tongue didn't meet any resistance when he pushed into her mouth and sought hers out. He couldn't think about anything except how much he wanted her. How incredible she tasted. Her gentle curves molding against his body. What it would be like to yank her scrubs to the ground, shove her onto the desk, and slide between her legs. His dick ached at the idea of being buried inside her.

Her palms rested on his chest, fingers digging into muscle. When her whimper vibrated through him, it was enough to wrap a leash around his desire, but only barely. He broke the kiss but didn't let her go. Her gaze held as much turmoil as raged in his own head.

She trailed her fingers down his chest, before drawing her nails up his back. Pleading hung heavy in her low voice. "Don't you dare stop."

This was bad. Everything he shouldn't be doing. And even knowing that, he still wanted more than anything to pin her to the desk and feel her wrapped around him. His cock strained against his slacks every time she rubbed her hip against him. His restraint almost collapsed when he spoke, but he forced his tone to stay steady. "I can't, Lys."

"Bullshit." There was a quiet fury in her response. "I want you." She slid against him again, her body taunting his erection. "You want me."

"You want happily ever after." He said the words aloud as much to reinforce them in his head as to remind her. "I can't offer that." Despite his argument, he couldn't make himself push her away.

"I want to be distracted for tonight. I'm not asking for anything beyond that. I don't expect it. Don't reject me again unless you really, honestly can't stand the thought of being with me. Please?"

The hint of pleading that leaked into her voice shattered her firm tone and the last of his restraint. A whisper in the back of his head said this was all about her. She needed him. But that was an excuse. He fucking wanted her, Goddammit.

FIVE

TATE YANKED ALYSSIA'S HEAD BACK, AND NIPPED HER EARLOBE. "Just for tonight." His growl vibrated against her skin.

Every inch of her body hummed in anticipation. She shifted against him, memorizing the way his hard lines imprinted on her, from chest to groin to thigh. This was really happening, but part of her refused to process it. What if he changed his mind? Again? No, this was different. She managed to keep her hands from shaking as she undid each button on his shirt, and pushed it off his shoulders, leaving in him in an undershirt and slacks. Wow that was sexy.

She leaned her head back to expose her neck and he kissed along the soft flesh, hungry and biting. There was too much clothing between them. She needed to feel his skin on hers. She grabbed the bottom hem of her scrub top.

He wrapped his hands around her wrists, holding her captive, and broke away. A teasing smirk danced on his face. "In a hurry?"

Embarrassment joined the liquid lust heating her skin. What was she supposed to say to that?

He kissed along her fingertips, one at a time on the first hand then the second. "If we're going to do this, you're going to enjoy it."

She clenched her toes inside her shoes at the heavy promise. She

217

was pretty sure she'd enjoy it regardless. "I'm not worried about that."

"Good." He trailed his lips down her palm, over her wrist, and then moved back to her neck. "That's my job." He pulled her top over her head with a fluid grace she didn't think she could have managed herself.

She wouldn't think about the fact that indicated what kind of practice he'd had. This was just them, and it was only for now. Nothing else existed.

He trailed his fingers down her spine, and under her bra strap. "You know." He kissed up her jaw, and nipped her earlobe, breath hot on her skin. "I've wondered for a while now what your nipples look like."

He'd spent time thinking about that? The realization sent flutters through her belly, and tingled between her thighs, making her wet. "You could have asked." Okay, that was a stupid answer.

"Not as much fun." In a single twist, he undid her bra. He dragged the straps down her arms, and tossed the garment aside. The way his gaze lingered on her chest made her desire spike. "Pink, big, and I bet a lot of fun. God, you're gorgeous." He cupped her breasts, and drew his thumbs over the already hard nubs. Each pass flooded her body with a tremor of pleasure.

When he pinched, she sucked in a sharp breath. Her frame tingled from the tug of pleasure and soft pain.

"You should know." His whisper caressed her skin. "I don't have any condoms."

Ambivalence warred inside, stealing some of her anticipation. She hated that she couldn't just say they'd be okay without. Did that mean this was only going so far? Was that his loophole? "So much for being a good boy scout." She struggled to keep the teasing in her tone.

He squeezed her breasts, rolling twin nubs between his fingers, and sucked hard on her neck. He paused long enough to reply. "There's nothing boy scout about what I'm going to do to you. I'll just have to improvise."

The promise filled her with anticipation, but her damned sense of reason wouldn't shut up. He really did expect her to be okay with it. "We can't without—"

"Give me some credit." When his gaze met hers, lust stared back at her. Heated, hungry, and unbound. She swallowed past a dry throat. He looked like he was going to devour her, and she didn't want to stop him. He kissed along her collarbone, lips vibrating against her skin. "I'm not that much of a presumptuous ass."

He wrapped his tongue around one nipple and drew it into his mouth, eliciting a gasp. It was all she could do to keep from crying out when he flicked and nibbled at the nub. Her panties had to be soaked by now. Each new nip and swipe sent another pulse of pleasure coursing through her.

He licked and sucked, alternating between each breast, until her head felt light. She almost thought she might get off just from that attention, but the need between her legs still pleaded for something more direct. She wasn't sure if he'd read her mind, or just the swaying of her hips when his affections shifted downward. He trailed over her stomach, hooked his thumbs in her waistband, and dragged her scrubs and panties to the ground.

The cool air brushed her heated skin and wet arousal. She'd never felt so exposed before, but the desire in Tate's eyes heightened the sensations. Hands on her hips, he turned, redirected her a few steps back, and nudged her onto the couch against the wall. The fake leather was a shock against her skin when it cradled her, and she gasped. Tate knelt in front of her, and kissed along the inside of her thigh, down to one knee, and up to the other.

So many sensations at once stole her reason. She'd never had a guy offer to go down on her. She'd begged a boyfriend once, and it had been so disappointing she'd never brought it up again. When Tate finally focused his attention on the aching need between her legs, a groan tore from her throat. He glided his tongue over her skin, and her breath came in short bursts.

"God, you taste amazing, Lys." His murmured appreciation tingled through her mound. With each pass, he drew closer to her clit, but never made contact. Impatience won out, and she couldn't take the teasing anymore. She tangled her fingers in his hair and pulled his head up. He closed around her swollen sex, and her entire body jolted at the contact. Her hips thrust in time with his sucking, and climax built inside.

When he shoved two fingers inside her, rough and hard, she had to bite the inside of her cheek to keep from screaming his name. She arched her back, and clenched around him when she came. He pushed harder and faster, still pumping her, until she shuddered from the pleasure.

Euphoria danced in her thoughts, and she wasn't ready for the encounter to be over. She stood, wobbling on unsure legs.

He was on his feet in an instant, steadying her. "Careful."

She used the opportunity to spin him so his back was to the couch, and press her frame against his. His erection dug into her stomach through his slacks, teasing her. She slid her fingers under the waistband of his slacks, and fumbled with his belt for a moment before finally unhooking it.

"What are you doing, Lys?" A note of warning lined his question, but he didn't move to stop her.

She undid his button and pulled down the zipper. "Returning the favor."

"You don't have to…." His words melted into a sigh when she wrapped her fingers around his shaft and freed it from his boxers.

"Nope, I don't." She fell to her knees, gaze locked on his, and flicked her tongue over the head of his cock, licking away a salty drop.

He bucked against her face, penis jerking in her hand. She stroked slowly, enjoying his every groan and sigh. When she took him into her mouth, she had to keep her hand wrapped at the base of his shaft to keep him from pushing too deep. He thrust in time with her pumping, eyes never leaving hers. The attention made her juices flow again, coating the inside of her legs. Watching him enjoy himself was turning her on all over again.

His grunts grew more frantic, and his speed increased. "Your mouth feels incredible on my cock." His stuttered breathing punctuated the words. "I'm so close."

If he meant for her to stop, or if it was supposed to be some kind of warning, she didn't care. She pumped harder, and caressed his wrinkled sac. He tensed under her touch, and a long shudder ran through him. Salty warmth hit the back of her throat in spurts, startling her. She'd never done that before, but for him she'd do it again.

No, wait. Reality was sinking back in. She wouldn't, because there was no second time for them. She'd promised.

Her thoughts evaporated again when he pulled her onto his lap. Hand on the back of her neck, he kissed her hard, claiming her mouth. That he wasn't bothered by tasting himself on her lips turned her on as much as anything. Mouth still pressed to hers, he slid his free hand between her legs. She gasped when he found her tender clit and rubbed hard and fast. He swallowed her groans, stroking and pushing her past the limits of her pleasure.

Climax tore through her, snatching away her reason. She shuddered as his touch became too much, and pulled away. She grasped his wrist, and raised it to her mouth, holding his gaze as she sucked one finger clean. His lips parted slightly as he watched her run her tongue along the pad before moving to his next finger.

She let go of him, and leaned into his chest, still struggling to catch her breath. That had been amazing, and she wasn't sure if it was just the things he'd done, or if it had as much to do with the fact it was him.

He trailed his fingers through her hair, heart hammering against her ear. This was too nice. She could get used to this. The moment the thought passed through her head, she pushed away. The last thing she could allow herself to do was get used to cuddling up to Tate. She pasted a smile on. "We're on a deadline, right?"

A flat mask passed over his face, before a pleasant expression flitted back in. "Right. Of course." He extracted himself from her couch and handed over her clothes. He turned away as she dressed, and she couldn't completely squash her disappointment at the heavy air that had settled in the room.

She straightened her clothes, skin still tingling everywhere he'd touched. That had been amazing. She struggled to pull her gaze from him as he put on his shirt. Fantasies taunted her of waking up next to him. Wandering around his house in nothing but that shirt.

She pushed the thoughts away, veins flooding with irritation at herself. She'd sated the teenager inside. The little girl who had been swooning over her older brother's best friend for as long as she could remember had gotten what she wanted. It had been incredible, but that just meant she could move on with no regrets. Right?

His eyes met hers, holding her attention captive. A wicked smile tugged up the corner of his mouth. He closed the distance between them in a few short steps, and knotted his fingers in hair again. His mouth crashed down on hers, and she yielded to the kiss without hesitation. He let her go far too soon for her liking, and stepped back. His teasing, seductive tone tickled her thoughts. "I'm feeling better. You?"

She ducked her head, heat flooding her cheeks. Was she supposed to say thank you? Tell him he was as much responsible as she was? Definitely not ask when they were doing it again. She forced confidence and professionalism to the forefront, despite the way lust kicked and clawed to maintain her attention. She was grateful her voice stayed even when she replied. "I take back anything I said yesterday. The random hookup was way better than trying to find a guy online." She plowed forward before he could reply, not sure she could maintain her mask otherwise. "We have a deadline, right?"

It would be good to stay focused. She'd keep from lingering too long on emotions she couldn't possibly unravel right now. Feelings she shouldn't have. If they dove back into work, everything could go back to what it had been before tonight. Was it last night that had been the catalyst? Or eight years ago? Or— she shook the rambling thoughts aside.

"Work. Right." He nodded at her chair. "There are storyboards and a script for you to approve." He let out a shaky breath. "You sure you're okay?"

Arrogant asshole. Irritation flared inside. Like she couldn't cope with a simple thing like a fling? A retort rushed to her lips.

He wasn't done. "With this whole Thompson thing and the news?"

Her angry comeback evaporated as her gut deflated in on itself. Right. That. The question was a more painful reminder than anything else that he'd been comforting her, and her entire world was about to crumble for more important reasons than her childhood crush didn't feel the same way about her that she did about him. She gave him a weak smile. "I'm good. If we get this done, it helps, right? Shows people the shelter is the real deal?"

"I suspect it'll help."

She focused on the sentiment, and the business of things, and dropped into her desk chair. She navigated to the files automatically. He would have placed them on their shared folder on the cloud.

A knock echoed through the room, and she jumped at the sudden banging. She giggled at her own antics. Tate gave her one more glance, furrowed his brows in concern, and smoothed down his shirt before unlocking the door. She pulled her hair back and twisted it into a knot, sticking a pen through to hold it in place. At least if it was a mess, tying it up would hide it a little. Would people be able to tell? Were her cheeks flushed? Mouth swollen and red? Her fingers twitched against the keyboard as she resisted the urge to trace her them over her lips to check.

Greg—the guy who was taking video of the animals—hovered in the doorway. She'd met him a couple of times at company parties. He was a nice guy. A little hard core when it came to his love of video, but Jared was the same about machines so it didn't faze her.

The moment her brother's name popped into her head, she dropped her face into her palms. Would Greg know what they'd been up to? Did the rest of the office know? He was going to tell her brother. Shit. She'd have to deal with another lecture about why she couldn't get involved with his colleagues, or anyone, really, as far as she could tell. Why he'd be happier if she joined a convent...

"What do you think?" Tate's question shattered her out of control thoughts, and she yanked herself back into the conversation. Greg was gone, and her office door stood wide open. Tate was on the other side of her desk, thumbs hooked in his pockets, watching her. "Do you need a couple more minutes to read?"

Right, she was approving the storyboard and script. "Yeah, give me a sec. Sorry."

She could stay as calm and collected as he was. What they'd done was meant to take the edge off her stress, and it had done that. She was going to ignore the new layer of tension that had drifted in instead. Besides, she promised Tate she didn't want more.

So she'd swallow the impulse—her preprogrammed desire to make sex into something emotional—and she'd move on, just like he was. She glanced up from her monitor, surprise filling her when she saw his fingers drumming on his leg, and his toes tapping.

She pushed the observation aside and went back to work. All she had to do was act normal and it would all be fine. Right?

SIX

Tate counted to ten as he breathed out. Last night's 'stress relief' session with Lys had been amazing, but the world kept turning during and after. If anything, the one thing it did for him was give him a painfully erotic fantasy to slide into every time he remembered how she tasted, her scent, her soft lips wrapped around his cock.

"Did you see the news about the animal shelter?" His assistant, Alan's voice floated from the speaker phone.

Tate shook the images away. He wouldn't let the question get to him—the implication that the news report last night was anything more than an irritating splash in the media pool. There was a solution, he just had to keep his cool. He spoke into his speaker phone. "I did."

"Do we need to worry about backlash?" Alan's voice was hollow, echoing through the Tate's office. "They're not live yet. Are we sure this is a good pilot group for us? If people buy into the hype, and that spreads onto us for supporting them… We look like we're backing animal abuse."

Tate choked back a snarl. This was why he'd hired Alan. Why the guy made such a great assistant. He thought of these things, and he didn't keep the thoughts to himself. But damn it, this wasn't what Tate needed to hear right now. The bad press wouldn't be an issue. He already knew Lys would be able to stop the rumors before they became an issue, and this wasn't just business, it was a good cause. "They're going live. We won't have any problems."

"Right. I'll update the time line to show they'll be live by tomorrow night."

Tate tossed a few instructions out about meetings that afternoon, and disconnected the call. He rubbed his face, but it didn't push away his gnawing tension. He'd already ignored the email from his mother reminding him how easy it would be for Alyssia to make this go away.

He needed to step back, do his job, and let the rest roll off. He'd make sure it all worked out. This business venture, and his test user, meant too much to him to let anything go astray.

A knock drew his attention, and he dragged his gaze to the doorway.

"Lunch?" Mikki—Jared's fiancée and the company's top developer, was leaning against the frame. Her black hair had a violent blue streak through it that week, and she'd pinned the locks back from her face with butterfly-shaped barrettes. While he still struggled to understand the attraction between her chaos and his best friend's unyielding order, he knew she was the best thing to ever happen to Jared. That kind of relationship was a once in a generation kind of fluke, like a sappy movie or something.

The idea made his brain twitch. Something unfamiliar and completely unpleasant surged inside and he obliterated it, focusing on Mikki instead. "I just have to be back by two." Alyssia was coming in to record the voice-overs for her promo video. The name summoned every positive and negative emotion he'd just stuffed inside. He needed to get a handle on that before she showed up. "I'll meet you there."

"Epic." She was already spinning away. "Microbrewery off one-forty-one."

He rolled his eyes and let out a short laugh. "Got it." Almost a year in Atlanta and she didn't care to learn the names of anywhere they regularly went. Said the world was too transient for things like proper nouns on buildings.

The moment she was gone, he sank back in his chair. The two conversations had summoned the one name and image he'd been trying to keep from his mind all morning. Or rather, the memories of last night. He could still taste Alyssia, like a phantom tingle on the tip of his tongue. Every exquisite inch. The woman he'd seen almost every single day since she was a kid, and now just her name made his cock twitch.

He swallowed the lust. The inching desire to figure out what else they could get up to if there were no strings. He had lunch to get this out of his system. No big deal. He was a big boy, and flings were his specialty. He could handle this.

He finished replying to a couple more emails, suppressed any lingering fantasy from the night before, grabbed his sunglasses, and headed out the door.

Fifteen minutes later, Tate strolled through the front door of the pub. The drive had been enough to clear his head, and he felt like his mind was working again. Never pausing, he nodded at the host and cleared the corner to head into the dining area. His friends would probably be at the same table they were always at, near the back of the room.

They were exactly where he expected, but instead of three heads he counted four. He hesitated, and then forced himself to keep walking at a normal gait. Instead of the standard one table they usually sat at, two tables had been pushed together because Alyssia had joined them. No big deal; she dropped by for lunch all the time when she was working night shift.

So why were Jared and Mikki sitting across from each other, Mikki by Alyssia, and Jared by Vivian?

"I don't get the point," Jared said as Tate drew within earshot.

The table between him and Mikki was clear. She flicked a sugar packet across the smooth surface, where it glided to a stop just short of Jared's edge, half on, half off the table. "If it lands like that, you score a point." Mikki explained.

"Of course." Instead of tucking the sugar packet away, like he would have six months ago, Jared flipped it back.

Mikki met Tate's gaze for just a moment before returning her attention to the game. "Look who we found."

Tate didn't have to look. Every time he tried to pull his gaze from Lys, it drifted back to the heat and doubt in her eyes.

"I dropped by to say hi to Jared before our recording session," Alyssia said.

Of course she had. Tate hid his grimace under a wide smile. "Awesome." His skin buzzed with memories of the night before, every nerve ending dancing to life in anticipation just from the way she caught her bottom lip between her teeth. That wasn't good. Apparently his rambling thoughts weren't under control.

He took the empty seat next to Vivian, rather than continuing to stand there and gape. Vivian was the director of operations for Skriddie Bust Media, and Mikki's boss. She, Jared, and Tate had clashed when she joined the company several years ago. However, a handful of crises that pushed them together, proved the three clicked on a whole new level when it came to problem solving, and they'd become solid friends. Jared was closer to her than Tate, but Tate still had nothing but respect and admiration for her skills. And she played a mean hand of poker.

When V raised her brows in question, he scrambled for the first excuse he could find that wasn't, *"If I sit next to Lys, I'm going to spend all of lunch with a hard on."* "I have a question for you about St. Louis."

He didn't mean the city. Before they hired Mikki, her former employer, NSS had used her skill without her knowledge to violate the Skriddie corporate network. Jared and Mikki had spent several months pulling together enough information to file a civil suit for the infraction. But the violation itself had already done damage to Skriddie's public image. St Louis was their code name for the PR campaign Tate was spearheading to update their image.

"What's up?" Vivian asked.

Shit. Now he had to come up with something. A long series of questions ran through his head in a millisecond. "How often does operations re-certify developers?"

"Every six months or as operating systems update, whichever comes first."

Jared jerked his attention from the makeshift sugar-football game. "Speaking of, we got a document discover request from Vicker today about intellectual property No clue how they found out we'd even done that."

Damon Vicker was the attorney defending NSS in the civil suit Skriddie had filed against them.

Tate was good—great even—with this line of conversation. It was boring, it was dry, and it would keep him distracted. "We all know there are other ears inside the company." It was part of the reason they called their PR project St. Louis instead of Fuck-NSS-Over-Publicly.

"Send me a list of what Vicker wants, and I'll grab you the documentation this weekend." Technically, Tate was balancing two jobs. He still held his senior VP of sales job at Skriddie, but was also president of the new venture. The extra work would be worth it, though, to get his sites off the ground.

"If everyone's here, are y'all ready to order?" The waitress's pleasant southern lilt drew Tate's attention. Her nametag said she was Brittany. Large blonde curls framed her face, and her lipstick was just bright enough to draw attention without being too gaudy. Her lips didn't look as kissable as Lys's, though. And Brittany probably didn't make the same guttural moans—

He shook the thoughts away. He wouldn't compare her to Alyssia. He'd grab her number instead, to remind himself how much he enjoyed having the option of hooking up with a different woman every night.

"I'm not sure, Brittany." He met her gaze, never breaking eye contact, and let his own drawl slide in. A trick he usually either saved to irritate his mother, or to give him that boy next door sound. Even though he'd grown up in Georgia, he'd never had the accent by default. His mother had taught him. She'd said when it was used at the right time, it could shape all sorts of impressions. He never had to use it around Lys. Which didn't matter because he wasn't thinking about her.

Brittany moved to his side, and rested a hand on his arm. "What can I do for you, sugar?"

He did this all the time, so why did it feel so unnatural now? Because he was over-thinking it, that was why. "Which do you recommend? Chef's special, or catch of the day?"

She twirled a strand of hair around her finger. "Depends. Catch of the day is fresh, but chef's special is spicy. You look like you enjoy a little heat." She winked.

"Quite a bit." He handed the menu back. She was hooked, he was almost certain of it. A couple more lines, and he'd have her number. Except he couldn't force out the next line. He couldn't close.

"Me too." Vivian passed her menu between, breaking a teasing gaze about to turn awkward.

Brittany turned her attention to the rest of the table, and after one last glance at him, moved on to other customers. The conversation shifted from work, to the Memorial Day barbeque his parents were holding in just over a week. When Jared shifted his attention to his sister to ask her something about their own parents, Vivian tilted her head toward Tate.

"I'm surprised you didn't snag her number." Vivian's voice was low enough only Tate would hear.

Tate glanced at Lys, her eyes bright, a genuine smile in place as she laughed at something Jared said. "I'm off my game or something. Work, stress, blah, blah, blah."

Vivian smirked. "That's never been an issue for you before."

Irritation surged through him at the prodding. "It is now." The words snapped out sharper and louder than he intended, and everyone's heads swiveled in his direction. Why was he even upset with V? She was being friendly, teasing the way they always did. "Sorry. Like I said, stress."

Vivian pursed her lips. "Apparently so."

Again, the conversation shifted and flowed as the food arrived, and then empty plates were taken away. At some point, Brittany slipped her phone number under his hand. Tate managed to bring his rambling thoughts under control by the end of the meal. He should be fine in this afternoon's recording session with Lys, especially with the sound engineer around. Which reminded him. "We have to get back." He realized after a glance at his phone to check the time. "Recording session."

"Everyone rode with me," Jared said. "Meet you back there?"

Alyssia's eyes grew wide, and she opened her mouth, but before she could speak, Vivian cut her off. "I'm going to catch a ride with you, if you don't mind. J's back seat is cramped, and I have an idea I want to run past you." Vivian fell into step beside Tate. He tried but failed to ignore the disappointment that flashed over Alyssia's face before a smile flitted back in.

"Sounds like plan." Did V have any idea she'd just bought him another fifteen minutes by asking for a ride before Alyssia could?

Mikki and Alyssia split off toward the other side of the parking lot with Jared, and Tate let relief trickle through him. He glanced at the waitress's number one more time before crumpling it and tossing it in a nearby trashcan.

"You're going to break her heart." Vivian's comment dragged him back into the now. Exactly where he needed to stay. He'd remember that.

Which meant she was talking about the waitress, not Lys. "She served me iced tea, V. I don't think she expects a ring for that." He held the car door open for her, and waited until she was seated before taking his spot behind the wheel.

Vivian laughed. "That's good. And not who I was talking about. What do you think J's going to do when he finds out you hooked up with his sister?"

She *had* figured it out. *Fuck.* He wanted to ask if it was that obvious, but he wasn't willing to confess. "He'd probably blow a fuse. Good thing we didn't."

Vivian raised an eyebrow.

"What?" Tate didn't like the defensive mechanism kicking in. "I'm not stupid. I've known her a lot longer than you have, and I know she's not a one-time kind of girl."

Vivian shrugged. "She wouldn't look at you during lunch, she barely said two words after you showed up, and she clenched her jaw every time the waitress showed up. Something happened, at least as far as she's concerned."

He didn't want to snap at V, but the last thing he needed was her voicing every argument his mind was already tossing at him. "Were you this bad with Jared and Mikki?"

"Considering they'd hooked up, and you two *haven't*"—she made a show of clearing her throat—"I was about fifty times worse. But my reasons with Mikki were different."

Of course they were. Because no matter how much she liked Mikki, or respected Jared, she still felt like he'd betrayed her by falling in love. Tate would have bet big that Vivian had never completely gotten over Jared, but as long as the two of them were still single, she could pretend it would be that way forever. He kept the thought to himself, not interested in picking a fight. "I've known the two of them for ages, I understand what a bad idea that would be—and that doesn't even matter because there's nothing going on with Lys."

"Right." Vivian's tone was flat. "Because if there were, you'd know eventually you'd have to pick a side."

"Did that a long time ago." He just had to remember that. Jared was his best friend, and Alyssia was a client. Vivian's reminder just cemented he needed to put as much emotional distance between himself and Lys as possible.

SEVEN

ALYSSIA LEANED AGAINST THE FRAME OF HER HOME OFFICE DOOR. "It's okay, really." It was true, two days ago, she had been irritated with Jared for insisting she upgrade her home network hardware to be more secure.

Now, that seemed like an eternity ago. A flutter raced across her skin, and her gut churned at the reminder.

"If you didn't do so much work from home..." Jared sat at her desk, fingers flying across the keyboard, rarely pausing even as he spoke. "Nah, that's just an excuse. You needed the upgrade."

"Really?" She kept a teasing tone. "So you've already upgraded everything in your house, and needed someone else to techify?" Even though she was trying to keep her attention on the conversation, it kept dancing with the one name she'd been doing her best not to think of since she left the Skriddie offices that afternoon.

Not that she'd succeeded. Every unoccupied thought, and even some of the occupied ones, were interrupted with Tate. Had last night been a mistake? It had taken her this many years to get used to how he flirted without shame with pretty much every waitress, hostess, anyone. Then today at lunch, watching him with their server had almost devoured her.

Still, the memory of what she had Tate had shared, the way they'd clicked, and the things he'd done, she wouldn't give that up for anything. She would stick to her promise that what happened between them was just physical. A one-time event, and all that. Which was why, when he'd asked if she wanted him to just email the promo video to her for approval, and launch the site without her, or if she wanted to be there for all of it, she'd invited him over.

His dropping by for whatever had never been a deal in the past, and there was no reason for that to change. The faster things got back to normal between them, the better.

"Hello?" Jared's insistent voice shattered her wandering thoughts. "Earth to Alyssia. You in there?"

She shook away the mental clutter and focused on her brother, who apparently had finished what he was doing, and was watching her. "Sorry, too much going on everywhere. What?" she asked.

"You're all done." He held up a blank post-it note, then stuck it to one of the frames he'd brought back for her from a business trip. The picture frame was from Busch Gardens. The blank note was his way of letting her know what her new network password was. She did adore that he always remembered to bring her something, wherever he visited. And each new trinket had a different memory attached to it, which was why he used them for her passwords.

"Thank you." She smiled. "I really do appreciate it."

"I know you don't so much." He stood and joined her, falling into step next to her as they made their way downstairs, to the living room of her townhouse. "But I appreciate you placating me. And yes, you're right. Even Mikki doesn't think we need any more new tech in the house. But if I can show her this router works for you…"

"I'm glad I could be your guinea pig."

Jared strode toward the door. "Good luck with your launch tonight. I know you'll do awesome."

Alyssia's heart leapt, hammering in her chest, when Jared opened the door to find Tate on the other side, hand half raised to knock. Tate slid a quick smile into place, never flinching. His gaze met hers for the briefest moment, and she swore she saw heat flash in his eyes as they flicked over her.

Or that was wishful thinking on her part? Why did he have to look so good?

"You get everything squared away?" Tate turned back to Jared.

"She's set." Jared glanced back at Alyssia, and she resisted the urge to stick out her tongue. She wasn't going to fall into a childish role with her brother. Not tonight. "I'm glad you're here to take care of her, though."

Heat flooded Alyssia's face at the rush of images associated with Tate taking care of her. He certainly had last night. She shook the thoughts away, and nudged Jared forward. "You're going, right? And keeping in mind how profusely grateful you are I gave you an excuse to buy something new?"

Tate clapped Jared on the shoulder before stepping around him. "I promise any trouble she gets into will be fully supervised by me."

This time when Tate's gaze met hers, she had no doubt mischief and desire danced behind his look. Damn it, she couldn't go back to casual flirting with him so soon after.

"Glad to hear it." Jared finished saying his goodbyes and seconds later, the townhouse door closed behind him.

Alyssia summoned every last ounce of calm and cool she could find, and dragged her gaze away from Tate. She couldn't spend the whole night staring. "Should we get to work?"

He raised an eyebrow, and she hid a wince. Maybe she shouldn't have had so much ice in her tone. "Nice to see you, too." His voice was pleasant, and light.

She could be civil, no big deal. It was the meaningless innuendo she'd struggle with. "Sorry. I'm just—" What? Desperate to relegate last night to a pleasant memory, rather than intense longing? No, she'd go with a different truth. The one she'd managed to ignore in favor of more fleeting, less stressful things. "I'm just eager to get this thing online, and put more distance between the shelter and Thompson's bullshit."

Tate's left hand clenched into a fist, and he gritted his teeth. "Right. Let's get that done. Lead the way." He gestured toward the stairs, and then paused, and wrapped a loose hand around her wrist.

"What's wrong with your arm?" He was looking at a large piece of gauze taped to her skin, below the elbow.

"I had a patient get a little excited, and he hadn't had his nails trimmed in a while. It's not a bad gash, but it's long."

"Are you okay?"

"Sure." She hadn't even thought about it, but his concern filled her with a soft glow. Injuries like this were status quo for her. "I'm on antibiotics just in case, but it'll be fine."

"Good. As long as you're all right." He rested a hand at the small of her back, his light touch all but searching her skin through her T-shirt. She did her best not to focus on the touch. Not to associate it with memories of his hands running over her bare skin. By the time they reached the doorway to her office, her imagination was working overtime, and her breathing shallow. She pushed aside the vivid images and tried to be subtle about pulling away from him.

"What first?" She cringed at the too-bright chirp that tore from her mouth.

"Have a seat." His tone was flat, any of the earlier teasing gone. "You do the setup, I watch and make sure it's all intuitive."

Her insides twisted in on themselves as she pulled up the admin panel for the crowd-funding site. Apparently, without the rampant fantasies of Tate, her mind was free to linger on Thompson's threats instead. The lawyer she kept on retainer had sent letters to Thompson and to the news station threatening a defamation suit if Thompson didn't retract the statements. She hadn't heard anything back, and didn't know if that was a good sign or not. But if they could get her campaign online tonight, and get promises of funding, that would help. It had to. It would be a chance for her to remind people the shelter did good things. That it was worth people's time and investment to support the animals.

She shoved aside the chaos tumbling through her head, and tried to clear her mind. "What first?"

"The art department had time to implement all your requests, so give this a look and make sure you're good with it." Tate rested his hand on her shoulder, leaned around her, and plugged a USB drive into her laptop.

His familiar scent filled her nostrils, and she inhaled deeply. His warmth radiated through her sleeve, and dragged her jumbled thoughts back to the surface. This wasn't the way to move on from last night. That would have to become her mantra if she was going to make it through the evening with her sanity and heart intact.

She leaned toward the screen, breaking the contact between them, and clicked the auto-run icon that popped up. After recording her voice-over that afternoon for the promo video, she'd sat with the art department, giving her feedback with each new tweak, so there would be as few surprises as possible tonight.

She played the video, pleased with the results. Tate told her all of the pilot groups had similar access to Skriddie's art and marketing departments, to help make the crowd-funding software launch go as well as possible. She still felt like she'd gotten a little extra attention. Not that she minded in this case.

The application was fairly easy to navigate. With only a little prompting from Tate, she finished setting everything up.

"That's it." Tate rested a hand on her shoulder, but pulled away too quickly for her liking.

Nervous energy hummed through her. Everything else aside, this project was going to take her shelter to new places. Owning the land they were on would give them new options for expansion, the opportunity to implement new projects for the animals. Her fingers twitched in anticipation. She inhaled deeply, then pressed the 'Go Live' button.

All the air escaped her lungs and she sank back in her chair, as the world continued on around them. "That was anti-climactic." She laughed at her own anxiousness. It wasn't like the world should have turned upside down just because she clicked *Go*.

Tate draped his arms over her shoulders and squeezed. "Congratulations." His breath caressed her cheek.

She wanted to sink into the hug, but forced herself to draw back. She navigated to her dashboard. "Do I take the system down if I refresh obsessively?" She forced her tone to stay light.

"No." A hint of strain lined Tate's response. "It's built for that. Refresh away."

She clicked the refresh button several times in rapid succession, just for fun, impressed when the system responded instantly each time. And then the system hung. It sat for several seconds before rendering in a jumble. "I think I broke it." She joked.

"It's a hiccup. Try again."

She did. Each time, the response took longer, until nothing was returned at all. "Nope, definitely broke it." Her teasing came out more forced than she intended.

"Can you get to other sites?"

She navigated to a couple without any issues, but still couldn't get back into her admin panel.

"Shit." Tate's curse was so soft she barely heard it. "May I?"

She stood and let him have her seat, furrowing her brow. What was going on? This shouldn't be a big deal, right? She'd been watching Tate and Jared work long enough, though, she knew something was wrong. "Do you want me to call Jared?"

Tate's fingers flew over the keyboard, new windows opening, including one with a black background and white text, and another that looked like a different computer desktop. "He and Mikki have plans." His voice was tight.

"You know he'll cancel. Is it bad?" She crossed her arms, and tapped her toes. What was going on? It was just a little glitch, right? So why did she feel like everything was about to go sideways? Her gaze drifted toward her phone, at the edge of her desk. Maybe she should call Jared anyway. Tate wouldn't let his ego get in the way of doing this right.

The high-speed clack of keys drew her attention back to what Tate was doing. Her limited understanding of what they did at Skriddie told her he was dialed into a remote computer, switching between a performance monitor and a window with text in different colors. "Fucking load balancing issue." Tate muttered a string of curses, and continued working.

Guilt joined the swirl of emotions in her head. She should have remembered, Tate had the same background as her brother, he just used it differently.

Watching Tate now, he really did shine when it came down to it.

At least, she assumed he was. He never paused for more than few seconds, and as the minutes ticked away, he clicked through more things she only vaguely recognized.

The light faded outside, until the primary source of light in the room was her laptop screen. A nudge at the back of her mind told her she should turn on the light, but she was too engrossed in watching Tate work.

It seemed like eons later, but according to her clock it was less than two hours, when he leaned back in her chair with a loud exhale. "So weird." Despite his quiet tone, the sudden statement was loud in the room.

She chewed on her bottom lip, not sure what to say. "So… It's fixed?"

He stood and gestured for her to take the chair again. "Yes. You're back online."

"What happened?"

"Do you want the technical details?"

She might feel smarter if she heard them and understood them. Then again, if she described the details of neutering a dog, he wouldn't be able to keep up either. "Not really."

He gave a light laugh. "Something was wrong with the server configuration. It wasn't set up to handle as much internet traffic as it should have been."

As in, none? She had to have been the only person on the site. The clench of his jaw and way he kept glancing back at the machine made her wonder what he'd found that bothered him so much.

"It's back online now. You're good to go," he said after a final glance at the laptop.

She reached for the mouse, then paused. He'd said it was fixed, she was being silly. Still, as she clicked into her admin dashboard again, her earlier enthusiasm was missing. A whisper of disappointment mingled with the rest of her thoughts. Of course there wouldn't be any donations. The site had technically only been online for a few minutes. Still, she clicked refresh again, bracing herself for anther slowdown.

Her heart leaped, and a smile broke her face. Was that a donation? She hit refresh again. Yup, it was. It was several hundred dollars, from an anonymous source. She had no idea how it had gotten there. A voice in the back of her mind asked how that had come in so quickly. Technically they wouldn't be live until tomorrow. Advertising would go out then. The social media campaign would start up.

But it was a donation. How was that bad? "Yay." She hopped to her feet, giddiness flooding her, and spun to Tate. She tossed her arms around his neck. "It worked."

His hands rested on her back, and he squeezed. "Congratulations." He didn't let go.

Heat flooded her as the seconds ticked away. His pulse hammered a beat against her cheek, and she extracted herself from his embrace, not able to meet his gaze. She really needed to get over this.

"Hey." He placed a finger under her chin and raised her head until she was looking him in the eye. "Enough. We both had fun last night, right? I know I did."

It was okay to admit to that. Fun had been part of the point. "I did too." Alyssia felt a touch of relief being able to say it aloud.

"I don't regret it. Not in any way." His expression was soft, attention focused completely on her.

She didn't either. She just had to say so, and things would go back to the way they were. So why couldn't she say the words?

EIGHT

Tate's heart froze for the briefest moment when Lys didn't reply.

"No regrets." Her words were a reassurance he didn't know he needed.

"Good." He intertwined his fingers with hers, and tugged her out of the room. He knew what his problem was. He'd been over-thinking everything since last night. He needed to step back, get an objective perspective, and just let instinct drive. "Let's go celebrate."

"What did you have in mind?" Lys paused by the front door long enough to slip on a pair of sandals, and grab her purse.

The one thing they always did. Something nagged at the back of his mind, asking how they had an 'always' anything. He shoved it aside. It's just the way things were between them. It didn't mean anything. "We grab a pizza and head up to the lake."

"Sounds perfect." Her grin latched onto something inside him, and send a wash of need over his skin.

Apparently he hadn't reached that objective point yet. He'd get there, though.

"You drive." She tossed him her keys.

He snagged them without missing a beat. The Bentley was nice for freeway and city driving, but Lys's ancient Suburban would handle the off-road lake paths a lot better, and he was more familiar with the route than she was.

An hour later, they'd found a quiet spot of trees, and a clearing with no one else around, and backed the SUV up several feet back from the lake. They finished the pizza and discarded the box half an hour after that, and then sat next to each other on the tailgate. Lys swung her legs in a lazy arc, and Tate leaned back, palms resting on the upholstery behind him. Once upon a time, Lake Lanier had been one of his least favorite places. His parents had a summer home that was really more of an excuse to show off than a reason to vacation. They'd sold it when the area got too crowded.

Spending time with Lys up there, though, helped him discover an appreciation for the beauty again. Especially when they could find an isolated spot of land and just unwind.

"Remember that night we came up here to study for my finals?" Her question blended into the calm of the night.

"Which time?"

She leaned into him. "Every time. I doubt I would have made it through undergrad without your help."

"I was zero help for vet school, so I guess that evens everything out. What about the time you ran away?"

"Oh, God." She scrubbed her face, laughter spilling through her fingers. "I don't even remember why I did that, but I know it was childish. I'm still grateful you never told them you found me up here."

"Right. Because I was going to tell J—anyone you hitchhiked to the lake." Tate wasn't sure why he stalled on Jared's name. Something told him he didn't want to ruin the mood that way.

She tucked one leg under the other knee, and turned to face him. "Or three years ago when I closed on the loan for the shelter."

Her eyes sparkled with amusement, holding his gaze captive. If he leaned in a few inches, he could lose himself in the soft perfume of her shampoo. His senses prickled at the idea, and he shelved the desire. "You mean the night you drank way too much champagne and almost puked in my car?"

"I don't remember it that way." She tucked a strand of hair behind her ear. His fingers itched with the desire to cover her hand. What was wrong with him tonight?

"You were wasted." He struggled to keep the conversation light, friendly, and as completely unsexy as possible. "I'm surprised you remember anything."

"I remember enough." She twisted her mouth in mock-irritation. "Was that really the last time we were up here?"

He had a feeling she knew the answer as distinctly as he did. "It was."

"Why did we stop?"

"Coming to the lake?" He was stalling. He knew exactly what she meant. "Our schedules got busy. Life got in the way." The excuse slid out without thought. It was the same one he fed himself every time he wondered why they didn't hang out more. With the question between them now, it bounced in his head.

He studied her closer. The flush of laughter on her cheeks. The smile tugged forward by the memories. Had they really spent so much time together? Up here. At home. He sifted through stacks of memories, and she was a part of so many of them.

She poked him in the arm. "What are you staring at?"

He shook away his rambling thoughts. "Just you."

Fuck it all. He was lingering too much on this one thing. Putting too much thought into a simple, physical response. She'd been open to no strings last night, would she go for it again? Once the physical wasn't taboo anymore, the tension between them would vanish, and they could go back to being casual and friendly, without the awkwardness.

Alyssia tried not to notice the sudden silence. Maybe she shouldn't have brought up the celebration night. She remembered it far more vividly than she'd ever let on. She'd actually only had a couple of glasses of champagne, but had definitely enjoyed the excuse to fall asleep on Tate.

"But you know." His voice was suddenly too loud in the still. It sounded too cheerful, but strained at the same time. "That's life, right? We'll drift our separate ways, you'll meet a great guy to bring up here, and he'll be one hell of a lucky dude if you give him a chance."

But she'd already met a great guy. She bit the inside of her cheek to keep the comment from escaping. "I guess."

He hopped to the ground, and disappointment spread through her at the sudden distance between them, even though he'd only stepped a few feet away. Was the moment ruined? Was he waiting for her to say something?

"However." The strain vanished from his voice. He stepped closer, and tugged her foot so both of her legs hung over the tailgate again. "If you want a distraction until then…"

Anticipation seared her veins and her pulse kicked into over-drive. She tried to keep the teasing in her reply. "I'm not sure I know what you're suggesting."

"I'm just thinking, waiting for Mr. Right has got to get lonely sometimes." He nudged her legs apart with his knee, and pushed between her thighs. Friction built, teasing her thoughts. "And I'm guessing a battery operated boyfriend doesn't always do the trick."

Her face warmed. "I don't—" His raised brows made her pause, mid-protest. "No, it doesn't."

He glided his fingers over the backs of her hands, up her arms, and along her jaw. "I'm offering something a little more… organic, from someone you already like and trust."

Like. Such a tame word. Desire glided under her skin, focusing in her belly, then spread outward again. Could she really have casual sex? Tate didn't do long term, but he was being up front about it. She could fool around, indulge her fantasies, and then they could both step back once their needs had been met. "It sounds like a perfect arrangement." She almost stammered on the words. Where had that come from?

He cradled her face in his hands, searching her eyes. "Couldn't agree more." When he kissed her, mouth pressed to hers, palms holding her head in place, excitement squeezed her chest. She could keep things casual if it meant more of this. More of this kind of attention from Tate. Definitely.

He trailed his lips along her cheek, and down her jaw. Traipsed a line of kisses over her clavicle and to her sternum. Each new, feather-light touch sent a pleasant shudder through her. She whimpered and tilted her head back as he moved lower. His touch through fabric teased her. She shifted her weight to bring herself closer, and he lifted his head to close his mouth over hers again.

One hand found its way under her shirt, and she gasped at the barely-there sensation of his palm on her bare skin. She rested one hand at the base of his neck. The short, blond hairs tickled her fingertips as she held his head captive. Sank into the growing hunger. She dug her fingers into his chest, memorizing each new line of definition as she grasped for something to cling to.

The desperation that had been there last night was gone, replaced with something steadier. More sensual. But need still bubbled inside her. She wanted to burn every touch into her memory to savor later. He brushed the bottom of her breast with his thumb, and a gasp tore from her throat. He dragged a path across her nipple, then back again, teasing through fabric. Dampness grew between her legs.

He kissed along the edge of her ear. "You make delicious noises when you're turned on." His voice was so quiet she felt it as much as heard it. "What kind of sounds do you make if I do this?" He dragged the cup of her bra out of the way, scraping lace and elastic over the tender skin.

She sucked in a sharp breath through her teeth. "That kind apparently." It was a struggle to find words.

"What if I do this?" He lowered his head, and flicked his tongue over the jutting pink nub. Slowly at first, but then building up speed.

She squirmed against him with a whimper. An ache called from between her thighs.

"That's good too." He blew lightly on the damp skin.

Her head felt light as the blood rushed from it. Squeaks and gasps pushed from her throat.

"I've got a better place for this." He covered her hand with his.

She managed a laugh. "Where's that?"

Palm against the back of her hand, he guided them both lower. Her fingers brushed a bulge, hard and long, outlined by denim, and he groaned. "Right there."

A new spark of desire raced through her, and she traced his erection through his jeans. Each time she brushed it from a new angle, or gripped his shaft, or caressed the head, he responded. Kissing her nipple, sucking, nipping the flesh with his teeth.

She wasn't sure how long they sat there, clothes half-out of the way, groping and kissing while she sat on the tailgate of her Suburban, him standing between her legs. But this wasn't making out with a boy at the lake. She could have more. She drew his mouth back to hers, and kissed him hard, tongues dancing around each other.

When she broke away, she met his gaze. "We should go back to my place. Or yours. Wherever."

His hungry gaze slid over her face. "What's wrong with here?"

Heat rushed to her cheeks. "We're outside." Except, did she actually mind?

He nipped at her neck with his teeth, and then her shoulder. "And no one's around. We have the area to ourselves. It's dark." He looked her in the eye again. "And tell me the idea of getting caught isn't at least a little exciting."

Her anticipation spiked. "It's more than just a little exciting."

"Good." He dragged a thumb across her nipple again. "Because I've tried. I really have. To put yesterday out of my mind." He covered her hand again, and squeezed. She followed his lead and tightened her grip on his bulge, stroking as he pressed against her hand.

He lifted her chin, holding her head in place, and locked her gaze on hers. "My best intentions have failed." His voice had dropped an octave, and the husky tone floated over her skin. His accent was back. The drawl he tried so hard to hide. The one that made her senses flare to life. "I can't stop thinking about your lips wrapped around my cock. How gorgeous you looked. How incredible it felt. But I'm dying to bury myself inside you. Knowing how tight you were, how wet you got? I want to feel your pussy squeeze around me."

He dipped his head in again, the heat from his breath hot against her cheek when he whispered, "I have condoms tonight. God, I need to fuck you, Lys."

Part of her mind snagged on the words. He'd planned to spend this evening with her. The entire night, right? But he'd stopped for protection? A smirk slid onto her face. She fumbled for the button on his jeans, and then slid down the zipper. "I like the sound of that," she said.

NINE

Tate was so hard, he could barely think. Every time Lys traced his cock, his entire system jerked with pleasure. When she finally freed him from his jeans, the combination of her warm palm and the cool air brushing his bare skin dragged a long groan from him. He wanted to draw this moment out, but his resistance hovered near empty.

She stroked his shaft, and he squeezed her breast harder. She made the most delicious whimpers with every touch. He made quick work of the button and zipper on her jeans, and tugged. She kicked off her sandals, and lifted her ass off the tailgate long enough for him to drag her pants down her legs. It was too dark to stop and drink her in, but her pussy—the way it looked, the way she tasted, was burned in his mind anyway. He moved a hand between her legs. When he pressed into her slit, his fingers were instantly coated.

"God, you're so wet." He dug his teeth into her shoulder, muffling his words.

"I blame you ahh—" Her teasing words faded into a gasp when he shoved two fingers inside her.

He slid in easily, pumping in and out. "You were saying?"

She shook her head, bottom lip caught between her teeth. Each time he pumped inside her, she squirmed and pushed back. He sought out her clit with his thumb. His dick throbbed in the night air, eager and waiting.

Her breathing grew more punctuated. Groans became gasps became panting. "Fuck, Tate. Oh, God."

She was close, he could tell from her rigid spine, the lilt of her sighs, and the way she clenched around his fingers. Climax rolled through her. He needed to be inside her, now. In a fluid motion, he pulled his hand away, and thrust his cock inside her.

Her fading cries peaked again, and she dug her nails into his back. He pounded her. She felt even better than he imagined. Spots danced in front of his eyes as his orgasm built. She wrapped her legs around his waist and kept the pace fast and frantic. She gripped his erection when she came again.

Every point of contact converged into a single spot in his mind. He couldn't last any longer. As much as he wanted to draw the moment out, it wasn't going to happen. He ground against her as he came, spilling hot and frantic inside her. Still driving hard until his legs were weak, and he was spent.

He rested his hands on the tailgate, on either side of her, to support his weight, and buried his head against her shoulder.

She rested her forehead on his chest, still sighing with each gasp for air as she brought her breathing under control.

He slid out as he softened, and something occurred to him. "Fuck," he muttered against her skin. What was wrong with him?

"Already?" Her laugh was light.

God damn it. He'd never done that before. Ever. "I forgot the condom."

Her frame froze beneath him, and then she pushed him back. Wide eyes met his. "You said you had one."

"I do. Still." He tried to keep his tone calm. Struggled not to let his irritation with himself leak into it. "I got caught up in the moment. I forgot…"

She lifted her clothes from the ground with her toes, and shook the dust off. The snap of denim was loud in the late evening. "Forgot."

He didn't know what bothered him more. That he'd gotten so caught up in the moment it had slipped his mind, or that he had enjoyed it so much he wanted to do it that way again. With her. "I'm sorry."

She raked her fingers through her hair. "Do you forget a lot?"

"Never." He poured all the emphasis into the word.

"So, you're clean, right?"

The question stung, but he understood her concern. If there was one thing he hadn't been for years, it was celibate. "Absolutely."

She nudged him back with her body. "I'm on birth control. We should be good."

A strange kind of ambivalence nudged his senses. What the hell? He was just a little drained. That was fantastic news. "Good. Great." He forced himself to relax.

THE RIDE back home started quiet, but conversation eventually flowed again. Alyssia leaned back in the passenger seat, watching the passing lights, and swapping random banter with Tate. A strange moment of panic and hope had passed through when she'd said he hadn't used protection. A bubble of fantasy. Of what might happen if her birth control failed. However, she knew that wasn't his dream. The last thing she wanted was for him to feel trapped, or obligated by something like… She didn't even dare think the words. She wouldn't do that to him.

They pulled up in front of her townhouse, and she met him outside the vehicle. In the dim light, streetlights highlighting his features, he looked as handsome as he ever had. She traced a finger down his cheek. "You heading out?" She swallowed the desire to ask him directly to stay. That wasn't *no strings*.

He intertwined his fingers with hers, and led her toward her townhome. "I'm a little wired, and I don't have anywhere else to be. If you're not busy, I might stick around."

She couldn't fight her smile. "I think I could make time for that."

He unlocked the door, stepped aside for her to enter, and hooked her keys on their hook. "Movies?"

"Sure. I'll find something. I have Coke in the fridge." This was better. It was the comfortable, laid back interaction she enjoyed with Tate. It was true, thinking his name still made her blood run hot, and she didn't know if she'd ever stop daydreaming about the way he kissed. And everything he'd kissed. But at least they were acting normal again.

"I'm good." He dropped onto the couch. "Something smart?"

"Something sweet." She grabbed the remote and pulled up a list of streaming videos. Moments later, *Silver Linings Playbook* started. She wasn't worried he'd argue. For as much as Tate swore no one in real life got a happily ever after, he enjoyed the fictional version. Only guy she'd ever met who didn't mind sitting through romance movies with her.

He patted the couch next to him. No reason to overthink this now. She took the seat, and tucked her legs beneath her. He draped his arm over her shoulders, and she leaned in. This was definitely doable.

The film started, and though she'd seen it several times, she let herself be sucked into the story line. They finished one movie, and picked another. Somewhere along the way, Tate nudged her forward, lay down in the couch, and then pulled her back into him. She didn't argue when he pulled her tight, pressing her back against his chest, and draping his arm over hers.

Within a few minutes, his breathing shifted. He'd drifted off— the realization tugged something inside her. She could get used to this. That was probably a bad road for her to go down. She adjusted her thinking as she snuggled into him. It wasn't like she wanted him there every night for the rest of their lives or anything. This was just comfortable. Nothing more.

TATE STRETCHED and tried to push the lingering fog of sleep from his brain. He couldn't believe he'd passed out on Alyssia's couch. He had vague memories of her warm body in his arms, but maybe he'd just dreamed that. No, he was pretty sure it was real.

Something clattered from the kitchen, jarring him more awake. Might as well investigate. He paused in the doorway, and his senses roared to life. Lys had her back to him, and was grabbing something from the counter. Her damp hair hung down her back, and she only wore a T-shirt and panties.

His cock roared to life, straining against his jeans. Fuck, that was sexy. And she probably wouldn't appreciate him staring. He cleared his throat.

She let out a small squeak and whirled to face him. She blushed and crossed her arms over her chest. He tried to drag his gaze away, and finally managed. "I didn't mean to startle you." He winced at his own drawl. He must be more tired than he realized.

"It's okay." She tugged down the edges of her shirt, sighed and then stopped, looking him in the eye again. "I'm not used to waking up with someone else in the house. I guess I forgot my pants."

"I'm not complaining." His erection was starting to protest at being ignored, though. "Have you been up long?"

"My brain is still on graveyards. I haven't been to sleep yet. I was just seeing if I had any food to make. Do you want breakfast? I can cook something. Or, well, not really. I can make oatmeal—"

She was adorable when she rambled. "Stop." He wasn't sure if he was talking to her, or himself. He crossed the distance between them, and dragged a thumb over her bottom lip. His fingers tightened, wanting another touch. He tried to be subtle about smothering his rampant arousal. "We're good, right? We got past this last night?"

"I think so." She chewed on the inside of her lip, and meet his gaze. "I mean, we totally are."

"Good." He rested his hands on her hips and nudged her back until she collided with the counter. "Because you look fucking hot, and I don't think you owe anyone any apologies for that." She shifted her weight, and her hip rubbed his cock through his jeans. The blood rushed from his head, and he struggled for a moment to form words. He dipped his head, and trailed his nose along her neck, inhaling deeply. She smelled intoxicating, like lilacs. "It's too bad you already showered." He nipped at her earlobe. Her gasp burrowed into his head, short-circuiting his thoughts. "I would have asked if I could join you."

She draped her arms around his neck, and pressed her entire frame to his. Her nipples dragged over his chest, teasing him through fabric. "You're welcome to use it now, if you want."

He cupped her ass, holding her as close as possible. "I don't have any clothes here."

"No one said you had to get dressed after."

A voice whispered in the back of his head that he was playing with fire. That this was crossing a line he needed to steer far clear of. His raging desire for another chance at the woman in front of him drowned it out. "You make a good argument. I think I'm going to take you up on that."

She brushed her lips over his. "Towels are in the closet, I'll be in the bedroom."

Tate was surprised he had any restraint left, as he stripped down in her bathroom. He couldn't stop fantasizing about spending the entire day in bed with Lys. Tasting every inch of her, finding out how loud he could make her scream if she wasn't worried about someone hearing her. His dick stood at attention. He was as bad as a teenager with an inconvenient boner.

He stepped into the shower. Hot water sluiced over him, and he grabbed the body wash. Now he was going to smell Lys on his skin all day. Did he really mind that much? His cock jerked when he gripped it, hand soapy. A low groan escaped his throat. He leaned his head back, eyes closed, and focused on the sensation. Memories danced in his head as he stroked. Lys squirming against him. Her lips wrapped around him the other night. How tight she was when he buried himself inside her.

His balls tightened, and he bit the inside of his cheek until a sharp pain echoed back in protest. It ached to let go, but he forced himself to stop before he came. He definitely wanted to save that until he had her company.

He finished the rest of his shower quickly, dried off, and wrapped a towel around his waist.

There was a knock on the door so soft, he almost wasn't sure he heard it. He toed it open, to find Lys on the other side. Disappointment tried to nudge its way in when he saw she'd dressed. He pushed it aside and summoned a smile. "Hey, gorgeous. Couldn't wait?"

She grimaced, shook her head, and held up her hand. She was holding her phone. "It's for you," she said.

Shit. That couldn't be good. "Hello." Tate kept his tone chipper.

"Gorgeous, really?" Jared's irritation rolled over him. "Couldn't wait for what?"

Double shit. "Breakfast. We were going out to celebrate that her site went live last night." The lie tasted fouler than Tate expected. As if he should be bothered he had to hide what he was doing. Ridiculous. This wasn't anyone's business but his and Lys's.

"Which is why your phone's off." The edge in Jared's tone grew sharper.

Alyssia perched on the edge of her bed, eyes wide, watching Tate.

"I left it in the car, forgot to charge it, it's probably dead." Which, when Tate thought about it might be pretty close to the truth. When was the last time he'd seen his phone? Last night sounded about right.

"You just let it die?"

"Yes. Not all of us treat our electronics like additional limbs." Tate gritted his teeth. Cold air swept over him, and he shivered. Right, he was still in a towel. Though at least he wasn't as hard as he'd been a few minutes ago. "You called for a reason. And it wasn't to get pissy because I complimented your sister." Lys raised her eyebrows, and Tate shrugged. "Why did you call her looking for me?"

"I called her because we're getting a hold of everyone impacted.

All of your crowdfunding sites are running slow, and since you're renting my rack space, I'm an emergency contact."

Fuck. "Let me get home. I'll call you back." Tate disconnected, and tossed Alyssia's phone on her mattress. He raked his fingers through his hair. So much for a morning with no distractions.

TEN

Alyssia didn't know if she was better off or not, only hearing Tate's half the conversation. Her attention drifted between Tate in just a towel, standing in her bedroom doorway, and what he was saying.

He snarled when he tossed her phone back.

So much for extending last night's play time into today. "Bad news?"

"Seems that way. Something's wrong with the crowd-funding sites. I don't have details yet." He raked his gaze over her, exhaled slowly, cheeks puffing and then deflating. "I have to get home. I really wouldn't if I had a choice."

Concern rolled over her disappointment. "My site?"

"All of them. Jared just said running slow. But it was bad enough someone called every emergency number until they got him. I'm sorry, but duty calls."

"If you're working on my stuff, I want to be in on it. Stay here."

"I get the feeling this is a more global thing." His towel slipped lower on his hips, and she couldn't keep her gaze from drifting. The corners of his mouth twitched. "I need to get dressed."

She really didn't want that, but she could compromise. "I guess."

She kept the teasing in her tone. "But do the work here if you can. You've got to remote into the office even if you go home." It wasn't because she hated to see him leave. Not even close. The clench in her gut was completely and totally because the future of her shelter depended on her site working. "I'll grab your phone. Is it really in the car?"

"Probably." He gave her a half smile. "Thanks."

By the time she got back, just a moment or two later, he was already logging into a remote computer. She plugged in his phone and set it on the desk next to him. When he grabbed her wrist, a shock raced over her, sending her earlier desires tumbling through her body.

He spun in the chair, tugged her between his legs, and rested his hands on her hips. "The moment's not ruined, just delayed." With each word, his breath caressed her stomach through her shirt.

She wanted to close her eyes and sink into the moment. Drop onto his lap, and see what they could get up to. That he needed to focus was only one of several reasons that was a bad idea. She stepped out of his grasp before temptation won out. "Jared's waiting for you to call him back."

Disappointment splashed onto Tate's face before vanishing just as quickly, and he turned back to her computer. "Yes, ma'am." He fiddled with his phone.

Seconds later, Jared's voice filtered through the speaker. "What did you do, punch it to ninety to get home so fast?"

"Decided I was too impatient. I'm staying here. What's up?"

TATE FORCED himself to concentrate on the conversation, and not the lingering scent of lilacs that still teased him.

Jared launched into an explanation. "Someone has tweaked your server configuration so you don't have any bandwidth. Mikki is working on it. Second, we had trolls in the comments. Most of them on the shelter's site, but because of the brand, it bled into the other sites as well. We had to shut down comments."

"Mikki's not in my budget." Tate had tried to snag her, but V held onto her top talent.

"Consider it a personal favor." Some of the irritation faded from Jared's voice. "They're Skriddie services, she's Skriddie operations, so we're blurring the line."

Tate smiled, despite the situation. It was nice to have good friends. He needed to make a call on what to do next.

"What kind of comments?" Alyssia asked.

It had been a controversial decision to add comments to the campaigns, but these were meant to be social platforms to show support for the small businesses using them. Letting people interact was meant to show that, knowing they had filters in place on each site, and their assigned community managers kept an eye on what was being said.

"Nothing." Jared's response came too quickly. "Explain again why you're at her place, Tate?"

Tate rolled his eyes at the screen, glad no one was watching. "Are we talking a dozen comments? A hundred?"

"Thousands. They're hidden, but not gone from the back end."

Tate suppressed a roar of frustration. He dialed into the database server. "I'm guessing we can delete them all." Next, he loaded an admin window, and clicked into the comments. He tried not to read the details.

I could never support a shelter that kidnaps people's dogs and refuses to give them back.

What the hell is wrong with you people?

You should all rot in hell, you sick, puppy-killing fucks.

His gut sank with each new note. So much for the issue with Thompson dying quickly and quietly.

"Oh, God." Lys's soft voice dragged his attention from the vitriol. He whirled in his chair to find her leaned against the far wall, raking her fingers through her hair. "This is bad. It's so, so bad. What am I going to do?"

He was on his feet in an instant. He closed the distance between them and rested his hands on her shoulders. "Look at me. It's okay. It'll be okay. We'll fix it."

"Right now, I'm having a hard time believing that." Her voice cracked.

"Fuck. We have another problem." Jared's voice sounded tinny coming from the phone.

Tate glanced over his shoulder at the computer, then back at Lys.

"Take care of it." Resignation hung heavy in her voice.

He kept his voice low. "I'm worried about you. It will wait a minute."

She dragged in a shuddering breath, and broke free of his grasp. "I'm fine." The emotion vanished from her voice.

"Tate." Irritation swelled in Jared's voice.

"Go."

A string of foul words spilled through Tate's head as he sat back in the desk chair. "What?" He couldn't help the occasional glance over his shoulder, at Lys pacing, and tugging at her hair.

"Mikki's doing work on the structure. She says someone's been making manual donation entries in the database. She's only found the one in here so far, but since it's wasn't added by the software, she's concerned there are more hiding out, and it's for a couple hundred dollars. Your development team followed security protocols, right?"

Tate risked one last glance at Alyssia, who had paused, and was watching him, brows knitted together. He didn't want her to hear this. How did they even find that? "Yes, and it's fine."

"It's not fine. It's—"

"It's not an issue." Tate barked. "I know exactly what it is. It's not a security breach." Please don't let him push the matter. Not with Lys listening. Now wasn't when he wanted to explain he'd slipped the manual donation in last night when he'd worked on her site.

"If you say so."

"Positive. Focus on the actual problems." Tate looked behind him again, but the room was empty. An invisible grip tightened around his chest. Nothing to get worked up over. "I thought you plugged all your security holes. Where's this coming from?" The dig wasn't fair, but Tate's frustration wouldn't let him hold it back. Between Jared and Mikki, they'd accounted for so many technical security holes they could fill volumes with the work they'd done. Still, someone had managed to bypass security.

"We did plug the holes. Someone's been screwing with your settings." Jared spilled off a list of details.

Right, the technical stuff. They'd done triage, it was time to step back and fix things more completely. Tate let his thoughts trip through a list of next steps. "I'll get a hold of someone to help with client and user-facing messages. We'll paint a pretty picture. Back in ten."

It was a good excuse to hang up and go check on Lys. Despite his tension, relief tickled his senses when he found her. She was in her bedroom, still completely dressed. Except she'd curled up on top of her comforter and fallen asleep. She snored softly.

Of course. She'd been up all night. He brushed her hair off her face, and the impulse to lean in and kiss her on the cheek raced through him. He banished the desire. That wasn't a casual gesture. It definitely fell outside either facet of their relationship.

After one last, ambivalent gaze in her direction, he pulled a blanket over her, and headed back into her office. He closed both doors, so he wouldn't disturb her.

He made a few calls, found someone on the Skriddie marketing team who didn't mind putting in the extra time—especially with the promise of compensation—and called Jared back. The morning melted into afternoon as they worked through configurations, strategies, handed out assignments, and monitored timelines that only had minutes of leeway depending on the task.

A hand rested on Tate's arm, and he jumped.

"Sorry." Lys's voice was soft enough only he would hear, despite the speakerphone. She set a plastic bag on the desk next to him, Chinese takeout boxes peeked out at him. The heavy scents of citrus, spice, and grease hit him, and his stomach growled in response. Maybe he should have eaten earlier. "I thought you might be hungry."

He put the phone on mute—they were in a lull anyway—and whirled in the chair to face her. "I didn't hear you get up."

"Then you didn't hear me go out, either. I snagged your keys so I could get into your apartment." She held up a second bag, and he realized it had clothes in it. His clothes. She shrugged, playful smile dancing on her face. "Wishful thinking."

The desire he'd squelched earlier rushed back. He stood, tangled his fingers in her hair, and crushed his mouth to hers. She whimpered against his lips and dug her fingers into his shoulders. His pulse roared in his veins, mingling with the desire to press her against the wall and strip her down. He subdued most of the response. "Thank you."

Pink dotted her cheeks. "How's it going?"

"Good. Getting it under control." He traced his thumb over the back of her neck, and twisted a strand of hair around one finger. "Still got a few more hours, though."

She nodded behind her, but didn't break his grip. "I'll be in the living room, watching TV."

"Do we have the new landing page?" Jared asked.

Alyssia shook her head, and stepped out of Tate's reach. "Good luck."

Tate wanted to chase her. He forced himself to unmute his phone instead. "Yeah. ETA to deploy, five minutes." He dove back into the grind, picking at his food, even after it went cold. The light outside faded, and computer clock told him it was after ten when they finally declared the day a success.

"This saved my project, and my ass today," Tate said, as he and Jared wrapped everything up.

"You're welcome. You owe me."

"Bullshit. This is you paying me back for that all-nighter in Vegas." The weekend Jared and Mikki met had led to a major crisis for the company as well. All of them had pulled an all-nighter to bring things back under control.

"Fine." Jared laughed. "You okay to make it home? Sleep in your *own* bed?"

Tate forced himself to ignore the emphasized word. "It's only ten. I'm not an old man. But now that you mention it… the couch here looks pretty comfy." A twinge in his neck reminded him he'd spent last night there, and that might not actually be true. Then again, he'd only slept a few hours, and he'd been hunched over a computer all day.

"I'm glad we got this sorted," Jared said. "And at least as glad you're not serious."

Tate ignored the lack of conviction in his best friend's voice. "Totally. Night, man." He disconnected, and leaned back in the chair. Exhaustion, combined with Jared's half-joke, summoned a doubt Tate had managed to suppress since last night. What was he doing? Carrying on like this wasn't helping either of them. He should have gone home this morning. Or last night. Whatever he was doing with Alyssia wasn't going anywhere. How had he justified it to himself?

So why did knowing that ache in his joints, and rattle uncomfortably in his head?

"How'd it go?" Lys's soft question startled him. "Sorry to interrupt. I heard you hang up."

He whirled to find her standing in the door. The way she leaned against the frame accentuated her lithe figure, and he let his gaze trip over her curves. "It's fixed. We'll put more permanent measures in place on Tuesday."

She hooked her thumbs in the belt loops of her shorts, pulling just low enough to tease. "So what now?"

She wasn't talking about work. He didn't need to clarify with her. That didn't make his answer come any easier, though. He needed to tell her he was leaving. Thank her for everything. Walk out the front door, and dial all the flirting back to zero. The words repeated in his thoughts on fast-forward until they were a scrambled mess of squeals. He was exhausted, still wearing the same clothes he'd been in yesterday, and hadn't had more than four hours of sleep any given night in the last several.

But watching Lys's chest rise and fall with each breath. The way she chewed her bottom lip. The tick of her thumbs against her bare stomach. It sent a new rush of energy through him, and the reminder they had unfinished business from this morning. He crossed the room, and rested a hand at the back of her neck. Lilacs teased him, and her warm skin against his palm jerked his senses to life. He brushed his lips over hers. "I was thinking this time, you join me in the shower."

Tomorrow. He'd walk away tomorrow.

ELEVEN

They shed their clothes quickly between Alyssia's office, and the bathroom. When she bent over to turn on the water, Tate glided a hand up her thigh, and over her ass, cupping the cheek.

She sighed and leaned into him, pressing her bare back against his chest. She wouldn't linger on how right this all felt, just on how good. He drew his palm up her stomach, and between her breasts, though he never touched them. He rested his hand at the base of her neck, and held her tight. Every touch was another claim staked on her skin. Another searing mark holding them together.

He drew back the shower curtain and nudged her into the tub. Seconds later, he stood behind her again, as the hot water sluiced over them. She reached behind her to grab the hard length pressing into her butt.

He grabbed her wrist with a, "Tsk," and then kissed up the side of her neck, lips vibrating against her skin. "Patience."

She ground against him, satisfied when his erection jerked in response. "I'll try."

He reached over her shoulder, grabbed the body wash, and poured a generous dollop into his hand before setting the bottle back on its shelf. A shock of cold raced over her when he rested his hand on her stomach again, and she squeaked.

"Sorry." He sounded anything but. "I guess we need to warm it up." He drew his palms over her skin. Up her chest, down her thighs, everywhere but the bits of her aching to be touched. She gasped when he trailed along the back of her legs, behind the knees, and groaned when he slipped over the insides of her wrists. With her entire body begging to be touched, new erogenous zones spread everywhere. She cried out when he finally cupped her breasts, and a new spark of pleasure filled her.

"God, I love your tits." His grip slid over her skin. "Gorgeous, pink nipples. Perky." He squeezed, and she squirmed in pleasure. "Sensitive." He kept one hand on her chest, and the other slipped lower. "But this." He pushed between her folds. "What do you sound like when you're not worried about someone hearing you scream when you come?"

She swayed her hips against his touch. "You're welcome to find out."

He pulled away from her clit. "I was hoping you'd say that." He moved both hands to cup her ass, and slid a finger between her thighs. Soap slithered down her skin, pooled at her feet, and then washed down the drain.

He reached over her, and grabbed the shower head. "I've always wondered, if you get the full enjoyment out of this."

Embarrassment and a new level of arousal pulsed between her legs. She fought the desire to confess he was frequently the focus of those fantasies. "I might."

He moved the head along her skin, letting the water flow over her, and rinse away the soap. He nudged one of her legs forward with his knee, and brought the shower head to rest between her thighs. "God, I'd like to watch that sometime."

The idea of putting on a show for Tate pooled in her belly, tugging at some of her more vivid fantasies of him walking in on her. With the water pounding against her clit, his other hand still sliding between her legs from behind, and the vivid pictures in her mind, orgasm threatened her senses.

He pulled away before she climaxed. "Not yet." He whispered.

She liked this teasing. She took the showerhead from him, replaced it, and filled her own palm with soap. "Your turn." She whirled to face him.

He raised his brows. "What did you have in mind?"

"It's a shower. So, getting clean." She tried to repeat what he'd done just a few moments ago. Soaping over his chest, up his legs, everywhere but his stiff shaft.

He leaned a hand on the tile, and lowered his head until his forehead met hers. "You're killing me, Lys. I need your hands wrapped around my cock."

His groan when she obliged tickled all her senses. She kept her grip loose, stroking slowly, deliberately, sliding over every inch of his member. He lifted her chin, and crushed his lips to hers, devouring her. Driving the kiss through her. He broke away, and held her gaze. "Turn around."

"I don't—"

"Turn around." He emphasized each word.

A pleasant shudder filled her at the command in his voice, and she spun away from him. He placed his hand between her shoulder blades, and pushed. She took the hint, bending at the waist, and pressed her hand against the edge of the tub for support.

"I can't behave around you." The head of his cock slid down the crack of her ass, then nudged her pussy. She let out a loud cry when he thrust inside without any further fanfare. "Fuck, you're so tight. So slippery." His words were punctuated by groans.

He gripped her hips, fingers digging into the skin, leaving more invisible marks. Each time he pounded against her, he hit something inside. Striking the pleasure spot hard, fast, and frantic. The orgasm she'd been drawn back from rushed forward again, and she teetered on the edge.

His other hand reached around her. When he bumped her clit, climax washed away her thoughts. It rushed over her, and penetrated every inch of her mind and body. She lost herself in the hard grinding from behind, and was only vaguely aware of him coming. Grunting and filling her.

Her senses slowly drifted back in, and her legs wobbled. He helped her stand, and pulled her back into him again.

He wrapped his arms around her, and kissed her neck. "Dirtiest shower I've ever had."

She chuckled, and pulled his arms tighter, sinking into the embrace. Burning the moment into her memories.

When they caught their breath, they finished showering. This time Tate was tender as he rinsed her off, and she returned the favor. They toweled off, and she led him back into the bedroom.

He tugged her into the bed, wrapped himself around her, and pulled the blanket over them both. He didn't speak, and she didn't dare shatter the moment by saying anything. If she could only have him for right now, she was going to enjoy the moment for all it was worth. Tomorrow, when he had to leave, she'd deal with that. Right now, he was still here.

TATE EXTRACTED himself from Lys's sleeping form. She frowned in her sleep and rolled over. An ache spread inside him, knowing that he had to walk away. Which was exactly the reason he needed to leave. He shouldn't have mixed business with pleasure. He gave her one last look, resisted the urge to lean in and kiss her on the forehead, and padded into the other room for the change of clothes she'd brought him.

His brows rose, and curiosity tickled his senses when he saw what she'd grabbed. On weekends—those he wasn't working anyway—he was a board shorts and T-shirt kind of guy. She'd grabbed him a pair of jeans, and a black and white button-down shirt with a dragon wrapped around the back and shoulders. He'd completely forgotten he had it. Vivian had given it to him as a gag gift.

And it planted a tiny, rebellious idea in his head for tomorrow, at his parents' Memorial Day barbeque. He finished dressing, left Lys a note thanking her for everything—but not saying anything else—and locked the door behind him on his way out.

It was best this way. For her, probably for him, and for the lucky, future Mister Alyssia Tippins.

ALYSSIA SHUFFLED through her town house, operating on autopilot. Her brain was spinning to grasp a thought, a feeling, or something just out of her reach. Waking up alone in bed left her conflicted. It wasn't a new thing, or an unexpected one, but it still drilled an empty pit into her thoughts.

She poured herself a glass of juice, struggling to make sense of what was going on in her head. This was who Tate was. For as long as she could remember, even being a girl and playing house. At the time his actions had just been those of a stupid boy who thought he was smarter than her because he was older. He'd always boasted that he was never having a wife, or a family, and that house was a dumb game for kids who thought cartoons were real life.

Even though his delivery had changed, his views hadn't much. In fact, she'd never seen Tate *date* anyone. He occasionally made a tabloid page, if he hooked up with the right celebrity, but he didn't do repeats. He was adamant about that.

Someone knocked on her front door and hope surged inside. She beat it back. It wasn't going to be Tate. What was wrong with her? She was sucking big time at this staying detached thing. She forced herself to walk at a normal pace to see who it was. Despite her mental insistence, disappointment flooded her when she saw a stranger on the other side of the peephole. She opened the door.

The guy looked up from his clipboard. "I'm looking for Lisa Tippins."

"Alyssia." She corrected him without thought. Years ago, the mistake bothered her. She was used to it now."

He handed her a stack of stapled, folded papers. "You're named as the defendant in the case of Bryce Thompson versus Alyssia Tippins and the Great 'n' Small Animal Shelter. Have a nice day."

"Thank you…" She trailed off when he turned away before she finished. His words sank in, and bile rose in her throat. Thompson was suing her now? Crap. She unfolded the complaint and scanned it. So much legalese. His lawyers probably made more writing this letter than she did in a week. Her insides knotted themselves until she couldn't breathe. She plopped into the middle of the floor, and folded her legs underneath herself. Calm down. She needed to calm down.

When the spots stopped dancing in front of her eyes, she read the letter again. It was so wordy, but as far as she could tell, he was suing her for keeping the dog after he'd brought it in for standard care, and for the slander and harassment that accompanied her calling the cops on his son.

Fuck, this was so bad. She needed help. The lawyer she kept on retainer would charge extra for a Sunday call. What was she going to do? She forced herself to her feet, and found her phone in the bedroom, on the nightstand. Her fingers were pulling up a phone number before she registered whose it was. She paused, thumb hovering over the *Dial* button, then cleared Tate's number from the screen. What was he going to do? It didn't make sense to call Jared, either. He'd be concerned, but it wasn't like he could do any more than tell her to call her attorney.

Her fingers twitched against her phone, tapping the plastic frame. What was she supposed to do? She couldn't just sit around. Waiting would devour her. She'd go to the office, catch up on some paperwork. Her mind whirred over the situation as she drove. Painting possible outcomes, making each scenario worse. Could she lose the shelter over this? What if the crowd-funding didn't pan out? What would happen to all the animals? She needed to update her list of where she could send them. What if the other local shelters didn't have room?

By the time she turned down the street for the shelter, her thoughts ran rampant, throbbing against her skull. Beating out a merciless rhythm. Her world darkened several more shades when the shelter came into view. Five people stood on the sidewalk outside the fence, holding signs.

Puppy-napper

Animal abusers like you should rot in hell

She forced herself to look away, and ignored their shouts and waved fists as she pulled into the parking lot. Fortunately, no one was near the back employee entrance.

Fuck. What was she going to do now? She settled into her desk, mind working at high speed for a solution. She needed to reply publicly. Regardless of what Tate said, these people had seen the shelter on TV, and that's where she needed to make sure people saw her rebuttal. She dialed Sara's extension. If her assistant wasn't in, she'd leave her a message.

Alyssia was surprised when she answered on the first ring. "Hey." Sara's cheery tone was strained. "I didn't think you were in today."

"Same for you." The small crowd outside must be impacting everyone. Of course, that made sense. Her employees were as dedicated to the shelter as she was. "I was just going to leave you a message, but since you're here… on Tuesday, will you call up the TV station, the same one that ran the piece on us last week, and tell them I'd like to talk to them. Clear things up?" There, that wasn't so hard.

"Actually, funny you should mention that." Sara's laugh sounded forced. "I just got off the phone with them about half an hour ago. They want the same thing, sooner rather than later, so they can air it on Wednesday night."

"That's great. Isn't it?" She didn't know if she was asking Sara, or herself.

"It seems like it, right?"

"Absolutely." Alyssia forced herself to smile, and hoped it would reflect over the line. "Tell them I'll make time, whenever they'd like between now and then." She exchanged a few more words about work and life with Sara, and then disconnected. That had gone easier than she thought. So why was her gut souring at the thought of doing the interview?

TWELVE

Every fucking year. Tate grabbed his ticket from the valet and made his way into the country clubhouse. He still didn't know why his parents threw this party every fucking year. He'd stopped attending in college. They invited so many people—neighbors, friends, upper and middle management from Skriddie—at the time he'd wondered what he was supposed to get out of the whole event. He'd figured it out since. It was about the networking, the meeting people, and if he managed to find the right people, enjoying Memorial Day.

He cut straight for the bar, made eye contact with the guy pouring drinks, and smiled. "Hey, man. How's it going? I'm Tate." He extended his hand.

"Gary." The bartender returned the handshake. "What can I get you?"

Tate's smile grew, and he leaned against the bar. One of the things he'd figured out was finding the right people meant being in the right place. "Whatever you're making today, I'll pay you that much more to let me slide back there and serve drinks."

Gary shook his head, easy expression never fading. "No can do.

Sorry, man. I was told whatever you offered, they'd double it if I didn't let you back here."

Tate hid his irritation. Avenue number one for enjoying his afternoon, blocked by the woman in charge. One thing he enjoyed about any gathering was taking a spot behind the bar, and getting to know people that way. "They?"

Gary grabbed a glass, and polished an invisible spot. "My employers for the day."

"Right." Yup. His mother wanted him mingling, not doing *common work*. Might as well make sure the bartender made some cash for the day and strap Marge's wallet at the same time. Tate counted five one-hundred dollar bills from his billfold, and laid them on the bar top. "Keep this, and stay behind the bar. Tell Marge Foster that's how much I offered you to let me back there. Don't tell her you took my money."

"I… you're kidding, right?"

Tate nudged the bills closer to Gary. "Not at all. Enjoy the party, man." Time to search out avenue number two. Something in his chest twinged, and he breathed deep to force it away. This was nothing. There was no reason to feel bad about plan B for keeping himself occupied during this party. He scanned the room, and then outside, on the sweeping lawn. There. The redhead keeping an eye on the buffet table. Several inches shorter than he was, at least from this distance, with full curves that filled out her white polo shirt and black slacks gorgeously.

Perfect distraction for the next few hours, and great way to remind himself the weekend spent with Lys was strictly a casual thing. Her name filled his head with memories of her moans, the scent of lilac, her smooth skin pressed against his, the way she squirmed when he touched her in the right places.

He dragged in another shaky breath. That wasn't a great path to wander down. Except his racing pulse said it was a fantastic place to let his thoughts linger. He stepped out of the flow of people, and leaned against a nearby wall. He should have had Gary pour him a drink while he was at the bar.

A movement caught his attention. His mother, standing all but nose-to-nose with Bryce Thompson, laughing, and running her tongue along her upper lip. His stomach churned at the sight. They could at least try to keep that private. He forced his gaze away.

He spotted a few familiar faces in the crowd, and wove through the small clusters of chatters. Lys and Jared's parents. "Holly. Robert." He held his arms out.

"You look beautiful, as always." He gave Holly a quick hug, and peck on the cheek. She did, too. An older version of Alyssia, gray around the temples, but still with a smile for everyone. "Sir." He clasped Robert's hand and pulled him into a quick hug as well.

"You look tired." Holly's voice was lined with concern. "You're working too hard."

The genuine tone warmed Tate. "I do what the job requires." The Tippins were more like his parents than his own folks. Growing up, they'd always welcomed him at home, and treated him as well as they had their own children. Sometimes he envied Robert and Holly's relationship, but they had one of those happily ever afters that only existed in fairy tales. The lucky one in a million. And a great reminder of what Lys deserved that he couldn't offer. "How are you both doing?"

"Wishing retirement weren't so far off." Robert chuckled.

They chatted for several more minutes, before someone else called them away. As they headed off, Holly hung back. She tugged Tate aside, voice low enough he barely made out her words above the din. "Don't let them drive you into the ground. I mean it. Take care of yourself."

"Thanks." He squeezed her hand. "I'll do my best."

Time to make the rounds, meet some people, have some fun.

"What are you wearing?" A familiar voice clawed its way under his good mood.

He froze a pleasant expression in place, and spun. "Mother. I was wondering if you'd pull yourself away from Mr. Thompson long enough to say hello."

She pointed a glare at his shirt. "Did you forget to have someone pick up your laundry? Oh, for heaven's sake. What's she doing here?"

He followed his mother's gaze back to the clubhouse, and his mind checked out. Lys stood in the doorway, blue sundress stark against her pale skin, and hugging every inch of her figure. It ended a few inches above her knees, leaving her long legs on display. He struggled to pull his attention away. It was a good question, though. Her parents still came to these parties because they were friends of the family. Jared showed up because it was a work thing. But Lys... She could have opted out ages ago. Yet he couldn't remember a single year he hadn't seen her there. "I have people to talk with." He stepped in her direction.

"Yes, you do." His mother grabbed his sleeve, and redirected him. "I want you to meet someone."

A snarl bubbled in his throat, but he followed where she was pointing. And then looked again. "Who's that?"

"The young woman over there." She nodded at a girl standing just a few feet away.

Tate raised his brows. "Is she even legal?"

"She'll be twenty this fall." Marge pulled him toward the girl. "She's the Senator's daughter, and she's dying to meet you."

"She's still a kid."

"When you wait as long as you have to get married, you can't be picky." She pasted on a plastic smile as they drew within earshot. "Bonnie. This is Tate."

Irritation bubbled inside. Bonnie didn't deserve his wrath, but so help him he wanted to ask his mother why she kept doing shit like this. God, it was going to be a long day.

———

Lys wandered through the clubhouse, making sure she made eye contact, smiling at anyone who noticed her, and trying to keep her expression friendly. Why did she keeping coming to this thing? She should be at the shelter, catching up on work.

It had been too good a chance to pass up, though. She'd always gotten along with the guests in the past, and had several of them tell her if she ever needed any help...

This was her opportunity to mingle, shake hands, and maybe let it slip that her shelter was raising donations to buy the building they were in. Except every time she told herself that was her goal, her gut churned in nervous protest. Networking wasn't her thing. Tate was good at it.

His name added a new edge to her apprehension. She hadn't heard from him since the note he left Sunday morning. Not that she should expect to. It wasn't like he called her every day, normally. This was just how things were.

She tugged down the skirt of her dress, and scanned the crowds. So why couldn't she stop searching for his face?

Her gaze landed on someone else instead, and acid rose in her throat. Bryce Thompson Jr., taking pictures of something with his phone. She wasn't sure what. One of the girls serving drinks, possibly. Or the food. Or… she didn't even want to know. She turned her attention back anything else. Keeping her distance from him would be important today.

She found Tate, and her heart sank. He stood next to his mother, chatting up a girl who was smiling as if she'd just won the lottery. She'd giggle, and then rest her hand on Tate's arm. Twirl her hair around her finger. Lean in closer.

If she got close enough, would she see the lines around Tate's eyes that always appeared when he was wearing a mask? Or would she see the genuine expression he wore when he was picking someone up? The same look he'd had with her the night before.

Why had she thought that? Damn it. She turned back into the clubhouse, and headed for the bar. Maybe a drink would help her relax. Or she could go hunt down Jared and Mikki. Mikki's tactics for meeting people tended to be more blunt that Tate's, but she still had a gift for it.

Alyssia ordered a glass of white wine, and wandered back into the gardens. So many people wearing so many masks. This was why she liked animals. They were sweet, and accepting, and non-judgmental, and totally not intimidating.

The longer she studied the crowds, the further she drifted from them, until she lingered in a corner. The din drifted toward her, but no longer so loud it kept her from being able to think. Why had she even come to this party?

"Hey." A rough voice assaulted her ears, and she looked up to see Bryce Jr. approaching. "You're that bitch who stole my dog.

Her lungs squeezed and she forced herself to draw a breath. She stepped to the side, to move around him. "I need to see someone. They're waiting right over there." She nodded at the general area behind him.

"Not until we're done." He blocked her path. Every time he breathed on her, the stench of alcohol assaulted her senses. Who the hell had given him a drink? Though he was only seventeen, he was at least six inches taller than her, and twice as wide in the shoulders. He poked a finger in her chest, and her breastbone winced both in pain and panic. "You're going down. You know that, right?"

"Bryce, buddy." Tate's voice cut through her spiraling panic. Bryce whirled. In a single motion, Tate grabbed his hand in what looked like a friendly grip—except Alyssia saw Tate's knuckles pale —and pushed the younger man out of her path. "I've been looking for you."

"Let go of me, queer-boy." Bryce jerked out of his grip with a growl.

Tate's smile never wavered, but Alyssia had never seen him show so many teeth. "Tell you what." The pleasantness vanished from his voice. "Why don't you walk away now, and go check out the banquet table."

Bryce stepped closer to Tate. "Why don't you leave and let me talk to the bitch?"

Tate growled, and faster than Alyssia could blink, his forearm was pressed to Bryce's throat, and he had the boy pinned to the wall. "Leave. Or I stop asking nicely."

Bryce choked out a response that might have been, "Fuck you." Tate pushed harder.

"Is everything all right?" Marge Foster joined the group.

Alyssia's head spun, and her pulse hammered in her throat. Why was her quiet corner suddenly the highest traffic area in the clubhouse?

"Everything's fine." Tate stepped back, and his expression went flat. No smile, no frown, just a blank mask. He straightened his clothes with a single shrug, and wrapped his arm around Alyssia's waist. The shock of his touch overloaded her already crowded thoughts, and she struggled with the desire to lean into him. She wasn't a helpless damsel in distress. Except right now she felt like one, and she wasn't sure she minded the possession Tate's grip conveyed.

"I was just walking Ms. Tippins to her car." Tate steered her around his mother and Bryce without hesitation. "Keep walking. Don't look at anyone." His voice was low, meant only for her ears.

He didn't say another word on the short journey to the valet, and she wasn't sure if she could manage any of her own. His flat mask never wavered. He waited by her side while the hop fetched her car, and walked her to the driver's door.

"Thank you." She managed the soft words as she slid into the vehicle.

He clenched his jaw. "Don't worry about it." Why wouldn't he look at her?

"Are you all right?"

"I'm good. You should probably get home."

She didn't like this. Cold, removed. Tate had never been like that with her. Awkward was one thing, but this cut deep, leaving gashes in her thoughts. She couldn't help trying one more time. "Are you sticking around? We could go somewhere. Hang out."

A tremor ran through the car, and she realized he was clutching the door so hard his fingers shook. He finally looked at her, and the dark cloud in his gaze dug deeper than his indifference. "Go home, Alyssia. Or, somewhere else. Just…" He inhaled through his nose. "Go."

Her full name. She forced herself to smile, despite the tears stinging her eyes. At least he was cutting her off fast and completely. No false hope or anything there. "Right. See you around. Or not."

She yanked her door shut before she could discover if he had a response. And tossed the car into gear. It was better this way. He probably knew that. She just had to convince her own heart of it.

THIRTEEN

Tate gripped the steering wheel so hard his wrists ached. He focused on the road, and struggled to clear all the thoughts from his head. He shouldn't have gone to his parent's barbeque—the entire thing was a disaster. That girl his mother tried to hook him up with. Bryce Jr.

Alyssia. Every time her name danced through his thoughts, his pulse kicked back up, and his frustration poured in. He'd wanted to brain Bryce for cornering her. That was bad enough. But when Tate had wrapped his arm around her waist, to lead her away. The light sag against him. The hint of her weight pressing into his body.

It had taken what little control he had left not to drag her into a bathroom, lift her onto a sink, and push her skirt up to see if she was wearing anything underneath.

Except that wasn't right. He didn't want to do that there. In that horrid place filled with bad memories. He'd wanted to take her back to his place, because what they did together wasn't anyone's business but his and hers.

And when she'd turned that hurt gaze on him, next to her car. He'd almost caved. Been seconds from tossing restraint aside. The only thing that kept him from acting on the impulse was knowing he'd hold her back. The longer they pretended to be anything more than casual acquaintances, the less likely that she'd find the guy she actually deserved.

"FUCK!" He pounded the steering wheel until it creaked. He forced himself to breathe. Inhale and exhale one, two, three times.

His phone rang, and he ignored it. He couldn't get home soon enough. Even if, for reasons he couldn't explain, he was dreading going back to his own house for the first time ever. Home was sanctuary. He was in control there. But now, it was a looming, empty box.

Damn it.

TATE WAS PRETTY sure he'd never been more relieved to see a weekend come to a close. Tuesday morning was his new savior. Work was safe. He'd dive into his never ending task list and lose himself in everything he needed to do. Check on all the other crowd-funding sites, make sure they were all online, touch base with his sales team.

Today would be better than yesterday. It didn't have much of a choice.

His phone rang, and he clicked the speaker button without looking. "Yeah."

"Mr. Foster is here to see you." Alan's voice had a more formal tone than Tate was used to. Then again, it would make sense, if the company CEO was standing next to his desk.

Fortunately, Tate wasn't quite so worried about what the man thought of him. His dad didn't expect the same formality at work as his mother did. "Send him in." He looked up at the snick of his office door opening, and nodded at the chair across from his desk. "Dad."

His father closed the door, and Tate's suspicion spiked. Ben Foster took a seat, rested one ankle on the other knee, and intertwined his fingers. Tate could almost hear the seconds ticking away as he waited. The silence dragged on.

Tate suppressed a sigh. "What can I do for you?"

Ben clenched his jaw, and his gaze narrowed. "The waitresses? That's fine. I don't know if you're just trying to piss off your mother, or you genuinely like those girls, but I don't care as long as you're all having fun."

That was new. Tate waited for him to continue, despite the dread building inside. "And?"

"But you can't mix business with pleasure. Ever."

Tate choked back a retort about hypocrisy. "Great advice. Thanks." He almost managed to keep the sarcasm from his voice.

Ben drummed his fingers on his leg. "Get it out of your system now. Whatever issues you've got with my advice. Work through this, and reconsider what a stupid idea it was for you to sleep with a client."

Tate raised an eyebrow. There was no way his dad knew about that. He was shooting in the dark. He opened his mouth to ask what the man was talking about.

"Everyone." Ben cut him off before he made a sound. "Your mother, the club staff, the maids at the house—know the Tippins girl has got it bad for you. That's fine. Kids outgrow crushes, she will too someday. But that display of yours yesterday? My money says you're taking advantage of the situation. Don't. I don't care if you are already, or are just thinking about it. Stop now, and put the idea out of your head. At least while she's one of our clients. After her contract is up, I don't care what you do to her."

Tate choked on an angry retort. Taking advantage of...? Realization spread through him. Was he? He knew how Lys felt. Was he really using her? The idea sat heavy in his gut, and gnawed at his thoughts. "Nothing's happening. I know better than that. Not that it's anyone's business."

"It is, though." Ben stood. "It's my business, because it's my company."

"Really?" Tate's irritation slipped out before he considered where he was going with it. But once the word was out there, he knew exactly what he wanted to say. "You're going to come in here —you of all people—and tell me not to mix my business and personal lives? Insult Alyssia Tippins for some imagined slight, when you're guilty of the ultimate blend of company and home?"

"Excuse me?"

He didn't have these arguments with his father, because normally, the older man didn't push those buttons. But he certainly couldn't talk about it with his mother. She'd gloss over it, tell him she was right and he was wrong, and brush him off. "You're going to tell me business and pleasure don't mix when that's the entire foundation of your marriage? A contract that makes sure you both get what you want in the boardroom, and doesn't care what you do in the bedroom, as long as the world sees you as a happy couple?"

Ben knitted his brows together, and let out a long breath of air. "Do as I say, not as I do. I'd hoped you would turn out better than we did."

"I didn't mean to." The answer snapped something inside Tate. A frustration crumbling over a week-long, emotionally exhausting journey. One of Tate's driving goals had always been to keep his personal life separate. Why had he let this happen?

A frown settled onto Ben's face. "Then you already know what I'm about to say. This entire affair. The issues with the Thompson's dog, the struggling animal shelter. It's gotten too personal for you. I know you and Marge are both stubborn, and that neither of you wants to back down from this."

He met Tate's gaze, eyes soft and sad. "But you're smarter than that. You know what decisions you need to make for the business. If I didn't trust you with that, you wouldn't be in the position you're in, and you wouldn't have gotten the sign off on this project."

Tate didn't know what was worse—the accusations based on a truth he didn't want to recognize, or the underlying hint of 'don't disappoint me' in his father's voice. He didn't bother with a smile, he just turned back to his computer. "Don't worry. I know what I'm doing."

"Make sure that's true." Ben walked out and pulled the door shut behind him.

Tate tried to throw himself back into work. To immerse himself in the onslaught. But his father's words echoed in his head, jumbled and cluttered and trying to grasp at thoughts just out of his reach. About Lys, about the choices he was making.

The one thing he refused to acknowledge though, was the unspoken implication he needed to cut the shelter from the crowd-funding pilot group. That was the last thing he would do.

FOURTEEN

Alyssia padded from one end of her office to the other, then
spun and retraced her steps. Her bare feet slapped against the cool
tile. She'd stashed her heels under her desk until she really needed to
wear them. They weren't conducive to pacing. She paused in front
of the full-length mirror on the back of her office door. The skirt
and jacket outfit were conservative, and professional looking. The
perfect thing to wear in front of a camera, and tell the local news
that her shelter was a good thing, instead of the spawn of some
greater demon of the billionth plane of hell.

She straightened her shirt, and pushed a strand of hair back into
her braid. Crap, maybe she should have worn her scrubs instead.
Something that made it clear she was a doctor, and not just a girl
playing a part. She squeezed her fingers together and then relaxed
them. Right now she felt like a girl playing a part. This had to go
well. The group of picketers outside was growing larger, instead of
shrinking, and her time was running out to raise the money to keep
the building.

Her phone rang, and Sara's voice followed. "Your visitors are
here."

"I'll be right there." Too late to change now. Alyssia took a deep breath, and opened the door.

The interviewer gave her a warm smile, and introduced her to the small crew. Alyssia's tension ebbed as the afternoon progressed. They chatted, it was friendly, no invasive questions asked—not really. The closest it came was asking for her side of the story when it came to the Thompson's dog. She told them what she was allowed based on the pending criminal case. That the dog had come in injured, and they'd treated him, and were holding him until he found a fitting home.

She walked through the kennels with the cameraman, let a few dogs out to play.

Almost two hours later, when she saw the news crew to the front door, Alyssia felt better about the situation than she had since that horrible news story almost a week ago. Time to change in to her scrubs and get some work done.

She strolled toward the back rooms, and a jarring crash spilled through the room. Her heart jumped into her throat, and she spun before her brain registered it was the sound of shattering glass. A large rock—twice as big as her fist at least—sat in the middle of the lobby. Fortunately the window was tempered, so most of it had rained straight down, but small shards had escaped, and littered the room.

Chants and cheers flowed in from the picketers outside. Alyssia forced her racing heart to slow. "Sara, call the police." There wasn't anyone in the waiting room besides staff—a fact she'd hated a few hours ago but was grateful for now. "Ricco, will you grab the broom? I need to change. Give me just a few and I'll help you clean up."

While she was changing, she grabbed her phone. Her thumb hesitated over Tate's number. What was he going to do? She pushed the bitter longing aside, and dialed Robert Tippins instead. "Hey, Dad. I know it's after eight, I'm sorry. But I need to board up a window at the shelter, and we don't have tools here, can you help?"

"A window? What's going on? Are you all right?"

She winced and held the phone from her ear. "I'm fine, Daddy. You still have some plywood from the remodel, right?"

"Of course, hon. I'll be right there."

She disconnected, and tossed the device back on her desk. A sob bubbled inside her, and she forced it aside. She wouldn't panic. She could handle this. Helping Ricco sweep up glass, talking to the police, making sure the window was secure once her dad got there, all of it kept her mind occupied.

When they left, her mind turned on her. Running rampant and taunting her with every fear and worry she'd swallowed that afternoon and evening. She gave Sara a weak smile, shuffled into her office, and collapsed into her chair. What was she going to do? The news interview better work out for her tomorrow. Something needed to go right.

Her fingers twitched toward her cell phone. *Call Tate*, chanted in her head. That wasn't an option. Not until she knew she could handle herself around him without caving again. She needed to get to work, instead. Bury herself in the job, and her mind would do what it needed to, just like cleaning up the mess in the lobby.

She pulled up the crowd-funding admin page. Donations spilled in slowly. A couple a day, but nowhere near what they'd need to meet their goal before their deadline. The largest donation—the anonymous one that had come in first—still sat at the top of the page. Taunting her. Something clicked in her thoughts as she studied the number. Something Jared had said the other day? Mikki had discovered…

She couldn't grasp the idea. It would come to her. Right now, she needed to concentrate on work, and not losing the shelter. The rest could wait.

TATE HAD a love hate relationship with short work weeks. On the one hand, taking Monday off meant all the good, obvious things like extra time away from work. On the other hand, it also meant five days of work compressed into four, and always feeling like he was a day behind. He scanned the messages waiting for him when he got into the office Wednesday morning. His eyes grew wide when he saw the newsletter from NetSafe Systems. He subscribed to all manner of industry mailing lists as part of his job, so getting the email wasn't the surprise. It was the content. *NetSafe Systems announces their newest offering—crowd-funding for your small business!*

Tate's irritation grew as he read the rest of the promo. Most of it was standard hype. It was the mentions of heightened security, twenty-four-seven community managers, and a fool-proof comment system. On top of all that, this was the first he'd heard of it.

He clenched his fist, glaring at the screen. He'd expected them to compete, it was what they did. The phrasing in the message gnawed at him, though. Heightened security. The phrase repeated in his thoughts.

Fuck. Time to take a stroll. Seconds later he stood a few doors down, in front of Vivian's office. She looked up at the knock, and gave him a half smile. "What's up?"

He took the chair across from her desk, pulled up the message on his phone, and slid it across to her. "What do you think?"

As she scanned, her lips drew into a thin line. She handed the device back to him. "So they already know what happened to you on Saturday."

"I assume. So much for non-disclosure agreements, right?" His question was flat.

"They could have seen the issues. All your sites were dragging."

Tate spit out his theory. "Could have seen, may have caused..."

She pinched the bridge of her nose. "Childish, unethical assholes," she muttered, and dialed a number on her desk phone.

"Yup?" Mikki answered.

Tate leaned in to speak. "The slowdown on Saturday. Can you take another look and see if there's anything suspicious about it."

"There was." Mikki's answer came too quickly. "Someone tried to take a bunch of websites offline that weren't doing anything but sitting out there all happy and boring like."

Tate might have laughed at the dry retort, if his suspicion and concern weren't mounting. "We're looking for more than that. A fingerprint."

"Give me ten." Mikki disconnected.

Tate leaned back in the chair, closed his eyes, and rubbed his forehead. He didn't do spite, but he still hoped if NSS was behind this, they'd left an ugly trail. Something else to crucify them with, in the upcoming civil case.

"Did you end things yet?" V asked.

Of course. She was back on the conversation from lunch last week with Lys. The last person he needed to be thinking about, and the one name constantly lingering at the back of his mind. Acknowledging her name sent a flood of memories through his thoughts, teasing him. He straightened, and met her gaze. "Pretty sure it's none of your business. But yes."

"No need to get defensive. I just missed seeing you both at the party on Monday." She said it so simply, as if it were the most innocent question ever.

"I couldn't tell you where she was." He couldn't say her name. Her voice in his head was already wreaking havoc on his senses. And it was true, he didn't know where she'd gone after she left the country club, though he still wished he could have gone with her.

Instead of replying, V looked over his shoulder, eyes focusing on something behind him.

Seconds later, Mikki claimed the chair next to him. "It's not what you think, but it is a good thing you had me look. Someone is screwing with your config, and they did it again today. Your bandwidth has been severely limited."

That didn't make sense. Tate mulled over the comment. "Someone is intentionally going in there and slowing my sites down. Over and over?"

Mikki nodded. "They've tweaked the work we did over the weekend, not as thoroughly as before, but someone's restricted access for your clients."

"Fantastic." Sarcasm dripped from Tate's voice. "Like, who?"

Mikki quirked her mouth to the side, and shrugged. "One of Jared's people. Whoever's got access to your servers, which is all of them. I'd ask if you pissed off upper management, but since you are…"

Could Marge be choking his sites, to force the crowdfunding site to fail? The thought surged into Tate's head, sounding absolutely ludicrous. This was still business, and even if she didn't like the idea, it was still surging toward successful, despite the problems.

"Do you want more?" Mikki asked.

V looked at Tate, apology in her eyes. "I'm sorry. After hours, maybe, but she's got her own work to do."

"I get it; it's fine. Thanks for looking." Tate sank lower in his seat. He needed to get to the bottom of this.

The moment Mikki was gone, V turned back to Tate. "Look, I know Alyssia is everyone's favorite baby sister. But this is business, and you need to consider shutting her down."

Tate was getting sick of hearing that. "It's not just business." The retort came out sharper than he intended. He needed to dial it back.

"It should be."

Tate rolled his eyes. "That's not what I mean. She's running an animal shelter, and they do good things. This isn't just about a bottom line. What about all those animals?"

"I'm not heartless." Vivian's expression softened. "I'll write them a check. I'm surprised you haven't done the same."

"She won't take my money. I'd fund the entire operation if I could."

Vivian raised her brows. "Strictly for the puppies?"

"Of course."

"If she won't take a perfectly legitimate donation, maybe Alyssia's the problem. I hate to say that, and I know you don't want to hear it. But if you do this emotionally, people are going to get fucked."

Tate dug his fingers into his leg, and squeezed in frustration. V was wrong. He knew it. He just couldn't figure out what was right.

FIFTEEN

When Tate stepped through the front door to the shelter, a painful sense of déjà vu washed over him. He shook his head to clear out the thought. The boarded up window already had his anxiety cranked to max. He'd been out since after lunch, dropping off paperwork with all their crowd-funding site pilot groups, and the shelter was last on his list. Because Lys's shift didn't start until later, of course. No other reason.

Sara's smile looked forced when she glanced up from her computer. "You might not want to go back there."

He nodded at the window. "Something I should know first?"

"That was a rock last night. Our friendly neighborhood picketers." Her usually chipper tone was flat. "But that's not the problem."

"Okay?"

"She did a rebuttal piece with the news station last night. It aired about ten minutes ago."

An invisible hand clenched around Tate's chest. "Do I want details?"

Sara just shook her head. "I heard some kind of primal-scream-type yelling. She's not answering her phone, and when I tried to check on her, she told me to go away. You should probably check on her."

Tate was already moving toward Alyssia's office, adrenaline pumping through him at a painful clip. She didn't look up when he stepped inside and closed the door behind him. Her attention was on her feet, as she traveled from one end of the office to the other, and then back.

Every impulse he'd struggled to suppress since Monday. The desire to protect her, to keep her safe, to wrap her up and never let go, flooded through him. "Lys."

She jumped and whirled to face him. Her eyes narrowed. "What?"

Not the reception he'd expected, but it was fair, all things considered. "Are you all right?"

Her laugh was bitter and sharp. "Your powers of perception are slipping if you don't already know the answer to that." She shook her head and resumed pacing. "But since it's not obvious, no. I'm not fucking all right."

Anger. He could deal with that. It meant she'd talk, and he could find a solution. "Fill me in."

"Is there something about me that screams stupid? Or gullible?"

"Absolutely not."

She finally looked him the eye. "In that case, tell me something, and be honest."

"Of course." He was losing control of the conversation, and he didn't like that. But he couldn't think of any alternative but to go along with things until he uncovered more of the situation.

"Did Sara tell you what was going on?"

The question was too easy. That couldn't be where things were going. "She gave me a brief run-down. I figured I'd get details from you."

"How many times since you walked in the front door have you told yourself you'd fix this?" Her lips twisted in irritated amusement. "How many different ways are you thinking *you'll* make this better?"

Tate didn't know what bothered him more—that she'd crawled

into his head and plucked the thoughts out so succinctly, or her irritation when she asked about it. "*We'll* make it better."

She shook her head, kicked out her office chair, and dropped into it. "I did what you told me not to. I talked to the news station. That crowd outside gets larger every day, and our numbers have slumped off noticeably in the last few days. I had to do something."

Tate had to clench his jaw to keep from interrupting.

"And they slaughtered me. Took everything I said out of context. Almost all of their footage was of the people on the sidewalk. What little they showed of me was clipped to make it look like I only do this to make people suffer. I take their pets in, never give them back, and call the police on the people I don't like. They spun it that way."

It was Thompson's TV station. What had she expected? "Call your lawyer. It's slander."

She slammed her hands on the desk hard enough to shake the floor. "I know it's fucking slander. The damage is done. And so help me, if you're thinking you need to rein me in, and make me calm down, I'll have Ricco throw you out."

Once again, he was bothered she'd read him so easily. "You're not solving anything this way." He struggled to keep his tone cool and calm.

"You think?" She breathed deep. Her chin quivered, and she clenched her hands into fists several times. She scrubbed the back of her hand across her cheeks and eyes. "None of this is solving anything." The fire in her voice wilted, faded, and ended in a crack. "Your ideas aren't exactly batting one-thousand either. If the site keeps taking donations at this rate, it'll be twenty-fifty before I've raised enough for the shelter expansion."

The conversation with Vivian tickled his memory. "So let me write you a check. I can get that out of the way now, and then we can focus on the legal problems, and setting things right."

"Let you. You can get. Do you hear yourself? I don't want you to make this all vanish. Nothing gets better if you sweep your magic money wand over the entire situation."

"Where's this coming from?" He'd been cold at the party on

Monday, and he owed her an apology for that, but this didn't seem even remotely related.

"You can't bail me out for the rest of my life, Tate. What happens when we grow apart?"

The question burrowed under his skin and drilled a hole into his thoughts. A wave of cold passed over him. "Why would we grow apart?" It was a stupid question. Of course they would. He'd just never thought about it before. Not seriously.

She tugged on her hair. "You keep talking about this mysterious Mister Right that I'm going to end up with. Do you think things are going to stay the same between us when he comes along? That we'll all be best buds, and our relationship won't change?"

She was just spitting his own words back at him. Reiterating the future he'd always seen for her. The one that didn't include him. But hearing her acknowledge it sank into his feet like concrete. He'd never hated an idea more.

"I'm not like you." She continued. "I don't like the idea of growing old alone. My life plan has never included not getting attached. I want kids, and a happy marriage, and a house with a big enough yard for dogs and cats. Maybe that does mean I'm stupid or gullible, but that doesn't stop me from hoping."

He couldn't think about her entire statement. Taking it in its entirety jumbled his thoughts. He zeroed in on the bits he could grasp. "I won't be alone. I'll have my friends."

"That's all fine and good. But it's not the same." She stared at him, gaze driving into his soul, as if she searched for something he was certain didn't exist. "Friends are great. But I want more."

How had this gone from being a conversation about the shelter, to the rest of their lives? He wanted to switch the conversation back to something more neutral. Bring it back to a place he understood and that didn't make him ill. Something told him that wasn't an option. Even though he'd always known her future was somewhere else, even though he'd been repeating it in his head and out loud for the last week, hearing her say it felt like betrayal. It wasn't fair to tell her that, though. Because she was right, and any other answer was selfish. "You're right. You deserve that. You deserve more."

She clenched her jaw, and her entire frame shook. Her eyes grew watery, and she sniffled. "You need to leave."

He couldn't. If he walked out now, this would never be better. But his own thoughts didn't make sense to him. He was contradicting himself, and he didn't have a response.

"Please. Leave. Have a different project manager contact me."

She was right, so why did he want to argue? He should be grateful she finally got it. This was the best solution for her, and staying was just him being selfish.

Alyssia dropped her face in her hands after Tate walked out the door. She wanted to be pissed at him for just going along with what she'd said—because it was best for her. She wanted to be furious at him for making her think about it in the first place. Most of all, she wanted to get rid of the feeling it would have been smarter of her to hack off her own arm with a butter knife than to pick that fight.

But blame had bounced back and forth in her head all night. Since the news story aired. It was her fault for not listening to Tate. It was his fault for always trying to do what was best for her. It was Jared's fault for treating her like a baby for so long.

Everyone was to blame, the world sucked, and she didn't even know if happily ever after really existed. She hated Tate most of all for putting that thought in her head.

If she was going to insist on doing this on her own, she'd better get started. At least it would give her a distraction. Tate's idea hadn't worked—a glance at her crowd-funding site told her she wasn't even five percent to her goal. Her idea hadn't worked—the news story that night was proof she couldn't compete with the Thompson's connections, and he'd put her entire shelter at risk because of it. Or she had. It was time she started taking credit for her own fuck ups.

It was time to explore other options. She should have done this months ago, but it was too easy to let Tate step in. Too easy to convince herself that even though she wouldn't take his money, she was being self-sufficient by letting him do the work. She'd find an investor group, or wherever money came from when banks didn't loan it. Where to start?

Search engines were her best friend, and it was time to dig her heels in and either fund her shelter, or make sure she had contacts in other places to send the pets she wouldn't be able to take in if she couldn't expand.

Armed with a plan, she banished thoughts of Tate to the back of her mind. Just thinking his name hurt in every inch of her body, but that would lessen with time.

She didn't have a choice. She'd get over him.

SIXTEEN

Tate wasn't sure how long he'd been driving. Long enough to get him all but lost in the back roads of Northern Georgia, and then turned around and heading back toward the city again.

He couldn't get the argument with Lys out of his head. Every time he managed to present himself with a logical reason to move on, his brain dragged him back to the fact he wasn't listening to himself. He didn't want to see her with another guy. That's what it came down to at every mental intersection. Thinking of her spending the rest of forever with some random guy—even if he was the nicest dude on the planet, made Tate clench his hands until it ached all the way into his fingertips.

Tate had always told himself he wasn't equipped to handle a relationship. That sat at the other end of his dilemma. His parents' marriage was a painful thing to behold. Two people bound by law for business purposes, who had only ever slept in the same bed long enough to conceive him.

So why couldn't he picture his future without Alyssia? The idea of growing old alone, of drifting away from her, of watching her fall for someone else, crushed him from the inside out.

That was what it came down to. He wanted her in his life.

Needed her. Couldn't do this future thing without her. And he had to tell her.

He turned the car back toward her shelter. At least it was late, so traffic was light. Half an hour later, he pulled into the parking lot. Most of the picketers had called it a night. That was something, at least. He strode through the front door, flashed Sara a smile, and headed straight for Lys's office. He knocked, and waited.

Several seconds passed. He glanced back at Sara.

"She's in there." Sara shrugged. "Not on the phone. At least not the office lines."

Tate frowned, and knocked again.

"Hang on." Alyssia's voice sounded tiny and raw. Several more seconds passed. "It's open."

Tate nudged into her office, ill-ease growing inside. His concern spiked when he saw her in her desk chair, knees pulled to her chest, and face pale and drawn. He closed the door behind him. In just a few steps, he was next to her. "What's wrong?"

She shook her head, and her chin quivered. She opened her mouth to speak, and a sob tore out instead. Her jaw worked up and down, but nothing intelligible came out.

What the fuck? He didn't know what was going on, but it was splitting him in two. He held out a hand, and she stumbled forward and collapsed in his arms. Ear-piercing cries echoed through him, gnawing at his calm, flooding him with concern, and a desire to make this vanish, even though he didn't have a target. He rubbed her back until the sobs slowed to body-wracking, and then tiny sniffles. Her muffled whispers drifted to his ears, and he strained to hear her.

"I didn't know," she muttered. "God, what's wrong with people? I didn't..." She choked on the words.

It didn't matter what he'd come there to tell her. This was more important. "Talk to me, Lys."

She shook her head, and pressed closer into his chest. "You can't fix this. Jesus, no one can fix this. What the fuck is wrong with people?" She finally met his gaze with red-rimmed, puffy eyes. "I just wanted... I was trying to figure out what to do if the crowd funding fell through. I stumbled on a site with an article about the shelter, going on about all of the lies Thompson's told. Spewing them like they were truth. And the comments. The things people said about me, about this place…" She swallowed, and nodded at her computer.

He kept her turned away, jarred the mouse, and pulled up her web browser. It took him a moment to register what he was looking at, and when he did his lunch threatened to repeat on him. Videos were embedded in several of the comments. Of animals being tortured. Holy fuck. He closed everything, and slammed the lid shut on her laptop. No wonder she was a wreck. He led her toward the couch, and lowered them both, never letting go. He couldn't find the words to ask anything new. Everything stuck in his throat on a surge of sickness.

She curled up against him. "I know people are saying bad things about the place, but I didn't realize how malicious it had gotten." She shuddered. "I didn't expect to find… God, what's wrong with people, Tate? I couldn't stop looking, and oh fuck."

He couldn't tell her it was going to be okay. Of all the lies he could come up with, that felt like the most insulting. All he could manage was, "I don't know what's wrong with people."

He trailed his fingers through her hair, desperately searching for his own calm and not willing to let her go. He'd stay with her all night if that was what it took. It still wouldn't give him a solution, but at least they'd both have something to hold onto.

ALYSSIA'S EYES felt like they'd been bathed in sand, and her throat wasn't doing much better. She couldn't think about what she'd seen. She'd known there were sick fucks out there, but having to see it firsthand… No, she wouldn't go down that path. Digging deep, she summoned the willpower to shove the mental images aside. She sat up enough to look at Tate. "I'm sorry."

He brushed a strand of hair from her face. "You don't have to apologize for anything."

She disagreed, but didn't have the strength to say so. "Why did you come back?"

He hesitated for the briefest second. "I had a hunch." He wasn't telling her everything. She didn't care. Right now, she was just relieved he was there. "Will you be okay for a minute or two?"

She didn't know if she'd ever be okay again, but it wasn't like she could curl up in a permanent ball because she'd seen proof of how ugly the world was. "Yes."

When he returned a few minutes later, he handed her a cup of water, and a damp washcloth. She let the cold liquid slide down her throat, trying to only focus on the physical sensations, then used the towel to sap some of the heat from her cheeks.

He set everything aside. She didn't like the pity on his face. Or maybe that was just concern, and she was overreacting. Panic surged inside again, and she squashed the visuals it threatened to bring with it.

He grasped her fingers, and tugged her to her feet. "Come with me."

She didn't have any strength to protest, or even ask where they were going. She couldn't meet Sara's curious gaze when Tate led her into the lobby. He reached over the front desk and grabbed something she couldn't see, then tugged her toward the kennels.

Most of the dogs were sleeping, but a few stirred when he let them into back room. One animal barked, and seconds later the rest joined the chaos. Her soul shrank from the sound. She wouldn't react. She loved that sound. It wasn't a bad sound. She squeezed Tate's hand tighter, and followed closely behind.

They stopped in front of Grim's pen. The dog had recovered wonderfully in the week since they'd taken him in. He still couldn't do a lot of moving, but he was happy and playful as much as was possible.

Tate unlocked the pen, knelt in front of Grim, and gestured for her to do the same. He lifted her chin until he was looking her in the eyes. Even amid the barking of a dozen or so dogs, his voice was distinct, and kind. "You can't protect the world, Lys." He licked his lips. "Not any more than I can lock you away from everything bad. But what you do matters so much." He held out his hand. Grim sniffed his fingers, then ducked his head. Tate scratched him behind the ears, and under the chin, affection rolling with the loll of the dog's head.

Images from the videos spilled back into Alyssia's head, and she gasped for breath. Grim whimpered and withdrew. Tate gave her all his attention. "Don't think about it. Look at me." His voice never rose. Never wavered. "This is here, and it's just us and the dogs, which you're keeping safe."

"But, the things I saw—"

Tate brushed his lips over hers. It wasn't hungry, or demanding, just soothing. "And the animals you've already saved. Like Grim," he said. "He's not going anywhere until his doctor says it's okay, and even then, only with someone you sign off on. Right?"

She nodded, and forced herself to draw a deep breath.

Tate scooted closer to Grim, and let the dog rest its head on his leg. Fur and bits of kibble dotted Tate's slacks. If he noticed, he didn't care. He never let go of her hands, even while he scratched the dog's ears and patted its sides.

As they sat there, the din around them died, and one by one the dogs drifted off to sleep again. Watching Tate with Grim, warmth leaked back into her fractured thoughts, sealing some of the cracks. She really was falling for him.

The words jarred her thoughts as they formed and solidified. It was a relief to finally let herself admit it. She'd focused on a crush for so long, she'd ignored the actual man behind her infatuation. The realization ached and soothed her at the same time.

"Come on." She stood, and pulled on Tate's hand. "Let the dogs sleep."

He locked Grim's door, followed her into the lobby, and set the keys on the front desk.

"Everything all right?" Sara looked between them, gaze lingering on the grime on Tate's suit.

Alyssia's jaw clenched, and a response died in her throat.

"Just playing with some of the dogs." Tate flashed her a smile.

Did she see the tight lines around his eyes? Or was Alyssia the only person who noticed that?

"Come on." Alyssia found her voice. "I have some scrubs you can change into. You're kind of a mess." Not only was he covered with Grim's fur, splotches of drool decorated his shirt.

Tate looked down, and his eyes widened. "Guess I wasn't paying attention."

"You know where I'll be," she said to Sara.

Back in her office, she grabbed a set of scrubs from a cupboard, and handed them to Tate. "You probably should change. I hope you didn't ruin your clothes." The normal conversation helped calm her further, and keep her in the now.

"They're pants. They're replaceable."

"I know I shouldn't ask. But, do you have anywhere to be tonight?"

He shook his head, and stroked his thumb over the back of her knuckles. "Just here."

"Are you fucking kidding me?"

Alyssia's irritated voice dragged Tate from sleep. He winced at the kink in his neck, and sat up. It took him a minute to focus his eyes. She stood in front of her computer, face contorted with fury. She wasn't back on one of those horrific sites again, was she? Tate's chest squeezed with concern.

She pointed to her screen. "What the hell is this?"

No, probably not. He climbed to his feet, to get a look at what had her so angry. It was a generic landing page from the crowd-funding site. Pretty, friendly—creative had spent weeks on the graphic. The one that said "Sorry, this campaign isn't running right now. Can we help you find something else?"

His own ire spiked. Someone had shut her down without his okay. "Son of a bitch."

She drummed her fingers on the back of her chair. "What's going on?"

"I don't know." All of the user agreements allowed the sites to be taken offline without consultation if there were legal or safety concerns. Lys's site wasn't either of those things. At this point he'd be tempted to tell her to go with another crowd-funding vendor, if there were enough time to spin her up with someone new, and get her donations in before the clock ran out. "I'll fix this."

"Of course you will." Her voice held a hard edge. She sighed. "I'm sorry. I'm not snapping at you."

"You should be. Someone needs to be reamed for this." He grabbed his phone, and dialed his mother's office line. It went straight to voice mail. Funny how it hadn't forwarded to her cell phone. She was either screening him or on the other line. "You can come with me to yell at someone, if you'd like."

She shook her head. "I don't know that I'm equipped for that this morning. Call me as soon as you have answers."

He squeezed her hand. "Of course."

He let his rage soar as he stalked to his car. He was half tempted to go into work dressed in the wrinkled scrubs Lys had loaned him, but that wouldn't help his case. If he was taking on his mother, he had to be cool, professional, and unflinching. This wasn't just about Alyssia's site, though the fact it had been shut down certainly resided at the top of his list. His mother never would have touched one of Jared's projects like this. Or Vivian's. This was about shutting his business venture down without conferring with him first. The hypocrisy that accompanied the decision infuriated him. That she thought she could do this to him because he was family.

For as long as he could remember, he'd yielded, caved, and gone along with her whim because she was his mother, and a parent should know best. It was out of respect and a sense of propriety. Her actions indicated she didn't hold him in the same regard. He was done being steamrolled, and it was time to put an end to it.

SEVENTEEN

TATE STRAIGHTENED HIS TIE, ASSUMED THE CALMEST, COOLEST AIR he could summon, and strode toward his mother's office. The door was closed. He wasn't surprised. He gave her assistant, Kat his warmest smile. "Is Ms. Foster in?" He was on her turf, so he'd follow her rules of formality regardless of the unprofessional way she was approaching their relationship.

"Hey." Kat's neutral expression shifted to warm and open when she saw him. "I'd let you in if I could, but she'll be on calls on and off most of the morning. I'll tell her you stopped by. Ping you if she pokes her head out for more than a few seconds."

"Don't worry about it." He let just enough of his drawl slide in to sound polite. "You know what? I'll just hang out for a couple minutes, if that's all right. See if she frees up before the top of the hour?"

"Stay as long as you'd like." Kat's smile grew. "I'll send her a message and let her know you're out here."

He covered her hand. "Don't worry about that. I'd hate to make her hurry just to see me. I'll just hang out for a little while."

"Tate." A familiar baritone snapped through the friendly facade.

Tate ground his teeth at the sound of his father's voice, but managed to keep most of the reaction from his voice. He whirled to face the older man. "Mr. Foster." Calling him Dad in public wasn't the same taboo as referring to his mother so informally, but Tate was already in that business frame of mind.

"Can it." Ben nodded toward his office at the other end of the hall. "Let's talk."

It wasn't the conversation Tate wanted to have, but it might do. He followed, keeping his mouth shut until the door closed them off from the rest of the world. He didn't bother with sitting. "Do you have any idea what she did?" That wasn't how he'd meant to open this conversation.

"I know what she didn't do." Ben took his seat, and leaned back in his chair. "And that's shut down the shelter's crowd-funding site."

Shock filled Tate. "You? Why?"

"You made this personal; I made an executive decision. This may be your spin-off, but ultimately it still falls under the Skriddie label. Think of it as an investor getting involved."

"This isn't just about business." Tate didn't have to bullshit here, or play sweet. That was one thing he appreciated about his father. "You know what happens to that place if they can't raise the capital they need."

"It is about business. Her business is dealing with bad media. Our business is dealing with bad media for entirely different reasons. If we're seen supporting her business, ours looks worse."

Tate understood the logic. He hated himself for it, but he got it. That didn't mean he agreed. "So this is all about the bottom line."

"Yes." Ben leaned forward, fingers clasped and arms resting on his desk. "Look. I don't care what you've got going on with Alyssia Tippins. Whether it's something, or nothing, or falls somewhere in the middle. That's between you and her, and despite what your mother thinks, there's no reason to marry you to a senator's daughter who isn't even old enough to drink."

Tate bit the inside of his cheek to keep a retort from slipping out. He was curious to know where this was going.

"But that's personal, this is business. Look me in the eye and tell me you don't understand my decision."

"I get it. But I still don't agree. This isn't just about return on investment."

"That's exactly what it's about." A sharp crack lined Ben's words. "We're not a charity. The things we do, we do to make money."

Tate didn't have a retort. He knew he couldn't win, but he wasn't willing to back down or give up. "I won't be in the office the rest of the day."

"Fine." Ben turned to his computer, indicating he felt the conversation was over. "Get this out of your system. When you're back tomorrow, I expect business as usual from you."

Tate was already reaching for his phone as he stormed from the office. He didn't have a plan, or even the inklings of one, and he wasn't going to find the answers here.

A text message from Lys waited for him. *How'd it go?*

What the fuck was he going to tell her? He shoved the device back in his pocket, and headed for his car. He'd figure it out.

ALYSSIA LAY IN BED, staring at the ceiling. Every time she drifted toward sleep, horrible images flashed in her mind, muddled with a lack of solutions, and the creeping dread that she didn't have a way out of this problem. She rolled onto her side, and her gaze fell on her cell phone. She would have heard if it had gone off, but that didn't stop her from clicking the button to see if she'd missed any calls or texts.

Nothing.

"Damn it, Tate." Talking to the empty room was better than being alone with her thoughts. He was supposed to keep her updated. He'd been so kind last night, and she knew that man was still in there. She also couldn't shake the feeling he was falling into old patterns.

Sleep wasn't going to happen. She climbed from bed, and pulled on some clothes. Maybe she'd have lunch with Jared, use that as an excuse to surprise Tate. That was a stupid idea. She wasn't being that girl anymore. Jared… Something clicked in her thoughts, chinking and whirring.

She knew what to do, but she couldn't do it alone. She grabbed her phone and dialed.

"This is Mikki."

A sliver of progress wormed its way into Alyssia's thoughts. This *would* work. "Hey, it's me. I need a huge, huge favor, and then maybe you can transfer me to Tate?"

"Like, the exciting, get into trouble kind of favor?" Mikki asked.

"Probably not. But it's a challenging kind of thing, and I can't pay you."

"Then yes. But no to the second thing. Tate's not in today."

Alyssia suppressed her disappointment—and that was all it was. No irritation mingled with the feeling. "Tate told me when he set up this whole crowdfunding thing that he rented Skriddie servers because he didn't have the people to build him a setup." The way he'd phrased it, it sounded like he couldn't find the talent. He'd slipped a few times though, that hiring that kind of skill wasn't in his budget. He'd even placed the hardware orders before his investors— she'd taken that to mean his mother—pulled their funding on the IT budget. He'd sworn he would set it all up once they had the capital. "I don't even know if I'm saying this right. How long would it take you to setup and configure an entire server array for the crowd-funding sites."

Mikki laughed. "Me, personally? Thirty hours. Maybe twenty."

"So, asking you to do this means you'd be giving up your evenings for a week or two." Alyssia couldn't do that. "Never mind."

"What are you kidding? I'm totally in. Hell, I have a friend or two back in Utah who will help."

"Are you sure?"

"I might ask you to chip in on Mt. Dew funds. But yes, one hundred percent. Tell me what we're doing."

Alyssia spent the next half hour laying out her idea, and making sure Mikki had all the right information, before thanking her future sister-in-law, and disconnecting.

Tate still hadn't answered her messages. She wasn't going to waste a phone call on this; it was a conversation that needed to happen in person. She headed to her car, pulled onto the road, and pointed it in the familiar direction.

Her determination wavered when she drew within sight of his driveway, and confirmed his car was there. Maybe he was just home sick, or sleeping off too many long nights. She should wait for him to return her messages.

She summoned her resolve, and parked her car next to his. No backing down. It was his decision if he was going to be a part of this or not, but he was going to tell her to her face, and she wasn't going to let him wrap it in excuses and faulty logic. She rang the bell, and waited, toes tapping inside her shoes.

The door jerked open more quickly than she expected, and she jumped. Tate stood there, shadows under his eyes, in a battered T-shirt and jeans, and a tired smile. "Hey. Shouldn't you be sleeping?"

He looked good, even exhausted. *Concentrate. Remember the plan. Get him to sign on, or walk away.* She repeated the words in her head. "I should be. I couldn't. Can we talk?"

"Absolutely." He stepped aside, and gestured toward the couch.

She hovered near the entryway. *No sitting until she had a better idea of how this was going.* "Did you get answers this morning?"

"Yeah, but don't worry about it. It's under control. I've got plan—"

"I am worried about it." She crossed her arms. "Do you remember yesterday afternoon? You don't get to have plans about my business without my input."

He sighed, and pinched the bridge of his nose. "I know. That's not what this is. This impacts my entire startup. I need to take care of it."

"Tate." She couldn't keep the frustration from her voice. "No. *You* don't. Is this a lack of respect? Do you not take me seriously? Maybe you think your friends are only there when you're the one taking care of them?" The words hurt, tugging at insecurities she hated to acknowledge. But she was so tired of dancing around *every-thing* when it came to him.

"No. Not at all." He reached for her, then dropped his hand. "I swear, that's so very far from the truth. I have so much respect for you. For everything you do. I've never met a stronger person. The things you see, every day, and the fact you still fight for something so good?"

His words flowed through her head and heart, warming her in a way she didn't want. What if it was just lip service? "Then what are we doing? You don't have to take care of everything on your own. You help me, and I do the same for you. It's who we are."

He dragged his fingers through his hair. "I want you to be happy. I want those animals to be safe. I desperately want to tell you I love you. To write you a check, to make this all go away, to move on so you don't have to deal with it. Not because you're incapable, but because no human being should have to put up with this shit, especially you."

She struggled to keep up with the conversation, but her mind was stuck on three words, skipping back to them. Replaying them over and over in her mind. "Did you just say…?" She couldn't force the question out. Already, her thoughts were working to convince her she'd imagined it.

"I did." He cupped her cheek, and her pulse threatened to burst through her heart. "I love you, Lys. For as long as I can remember. I've just never felt like I could give you what you needed. I still can't."

She pushed him back, anger and confusion mingling with the relief of the revelation. "You fucking asshole. What the hell is wrong with you? I don't even understand why you think you can't give me what I'm looking for."

He clenched his jaw, then dragged in a shaky breath before replying. "Can you really picture me being tied down?"

"I can and I do. You're already anchored here. Maybe it's easier to think that's me being delusional, and seeing things that aren't there. But you just admitted it. You're as tied to me as I am to you. You don't get to make a confession like *I love you*, and wrap it in a bullshit line like '*I know what's good for you, and it's not me.*' You don't get to dump that on me and in the same breath remove my right to tell you I feel the same.

"In fact, I'm tired of you making all sorts of these decisions without my input. Faking that first donation on my website? Okay, I convinced myself you hadn't actually done that. Loaning Jared the money years ago, so he could tell me it came from him, when I bought the shelter? I pretended I didn't know you'd done that." Her words spilled out, surprising her. How did she know that? But the look on Tate's face told her she was right. He'd been there the entire time, making sure she succeeded. Helping. Finding ways to keep her from turning him down.

He shrugged. "This is your dream, and it's a good one. You won't take the money from me."

She hadn't wanted to approach things this way. Especially not with Tate's confession—wonderful, amazing, infuriating as it may be—hanging between them. But she was laying it all on the line. "I will now." Wow, that was harder to say than she'd expected.

"What?"

She shoved her hands in her pockets to keep them from shaking. "I need a loan, Tate. Enough to move forward and make this shelter grow." Now that the words were tumbling out, it was easier. "But I need more than that."

"Of course." His shoulders relaxed, and the lines faded from his forehead. "Whatever you need."

She shook her head. "It's not about me. You need to make this idea take off. What you can do for companies like mine? It's important. These sites of yours can make a big difference and you're doing it right. So we're going to make sure your idea takes off. You, me, Mikki, and she's even going to pull in her friends. We keep failing miserably when it comes down to what I need, or what you want to do. This is about us." She hadn't meant it that way. But she liked the way it sounded.

"Slow down. I think I missed a few steps."

"Right. Sorry." She paused, dragging her thoughts together. "Everything that you've struggled with since you tried to launch these crowd funding sites—or at least a lot of it—goes away if you have your own hardware. You've said you don't have the manpower, but you have technical knowledge, and I found you people who will work for free. You do that, you keep my donation site online, and I'll make sure my expansion happens."

"You've thought this out. Thank you for that."

She felt better than she had in weeks, but she wasn't done yet. "And Tate?"

He met her gaze, eyes widened in question.

She stepped in. "I love you, too."

He grinned, and rested his hands at the small of her back.

She pushed him back playfully. "And if you ever pull this '*I know what's best for you*' bullshit on me again, we're going to have problems."

He grabbed her wrists, and pulled her in. "Yes ma'am." He cupped the back of her head, and crushed his lips to hers. Hunger, need, and security surged through her and she pressed back. She wasn't sure if their new plan was any better than any of the old ones, but this—what she had with Tate—was the one thing she wasn't worried about.

EIGHTEEN

Tate drew Lys into him, and trailed his fingers through her hair. God, he loved having her in his arms. Her warmth, weight, and lilac scent. And right now, he was almost as grateful she wasn't as stubborn has he was. Relief still flowed through him at her acceptance of his financial help. She'd just gotten off the phone with her contractor, letting them know she was ready to move forward with the building expansion.

Tate moved his lips against the top of her head. "When do we start work on this plan?"

"Tonight, when Mikki's done with work and before my shift starts." Her breath was hot against his skin, teasing and comforting at the same time. "Because she'll do it for the challenge instead of trying to talk me out of it for whatever reason."

Tate didn't have an argument for that. "If I might make a suggestion until then."

"What's that?"

"You should probably get some sleep."

She pulled back enough to look him in the eye, and her gaze traveled over his face. "When was the last time you slept an entire night?"

God, he wasn't even sure he remembered. "Not a clue."

"In that case, only if you join me." She pulled him toward the bedroom.

Tate shook the sleep off at the sound of his doorbell chiming. After five. He hadn't meant to sleep that long, but he felt good.

Lys watched him through lidded eyes as he climbed from bed. "What's up?" she asked.

He kissed her on the forehead. "Don't know. I'll be back." He fastened his jeans and pulled on his shirt as he crossed the house to the front door. The remaining haze of sleep evaporated when he saw Jared on his front porch. "Hey, man."

Jared was dressed as if he'd just come from the office, which made sense given the time of day. He held out a USB drive. "I wouldn't bother you at home on a sick day, but you weren't answering your phone. I need your okay on some documents by tomorrow morning."

Sick day? Right. What other reason would he have for vanishing without notice in the middle of the week? Tate grabbed the thumb drive. "No worries. Do you want input, or just an okay?"

Jared shrugged, his expression neutral. "If anything needs to be corrected, use track changes. Meeting's at eleven, so as long as I have it first thing, I'll be set."

"No problem. See you tomorrow."

Jared didn't move, and his jaw tightened.

"Something else I can do for you?" Uneasiness flitted through Tate.

"I just wanted to say hi to your guest. Where is she?"

Tate's gut sank. "Who?"

"Alyssia. Her car's in your driveway."

It was going to come out eventually, and Tate wanted to shout about their relationship to anyone who would listen, but he'd rather have this conversation with Lys's consent, and definitely not while she was half-naked in his bedroom. "Oh, she's…you know." He waved his hand vaguely toward everything behind him.

Jared crossed his arms. "I don't, actually. I can make a lot of assumptions, but my sister accuses me of jumping to conclusions, so I'm hoping I'm wrong. You're not good for her."

Was that what Tate had sounded like? No wonder she'd been pissed. "It's not your call."

Jared made a noise that landed somewhere between a growl and a bark. "Tell me I'm wrong."

"It's okay." Lys's voice greeted him from behind. Tate glanced over his shoulder to see her leaning against the far wall, hair mussed. At least she was dressed, though. "I'd rather tell him now than later."

"What are you doing, Alyssia?" Jared stepped into the house.

Tate blocked his path, and prayed he wasn't about to get socked. Not that he'd ever seen Jared hit anything, but there was a first time for everything. It's what he would do if he were in Jared's shoes. He took a deep breath. "Hear me out."

"I'm listening."

Great. So what was he supposed to say? 'But I love her' was a good start, but it didn't feel very solid. Not given his history. The words flowed into Tate's head, and he spoke without filtering them. "I know you and I have had each other's backs since we were kids," he said to Jared. "But she's my best friend. Honestly, that's the best way to put it. I can't imagine not having her there to celebrate with when things go well." He turned to Lys. It was more important she hear this than Jared. That she know how he felt when they weren't in the middle of a heated argument. "I can't imagine you not being there when I have news of any kind. It wrecks me to think I might have to share you with another man. Let alone your—"

"I get it." Jared interrupted. "Please don't give me any details."

Tate turned back to him with a shrug. "I know she's your sister. I get that you're looking out for her. Thing is, I've thought for a long time about this. Probably longer than I should've. I know what I'm doing, and what I'm saying when I tell you I love her."

Jared's expression was cold, and unyielding. "Can we do this outside?"

"Go," Lys said, before Tate could answer. "Get this out of your system, Jared."

Tate stepped onto the porch. The moment he shut the door, Jared's mask shifted, lines marring his face, brows knitted together.

The almost-calm disappeared from Jared's voice. "You've got a really pretty speech rehearsed. It's almost believable. But out of all that, you only said one thing I agree with. We have known each other since we were kids. You've never been with a woman longer than twenty-four hours. And now what? I'm supposed to just step back and tell you, knowing what I do about you, that I'm fine with you hooking up with my sister?"

A part of Tate expected this conversation to be difficult, but he hadn't lingered on the details or logistics of it. Maybe he should have thought about the repercussions a little longer. Not that it would have changed how he felt about Lys, but it may have changed his approach to the rest of it. "I'm being sincere. I don't know what else to say."

Jared clenched his jaw. "Honestly, I shouldn't make you convince me. God, it hurts to admit that. But I know you're right. You and she... I know you're close. I'm not blind. I was just hoping you wouldn't ever figure it out."

Tate ground his teeth together, measuring his response. "Because I'm not good enough for your baby sister?"

"Because she is my baby sister, and this means admitting she's grown up."

Tate almost smiled at that. He swallowed back a jab about her having grown up a long time ago. "You have to let her make her own decisions sometime."

"That doesn't mean I have to like it."

This could have gone better, but it also could have gone a lot worse. He looked at Jared. "It's not like I have a choice but to show you I mean it. I'm not going anywhere without her."

Jared stared back, jaw set. "If this goes bad, that's the point where you'd better lose my number. But I have a feeling I don't need to worry."

"Not that she needs your blessing, but I'd kind of hate to lose your friendship. So, thanks."

They exchanged a few more jabs, the tension lessening between them, and Jared left. Tate headed back inside.

Lys sat on the couch, fingers intertwined, elbows resting on her legs. "You look like that maybe went well?"

"He didn't even hit me." Tate pulled her to her feet. "Really, though, I'm glad he's not too pissed, because I'd hate to choose sides, but I wouldn't have chosen his."

She wrapped her arms around his waist, and rested her cheek on his chest. Her voice was soft. "I'm glad you don't have to. I'd hate to make you regret us."

"I don't, and I wouldn't. Not ever." He hugged her back, holding on tight. "I still meant everything I said. This doesn't change how I feel." He kissed her. "As long as you know I mean it, when I say I love you, that's what matters."

"I do." She squeezed his hand. "And I'd stay here all night and let you show me, but we have an appointment."

Right. Time to put their plan into action. "I'll meet you at the shelter?"

She nodded, and stepped away. He grasped her fingers, pulled her to him, and rested a hand on the small of her back. He kissed her, pouring everything he felt into the gesture. Memorizing each curve of her body, and the way her frame molded to his. This was what mattered. Making sure Lys had whatever it took to make her happy. He finally let her go, and the absence of her touch lingered on his skin. "See you soon."

NINETEEN

Mikki sat on the couch in Alyssia's office, legs crossed, and laptop balanced on her knees. She had a friend—Jaycie—on speaker, but mostly what echoed through her phone was the clacking of keys.

Alyssia scrolled through lists of supplies—purchases she needed to grow the shelter. Tate was working his contacts to find a storage facility for his hardware. So many servers had to be on and online all the time, and they needed a secure location to live in.

It was the same scene as it had been for almost two weeks, and Alyssia found it comforting. That, and—now that she was back on daytime shifts—she loved waking up next to Tate, regardless of whose place they stayed at.

Tate reached around Alyssia for a pen. He brushed his lips over her cheek before scooting away again, and going back to his pacing and whatever he was looking up on the tablet he held. Heat flooded Alyssia's face when she realized Mikki was watching, mouth twisted in amusement.

Mikki shook her head and turned back to her work. "You two are cute."

"Are they at it again?" Jaycie's teasing voice came over the phone.

Alyssia flushed at playful exchange. She needed to meet more of Mikki's friends.

"Like, non-stop." Mikki glanced at Alyssia again. "I don't know why Jared's still grumpy about it."

Alyssia tucked away the sliver of hurt at the reminder. He'd told Tate he was okay, but he still snarled when he saw the two of them together. She knew it would take time, but Jared still meant the world to her. She couldn't ask for a better older brother. "It's probably hard to get if you don't have siblings."

Mikki shrugged. "I guess. Personally, I think he's just jealous. When Holly and Robert find out, he's going to have to share the 'when are we getting grandkids' conversations with you."

"I don't envy that," Jacyee said. "Dealing with developers is all the exposure to children that I want." She had been vague about what she did, but apparently it had to do with video games.

A nervous pit sank into Alyssia's gut. It had been there a lot lately. A hint of nausea that surged at certain times of the day, then ebbed again as she lost herself in work.

Sweet, heartfelt confessions of love were one thing, but it wasn't like they were even living together yet, let alone having a children conversation. It was true; Tate said he wanted to be her future, but they hadn't talked about things like that. And as much as she wanted kids, she wasn't sure that fell in line with his vision. She risked a glance at Tate. He stared at his tablet, his face a flat mask, and his finger tapping on the screen.

"I'm pretty sure he's not jealous." Tate finally looked up. "Really? You get the grandkids question already? You're not even married yet."

Mikki held up her left hand and wiggled her fingers. The overhead lights sparkled off diamonds. "I'm just saying, join us for Sunday dinner holding hands, instead of sitting at opposite ends of the room pretending you don't see each other, and things will change. It's not like it's a big deal, we're just running out of polite excuses."

"Kids aren't in your future?" Tate asked.

Alyssia tried not to pick apart his question. There was no reason to analyze the words, examine them for inflection. That wasn't uncertainty or disgust she heard in her voice.

"I don't know." Mikki turned her attention back to her work, typing as she talked. "Maybe. I know, he's ten years older, they've been waiting for a long time, but we're not sure if we want to do that."

Alyssia hadn't ever heard that from Jared before. Not that they spent a lot of time talking about his baby plans. Still, she'd always just assumed it was something she'd do, it was something Jared would do. "So are you saying you'll never…?"

"Maybe. Maybe not. I've still got time, and we're still having fun, you know?"

"I completely understand." Tate was making scrolling motions on the screen now, instead of random taps.

Currents of uneasiness rocked through Alyssia. "Which bit?" She tried to keep her tone casual. "The not knowing for sure, or the 'it's probably never going to happen?'"

He looked up, and his gaze met hers. "I have a press release explaining your situation with Thompson's dog. Something to help you change the perception of the shelter back to positive. Do you want to hit up the online news outlets with the information, or stick to local television stations?"

"Online too. Everyone who'll listen." She squashed her rising disappointment. She shouldn't jump to conclusions. It wasn't as if he'd said it was never going to happen. And again, it wasn't even like they had moved that far in their relationship. But she'd struggle to make things work, even with him, if kids weren't an option. Had he really thought this confession of love thing through? Had she?

She'd never kept what she wanted from her future a secret. Was she overreacting, or was this just one of many things they were about to clash over?

"So." Jaycie's voice was loud and hollow. "Speaking of media outlets, any news on Thompson?"

Tate shook his head. "Certified mail says he received the letter."

They'd decided to give him one more chance to rescind the stories about the shelter, and to drop the lawsuit. To issue a public apology, and then just let the issue die. The alternative wouldn't quite be as brutal as what he'd done to the shelter, but it certainly wouldn't paint Thompson or his local TV station a good light, and Alyssia's attorney already had a counter-suit drawn up if needed. "No response. He won't take my calls, and has refused any in-person meetings."

"Bryce Thompson was not available for response," Jaycie said in chirpy voice.

Alyssia stifled a laugh when the Mikki woman flipped her hair over her shoulder, and adjusted an invisible jacket. It was Mikki and Jaycie's anchorwoman impersonation. Mikki played the face, and Jaycie provided the voice. They'd been sliding into it off and on for days.

"So, we crucify the bastard." Tate tapped out something on the screen in front of him.

"You've got one more avenue." Alyssia didn't want to bring it up. Tate would hate the idea. But she still felt like Thompson deserved a chance. His kid didn't. That sadistic fuck needed to pay, but just because his dad was delusional didn't mean he should lose the things he'd worked for.

"No, I really don't." Tate rubbed his eyes. "All right, fine. She's out of town until Friday, though. I'll talk to her then. She's not going to listen. Especially when I tell her we don't need Skriddie's hardware anymore."

"I'm missing something," Mikki said.

"His mother has certain ins with Mr. Thompson," Alyssia explained.

"They're fucking. Have been for years." Tate made himself comfortable in a nearby chair.

Mikki's brows rose. "And I thought my family was dysfunctional."

"You have no idea."

Alyssia frowned at the resignation in Tate's voice. The entire evening of conversations was just one bad reminder after another. A nudge, asking if she and Tate knew what they were doing. Or worse, reminding her this may be far more temporary than she'd like. She didn't want to think that way, but every time she banished the insistent voice in the back of her head, it pecked at her resolve until it was free again.

TWENTY

Alyssia stood in front of her bathroom mirror, stomach clenched in knots. Which was the entire reason she was doing this. To convince herself the nausea she felt on an almost daily basis was the stress of working so hard, and not something deeper. More... internal.

Tate. His name twisted her insides further. She looked again at the piece of plastic in her hand, and the pink plus sign in the middle. Two weeks of bliss, and everything was going to fall apart again when she told him she was pregnant. He may have made the leap to committing to her, but she couldn't imagine he was ready for a family. Not after all the protests he'd put up over the years.

She might have thought it would be all right. Maybe it would be, and she was just overreacting. But after his conversation with Mikki the other day...

She sank onto the toilet seat with a sigh. How was she going to break this to him?

As if her thoughts had summoned him, her phone rang in the other room, and the familiar song she used as his ringtone drifted toward her. She shoved the pregnancy test deep into the trash, and jogged to answer. "Hey."

"Hey, gorgeous." Tate's smile carried over the line. "You sound out of breath. Are you okay?"

Just questioning everything, from herself, to him, them. She shouldn't doubt him. Things were going well, and she was just being paranoid. "My phone wasn't in the same room as me. I had to track it down. What's up?"

"Are you free this afternoon?"

It was her day off, but she was on call. "Until someone tells me otherwise."

"Have lunch with me at that little diner in Gwinnette?"

The invitation eased her doubt. She was definitely being paranoid. "Absolutely. When?"

"One thirty, hopefully. Marge Foster pushed my appointment back to noon." If he was calling his mom by her full name, instead of Mother, that wasn't a good sign. The full name treatment was reserved for when he was irritated with her, or trying to pretend they weren't related. "I wonder sometimes if she wishes she'd had the mailman's kid, instead of me."

"It'll be fine." Alyssia tried to keep her reassurance vague. "Say your bit, you know you'll keep your head, and I'll see you after."

"Good point. I love you, Lys."

The simple reminder helped calm her, but it didn't completely erase her doubts. "I love you, too."

***

TATE SAT in one of the waiting room chairs outside his mother's office, doing his best not to check the time. It was almost twenty after twelve. The door never opened, but her assistant, Kat, finally looked up. "Ms. Foster will see you now. Sorry for the wait."

"It's not a problem." He gave her a warm smile, a retort surged in his throat, and he choked it back. It wasn't Kat's fault, and he was doing his best to keep his cool through this. He stepped into the smaller room, pleasant airs still painted on.

"I'm so sorry to keep you waiting." Marge's southern lilt was back. "Important people demanding my time."

"Of course." He ignored the subtle implication he wasn't part of that list. "Thanks for making room in your schedule. This won't take long."

Her eyebrows twitched up, and she nodded to the chair across from her desk. "Then let's talk business."

He made a point of closing the door before he took a seat. Keep calm, play it cool, don't let her ruffle him. That was all he had to remember. "I've been trying to get a hold of a mutual associate, and haven't been able to reach him. I'm hoping you can help me."

She muttered something that sounded like, "Of course you can't." Out loud, she said "Bless your heart. Give me their name, and I'll see what I can do."

Time to tip his hand. "I need to get a message to Bryce Thompson."

Her eye twitched, and her mask slid back into place. "I'm sorry. I was under the impression this was a business meeting. I made room in my work schedule for this."

"It is business, Ms. Foster." He leaned back in his chair, posture casual. "He's impacted a critical Skriddie Bust Media project. One that's estimated to increase our quarterly revenue by at least five percent, and that's guaranteed to challenge our strongest competitors and give us a new foothold in the market. I'd like to speak with Mr. Thompson, and see what kind of an agreement we can reach. I think his taking the time to sit down with me would be in his best interests."

"Not yours?" Her lilting accent was gone, replaced with a hard edge.

"This isn't about me, it's about the company, and Skriddie comes out on top either way. This is just a professional courtesy."

Her jaw clenched, and she leaned in. "It's a clever game, Tate. And I'm not sure what you're doing, but disguising your little friend's problems as *business* isn't going to cut it."

He stood. "I see. Then you won't help me get a hold of Mr. Thompson."

"Why don't you reach out to him yourself?"

"I tried. I haven't been able to connect with him." The conversation was going almost exactly the way Tate had expected. Disappointment welled inside. It was naive of him to think she'd cooperate, but he'd still hoped. "I'd thought maybe if you were seeing him soon. Tonight, for dinner maybe, you could drop my name."

Her upper lip pulled into a sneer. "I will, as a matter of fact. I'll pass your concerns to him, along with the opinion that my son is chasing a dream and living in a fantasy world."

The insult sliced under Tate's skin, and he forced himself to ignore it. "I appreciate it. Thank you for your time."

He started to rise, and then paused, as if he'd remembered something. "One more thing. We've discovered Skriddie is in breach of contract for the hardware they rented to the new venture."

Her brows rose and her self-satisfaction vanished. "I doubt that."

"I did at first, too." He slid her a folder. The paperwork inside was from Mikki and Jaycie—evidence that Marge had been responsible for throttling the crowdfunding sites' bandwidth and server space, he assumed to make a point about...something? He knew other companies used negotiation tactics like that, but he hadn't expected it from his own.

"If there's an issue, I'm sure we'll resolve it." Her snideness was gone, as was her pleasant tone. A mask had slid in, flat and expressionless.

"That won't be necessary. The contract has been violated, and is being terminated. Notarized documents will arrive this afternoon."

She gave him a wicked smile, eyes narrowed. "You can't bring this to life on your own. If you burn this bridge, your venture will fail."

He shrugged, not feeling nearly as casual as he was trying to look, and stood. "I'm not worried about it."

His hands shook as he strode from the office, irritation and satisfaction warring for control of his thoughts. It was true, she'd never stopped condescending while he was in there, but he hadn't flinched, or sunk to the same level.

Besides, he had a lunch date with a wonderful woman. The

adrenaline racing through him ebbed as he headed toward his car. He'd be a little early, but he needed the drive and the fresh air to clear his head.

When Lys pulled into the parking lot of the diner, almost an hour later, he'd replayed the conversation in his head to the point of exhaustion. He couldn't think of a way to have handled that situation better, all things considered. But seeing Lys walking toward him, hair pulled into a loose bun, sway to her hips, erased the rambling thoughts. He met her halfway, pulled her close, and kissed her hard. She let out a tiny whimper, and leaned into him. God, he loved everything about kissing her. He intertwined his fingers with hers, and they headed toward the restaurant.

"How'd it go?" she asked.

"About like I expected."

"I'm sorry."

"Nah." He'd had enough time to make his peace with it. "We knew it probably wasn't going to happen. If Thompson is going to be an asshole about this, he can deal with the fallout. He never even considered you."

"I know. But…" She shook her head. "You're right. His choice."

The hostess led them to a table outside, and he took the seat across from Lys. "It's done and over. Did you get up to anything interesting this morning?"

She flipped the menu open and gave it her full attention. "Not really. Boring house stuff."

Doubt brushed his senses. She was just hungry. Not lying to him. "Like what?"

"Hmm?" She glanced up, but never met his gaze. Whatever she was studying seemed to have stolen her interest. "Cleaning. Laundry."

He knew he wasn't reading her wrong this time. She was keeping something from him. But what? Fuck. "What aren't you telling me?"

She finally looked him in the eye, corners of her mouth turned down. "I'm just." She pushed her menu aside. "I feel like this whole thing is going too well. There were so many road bumps to get to this point. And now it's just smooth sailing? I guess I'm just waiting for the other shoe to drop."

That was something he understood. He reached across the table and covered her hand with his. "Maybe it will, maybe it won't. We'll make arrangements for the stuff we can predict, and deal with the rest of it if it happens."

"I guess."

"Lys." He tugged her thumb. "We'll make it work. That's what we do, right?"

"Of course." Her expression relaxed. "You're right. We'll be fine. Are you coming over tonight?"

Tate still felt like he was missing something, but she said it was just stress, and after his morning, he might be overreacting. "Of course. I'll be there after work."

***

"Lys." Tate's voice drifted from the kitchen. "Are you sure you're all right?

The question filled her with an uneasiness she didn't expect. She set her glass of ice water on the table, and looked in his direction. "Not unless you know something I don't."

He wandered back into the living room, and held up an empty box. It was from her pregnancy test. Her gut sank. Why hadn't she hidden that better instead of just leaving it on top of the trash? Or maybe she should have just owned up to it right away instead of trying to hide it.

"So this was negative?" he asked.

That wasn't the way she wanted him to lead. "Would negative be better?" Not that she had planned for him finding out this way, but in a perfect, everything is going smoothly now world, he wouldn't be wearing a scowl, and he'd have asked if it was positive.

His mouth twisted in irritation. "Negative would justify the 'no there's nothing to tell you' response. I'm pretty sure positive is the kind of something you don't just dismiss."

"So what would you prefer the result was?" Alyssia knew this was childish. Coming clean was her best option, but concern twisted her from the inside out. They hadn't been together long enough for her to lose Tate.

Wait. Lose him? The phrase gnawed at her. Why would she think that? It was true, they'd had some bumps, and they hadn't officially been together for long, but even before they were a couple, he'd always been there. Since she was young, he looked out for her. And what he told Jared resonated so deeply with her. It wasn't that she always called Tate first because he was the crush she never got over. She didn't think his name first when the news was good or bad or even just mediocre because he was her brother's buddy.

He really was her best friend, and even though she'd only known about the baby for a few hours, if it had been any other news at all, she would have dialed him before anyone else, just to shout with joy and share.

The words stuck in her throat, and she forced them out. "I do have something to tell you. My birth control failed. I'm pregnant." It terrified her to say it out loud, but at the same time, it was comforting to have it off her chest. "I'm sorry."

The irritation vanished from. His face, replaced with a blank mask of nothing. "Sorry for… keeping this from me? For not trusting me with this information? For thinking… I don't know. What were you thinking, Lys?"

"I was scared. I think that's fair. This isn't something we planned for. We're still new as us. I figured the 'do you want kids' conversation was at least a few months off."

"So was the plan to keep it to yourself until you thought we were in a good place for that talk?" His mask slipped, and hurt flitted across his features.

"I haven't even known for twelve hours. I'm still adjusting to the news, and you've always made it clear a family wasn't in your future. I assumed that included kids."

"My views on my future have changed. Or did you think I was making up all everything I said about wanting you by my side? I've listened to and heard you, Lys. I know what you want out of life."

"But what do you want?" The question knocked a fear loose that she hadn't been able to name before now. Tate spent so much time worrying about her. It was sweet, but it wasn't a foundation for long term if he put his own needs aside.

He raked his fingers through his hair. "I don't know. Honestly, I haven't thought about it. The one thing I do want is what you said before. To do this together, whatever *this* entails. I know Jared doesn't believe me when I say that, and I'm sure he's not the only one. You and I have a spotty history. But you're the one who said we were doing this with each other; I thought you meant it."

Alyssia frowned. He was right. But even considering all that, "I'm still scared, Tate. And I'm still processing."

He drew his mouth into a thin line and leaned against the wall. "I get that. But…" He crossed the room, took her hand in his, and looked her in the eye. The test was positive, really?"

She nodded.

A smile cracked onto his face, and he squeezed her hand. "That's amazing."

A huge cloud she hadn't realized was haunting her lifted, and relief flooded her. She threw her arms around his neck and kissed him. This was going to be okay after all. She never should have doubted.

TWENTY-ONE

ALYSSIA POWERED DOWN HER WORK COMPUTER, AND GATHERED HER purse. Going home before the sun set, instead of as it rose, she liked that. Besides, Tate was picking her up, and she liked that even more. He was already waiting in the lobby, chatting with Sara.

The moment Alyssia stepped into the main room, his attention was on her. Her cheeks flushed at the smile that spread across his face.

"Don't keep her up too late." Sara warned. "She's got an important eight a.m."

"I'll do what I can. No promises." Tate stepped closer, wrapped an arm around Alyssia's waist and kissed her.

She moaned against his mouth. Such an amazing feeling.

Sara sighed. "So perfect," she said. Alyssia looked up just in time to see Sara snap a picture with her phone.

Alyssia held up a hand. "Delete that."

"Nope. Cutest couple of the year."

The front door slammed open, smashing into the far wall, the noise reverberating through the room. Alyssia spun, heart hammering at the abrupt interruption.

Bryce Thompson Jr. stood in the front lobby, face contorted. His cheeks were red. His mouth was twisted in a sneer. "Give me back my fucking dog."

Tate stepped in his path, fists clenched, and advanced forward. "You need to leave."

Alyssia was aware of Sara grabbing the phone, and dialing. But most of her attention was on the scene in front of her. Her stomach flipped in on itself, adrenaline spiking.

"Not until I have my dog." Bryce stepped forward and Tate met him.

Tate grabbed his arm, and pushed back. Bryce wrenched free, and let a fist fly, clipping Tate in the jaw.

"Stop." Alyssia looked for an opening. Something she could do to step in.

"Yes, we have an intruder," Sara told the person on the other end of the line. Alyssia assumed 911. "Violent. Assaulting a customer."

Tate growled, and dove his shoulder into Bryce's chest. The teenager returned the favor with a direct punch to Tate's gut. Tate grunted and doubled over.

Alyssia looked around the room for something, anything she could use to stop this. Bryce advanced on her. "Give me back my fucking dog."

She retreated as he advanced. Her pulse hammered in her ears, drowning out the background noise.

"It's not your dog." Bryce's voice was low and threatening, but a slur running through the words. "He's mine. I get to do what I want with him. If he's a bad dog, I get to beat him. I bought him. I'll buy you, too, bitch." As he got closer, a wash of alcohol on his breath hit Lys, making her eyes water.

Tate approached him from behind, hooked his arms under Bryce's and, pressed his interlocked fingers into the back of the kid's neck. He dug his knee into the back of Bryce's leg, and forced him to the ground. "Don't touch her."

"Let go." Bryce struggled against the grip, but Tate held fast.

The door swung open for the second time in as many minutes, and two officers stepped in cautiously, hands on their holstered guns.

"We got it from here," one said. Alyssia knew the man—he almost always took her reports, and had stopped by the shelter several times in the last few weeks to make sure things were going all right despite the protesters out front.

They extracted Tate and Bryce from each other, and cuffed the teenager. Relief shuddered through Alyssia, and she wrapped Tate in a hug, holding on until they both stopped shaking.

ALYSSIA GRABBED a handful of ice from the freezer and stuffed it inside a bag. She returned to the living room to find Tate leaned back on the couch, staring at the ceiling. Sara had canceled the 8 a.m. After spending the last several hours answering police questions, filing a report, and having a doctor tell Tate nothing was broken, but his face would look pretty nasty for a while, Alyssia knew they weren't going to be getting up early.

She knelt on the cushion next to Tate, and pressed the bag of ice to his eye. "My hero." She was only half teasing. Investing money he already had in her business was one thing, but taking a fist for her... Something she never thought she'd have to see, but she couldn't help being warmed by the gesture.

"I wasn't really thinking about being a hero." He covered her hand with his, the heat of his palm searing, where the ice bag chilled. "I was more concerned about you."

"That's what makes it heroic."

He pulled the ice pack away, and focused on her. "If you say so. Personally, I've got better things to think about."

She raised her brows. "Really? Like what?"

"Like why I'm the only one with a cold face right now."

"Because you're the guy with the black eye."

"So?" Tate plucked an ice cube from the pack. "I'd rather focus on you than that tiny purple bump on my face." He traced the frozen liquid over her bottom lip and then her top. His voice dropped an octave, gaze locked on her face. "Like how kissable your lips are."

Her mouth parted at the shock of cold and she gasped at the tease of melting water against her skin. "How long your neck is." He popped the cube onto his tongue, and lowered his head. Ice and his lips caressed a line down to her collarbone. She arched her back and whimpered. Her nails slid up his back, and she shifted her weight to get closer.

He lowered one hand to the back of her knee. She moved her leg, until she was half wrapped around him, urging him on.

"This bit is always fun, too." His icy lips brushed her ear, and she gasped.

"That does seem like a lot to think about." Her comment was cut short when he nipped her earlobe with his teeth. Her fingers wrapped in his thick hair and she pulled him back to her, crushing her lips against his. An insistent need grew between her legs.

She covered his other hand and pushed it further up her thigh, her knee hooking on his hip. His hand moved up the back of her thigh, sliding over the curve of her hip. He traced along the waistband of her jeans, a chuckle rumbling in his chest. His mouth moved back to her neck, words tickling her skin. "Good point. I guess we'll just have to cover multiple spots."

She fumbled for a comeback, attempts failing when his teeth grazed the soft spot between her neck and shoulders, and he sucked on the sensitive flesh.

His fingers brushed her crotch through denim and she whimpered. Her nails dug into his back, holding him close. He pressed two fingers against the seam of her pants, and pressed into her slit. She squeaked and shifted her weight until her clit rested under his touch. He massaged harder, and she ground against his hand.

He pulled away abruptly, and tugged her to her feet. "We need a little more room than the couch." He led her into the bedroom, spun her to a stop, and rested his hands on her cheeks. When he pressed his lips to hers, her chest threatened to burst. His tongue pushed into her mouth, massaging and twisting with hers. Wet need throbbed between her legs, wanting more attention, and her nipples pressed against the lace of her bra.

She glided her fingers down his chest, undoing each button she encountered, then pushed his shirt off his shoulders. Hunger swelled inside, combined with the lingering adrenaline from earlier. Each touch sent fire over her skin, and his comforting scent filled her thoughts.

He broke the kiss long enough to let her yank his undershirt over his head. He gripped her hair, and she gasped at the sharp jerk when he lowered his head to the hollow at the base of her throat. Her pulse threatened to run away when he cupped her breast, and squeezed a nipple through her bra.

His strong touch coaxed every nerve ending to life. She dragged her thumb over his chest, and flicked a small brown nub, slowly at first, then faster in response to his moans. He stripped her shirt and bra off, and tossed them aside. He guided her to the bed. Her sex pulsed, wanting attention. He massaged her breast, then drew a pink button into his mouth. When he flicked his tongue back and forth at a rapid pace, she tilted her head back with a gasp. God, that felt amazing. It tugged a chord inside that ran from her nipple straight to her aching center.

He continued the motion for several minutes, switching between breasts, until her thoughts swam with so many sensations she couldn't process them.

She wanted more. To feel his entire body pressed against her. She undid his belt and slacks, and slid her hand inside his boxers. His mouth vibrated against her rigid nipple when he groaned. She worked him as free as was possible, given they were both sitting, and stroked his shaft in time with his sucking. He thrust his hips against her.

Without warning, he unsnapped her jeans, jerked the zipper down, and nudged her onto her back. He yanked her pants down her legs, then leaned over her, voice deep and gravelly. "I need to fuck you."

She nodded at the hunger in his voice, not sure she trusted herself to speak. He shed the rest of his clothing. She scooted back on the bed, already slick with anticipation. With a single thrust, he drove inside her. She arched at the sensation of being spread open, drawing him in farther. He leaned forward, hands on either side of her head, and worked his hips slowly, keeping the rhythm steady. She pushed against him, trying to increase the pace.

He dipped his head in, mouth hovering over her ear. "If you do that, I can't last long."

She smiled. "I don't mind."

He sat straight up, pushing himself deeper with a sudden thrust. "I do." He grabbed one of her knees, and drove it to her chest. With his free hand, he reached between them, and found her clit. He bumped his thumb over the button, pressing harder each time he thrust into her.

She gasped, each breath growing shorter as the combination of him hitting her G-spot and fingering her pushed her to a fast climax. She wanted to draw the moment out, though. Sink into the pleasure. She pounded against him, and this time he let her set the pace. Orgasm flowed through her. Her pussy clenched around his cock, spasming, milking him. He pulled away from her swollen sex, and pushed her other knee forward. His grunts grew more labored and thrusting more frantic. She recognized the familiar sound of him coming, and seconds later, he spilled inside her.

He continued to pound a moment longer, until the edge faded from her ecstasy. He finally slowed, then stopped and let go of her legs. Still inside her, he bent in and brushed his lips over hers. "I want this for the rest of our lives. This… everything. This us." His words were punctuated with him struggling to catch his breath.

She nodded. "Me too."

He rolled off, and they shifted on the bed until she could rest her head on his chest. She could only focus on a single thought, as they intertwined their fingers and rested their hands on his chest. This was absolutely perfect.

TWENTY-TWO

Consciousness trickled into Tate's thoughts, bringing the ache of a black eye with it. He groaned and tried to ignore the throb as he forced himself to sit. He was the only one in bed. Sun shone through the window, striking his face and making him wince.

"Lys." He called through the apartment.

"Living room. You need to see this."

He couldn't tell if she sounded stressed out, or excited, or something else. He stumbled to his feet, and pulled on his clothes as he walked. For a moment he considered leaving it all behind, but with his luck Jared would be out there, or something equally as awkward.

Lys sat on the couch, wearing one of Tate's button-down shirts, and possibly not much else from the look of her bare legs tucked beneath her. She nodded at the TV. "Sara texted me. Said we made the morning news."

It wasn't Thompson's affiliate, it was the competition. And as Tate watched the clip, he understood why. It was a shaky, low quality video of the brawl last night, complete with subtitles of every abusive, arrogant comment Bryce Jr. had made.

Tate sank onto the couch, blinking back his surprise. "How'd they get this? It's not security footage."

"Sara. She said she was sorry, but not really."

"Wow." He listened to the newsman explain Bryce Thompson Jr. had been arrested. Bryce Thompson Sr. had issued a public apology for the unknowingly false reports they'd done on the shelter, and had refused any other comment.

"Thompson is going to be pissed," Tate muttered. "He won't let this drop." Not that it mattered.

Lys leaned her head against his shoulder. "We'll deal with it." Her words echoed his thoughts. "If there's backlash, we'll handle it together."

———

Tate held out Lys's chair for her, then slid it in as she sat, before taking his own seat across from her. It was taking a large part of his focus to keep his pulse from galloping away. He could be patient though. Only a few other diners were in the restaurant, and all sat several tables away. He'd made sure their reservations tonight would be perfect. Already discussed the meal with the chef, made sure they'd have the alcohol-free sparkling wine on hand for Lys.

The whole evening had to be just right. Though, given the company, he would have been okay with a crowded cafeteria off the interstate. Her black dress hugged her figure perfectly, flaring out at the waist, ending just above her knees. She was only seven weeks along, so she wasn't showing yet.

He'd struggled with the news of the baby. It had come as a huge shock, and he had to admit, he'd been terrified during the entire conversation with Lys. But the longer he thought about it, the more it felt right. He might not have enjoyed his childhood, and he had issues with his parents, but he'd seen other examples of amazing families all around him. Their child was going to have the same thing—a good, caring home. And he knew he didn't want it any other way.

She draped her napkin over her knees, and sipped her drink, looking everywhere but him. That was odd. He beat back a creeping smidgen of doubt. "I wanted to talk to you about something." She finally met his gaze.

His mind produced about five billion scenarios simultaneously, and he banished them all. No reason to jump to conclusions when she was sitting right there, about to finish her thought. "Sure. What's up?"

She tapped her fingers on the stem of her glass. "Now that Bryce Jr.'s preliminary hearing is over, the shelter can settle up some of our outstanding paperwork."

It hadn't been easy for her to testify when they determined whether or not the teenager should stand trial—reiterating what was wrong with Grim when he'd been brought in—but thanks to her, and Sara's video, the prosecution had a solid enough case to proceed.

She chewed on the inside of her cheek. "We need to place Grim. And I think I've found the perfect spot for him."

She would have found Grim a new home before now, but because of how public the case had become, the shelter held onto him until everything was legally finalized. Something sad tugged at Tate's chest, masking the giddy nervousness that had been there seconds earlier. He'd spent a lot of time playing with that dog during recovery. "That's fantastic." His tone came out flatter than he intended.

"The thing is, I'd like to see him with you. You've got the yard, he already loves you, and, well…"

Tate couldn't help his grin at the suggestion. He'd never even considered the idea. "I'd love to keep him. Are you sure? Am I allowed to do that?"

"Of course you are." She laughed. "There's a probationary period, but since you've spent half your free time with him, I'm not worried."

He let his joy mingle with his growing anticipation. He hadn't been sure when he wanted to do this. The meal was planned, the details were supposed to be spontaneous. Now seemed like as good a time for a segue as any. So why had his heart just paused? An unfamiliar nervousness fluttered through him "Speaking of having a lot of room…" He fumbled with a velvet box in his pocket, fingers suddenly feeling flimsy. "I want you to know, I'm so happy about the baby. And your pregnancy doesn't change how I feel about you."

She furrowed her brow, and tilted her head. "I know."

He finally grasped the box, and knelt next to her. "We've only been dating for a few months, but you've been my world for a long time. My best friend, my confidant, my everything. Alyssia Tippins, will you marry me?" He opened the box, to expose a ring with a recessed band of diamonds.

She gasped, and nodded. "Yes, and a million times over, yes."

He shouldn't have been nervous, of course she'd agree, but the reassurance didn't stop relief and joy from filling him. He slipped the ring onto her finger, stood, and brushed his lips over hers. She hooked her fingers at the back of his neck, and held him close for several more seconds, deepening the kiss.

He couldn't think of a better future. Things would only get better from here on out.

To KEEP up to date on new releases and other news from Allyson Lindt, subscribe to my mailing list.

PLEASE HELP this author's career by posting an honest review wherever you purchased this book.

HER SURRENDER

ONE

Vivian hooked the heels of her shoes on the rung of the tall stool, leaned against the high table, and let her gaze wander around the bar area of the restaurant. She'd thought about going home to change after work, before heading here, but if she walked into her condo, she wouldn't want to leave again. Tonight, she was determined to enjoy a night out, to prove to herself she still knew how to have fun, even if her two closest friends were getting married and had their own lives now.

Which, when she thought about it, was sad. Not that they were engaged—she wished Jared and Tate nothing but the best of luck and adored their fiancées. What struck her as a little pathetic was that the only people she called true friends were her two executive counterparts from work. People she didn't even know until five or six years ago.

She tucked the journey into poor-me-ville aside, and took another sip of her cranberry and vodka. Her career was as important to her as not surrendering her individuality to someone else. Of course her colleagues were her best friends. Which meant she missed their company, as much as she tried to deny it.

If Jared were here… He'd probably have Mikki with him, who

would be showing him how to play some game with saltshakers or something. Vivian couldn't even begin to predict what that woman was thinking half the time. There was Tate, who wouldn't be here without Jared—or rather, these days, without Alyssia, who was about eight months pregnant and looking every bit like a glowing mother to be. Vivian never thought she'd see the day when Tate fell into fatherhood, but she could tell he was going to be awesome at it.

Maybe heading out tonight was a bad idea. She downed the rest of her drink in a single gulp, eyes watering as the liquor burned down her throat. She'd get dinner to go, find a movie at home to watch, and not let herself sink into self-pity.

"Vivian?"

The familiar voice dug something from deep inside her and twisted her insides in on themselves. Not because she'd know that voice anywhere, and not because hearing him still sent chills through her, after all these years—which it didn't at all—but because he was supposed to be on the other side of the country, in his hometown. If Damon was here, it could only mean trouble.

She summoned a smile and turned toward him. "Counselor, we didn't expect you in town for this." Through the pleasant formality, her mind worked overtime to figure out how much disruption his presence was going to cause tomorrow, in the office.

He raised an eyebrow. How was it fair he pulled off gorgeous after all this time? Mid-thirties, and he still looked like he did when they were in college. Brown hair trimmed close. Captivating eyes. The biggest difference from back then was a button-down shirt hugged his broad shoulders now instead of a T-shirt, and slacks covered a sexy ass, as opposed to the jeans he'd preferred back then.

"Counselor? Really?" Amusement lined his tone. "That's the best I get?"

She wasn't going to fall into flirting with him, as much as part of her itched to. Even though she knew better, every time they'd run into each other in the last couple of years, there had been flirting. It wasn't professional, and not starting was the best way to keep it from happening. "You'd prefer…?"

He slid out the stool next to her, and took a seat at her table.

"My name would be nice. Are you alone tonight, or are your boys around here somewhere?"

A short laugh slipped out before she could stop it, and she tried to cover it with cool irritation she didn't feel. "My what?" She knew exactly who he was talking about.

"I apologize. Your colleagues. Not that you need the clarification."

"They're home. They have other lives now."

His smile grew, and the corners of his eyes crinkled. "Then it's my lucky night twice over. Running into you. Alone. I don't think they like me very much."

She reached for her drink, more to give her hands something to do, than because she was thirsty. Right. She'd finished it. She twitched her fingers against the glass. "You're Head Legal Counsel for the company that spends entirely too much of their money and time trying to rip us off. Can you blame Jared and Tate for not liking you?"

"That's not it. I think they just don't like me." Damon's tone was teasing, with no hint of malice. He waved down a waitress. "Guinness for me, and another cranberry and vodka for my friend."

The girl nodded and scurried toward the bar.

Vivian wanted to protest the assumption, but it warmed her that he knew her preferred drink. She shook aside her buzz of appreciation for his attention. Maybe she should have had something to eat, along with the two drinks she'd already polished off.

Damon squeezed her fingers, his touch sending a pleasant shock through her. "It's good to see you, Vivian."

The simple compliment clenched in her gut and dragged up her earlier loneliness. She squelched the reaction. She wasn't opposed to picking up a random guy in a bar—*no strings* was her preferred lifestyle—but Damon wasn't random. "Same here." She kept her words neutral.

"I mean it."

How was she supposed to respond to that? Change the subject. "I'm surprised you're in town. I thought you'd leave something tedious like discovery depositions to someone else."

He drew a finger along the back of her hand and up her arm, gaze locked on hers. "I thought I'd be a little more hands-on this time."

Heat jolted through her, filling her veins and tingling in her skin. *Don't react. He's testing your limits.* Telling her body to calm down didn't have as much of an impact as the searching look he gave her. "We're talking about the depositions still. Right?" She forced herself to sound calm, but didn't pull away from his touch.

He nodded at the waitress, when she set their drinks in front of them, but never pulled his attention from Vivian. "The thing is, if we talk about the depositions or work, or anything professional, we have to take almost all of it off the table, to avoid any kind of conflict-of-interest issues. Which means we run out of things to talk about in an instant. So I was hoping we could shelve that and be old friends catching up on everything except work."

Her brain stalled. She was used to small talk at business gatherings, but that had never been her relationship with Damon. Even after they broke up, whenever work brought them back together, the conversation got intense fast. Not necessarily because of flirting, but more because they tended to delve into every topic under the sun when they had time. Tonight, as much as she wanted company, she knew falling into that kind of familiarity with him was a bad idea. "Like… what you're doing here?" There. That was small-talky.

He looked around in an exaggerated motion, before turning back to her. "I'm in the restaurant, because it's near my hotel and I wanted dinner. I'm sitting with you, because who am I to laugh in the face of whatever fate stuck us in the same place, on the same night?" He covered her hand with his, and traced tiny circles with his thumb. "If I talk about why I'm in town, it'll lead to work, and… You already know the answer, anyway."

She wouldn't be dissuaded that easily. If he stayed, they'd make small talk. *You could always leave.* Except, despite the mental reminder, she didn't want to. It was an irrational response. Not as if anything beyond chatter was going to happen with Damon. But knowing this didn't motivate her to pull away. Maybe the alcohol was fuzzing her senses; she did feel a little lightheaded. Then again, maybe she didn't care. "How's your brother?"

Amusement danced in his eyes. "Fighting the good fight, I suppose. Social justice warrior through and through."

Vivian could do this. She didn't know why she'd been flustered. It was a normal, vanilla conversation. "I've been following this new project of yours. The legal-defense fund, to help those discriminated against in the workplace." She wasn't keeping track of it because Damon was involved—and that wasn't denial. It was because she fully supported the idea of helping people take a stand, especially in technology, against the kind of issues that kept a lot of women and minorities out of the business, or at least from speaking up when they were treated wrong.

"Ethan's girlfriend came up with the idea. She reminds me of you." Damon dragged his gaze over her, and friction rose in its wake. "Intelligent. Witty. But she doesn't have to pretend she enjoys the life she's built for herself. She means it," he said.

Irritation flitted into Vivian's thoughts. There it was. If Damon couldn't immediately find a way to chink someone's armor, he kept poking from different angles until he figured it out. It made him a fantastic attorney, but it also made him dangerous, as far as Vivian was concerned. She wasn't interested in having her walls broken down. Not by him. Not again. It took her far too long to rebuild, after they broke up. When she left home right after high school, only seventeen years old, she swore to never make the same mistakes as her mother. Never let herself get so lost in loneliness, she clung to any man who paid attention to her, regardless of how abusive or neglectful they were. Never surrender her identity to another human being.

She pulled her hand from Damon's, secured her glass, and gave him a fake smile, not caring if the phoniness showed. "They sound like a perfect match."

"Come on." Damon leaned back with a chuckle. "I don't even get an eye twitch for that?"

Bonus points for being honest about what he's trying to do. "Nope."

"Fine." He leaned back in his seat and took a drag off his beer. "You already know what I'm up to. What are you working on?"

She had to be misunderstanding the question. She rolled it over in her head but couldn't figure out why he'd ask after insisting they not talk about the office. "Well, we're involved in this lawsuit—"

He shook his head. "I mean at home. You haven't given up dancing, have you?"

A new kind of heat flooded her. Pleased that he remembered, and not a physical reaction to his presence. She danced in her free time. Jazz, ballet, modern, or whatever mood struck her. She'd never been good enough to do so professionally—well, not the kind of professional that went on a resume—but she enjoyed moving to the music. It helped her find her center, when nothing else could. "I haven't given up, no. I found a new remix a few weeks ago that inspires me every time I hear it. It's nice to unwind to at night."

He shifted in his seat and rested his knee against her leg. "I'd love to see your interpretation sometime."

"I'm not sure anyone else would appreciate me dancing in the deposition room."

"Who cares what they think? If they have any taste, they'll be grateful for the break from the norm." He loosened her fingers from her glass and intertwined them with his own. "Or, if you'd prefer, I don't have any other plans this evening."

Vivian struggled with her response. Which was irrational, because she already knew the answer, and didn't know why she was debating with himself. His offer wasn't tempting. Maybe if he weren't head of Legal for the NetSafe Systems, the company her employer, Skriddie Bust Media was suing. And maybe if she hadn't almost lost herself in him when they dated. And maybe—

She benched the string of thoughts. None of them mattered, because she wasn't seriously considering his offer, even if he was only testing her defenses again. She pulled away from his touch and couldn't ignore the disappointment that raced through her. "You've probably got paperwork to review before tomorrow. I know I do." She stood and dropped her money on the table. It was more difficult than she expected to put her cool mask back in place. *You're lonely, so you're looking for someone to fill the void. You know it's not him. You know what he does to you.* She repeated the mental reminder, until it was stuck on a loop in her head. "Good night, Counselor."

"Vivian." A frown creased his brow, and a hint of request leaked into his voice.

"I'll see you in the office tomorrow." She turned on her toe, and cut a straight line for the door. It took the last of her restraint not to look back at Damon. Not to go back and join him. Not to invite him back to her place, for a private performance.

Seriously, what was wrong with her tonight?

TWO

Damon stared back at the girl, unflinching. Maybe *girl* wasn't the right word. He let his gaze travel her frame again. She was probably his age, filled out the cut-off shorts and tube top with subtle but gorgeous curves, and he didn't see a single inch of her not toned. Her low-rise waistband dipped low enough he should be able to tell if she was a natural blonde, but there was no hint. Still, he'd bet money she was.

He dragged his gaze back to the stripper's face. "It's not fake."

She tossed his ID back on the table. "Your guy lied to you. The state logo is wrong. And that means I'm not serving you beer or anything else with liquor in it."

He wasn't going to look at the card. Looking was almost the same as admitting guilt. "It's not fake," he repeated. Fuck. He didn't want to get thrown out of this place. So what if he was only eighteen? He only wanted a drink and maybe a table dance. Something occurred to him. "How do you know that about the state logo?"

"I'm smart." Her posture and tone screamed *attitude*. Combined with that sexy body... if she didn't get him kicked out, he wanted the table dance from her.

"Or you're not as old as you say, either"—he dropped his voice, only meaning the accusation for her ears—"and you know what to look for."

"I'm twenty-two." Her answer came quickly, but she looked away, and pink dotted her cheeks.

"Me too. Which means I get a beer, and we keep each other's secret." He wasn't interested in getting her thrown out or fired, or anything like that. He was about to spend the next four years here, for college. It wouldn't hurt to know a pretty girl who could show him around town, who wouldn't call his bluff again on the ID.

She met his gaze again, amusement and defiance dancing in her eyes. "Fine. But don't get caught."

Moments later, she returned and set his drink in front of him.

"Can I see it?" he asked.

"I go on in half an hour, or you can see it up close for twenty-five dollars." She winked.

He chuckled at the innuendo. "Your ID. I want to see what a masterpiece looks like."

"I don't keep it on me while I'm working."

"Meet me after your shift is up, then."

She raised her brows. "I also don't date customers."

"I never said it was a date." He leaned back and took a swig of his drink. "Your assumption."

She rolled her eyes, but she was smiling. "I'm done at ten. They're not going to let you sit in here all night if you don't spend money."

He hid his wince. His wallet would hate him, but it was worth it. "I'll spend. That won't be a problem. Who am I waiting for?"

"Violet."

***

Now

Damon took a slow drag off his beer, as he watched Vivian stroll away from the bar. Her jacket pinched in around a narrow waist and ended right above her ass—gorgeous, firm, accentuated by her slacks. She never stopped looking incredible. Maybe he wasn't completely irritated with Hayden, for requiring him to be on-site.

It didn't matter that his history with Vivian was exactly that—history. There were times he wished they'd figured out how to stay friends. He missed her company. But knocking heads with her over work could be almost as much fun.

Even though *they* were ancient history, he wouldn't have complained if they moved their conversation somewhere more private, took their professional lives completely off the table, and re-enacted a few memories. Images flashed through his mind. Her, stripping off her top. Him, loosely binding her wrists. Running his fingers and tongue over every inch of her body, until she begged for release.

His cock hardened at the thought, and he adjusted himself, to relieve some of the pressure. He finished his beer. If he couldn't have intellectual stimulation, he'd have to settle for physical. The next question was, *here or somewhere else?*

"Is your friend coming back?" A teasing voice drew his attention. The waitress stood next to the table and studied him with wide blue eyes, as she traced a finger along the V-neck of her shirt.

She'd do. Sure, she was a little young—mid-twenties, most likely—but he wasn't looking for scathing conversation. That had walked out the door for the night. "You know"—he flicked his gaze to her nametag before locking it on her face again—"Emma, I don't think she is. Which…" He sighed and raked his fingers through his hair. "Never mind. Can I get another beer?"

Emma hesitated a moment, as if trying to decide whether or not to say something. Then she nodded. "Sure. I'll be right back." She was, too. Less than thirty seconds, if Damon had to guess. She set the fresh bottle in front of him on a coaster and brushed his hand as she withdrew hers. "Can I get you *anything* else?" She caught her bottom lip between her teeth.

This was too easy. Damon shook his head and drummed his fingers against the edge of his beer. "I'm only in town for a few days, and I don't really know anyone." He looked at her directly, holding her gaze captive. Each new twitch, either nervous, confident, or downtrodden, was part of drawing her into the conversation. "I bet you could do a much better job of showing me around, than she would have."

Pink spread over her cheeks—that was kind of cute—and she ducked her head. "Maybe."

"In that case…" He tilted his head toward hers and dropped his voice so she had to lean in, to hear him. "You tell me what time your shift is over, and I'll figure out when you get off."

She giggled. Not quite as endearing as the blush. "In a couple of hours," she said.

"Sounds perfect. I'll wait."

VIVIAN PROBABLY SHOULD HAVE TEXTED Jared and Tate when she left the bar last night, and let them know she'd run into Damon. She'd been distracted though, so she snagged Jared when he walked in the office this morning.

"What are the odds Damon only knew about the change in plans—I don't know—yesterday, as he caught his flight?" Jared asked Vivian. He sat in one of the chairs across from her desk, making notes on his phone every few seconds, in response to things said or files exchanged.

"He's known for weeks. I'm certain of it." She clicked up another file, scanned the contents, and stashed a copy in a new folder. The encounter in the bar had played in her head all night. If she hadn't run into Damon there, she had a feeling his being in office would have been kept a surprise up until the moment he walked in the door. She wouldn't linger on that now; she was in work-mode. Things needed to get done. Banter was a pleasant way to make the work go faster. Dwelling on what kind of games Damon was playing wasn't.

Someone knocked on her office door, and Vivian dragged her attention from her computer and focused on Tate.

"Alan said you were looking for me." Alan was Tate's administrative assistant, and as far as Vivian was concerned, a fantastic hiring decision. Then again, Skriddie Bust Media had a great track record with that. She'd never been with another company that had the same knack for finding the right people for the job.

Jared and Tate—and she, if she was listing people—were perfect examples of that. Even though the two men grew up together, and Tate's family owned the company, both men had worked as hard as she had, to secure their jobs. Now Tate ran a new arm of the company, focused on crowdfunding websites, Jared was half a step from being named Chief Technical Officer, and Vivian was senior Vice President of Sales and Operations.

She nodded at the empty chair next to Jared. "Change of plans for the NSS discovery depositions."

Jared held up a single sheet of paper. "Lead counsel is gracing us with his presence. And apparently visits start this morning, instead of tomorrow."

"Really." Tate snagged the legal-team roster and dropped into the chair. Unlike Jared, who sat straight-backed, Tate slouched a little and rested one ankle on the other knee. He looked at Vivian, rather than the paper he held. "I assume you're to thank, for him fitting an office visit into his busy schedule."

"My money's on Hayden. I'm guessing he thought this would be funny. Or something." Vivian expected last minute surprises from the upcoming legal sessions, but this one threw her for a loop. During a painful year of discovery documentation changing hands, she'd managed to keep contact with Damon to a minimum. Strictly to keep things simple. Skriddie's legal department said it probably wasn't an issue, given the relationship ended more than a decade ago, but it was more of a playing-it-safe measure.

"So you want me to play point while he's in the office." Tate snagged a pen from the holder on her desk, turned the paper over, and rested it on his leg, as if to take notes. "You know you can't avoid him completely."

She knew Tate would get it without her explaining. There was a lot more than running into an ex-boyfriend riding on this case. It had already cost Skriddie hundreds of thousands in man-hours, to pursue, and they bled more cash, the longer things dragged out.

They couldn't walk away, though. Losing meant NSS won their countersuit, Skriddie footed the entire bill, and they lost a lot of intellectual property and business they'd worked hard to earn. Caving to NSS could cost the entire business. "I can't avoid him the entire time; it's true. But if you're the one sitting in the room during depositions…"

"They can't claim you gave him dirty looks or something equally ridiculous, and it's one less thing for NSS to try and haggle about." Tate tapped the pen on his knee.

"Exactly." She loved the connection she had with these two. "You did most of the discovery paperwork, so you're already familiar with the case."

"And you won't get all technical and talk over their heads." Jared added.

"Lucky me." Tate's voice was heavy with sarcasm, but his smirk softened the tone.

"Luckier than watching the two of them stuck in the same room, for eight-plus hours." Jared didn't look up from his phone, but a smile twitched on his face.

With anyone else, Vivian would have questioned if they were being cruel, but she knew Jared was teasing.

"Sparks?" Tate asked.

Vivian couldn't hold back a snort of laughter.

"Ice," Jared said.

"From V? Nah." Despite the sarcasm, Tate grinned.

Vivian tossed a pen at him. "Love you too, asshole." The back and forth helped take her mind off the pending stress of the next couple of weeks. Even if she wasn't going to be sequestered in the deposition room, it wouldn't be easy. Skriddie had filed a lawsuit against NetSafe Systems, for a series of security violations to the Skriddie network. NSS had counter-sued for theft of intellectual property, and now a court reporter was recording a series of questions asked by legal counsel for both companies.

She should thank whoever thought to bring Damon in for the event, for getting her out of that room most of the time.

———

Damon straightened his suit jacket, stapled a smile in place, and stepped from the elevator. If he had his timing right, he'd be in the Skriddie offices before any of the other out-of-town guests, which meant he could get settled in the conference room before things got too crowded and hectic.

Last night, after fielding a series of questions about the weather, the football game on TV, and the weather again from Emma, he'd decided he wasn't in the mood to get laid after all. He went back to his hotel alone.

The receptionist flashed him a smile as plastic as his felt, and asked, "Can I help you?"

"I'm Damon Vicker. I'm here with the NetSafe Systems legal team." Another day and another office, he might be tempted to flirt. Strictly to stay in practice. He shifted his weight and adjusted his slacks. Maybe he shouldn't have acted like a horny teenager in his hotel room last night, unable to get Vivian out of his head. He was still raw this morning, from jerking off. What the fuck was wrong with him?

"Of course." She pressed a few buttons on her phone and spoke into her headset. "Mr. Vicker is here… No problem. I'll let him know." She looked at Damon again. "Someone will be right with you."

Vivian had been point on this case so far. What were the odds either she or her assistant were greeting people? A jolt raced over Damon's skin. *Calm down.* He stashed the unreasonable reaction and stopped fidgeting. He was on the clock now, and that meant being calm, collected, and unreadable.

"Vicker. Pleasure to have you in the office."

Damon spun at the familiar male voice. Tate. Damon extended his hand. "Foster. You get reassigned to administrative assistant? Step up for you. Isn't it?" It wasn't that he had a problem with Tate. He'd probably like the guy fine, under other circumstances, and compared to Hayden, Tate was a saint. If Damon had to work with the rich kid helping run Daddy's company, Tate was an easier choice. But the habit to throw the opposition off balance was always there, hovering at the front of Damon's mind.

"Nah." Tate shook his hand, grip firm enough to convey he wasn't interested in backing down, before he let go and nodded toward the conference room. "I've been promoted to Babysitter. V's got too much going on right now."

Or their Legal had advised her to keep contact with Damon to a minimum, to avoid accusations of conflict of interest. He'd guessed this would be the result, though no one at NSS had cared. "Speaking of babysitting, is Hayden in yet?"

Tate let out a barking laugh. "Nice, and no. You're here first." He gestured into a large room, with a table in the middle and a row of cabinets against the far wall. Coffee and bagels lined the counter. "Make yourself at home. IT's got independent Wi-Fi set up. Password is the zip code."

"Thanks." Damon knew better than to ask why they were on a separate, fairly insecure, network. Since one of the accusations against NSS was that they breached Skriddie's network, he suspected a lot of things would be off limits. A couple of laptops were already set up on the window side of the room. He picked a spot that looked least likely to get hit by the afternoon glare, found an outlet, and set up his computer before grabbing himself a cup of black coffee.

Over the next half hour, people spilled in, situated themselves around the table, and settled down to work. Damon kept half his attention on the questions and answers, and the remainder on how people reacted to both. They weren't actually taking depositions this morning. They were discussing their schedule and plans. Some faces were new, and others familiar, but as time passed, he got a better handle on each of them. Basic tells, nervous tics, and how comfortable each of them was with their involvement in the case.

When they took a break, Damon slipped away. He'd only been in the Skriddie building a few times, but the large, sprawling office was simple to navigate. He wandered through the halls, enjoying the mid-morning stillness of heads bowed and working, and found his destination without too much trouble. The soda machine.

"Did you get lost, Counselor?"

That was the familiar voice he'd wanted to hear all morning. He couldn't help the genuine smile that spread on his face, as he grabbed his drink from the machine and then turned to face Vivian. "Nope." He held up the bottle. "But a man can only drink so much water in a single sitting, and I think I've had too much coffee."

She raised her brows and shot a look at the can in his hand. "So you're going for the sugar instead. Smart." She leaned against the far wall, and the pose accentuated how well her shirt fit, hugging her breasts but looking professional. And when she twisted her body just right, Damon caught a hint of red lace under the peach-colored top.

Fucking sexy. He shuffled the thought aside. "Are you joining us this afternoon?"

"No." She crossed her arms, but instead of closing her off, the gesture showed off enough cleavage to tease. "Tate will handle things."

"You've got a different touch than he does." Damon was glad no one else was around. He had two choices—end the conversation quickly, or have a little fun. Impulse raced through his veins. Fun it was. "Not lighter, necessarily, but his experiences are different than yours."

The corners of her mouth twitched in an unformed smile. "He does fine with the tools he's got."

"I want someone who's more familiar with the tools I've got."

She covered her lips, but her snicker slipped out. "There was an information share. He's been filled in."

"Really?" Damon's grin spread. "Did you tell him *everything*? Because I'd like to hear that conversation."

"He knows enough to do what he needs to."

"But he's not my type." Damon stepped closer, so he could drop his voice, and not at all to catch a hint of the intoxicating violet scent drifting from her. *Watch yourself.* Nagging voice of reason. He knew what he was doing. This was innuendo at its vaguest. Nothing more.

Vivian wagged her finger, but she made no motion to step away.

"Careful, Counselor. Don't tie your own hands before this even starts."

He finished closing the distance, and dipped his head close to hers. He spoke quietly but couldn't keep the gravel from his voice. "Are you volunteering to let me tie yours instead?" All right, so this wasn't quite so vague or innuendo-y.

She straightened, leaving less than an inch between them. Her heat radiated, teasing him and drawing his imagination to life. She met his gaze. "I'm not. So I hope you got your fill from the waitress last night." Her tone was low, amusement lining it.

He was entertained she'd guessed him so right, and didn't bother to correct her assumption. "I never kiss and tell."

"Lucky me. I'll see you around, Counselor." She stepped around him.

Damon followed her into the hallway, where he almost collided with Hayden. Vivian gave the other executive a cool smile. "I have to get back to work."

Hayden's whistle echoed through the halls, as she walked away. "And you used to tap that."

Damon clenched his jaw and bit back a string of curses. Fuck. Hayden was the last person he needed to overhear that conversation.

THREE

Damon was tempted to bump Hayden aside when he brushed past, but as much as he disliked the man, Damon did work for them, and until his firm either left NSS's employ or fired Damon, he was stuck being civil. "We should get back."

"Hang on." Hayden grabbed his arm. Damon turned a glare toward the hand wrinkling his suit, and Hayden let go and shoved his hands in his pockets instead. "We've got a few minutes." His voice was low and he looked left and right between sentences. Which meant he didn't want to be heard.

The body language both piqued Damon's curiosity and set every inch of him on high alert. "Right. What can I do for you?"

"Hands tied. Vivian?"

God damn it, he *had* heard. Damon thought he'd been quieter. He had to assume Hayden heard everything, but at the same time, Damon should give away nothing. Irritation churned inside, mixing with concern this could get out of hand. Better defuse the situation fast and get back to work. "Our past isn't on trial. We've never made it a secret we used to date."

"Right. But Vivian, tied up? Literally? I can't even picture it. Well, I can, but not with her as a willing party."

Damon clenched his jaw and tried to be subtle about drawing in a deep breath and counting to ten. "Your sick fantasies are none of my business."

"She'd never do that now."

He needed to change the subject, cut the conversation off, and get back to the conference room. Damon summoned the calm exterior he used in tough cases and pasted it in place. "I'm not interested in what you think the people in this office would or wouldn't do. You're not as good at reading people as you think."

Hayden raised his eyebrows. "You're saying she'd do that. Submit."

Fuck, fuck, fuck. Damon's mind spilled through a twisted combination of irritation, fantasy, reason, and the desire to deck Hayden. The latter was winning, and that wasn't good. "I'm saying, if you had this gift you believe you have—to look at someone and know what they're thinking—the young lady whose job you threatened and code you appropriated would still be working for you. Instead, she's engaged to the Skriddie head of IT and is their primary witness in this case."

Hayden snorted and shook his head. "Bet me whether or not Vivian would still do anything bondage related."

"No."

"Because you know I'm right."

"Because it's none of your fucking business." Common sense Damon to step back, but he wouldn't be the first to turn away. If he were a better man, maybe not so stubborn, he might convince himself to leave without finishing this conversation. Since he couldn't hit Hayden, Damon's pride refused to let him go without getting in the last word.

"You're wrong about her, and your ego won't let you admit it." Hayden dropped his voice another notch in volume. "Or maybe when the two of you say you dated, it's an exaggeration. I see the appeal in that. Meet an attractive girl in college. Take what you want, with or without her permission. Force her to yield. Convince her to write it off, years later, for the sake of *career*—"

Damon grabbed a fistful of Hayden's jacket and guided him into the closest empty office. It took effort to move his jaw when he replied. To not speak through clenched teeth. "A few things. Speaking as your attorney, never let anyone hear you talk like that. Speaking as the guy who *did* hear it, if you ever imply that again—about me, yourself, anyone—you'll wake up on the floor, with a mild concussion. First time's free. Lucky you. My relationship with Vivian or any woman was, is, and always will be consensual."

Hayden jerked free of his grasp. Despite his squared shoulders and the hard set to his eyes, he stayed out of arm's reach. "Protesting much? Thinking a thought doesn't make a guy guilty."

Damon growled, clenched his fist, and took a step forward.

Hayden held up a hand. "So prove me wrong, tough guy. You don't want to be here anyway. You made that clear. Anyone can see the tension between the two of you goes both ways, but I call bull-shit that she surrenders control anywhere. If I'm wrong, you fly home early. Your team handles the depositions, like they were supposed to, and you go back to that little charity case of yours."

A million options raced through Damon's head, including several ways he'd punch Hayden right now and how much jail time he'd do for assault. Damon knew better than to let his temper take control, especially when someone tried to rile him up. He'd learned from his father at an early age that appearing to yield up front, while finding a smarter way out, was sometimes the best solution. "If it's a bet, you want equal wagers on the table. You're not right, but what do you get if you are?"

Hayden smirked and brushed past him. "Your job. Bet's on, asshole. Don't touch me again."

Damon snarled at the back of Hayden's head, and then composed himself before stepping back into the hallway. It was a bullshit wager. Vivian didn't deserve to be in the middle of it. He needed a little time, to cool down and figure out how to deter Hayden, and the details wouldn't matter.

The clenching rage and frustration in his joints disagreed, but it was ebbing adrenaline, not a nagging feeling this was a horrible idea.

VIVIAN COULDN'T GET the morning encounter with Damon out of her head. She knew the teasing was a bad idea, and she fell into it anyway. The attention was nice. Their shared past didn't have anything to do with it. Or at least not much. She was really letting this loneliness get to her.

She shook aside the rambling thoughts and focused on her work again. Chatter and laughter rolled into her office from the hall, and she glanced at her computer clock. Almost two. The legal team had to be wrapping up a late or long lunch, or both. She felt bad about shrugging the work off on Tate; his schedule was as busy as hers. At the same time, she was relieved she had some distance from Damon, to deal with this glitch in her brain.

"Got a minute?" Tate's question and knock drew her attention.

Good. A distraction. "What's up?"

He stepped inside, closed the door, and took a seat. He hesitated before answering. "You remember that night in Vegas?"

Tate's stiff posture, combined with the wandering thoughts of Damon that Vivian didn't want to entertain, made the muscles in her neck tighten. She wanted to make a joke about having been too drunk, but she knew exactly what he was talking about.

"Sounds familiar." The one that lead to these depositions. The cramfest of uncovering how NSS gained access to the Skriddie networks, and making sure the threat was removed and prevented in the future.

Tate sighed and sank further in his seat. "Apparently the four of us aren't the only people who do."

If she'd been on alert before, it was nothing compared to the alarms clanging in her head now. She didn't think any of the four of them said anything then that could be used against them in this lawsuit, but they'd pulled an all-nighter, and like now, tensions had been high. She didn't want to ask, but she had to know. "What are the claims?"

"They've got some kind of evidence that Mikki gave us proprietary information about the NSS network. Now they're suggesting she always worked for us and took your offer back then, and that her signing on with NSS was nothing more than a front."

Vivian swallowed a frustrated growl. "They know this is a business, not double-oh-seven, right? Only spies and corrupt companies come up with that kind of convoluted, double-agent bullshit."

He shrugged. "We argued that, when they dumped this in our laps during scheduling, this morning. Their response was that's the reason it never occurred to them until this whole legal mess started."

"Jerks," Vivian muttered. "How did they even get that information?"

"They're holding their source close for now. I was hoping you might have some thoughts."

Defensiveness spiked inside her. Or was that guilt, over flirting with the enemy? "Why are you asking me?"

"Because your office is closest to the conference room, and I kind of hoped this had already come up but wasn't in the hand-off information. I'm asking Jared and Mikki next."

"Right." She blew out a long breath. "Sorry."

"Vicker's really knocked you off your game."

"It shows, huh?"

"Only to me."

That was something. "I'll dig while you're in there. See what I can find. It's the least I can do, for dumping this on you last minute."

"You'd do the same for me."

It was true. Vivian would pull out the stops for any of them, which was why she wouldn't let them crucify Mikki, for doing what was right. "Regroup tonight? Dinner?"

"It'll have to be tomorrow morning, before the meetings start. Lys finally found the crib she wanted. I made her promise not to move any furniture around on her own."

Vivian was surprised he got Alyssia to agree to wait, even eight months into her pregnancy. The woman wasn't comfortable sitting and waiting for someone else to do things for her.

Tate paused with his hand on the doorknob. "Speaking of tonight, though..."

"Hmm?" Vivian didn't like that oh-by-the-way tone.

"The entire group—their legal, ours—is going out for dinner. If you want to join them. Off the clock, no talk about the case—all that stuff."

Perfect. This gave Vivian an excuse to ignore how much she didn't want to spend the evening alone. As long as she could get her head on straight before spending that much time with Damon. "Everyone?"

He gave a half-shrug, half-nod.

A muddled mixture of anticipation and dread spilled through her, souring in her gut and making her pulse race. No reason to let that show, though. "Absolutely. I'll make sure the boys don't get into any trouble."

Just keep yourself out of trouble in the process. Irritating voice. She'd be fine.

FOUR

Fꜰᴛᴇᴇɴ Yᴇᴀʀs Aɢᴏ

Damon's fingers hovered above her skin, millimeters from her fresh ink but not touching the new tattoo of a violet on her breast. "Don't get me wrong, it's sexy as fuck, but why?"

Vivian draped her arms over his shoulders and settled in, straddling his legs. "It's a birthday present to myself. I wanted to surprise you."

He trailed his lips up the side of her neck, breath hot against her ear. "You let someone inflict that kind of pain on you, without letting me watch?"

She laughed at the implication, unable to ignore the spike of heat it sent through her. "I thought of you the entire time."

"Naughty, naughty girl. Now that you're back, do I get to buy you your first legal drink, to celebrate you turning twenty-one?"

"I took the night off, so I wouldn't have to spend my time surrounded by drunk idiots. In other words, no."

He nipped at her earlobe, sending tingles of want through her. "It's your night. What do you want to do instead?" His voice was so low, she barely heard him, even with his mouth right next to her ear.

She shifted her weight against his legs and ducked her head. "I want to be yours for the evening." Even though her boldness came easily most of the time, this was the one thing she was embarrassed to ask for. She still struggled to get past the fact she willingly let him —wanted him to—do certain things to her, and enjoyed it. "Use me however you'd like, until I can't think straight."

A heavy current undercut his chuckle. "You're so wicked."

"It's one of the things you love about me."

He grasped her wrists roughly in one hand, and held them tight behind her back. "Arrogance gets you extra attention from the belt. And yes, it's one of many reasons I love you."

One-by-one, his words sank into her thoughts, warming her skin and heightening her senses. She didn't know which she enjoyed more—the sharp sting of leather, raising red on her ass, or the tender, almost reverent way Damon brought her to orgasm after. Wait. That wasn't true. She did know. Neither meant anything without the other. She squirmed, already slick in anticipation, and his cock hardened against her. "I love you too," she said.

"Stand in the middle of the room and take off your clothes for me." His whispered tone vanished, replaced with a low, commanding growl.

Vivian's heart hammered against her ribs, and desire pulsed between her legs. "Yes, Sir."

***

Now

"The blonde starts sobbing, and when the other two women ask her what's wrong, she cries, *I'm having puppies.*" Hayden laughed at his own punchline.

Damon didn't try to hide his eye roll, and neither did anyone else at the table. A few nervous chuckles rolled around the hibachi grill, but all the others appeared disgusted or did their best to look anywhere but at Hayden. No surprise, Hayden got worse when he had a few drinks in him. Vivian tightened her jaw, but her expression relaxed again so quickly, Damon almost didn't catch it. She seemed the least flustered.

Damon's phone vibrated against his thigh, and he reached for it. A glance at the screen told him it was his boss. Damon didn't know if he'd ever before been so relieved to get an after-hours call from work. He looked around, to excuse himself, but everyone was otherwise distracted.

"This is Damon Vicker," he said as he strode toward the exit. It was too loud in here for any conversation. That, and maybe the fresh air would help him clear his head.

"How's Atlanta?" Camille asked.

"Fantastic." Damon kept the pleasantry genuine, despite the snide tone in Camille's voice.

"Glad to hear it." She sounded anything but. "The boss's son behaving himself?"

"Not even close." He found an out-of-the-way spot along the side of the building, and leaned a shoulder against the brick. He could see the parking lot, but the rush of traffic was muted. "You walking out for the night?" It was nine here, which made it six back in Portland. He had a feeling if she was calling now, she'd be working late.

"It's funny you should ask that." The growing irritation in her voice set Damon on edge and tensed his muscles. "I'm actually going to be here a while."

Fuck. "What's up?"

"Well... I'm looking at a lawsuit from the GG foundation, accusing IasoChem of harassment, discrimination, and promoting a hostile work environment."

Damon pinched the bridge of his. IasoChem was one of their biggest clients, and Camille found every excuse she could, to force Damon through the ringer, for starting the GG Foundation without approval. "They simply need to go through the mediation and show they've learned their lesson. That's why we give them that option." She knew that, but he reminded her anyway. It wasn't as though the request was unreasonable. People deserved to be treated like people.

"IasoChem isn't interested in that. They want us to crush the plaintiff. Can you say *conflict of interest?*"

Probably better than you'd like. Images of Vivian flashed in his mind.

"I'm not handling their case. You've got me answering to someone else's whims right now."

Her sigh rocked through the earpiece and echoed in his skull. "Because you keep saying bullshit like this in earshot of Hayden, and he doesn't think you respect him."

"I don't."

"Damon." Her voice was sharp. "Deal with Hayden and get back here. You need to make this GG Foundation thing vanish."

"I'm not doing that. It defeats the purpose. The foundation is a safe place for people to come forward."

"It's been a year. The press doesn't care about this bullshit anymore. Sweep it under the rug and focus on helping someone not suing one of our clients, if that's the only way you can sleep at night. Her job or yours. Think about it."

The line went dead. Damon glared at his phone, a dozen foul words repeating over and over for several minutes in his head.

If Vivian had to hear another blonde joke, she'd scream, and she wasn't interested in letting any of these people know they got under her skin like that. Speaking of cracked composure, the paralegal who was part of Damon's group looked as if she wanted to crawl under a table and hide until this all stopped. Poor girl wasn't going to get anywhere, if she didn't learn to shrug off the blonde jokes.

Vivian stood and changed seats, taking the one Damon had abandoned a few minutes earlier. *Lucky bastard, getting a reprieve.* It put her next to Vanya, the paralegal.

"Hey." Vivian kept her voice quiet, not wanting to disturb the raucous laughter. "No one's going to be offended if you slip out for the evening." And Vivian had every intention of doing the same. Preferably before Damon came back, because she didn't want to deal with his attitude. *Not because you're worried he won't notice?* She crushed the ridiculous thought.

Vanya gave her a tiny smile, already pushing back from the table. "If you're sure..."

"Hang on." Vivian rested a hand on Vanya's arm, and Vanya's smile froze. "Can I borrow a cigarette?"

"Yeah, sure." Vanya fished one from the pack in her purse, said she'd see Vivian tomorrow, and vanished in the dinner crowd, on her way to the exit.

Vivian made sure the restaurant had her corporate card on file, to pay for the meal, said her goodnights, and moments later made her way outside as well. She didn't want the cigarette smell in her car—it had been ages since she had a smoke—so she wandered toward a picnic-style table at a neighboring cafe that was closed for the evening. She lit up and took a long drag. It had been long enough since she smoked, the puff left her lightheaded. But with nicotine feeding relaxation through her veins, it was worth it. It was going to be a long few weeks.

The lawsuit had already been taxing. Answering requests for documentation. Dealing with accusations that Skriddie was the one at fault. Their professional lives stuck under a magnifying glass. Having NSS in the office made the stress around the entire thing even worse. Go figure.

She inhaled another puff, her nerves calming further. Being away from the noise helped as well. Not that it was quiet out here. Music from the dance club next door spilled into the night, the bass sending a light tremble through the ground. She tapped her toe in time to the beat. As she smoked, she wiggled her hips to the music. Maybe she needed to go home and crank up a dance tune there. Something to fling herself into and forget about the world around her. Except she didn't want to dance alone.

She muffled the desire to fall into the music, and stilled herself, to finish her cigarette.

"That bad, huh?" Damon's question cut into the calm night. Sympathy, not disdain, lined his voice.

She tilted her head back, to look at the sky, and blow out a puff of smoke. "What do you think? These people are my friends and family, and they're being dragged through the mud, their ethics questioned and their time consumed, because y'all are greedy assholes."

Damon sat next to her on the bench but left at least a foot between them. "How did I get lumped into the same group as them?"

"You work for *them*." She held the smoke near the ground, used the toe of her shoe to make sure the cherry was out, and set the cigarette butt on the table, so she could throw it away later.

"Exactly. It's work; it's not personal. Sorry we can't all work with our replacement families."

She snapped her head toward him at the bitterness that crept into his tone. Was he playing a part? Digging for sympathy? It didn't matter, she wasn't getting sucked into whatever manipulation he had going on. *Unless he's not manipulating anything.*

Right. "Because this is all about the money."

"Money and fame." No emotion lined his words now. "You know that as well as I do. You got lucky with your job, and get to like it at the same time. Sorry to be a part of the tiny waves in paradise."

That was what she thought. He was trying to tug on her heart-strings. "If I wasn't happy with Skriddie business practices, I'd leave. I have that option, and so do you," she said.

"You'd pick up and leave your *family*? I forgot. Loved ones come first until you get a better job offer."

She glared at him. As much as she tried to keep her delivery cool, his words dug deep. "I need to get home."

"Wait." His single word made her pause. "I'm sorry. I didn't come over here to pick a fight."

"No. You're right." She turned to face him, tapping her toes inside her shoes in time to the beat. God, she'd rather be dancing right now. "I do hope I don't have to give up this family, though."

"Lucky them." He grinned, but sadness lingered in his eyes. "Listen, I didn't want to come on this trip. I'm trying to hand the case off, but Hayden keeps pulling me back in." He almost sounded sincere.

An ache echoed in her chest. Not that he was chipping away at her defenses, but maybe she could be a little kinder tonight. "I'm sorry you have to put up with that."

"It is what it is." He waved a dismissive hand. "It's all about the money and fame, right?"

"Do you ever think about leaving it all behind?" She didn't mean to say that aloud. It was a question meant more for her than anyone.

"Sometimes. But then I remember—"

"I know." She couldn't let him finish the thought. Doing so meant diving into a shared past, and the twisting in her gut told her that was a bad idea.

Back then, when the two of them were together, she shared secrets with him no one else knew. Not Tate or Jared or anyone. She was pretty sure the things she knew about Damon fell into the same just-between-us category. For instance, once upon a time he wanted to major in history, and maybe teach after he graduated.

His father's stance had been straightforward, though. He hadn't built his boys a life and a college fund from nothing, to see them struggle in go-nowhere jobs. So his father refused to pay for Damon's college, unless Damon went into medicine or law. Damon started law school at the same time his brother, Ethan, decided to major in computer programming and said he'd foot the bill himself.

Vivian knew Damon both resented and respected his brother for the decision, but also that Damon was content with his own choice, for the most part.

The things that happened to them before and during college might have molded them, but that didn't mean dwelling on the memories was healthy. She stood, and he did the same. "I should let you get going. We have weeks of long days ahead of us," she said. A new song pounded into the night, and her attention drifted toward the club. She knew the tune. It was one of her favorite to dance to, when no one was looking.

"Home?" Damon asked.

She dragged her gaze back to him. "Where else would I go?"

He closed the distance between them and rested a hand on her hip. Even through her skirt, the heat of his palm seared her senses. He nudged, prompting her to turn back toward the noise. "There, probably."

Dancing sounded better than the cigarette. Loud, mind-numbing, and all consuming. "I was thinking about it."

He slid his hand to the small of her back, and stepped close enough the faint scent of his cologne filled her thoughts. It mingled with the beat and the sound, and fuzzed her logic. "Do you need a dance partner?" he asked.

She shrugged, trying to look casual, but unwilling to pull away from his touch. "I'm sure I can find someone inside."

He pressed into her, arm hooking around her waist, hip bumping hers. "Someone who moves with you as well as I do?" His question, low and confident, blended with the night.

A smile rushed to her face, and she reached back to intertwine her fingers with his. "Haven't met anyone else yet, who does." This was a bad idea. Maybe. Probably. It certainly could have repercussions. Except, when it came right down to it, she trusted Damon. It might not be smart, and she wouldn't make the mistake of thinking they were more than associates, but he wouldn't use this against her.

And damn it, she wanted to enjoy herself for the night. They both knew what they were doing, and no one was going to get hurt. It would be fine.

"Come on." His warm breath caressed her cheek, as he led her toward the building. "Check your second guessing at the door. Let's go be other people for the night."

That was the best idea she'd heard in ages.

FIVE

Damon paused when Vivian did, immediately inside the club. She took a step back. Only his arm around her waist stopped her from retreating.

Even on the edge of the dance floor, he needed to dip his mouth to her ear, to hear and be heard. "Something wrong?" Besides the fact they were probably ten years older than anyone else in the room, and grossly overdressed compared to the jeans, short skirts and sometimes T-shirts—but just as often no shirts. Still, hesitation wasn't like Vivian.

She shook her head, said, "This is perfect," and pulled him onto the dance floor.

Within moments, she lost herself in the music, and he was happy to move with her. She draped her arms around his neck and slid her entire frame along his. She whirled and ground against him, ass pressing into his cock until it was rock hard and straining against his slacks. He didn't have the fluid grace or skill she did, but this wasn't the Atlanta Ballet, and he'd always matched her beat for beat in the clubs. Apparently and fortunately, his body remembered after so much time.

Eyes were on them—on Vivian, really—and that heightened his enjoyment. He wouldn't be surprised if half the club watched the slender woman, flowing like water from one song to the next, making her silk shirt and pencil skirt look better than any lingerie.

The occasional guy or girl drifted into their tight space, vying for attention. Damon was only interested in Vivian, the scent of her perfume and the sheen of exertion on her skin tempting him to lean in and trail his tongue up her slender neck. She danced with anyone who floated close, but never pulled away from Damon, always keeping a hand, arm, or hip in contact with him.

He lost track of the time. Somewhere along the way, she managed to undo the top two buttons on her blouse. Whenever she twisted in a new direction, he caught a glimpse of the tiny tattoo on her right breast. A violet. Her gift to herself on her twenty-first birthday. She'd laughed at her choice, because it was her stripper name, and she was sure she'd regret it in a few years, but that night she hadn't cared.

Did she regret it? He shook the question away and dove full force back into the now. No reason to linger on the past or tomorrow, or anything but how incredible it was to move against her and feel her press back. Over the course of the night, he resisted the desire to find a dark corner, shove her skirt up to her waist, and push inside her. It was only a fantasy, but since they checked the outside world at the door, he let it run rampant through his thoughts.

They didn't exchange words. It was too loud for talking, and he didn't want to ruin the moment with the kind of thought speaking required. It had to be after midnight, when they reached a non-verbal agreement and extracted themselves from the thinning crowds, to head outside. Heat from the packed room and from arousal flushed Damon's entire body. When they stepped into the night, the humid April air rushed over him, cooling him but not erasing his lust.

Across the street, the hibachi-grill parking lot was empty, and the lights out. They didn't have to worry about running into their colleagues. Pink decorated Vivian's face and chest, and her smile looked etched in place. She whirled and let out a light laugh, as they strolled down the sidewalk. They were walking away from their cars, and he was fine with that.

She spun back to him, pulled his arm around her waist, and leaned her head against his shoulder. "I'm going to be beat in the morning." Despite the words, she sounded infinitely less stressed than before they entered the club.

Her frame pressed against his and restarted his finally-slowing pulse. Ambivalence raged inside. If she were anyone else, he wouldn't hesitate to ask if she wanted to join him in his hotel room, but if she were someone else, the desire wouldn't be the same. "Worth it?" he asked, more to keep his mind focused on things besides her stripping her clothing off a piece at a time.

"Hell, yes. I may not ever do that again, but it was worth it. Thank you."

"For what?"

"I wouldn't have gone in there on my own." With each step, she bumped into him. Her perfume had faded in the club, and the scent was now mingled with that of alcohol and cigarette smoke. It shouldn't smell right, but it drove his senses nuts.

Without missing a beat, Vivian stepped in front of him and ground her ass against his cock. "I'd ask if it was good for you, too, but I'm making assumptions, based on the erection digging into my behind."

Their wandering had taken them to a nearby business park and a stretch of lush grass tucked away from lights or traffic. He dug his fingers into her hips and stopped them both. He dipped his head and traced his nose along her neck, barely touching her skin. "I had an amazing night." His voice came out more gravelly than he intended.

She pranced out of reach and turned to face him. "More fun than the waitress last night?"

The who? Oh, yeah. "I'd forgotten about her."

Vivian raised her brows, blue eyes sparkling with amusement. "I'm sure she appreciates that."

With the night air filling his lungs and the distance between them, reason and reality were sinking in. Damon wasn't sure he liked it. Tomorrow they could go back to being on different sides and not talking. "Probably no more than she appreciated me deciding I wasn't interested, after all."

Vivian sank to the ground and tucked her legs to one side. She leaned back and rested her weight on her palms, the posture accentuating her breasts and the fact she'd never redone the top two buttons on her blouse. "You really didn't pick her up."

He sat across from her, enjoying the view. "I did, actually, but I couldn't follow through. Her closing argument didn't move me the way it should have."

Vivian had no right to be jealous of anyone Damon hit on, regardless of whether or not it went anywhere. That didn't stop relief from whispering through her. "I'm sorry to hear it."

"No you're not. You're even less sorry to hear it's because I enjoyed talking to you so much, she couldn't compete."

Every time he swept his gaze over her, Vivian's heart beat faster, and her temperature rose. The dancing had been amazing, not only because she needed to let loose, but also because Damon was right. No one moved with her the way he did. And his physical response… Thinking about his cock pressed against her and the possessiveness in his grip made dampness grow between her thighs. It must have been something in the air. She knew better than this. "It doesn't hurt my feelings."

"Do you ever miss it?" He looked her in the eye, expression suddenly serious.

"Having my feelings hurt? Nope. Walled that off a long time ago." Speaking of keeping her defenses up, maybe it was time to dial it back. The problem was knowing she needed to keep her distance and wanting to do so different things, which happened to be very much in conflict with each other.

"I meant college. Do you ever miss it?"

"God, no." The answer tumbled to her lips without hesitation. "Cramming, working, never sleeping, drinking too much alcohol to relax and too much caffeine to stay awake."

He plucked a piece of grass and pulled apart a strand at a time. "Are you describing back then or now?"

"Touché."

"What about dancing?"

"I still dance. I've got the studio in my condo."

He chuckled lightly. "I mean *dancing*." Of course he did.

She snorted derisively, but her denial didn't come as easily this time. "Do I miss taking my clothes off for strangers, to pay my tuition?" Stripping was one of those things only Damon knew she'd ever done.

He studied her again, something darker, more intense in his gaze. "It wasn't all bad."

"No, it wasn't. It had its good points." She shouldn't have admitted that, even to him, but desire tingled through her body, tightening her nipples and uncoiling in her belly.

"And you were amazing at what you did. I have no doubt you still are."

"Putting on a show, to turn guys on, you mean?" The flattery added to the need aching between her legs and flooding her sex. She shifted on the grass enough that her skirt slid up several inches. A tiny part of her argued she didn't know what she was getting herself into, but she knew exactly what she was doing, and the urge to stop was non-existent.

"I don't care about them; I'm a selfish asshole like that. This is about you and me. Watching you move tonight, the way you ground against me, reminded me how much I miss the private shows."

Memories of *then* mingled with *now*, making her wet. A creeping concern grew inside that she was giving into this too easily. But they cut all the bullshit. It didn't matter his ego showed, he'd set aside pretenses, and she wanted to do the same. "I miss it too."

"Would you consider a command performance?" The corner of his mouth twitched into an evil, hungry smirk.

Her heart hammered against her ribs at the idea, and every inch of her begged to give in. She hadn't completely lost her mind, though. They needed rules, and then she could yield. "A private peep show? No touching? No taking it away from here?"

"Exactly."

"What are we doing?" Hesitation shoved the question out before she could stop it.

"We're college friends, catching up on old times. Nothing else. Nothing hanging over our heads in the morning, and the only thing keep is refreshed memories." He spoke so smoothly, he erased the last of her doubt.

She inched her skirt higher. "We're in a public place." Which should be enough of a deterrent on its own. Even though the place was deserted, they were within walking distance of the club and traffic chugged away on the other side of the hill, just out of sight. Logic told her that should be reason enough to stop. The indecision warred in her head, screaming to back away now.

"There's no one around. Besides, tell me the idea of being out in the open isn't turning you on even more."

"It absolutely is." Screw walking away, she'd take her chances. Something almost surreal seemed to envelope them, and while Vivian knew it wasn't real, she wanted to lose herself in it. In him. Just for the night. She reached under her skirt, hooked her thumbs in her panties, and slid them down her legs. She tossed the undergarment to him.

"Watching you dance reminded me of all those nights." His voice slipped into a soothing, almost hypnotic rhythm. "When you'd show up at my apartment after work, horny as hell."

She sank into the words, enjoying the way they reverberated through her thoughts and summoned pleasant sensations from the past. She undid two more buttons on her blouse, cupped one breast, and massaged lightly through the lace. "I never broke the no-touching rule in the club, but God, sometimes feeling those hungry gazes on me turned me on so much."

"My favorite sound was the key in the lock, at three in the morning, and then the slight creak of the floor, as you crept into my room."

The past blended with the present in her head, intensifying the tingles racing along her skin. She squeezed harder, pinched her nipple, and rolled it between her fingers. "I used to feel bad about waking you up."

"Never feel bad about that." He rubbed a visible bulge through his slacks. "Everything about those nights was fantastic. Telling you to take your clothes off. Watching you expose yourself. Seeing your gorgeous pussy when I told you to sit."

She spread her legs, pushing her skirt over her hips in the process, to give him a view. "I'd get so wet." She trailed a finger along her slit, and a gasp tore from her throat. "I still do. Knowing you were as turned on as I was. Following your commands." She faltered on the last word but swallowed the visceral response. It wasn't any sort of promise or commitment, simply a mention of how things had been.

"The way you'd drag your fingertips up your smooth, firm thighs." As he spoke, she mimicked his words, dropping back into the memories.

She scraped her nails up her skin and groaned at the touch.

"Shove two fingers inside yourself."

She did as ordered, inhaling sharply through clenched teeth at the self-penetration. "It's not as good as the real thing."

His laugh was strained. "But it's delicious to watch." The sound of his zipper dragging down was loud against the backdrop of the night. He worked his cock free and stroked slowly, always watching her. "Show me how you like it these days, but not too fast. Give me a slow buildup. No coming until I tell you."

"Yes, Sir." She bit her bottom lip and withdrew her fingers. She glided them along her slit lightly, enough to make herself gasp, but never touching her swollen clit. She drew closer then pulled away, her breathing growing shallower with each pass.

"Fuck. I love watching you." Damon worked his shaft in a steady rhythm. "So hot."

She tried to keep her pace slow, even as the ache between her folds increased. When she bumped her sex, it made her whimper, but she didn't indulge in the desire. Not until she had permission. Need and delicious tension tightened her muscles, flowing over her entire body. Damon's grunts heightened the throbbing begging for her touch.

Her pussy clenched when she trailed her fingers over her clit again. The oxygen stole from her head, making her feel like she was floating.

"I bet you're close." Damon's rough voice amped her senses further. Each new touch tingled in her fingers and twinged in her nipples.

"Yes." She couldn't say more.

"Do you remember bending over the back of that chair?"

New images folded into the existing ones. The enticing sensations of the past made her pulse race faster. The sounds. The feelings. The everything. "Yes."

"The sting when I slapped your ass." His tone was ragged, punctuated by heavy breathing. "The delicious squeals you made."

She did remember. Every minute. Every sharp smack. The combination of pleasure and pain. "The way I lost myself in the agony, until I begged you to fuck me."

"Are you ready to beg now?"

"Yes. God, yes." She panted, fingers slick with her own juices, and sex swollen. Any touch might push her over the edge.

"I want to hear it."

"Let me come for you, baby." She spoke between breaths. "I'm so close. Please?"

"Play with your clit. Get yourself off."

The moment she brushed the focus of her arousal, pleasure jumped through her. She leaned her head back, eyes closed, and bit the inside of her cheek to keep from crying out. Climax spilled over her in waves, and still she stroked herself. In the background, she was vaguely aware of Damon's familiar grunts. The punctuated sound that told her she wasn't the only one who had reached orgasm. She fingered herself until the touch became too much, and even then didn't pull away, until her own body shuddered from over-stimulation.

She sank back onto the grass with a tiny sigh, exhaustion flitting in to mingle with euphoria. A new urge filled her—or maybe it was a very old one—to curl up next to him. Crawl into his embrace. Feel his fingers trail through her hair. Lie beside him until the glow faded and the buzz quieted, and then fall asleep. She did her best to squelch the impulse. Reliving a few memories didn't mean she had to fall into old habits. Neither of them spoke for several minutes. She finally summoned the will to sit, and met Damon's gaze.

"Fantastic." He smiled and held up a crumpled ball, and it took her a moment to realize it was black silk and lace. Her panties. "I, uh…think I owe you a replacement." He almost sounded sheepish. Almost.

"Don't worry about it. It was worth it." A giggle worked its way from her chest, and she shook her head. She hadn't felt this good in ages. It was like her mind was clear.

He stood and zipped up. Seconds later, he was by her side, offering a hand. She accepted, memorizing the feeling of his firm grip, and then straightened her clothing.

As if by some unspoken agreement, they fell into step beside each other. As they made their way back to the parking lot, Vivian was conscious of how much space was between them. They walked close enough she felt his warmth through her sleeve, but there was no contact. "I can't believe we did that. In the middle of an office park." She felt subdued but content.

"If it were any other time or place, I'd tell you I knew it would happen." Damon glanced sideways at her. "But, neither can I. Not that I'm complaining."

A comfortable silence settled in, punctuated by the chirp of cicadas. When they reached their cars, she turned to face him. "I had a lot of fun. I meant it when I said *thank you*, earlier."

He tucked a strand of hair behind her ear. "Me too. Back to masks and indifference tomorrow?"

Forcing a smile into place was more difficult than she expected. Might as well start now. What had happened was only a blip in time, so there was no reason to linger. "I'll see you in the morning, Counselor."

Something flickered in his eyes, vanishing before she could define the expression. His face shifted, to reflect her grin. "See you in the morning."

No reason at all, for her to linger.

SIX

Fourteen Years Ago

Damon paced the floor of his apartment, struggling and failing to keep a haze of frustration and rage at bay. "Fucking bullshit. I can't believe—" His words faltered, and he hissed in irritation.

Vivian studied him, sympathy in her gaze. "How'd he find out?"

"I don't know. Ethan told him?"

She shook her head. "He wouldn't do that." She took a deep breath, chest rising and falling in her low-cut tank top, and temporarily distracting him. "And I hate to be the one to say this, but your dad was going to find out."

He sighed, sank onto the couch cushion next to her, and tossed the printed email on the coffee table. The message was from his father, and reminded Damon minoring in education wasn't part of their agreement. If Damon didn't get his applications into the law schools of his choice soon, he'd be footing a pretty hefty college bill when he graduated and tried to do something ridiculous, like *teach*.

Damon rubbed his face, and a low grumble worked up from his chest, leaving his throat raw.

Vivian shifted so she sat on his lap, both legs draped down next to his, her head against his chest. "Maybe we can make it work."

He trailed his fingers through her hair, the repetitive movement helping bring his fury under control. He let his thoughts solidify, before speaking again. "You're right; I knew it was going to happen. Maybe I wanted it to. He's got a good point. I'm not going to make money teaching, and there's no way I can pay off my student loans. I like law. I'm good at it. He's pushing me toward my potential."

Her spine stiffened against him for a moment, before she relaxed again. "It sounds like a good plan."

He knew she was lying, but he wouldn't call her on it. This was one thing he needed to work. "And you're with me?"

"Of course. Always." At least this time, there was nothing but honesty in her words.

———

Now

Damon kept half an ear on the conversation in the Skriddie conference room. They were reviewing the tentative schedule for the day—whom they wanted to talk to first, when breaks and lunch would be … everything they covered yesterday, but with fewer words. More than a day in town, and they hadn't started a single interview.

Camille's voice echoed in his head, nagging that this was the client's dime, and the firm got their hourly rate either way. He didn't have to care if they wasted a day or even a week. When it came right down to it, he and Camille both knew this case was—

"Sorry I'm late." Hayden sounded anything but. All conversation in the room stopped, as he dropped his laptop bag in an empty seat and headed straight for the coffee on the back counter. "Had a hell of a time waking up this morning. Anyone else get laid?" his gaze landed on Damon.

Laid? Not quite. Best night in ages? Without question. It was half a shame, half a relief that Vivian was back to her professional, aloof self this morning. It made it that much easier to keep in mind last night wasn't the start of something new.

He stared back at Hayden, unflinching. "If you'll have a seat, instead of toeing the line of sexually harassing an entire room" —*especially in front of a fucking court reporter*—"we've already started, and we have a full schedule today."

Irritation flitted onto Hayden's face but was quickly replaced with a sneer. "Yes, *sir*." He took his seat with no more delay.

Brian Wicker, one of the Skriddie lawyers, scrolled through something on the tablet in front of him, smirk barely hidden. "If you'd like to talk to Ms. Elford, we're requesting you get her in here soon. She has her schedule on hold until you've finished with your questions."

This was where Damon was supposed to say someone else was on the docket first. Delay things. Turn schedules around. Toss up a casual wrench in the schedule, to make sure the process dragged on. However, Camille's not-so-subtle threats from yesterday lingered in his thoughts, and Hayden's attitude had killed most of Damon's lingering buzz from last night. "That's fine. Let's get started."

They called Mikki Elford, swore her in, explained the process to her, and started asking questions. Damon's people knew what they were doing, and unless Hayden said something stupid, things should run smoothly without interference, so Damon kept half an ear on the deposition and let the rest of his thoughts wander. As much as he wanted to put the night before out of his head, it stuck with him. Not only the fantastic everything, but the way Vivian could flip a switch and go from willing submissive to a woman surrounded by walls, in a flash.

"Did you actually turn down the original employment offer from Skriddie Bust Media?" Vanya asked.

"Of course I did." Indignation hung heavy in Ms. Elford's response.

Damon didn't doubt it. Though he was curious where Hayden got the information about what happened in the hotel room, that night in Vegas. Camille knew and had promised documentation the moment she had time.

The exchange faded in and out of his awareness, and he fell back into his own musings. He understood why Vivian kept her walls up, and refused to take any shit in her professional life. Her upbringing was part of it. The bit of her past he was almost certain she'd never shared with anyone else, no matter how close she'd grown to these people over the years. Who she was played a key role as well. A lesser person wouldn't have come out of her childhood on top.

Growing up, Vivian had watched her mother drag through a string of bad relationships, some of them physically so. Men who slapped her mother around, and frequently Vivian as well. Hell, she took up dancing when she was ten, because when one man broke her leg, the doctor told her she'd probably never walk straight again. Her defiance was to prove she'd do more than that. Just the memory of hearing the story made Damon clench his fist so hard, his knuckles ached.

She and her mom had struggled to get by. Her mother was never the person to end a relationship, and Vivian knew there was something better out there. She graduated high school at seventeen, took the couple thousand dollars she'd saved from flipping burgers, and moved several thousand miles away to attend college and escape that life. She told Damon on more than one occasion she'd never let someone control her or erase her identity to the point where she became her mother.

Which, after Vivian and Damon dated for several years in college, was the same thing that tore their relationship apart. He shoved the thoughts aside. Dangerous path to walk down *ever*, but especially now.

"You're saying you never asked to attend the Vegas trade show?" Vanya asked. "It was completely Hayden's idea. Although on your first night there, before the official activities began, you'd already made contact with Skriddie executive staff. Remember, Ms. Elford, even though this isn't trial yet, you're under oath."

Damon felt a twinge of regret for the way they were attempting to shred the girl's naiveté. Yet another emotion he couldn't afford to linger on.

"You made contact with them your first night there, you spent a large portion of your free time talking to them, and yet you insist you weren't there to tell them what you'd learned, working at NSS," Vanya said.

Mikki flared her nostrils and clenched her jaw. She wasn't looking at Vanya; her gaze was focused on Hayden. "Yes. I'm saying all of that. Because, silly me, I tend to trust people. And I'm sure you think that's pathetic, but every time, right up until the end of my employment, I wanted to take Hayden at face value when he told me something. Because that's sure as hell easier than spending my entire life wondering who's trying to fuck me over."

Hayden leaned in, arms on the table and upper lip pulled into a sneer. "Which is why you'll never be more than a lackey, doing the brain work but not the smart work. And why your fiancé will continue getting screwed, and—"

"Let's take an early break and take this off the record." This was what Damon had been listening for, but he'd hoped it wouldn't rear its head for at least half a day.

"Don't stop on her account," Tate muttered.

Damon resisted the urge to roll his eyes. They weren't stopping for Mikki's sake, and he suspected Tate knew that. It was so Hayden wouldn't say something—on the record, even—that would blow up this entire case. Damon gave a general smile to the room. "We need ten minutes." He looked at Hayden. "A word?"

Moments later, Hayden joined him in one of the offices they'd been assured were private and available for such discussions.

"Do you want this case to be over now?" Damon kept his tone cool and free of emotion. "Because I promise, if it stops right now, the outcome isn't going to be in your favor."

Hayden leaned against the wall, arms crossed. "Or theirs. Thrown out, at the worst."

Which Damon was avoiding at all costs. "Really? When did you get your law degree? This is simple. Unless someone asks you questions, keep your mouth shut in there, especially while we're on record, or you won't be allowed in the room."

"I noticed both of you left early last night." Hayden didn't look fazed by the threat. He didn't blink, as he completely changed the subject. "I don't suppose you've already won our bet. Or lost. She shot you down, and that's why you're in such a foul mood?"

Fuck. Damon had already forgotten about that stupid thing. "There's no bet. It's bullshit, and it's not happening."

"You're giving up already? You really hate your job that much?"

This was stupid. Damon lost his temper yesterday, but the ice was back in his veins now. "What are you going to do, Hayden? Walk out there and tell everyone? That only reflects poorly on you."

Hayden hesitated, and when his smugness returned, it was strained. "Nope. I only have to tell Vivian and Camille you bet you could tie Vivian up in bed. Fucking the plaintiff? Not very professional. Hell, I don't know if I have to do more than tell Camille what I overheard. Doubt's enough."

"Keep thinking that"—Damon stepped around him—"and keep your mouth shut during the depositions."

What if he does tell Vivian? A horrible, tiny voice squeaked from the back of his mind. It didn't matter. She'd know Hayden was talking shit. Still, no reason to let her find out from another source. Damon sent her a quick, intentionally generic text, before he walked back into the conference room. *We need to talk.*

JARED KNOCKED on Vivian's office door. She dragged her gaze to where he stood. She'd like to think he startled her from the deep focus her work demanded, but Damon's message did that almost an hour ago. Every time she tried to get back to work, the words bounced in her head, in Damon's voice. She wasn't going to respond. Anything he had to say to her could be done in front of anyone. Unless it was about last night, which it wouldn't be, because they both knew what that was. Amazing and over.

She tucked the rambling thoughts aside. "What's up?"

"Lunch?"

So she could listen to him get into some ridiculous not-argument with Mikki, over Pentagon technology, guaranteed to bore anyone else within ear range, while the two laughed at their own jokes? The bitter thought made her cringe internally. She honestly loved their company, so why was she even thinking like that? Tate was right; Damon had gotten under her skin. Time to nix that, spend some time appreciating that she could go where she wanted, with whom she wanted, and when she wanted, by taking tonight for herself.

She gave Jared a smile. "I have to keep an eye on the catering they're bringing in for lunch—make sure clean up happens. You know, the exciting details."

He took another step into the office, searching her face. "You okay?"

Great. Now everyone could see her brain was tweaking on her. "Fine. Tired. Wishing this weren't happening. You know."

"If you want to talk, my door's open. Can I bring you back something, besides stale sandwiches?"

"Nah. I can eat what our guests eat. It's only fair." She tried to make her smile more genuine. "I'm fine. Really."

"All right…" He gave her one last glance before turning away.

She dropped her face into her palm. Tonight definitely needed to be a clear-her-head night, so tomorrow she could go back to being herself. She sucked in a few slow, deep breaths, to calm her mind, and dove back into work. She helped Heidi, the receptionist at the front desk, set up a second room with the buffet-style food, so their guests could get in and out, and work through lunch. She managed to ignore almost all of her trepidation about running into Damon, as well as her ambivalence when she didn't even catch a glimpse of him.

The clock ticked up on two, and she'd managed to make it through a large portion of her task list, the cryptic text message barely a buzz in the back of her mind. It was time to have Heidi clean up and consolidate the leftover food, and let the staff know they could help themselves to whatever was left in the room. An email would suffice, but Vivian needed to walk away from her computer for a few minutes.

As she drew closer to the front desk, she heard a voice she struggled to decipher. A few more steps, and she realized it was a child speaking. Reception came into view. Heidi sat with a boy next to her. He looked maybe five or six, and was holding up a car and a doll, and telling Heidi a story.

"Who's this?" Vivian asked.

Heidi looked up, eyes wide. "I'm so sorry, Vivian. My husband is working today, and it's spring break, and the babysitter had an emergency, and I couldn't find anyone else to look after him. I was going to call and ask if it was okay, but I hadn't had a chance yet."

"It's okay." Vivian approached the desk and rested her arms on the top. "I know Alan's a little lost with Tate in the depositions. I can get him to watch things here, if you need the rest of the day off." Heidi opened her mouth, but Vivian wasn't done. "I'll make sure you get paid. I promise."

"Thanks." Heidi gave her a grateful smile. "Come on, Tony. Let's go home, and you can tell me all about your car and his girlfriend."

"Ms. Graff, may I have a word?" Damon's smooth voice cut through Vivian's shell and sent her pulse racing.

She tried to be subtle about taking a deep breath, and turned to face him. Something short brushed past her legs, and Tony strode up to Damon.

"Who are you?" the boy demanded.

Damon knelt, bringing himself to eye level with child. "I'm Damon. And you would be?"

"I'm Tony, and that's my mom, and that's the lady who pays her." He pointed behind him. "And you talk funny."

Damon shrugged, expression kind. "It's a habit. I have to talk that way for work."

"My mom talks funny for work too. She answers the phone, and her voice gets all high and squeaky, like she's sick."

"Oh, God," Heidi muttered so softly, Vivian was sure no one else heard.

Vivian struggled to hide a smile.

Damon kept his attention on Tony. "That's one downside of having a grownup job. What do you have there?"

"This is Sam"—he held up the cast iron, black Impala—"and

this is Dean." He presented the doll." They're married and have lots of kids, but they have to work all the time."

The longer the child talked, the more intently Damon appeared to listen, nodding and asking questions whenever was appropriate.

"Don't tell my husband I said this." Heidi spoke in a whisper. "He's really gorgeous though, isn't he?"

"He's not bad." Vivian agreed before she realized what she was doing. "I mean, objectively, of course."

"Of course." Heidi laughed. "Come on, honey. Let's go home."

"Okay. But I want chicken and fries." Tony waved to Damon. "See you later."

A lump formed in Vivian's gut, and she ignored it, as she watched child and mother leave. She tried not to linger on how well Damon interacted with the boy. It didn't matter that her past was determined to haunt her this week; she wouldn't dwell on the fact she'd never have children of her own.

"Do you have a minute?" Damon asked.

"No. I'm sorry." Vivian kept her tone cool, as she stepped around him. "Too much work to do. Email me if you need my time, and we'll set up an appointment."

"Vi—" The single syllable that sounded suspiciously more like *Violet* than *Vivian* was cut short. "I'll do that."

She didn't trust herself to turn around. There was no reason to acknowledge he'd slipped into using his old nickname for her. She'd get Alan to straighten out the other room. It took the last of her control to stay calm and removed, and it shouldn't. That bothered her as much as anything.

SEVEN

Fourteen Years Ago

Vivian stared at the little plastic stick, nausea growing in her gut. She couldn't do this. She had at least a year before she earned her MBA, and Damon started law school in a few months.

"Talk to me." His voice was gentle and kind. "What does it say?"

"Yes." Her voice came out a weak croak. She swallowed to rid herself of the lump in her throat, but it wouldn't go away. He wanted this. He'd never kept that a secret. But she didn't know if she did.

"This is great." His enthusiasm made up for her lack thereof. Almost. "You don't look like it's great."

"We can't have a baby." She struggled to keep her voice from wavering, but wasn't sure she succeeded. "Even if I thought bringing a kid into this kind of fucked-up world was a good idea, we don't have money. This means I can't work anymore. No, it's not great."

He knelt in front of her, cradled her face in his hands, and forced her to look at him. "You can still work. Get a respectable job…" He winced. "I mean—"

The slip dug deep, gouging an ache into her body. "You've never had a problem with it before. I thought my job was sexy. A turn on."

"It is." He tried to kiss her, and she pulled back from his touch. He frowned. "Other people…"

"I know. Appearances are important. Especially with a kid, who has to grow up with the stigma of a stripper mommy." She scrubbed everything negative to the back of her mind, and focused on feeling nothing. "You want this."

"Don't you?"

"We didn't plan it." She didn't have another answer. Did she want it? A baby. Something about the idea both warmed and chilled her at the same time. "I don't know."

"That's not a *no*." He pulled her into his lap. "We can make it work. You've got brilliant skills, and you'll have your Bachelor's in a few months. You can do office work. We only have one set of student loans to pay off. I'll work. It'll be wonderful."

He made it sound so easy, but she couldn't sink into his touch. Every inch of her skin felt lined with pins, jolting and jarring her. Maybe she was being irrational. "I'll think about it."

He kissed her cheek. "Make sure you keep me in the loop. We're in this together, whatever it is."

She swallowed and said, "Okay." Would he be able to tell she didn't know if she meant it?

Now

Damon adjusted his tie in the hotel-room mirror, irritation spilling through him. He still lingered on Vivian's brush off yesterday, but he refused to beg for her attention. She needed to know what Hayden was up to, and Damon would sit her down and make her listen, regardless of what it took.

He shrugged into his suit coat, grabbed his laptop and everything else he needed for the day, and headed for the door. His phone rang before he could leave, and he snarled at Camille's name on the screen.

"This is Damon Vicker," he answered in a cool tone.

"Did I catch you before you got to the office?"

"Still at the hotel." He wasn't in the mood for small talk with anyone. He slept poorly last night, his neck was stiff, and he wasn't looking forward to another day of questions and Hayden's stupidity. He'd known for more than a year this entire case was bullshit. Camille knew it. A handful of the other senior partners knew it. NSS had no way of winning; they'd hacked the competition's network, tried to sabotage them with a combination of rumors and software, and blackmailed a handful of employees along the way.

Damon's job was to drag the case out as long as possible. Go for every delay he could file for, every hour he could bill, until their only move was to advise NSS to settle and try to put this behind them. He didn't have a problem with it before now. Or at least, he convinced himself he was fine with it. Today, though, it was another reason he was stuck here, babysitting the executive who threatened his career.

"Fantastic." If Camille caught his less-than-enthusiastic tone, it didn't seem to impact her cheerful mood. "I need you to get Skriddie to pull this Dewson guy from their witness list. Tell them everything he knows has already been covered. Do what you do. If they insist, make sure our people don't ask him anything."

Damon's *Why?* Stuck in his throat, and pieces fell together. "He's the NSS source. How they knew what was said that night, in Vegas." Son of a bitch.

"Of course not." Camille's tone clashed with her denial. "And we don't need him to say it, anyway. I saw the transcripts from yesterday. Ms. Elford came clean the moment she was asked. Confessed without hesitation that she gave them proprietary network information, despite her NDA."

"Got it." His mind whirred too fast, to manage anything more eloquent. "Anything else?"

"Nope. Talk to you later."

Damon hung up his phone, tossed it on the mattress, and clenched his fist. He swung at the wall and stopped short of punching a hole through the plaster. This shouldn't bother him. His entire day

—week, month, life—skirted the line of ethics, but something about the information gnawed deep inside. *Am I growing a conscience?*

Worse, he wanted to tell Vivian. She needed to know they had a mole working for them. Holy fuck, NSS was really playing spy games. Who the hell did that? There were all sorts of technicalities around whether or not Dewson should have told them anything, but unlike Mikki, he didn't spill proprietary information. And Damon couldn't say a word to anyone. For now, the knowledge was subject to client-attorney privilege.

Damon could make a case to the contrary, if he wanted to put his job further at risk. Which he didn't. Whatever was screwing with his head, he needed to get over it. This was business, and he was a part of it.

He fetched his phone again and made his way toward the lobby. Despite his decision to move on, conflict warred in his thoughts the entire drive to the Skriddie offices. *God damn it.*

VIVIAN WAS ALMOST THINKING STRAIGHT this morning. It was true, sleep last night was less than restful, but spending the evening without any pressures of work pounding down on her helped. With a large dose of espresso and some quiet, she'd be able to get back on task.

An email chimed in from Jared. *We're checking out that new sushi place tonight. You in?*

She paused, waiting for the bitter surge her mind taunted her with the last few days—her inner commentary about being a third or fifth wheel. Nothing was there, except an appreciation for the idea. She sent back a quick response. *I'm in. Three of us or five?*

He answered a few minutes later. *Just three. Meet us there at seven?*
I'll be there.

Was she actually looking forward to the evening? Yeah, she kind of was. Her mood improved, as the morning ticked away. After a few days of being in that bizarre haze, she had a backlog of messages to respond to, but she ticked through the list quickly and efficiently.

Tate said things were going well with the depositions, despite their concerns about what Mikki would be asked. Their legal team didn't feel she'd revealed anything damning. Vivian asked Tate why anyone brought it up. He said—based on the questions NSS Legal asked—the entire case looked like more bullshit than ever. The line of questions almost felt like a distraction, and if Skriddie had a little more information, they could demand a settlement and wrap this up.

Vivian's phone beeped with an incoming call, and she hit the speakerphone button, to listen to her assistant while she worked. "What's up?"

"Your eleven-thirty is here."

She furrowed her brow and turned her attention to her calendar. Sure enough, there was an appointment there, without much information. She clenched her jaw, good mood evaporating when she saw the subject header. *Legal discussion.* "Send him in." It was tempting to tell Damon to go away, but he'd gone through official channels to set up a meeting, so the sooner she got this over with, the better.

Are you sure you want it over that quickly?

Of course she did. Ridiculous question.

"Black, hot—nothing froofy. We'll be fine for a few minutes." Damon's voice drifted into her office, smooth, confident, and unwavering. "Grab something for yourself, too." Seconds later, he stepped into the room and closed the door behind him.

Vivian crossed her arms and fixed a hard gaze on him. "Did you flirt my assistant into going out for coffee?"

"Only when she's done grabbing herself lunch on my dime." He dropped into the chair across from her, without waiting for an invitation. "She was heading out soon, anyway."

Something pleasant fluttered in Vivian's chest at his effort to get her alone, and she squashed it. That was behind her. "You went out of your way to talk to me. What's up?"

He drummed his fingers on his knee for a moment, before answering. "I can't say."

"Are you serious?" She let her frustration leak in. "Cryptic messages and sneaky meetings, so you can tell me, *I can't say?*"

"What's your schedule like this evening?"

Free for you. Stupid, childish voice. "I have plans." At least it was an honest answer. "All this just to ask me out? I suppose I should be flattered."

He narrowed his eyes for the briefest moment, but his expression returned to normal again so quickly, she wasn't sure she meant it. "Don't be." His tone was ice. "This is important and private, and not what you think."

A wounded snarl rose in her chest at the brush off. *Why? You did the same to him.* "Give me a hint."

He paused, and silence stretched between them. She would have prodded him again for an answer, but she could tell from the twitch of his mouth he was measuring his words. "Monday morning, there were more than two of us involved in the conversation near the breakroom."

Her gut reacted to the statement, churning with nausea, before her brain finished processing the words. "Not...?"

"Yeah."

No need to fill in the words. Hayden. It made perfect sense. He was there when she walked out. "Fuck."

"Tonight?"

He'd sent the closest ears away, but she knew he was keeping the conversation vague and brief just in case someone else was listening in. Which apparently, was more important than she believed five minutes ago. "I really do have something else scheduled," she said.

"Will you be done by nine?"

She wanted to shrug him off, but this was one thing she couldn't ignore. "Yes."

"I'll send you an address." He stood and straightened his suit. "Thank you for your time, Ms. Graff."

She swallowed the bile rising in her throat. With any luck, this was nothing, and she'd find that out tonight. "Of course, Counselor. We're here to help." Too bad she didn't believe any of her own self-assurances.

EIGHT

Damon stood outside the restaurant a few blocks from his hotel, waiting. It was late spring, but the evening air was heavy with humidity, which held in the exhaust of traffic. He should have changed when he got back to his hotel room, but something—he wasn't sure what—kept him in the suit. The dense air made him regret the decision. He was early, but he couldn't sit in his room any longer, and the company at the hotel bar had been non-existent.

It was true, large parts of the day had been filled with more of the same bullshit from both Hayden and Camille, but the depositions couldn't have gone better. Mikki was a painfully honest witness, even for someone under oath. She gave answers that caught the Skriddie lawyers off guard and made the case look almost legitimate… if examined through squinty eyes, from a long distance, through a dirty window. Which was better than the brick wall that had been there before they started.

But the irritating conscience he'd grown over the last few days chanted louder than ever in his head. It taunted him with reminders that not all people had to deal with this kind of ethical gray areas in their jobs. Hell, he didn't deal with it the same way in GG Foundation cases.

The people on the other side of the table pulled this stuff, but he didn't have to.

"Wherever you are, I hope the scenery's nice." Vivian's lilting voice tugged him from his musings.

He shook the irritating haze aside… mostly, and focused on her. "Not nearly as gorgeous as the view here." She wore jeans that showed off her long legs, and her t-shirt hugged her torso and firm, round breasts.

Her smile shifted from polite to genuine. "Should we go inside?"

He held the door open. "After you." God, her ass looked good in these jeans. Fantasy mingled with memory, teasing him with images of stripping her clothes off and leaving a mark or two, hearing her sweet gasps, then bringing her to orgasm. *Not the time or the place.* The mental reminder didn't stop his dancing thoughts.

Seconds later, they were seated. Because it was after dinner on a weeknight, the place was practically deserted. At least that would make it easier to talk privately. It'd be a nice change. Maybe they could get up to a little more pretending they were still in college, the way they had in the dance club.

They ordered drinks and swapped random banter, until their waiter set a Coke and rum in front of Damon, and a cranberry-juice vodka in front of Vivian.

She sipped her drink, twirled the swizzle stick in the glass, and sighed. "How bad is it with Hayden?"

Although Damon had pushed for this and knew she had to be told, his involvement in the situation made him pause. Might as well get it over with. "He overheard the comment about tying your hands, and he wanted to bet me you weren't that kind of woman."

"But you told him *no*." There was no question in her tone, but she watched him expectantly.

"Of course I did. Shot him down immediately." Fuck, he hesitated a second too long. Did she catch it?

Her raised brows said she did. "And… then he goaded you into agreeing anyway."

"Absolutely not."

She took another sip of her drink. "Until he did. I get it. Hayden has that effect on people."

Damon couldn't help his chuckle. "I never intended to carry through. I needed to buy myself some time, to cool off."

Her expression faltered, shifting into something that almost looked like disappointment, before the half-annoyed mask slid back in. *Or did I imagine that? Must have.*

"You bet him you could get me to…?"

"He said you'd never submit, and that if I couldn't prove otherwise, he'd have my job." Saying the words didn't feel nearly as threatening as he expected. He should be furious at the thought, not wondering if it sounded like an okay idea. This was insane. He'd worked hard for his partnership and wasn't letting some spoiled rich fuck take it from him.

She twirled a strand of hair around her finger. "And we're here to make sure you win?"

That tempted every inch of him. "No. Never under someone else's terms. I'm telling you, so when he comes to you, you're not surprised, and you can call bullshit. Because you know he's not going to keep his mouth shut."

"I appreciate the heads-up." She sank a little in her seat. "Does that mean the drinks come without seduction?"

Vivian's words bounced back at her, and the innuendo sank in a moment too late for her to take them back.

"I'm not worried about the drinks coming." He traveled his gaze over her. The attention left shivers in its wake. "But I'd love to see you come again."

Damn it, she didn't want to be flattered by that. Or turned on. Or sucked into the flirting. "I can't say it's a driving motivation for me, these days." Intellectually, this was the last place she wanted the conversation to go. The way her pulse pounded in her ears and her senses hummed in anticipation felt different.

"Maybe you're not doing it right."

Vivian raised her eyebrows and stared at him in disbelief. "It's straightforward. Stick goes in the hole, stick slides in and out a couple of times, and then it's over." It was crude and blunt. With any luck, it would keep the tone of the conversation light and Damon removed.

He leaned in, forearms resting on the edge of the table and voice low. "If you really felt that way, you'd have stopped doing it with anyone but yourself. Or maybe you have. I'm not asking, unless you're sharing details. Besides, those are the basics. With each person, you especially, it's the details that matter. Maybe you're missing someone who knows those details."

His arrogance infuriated her, but there was a challenge in his tone, along with scores of unrealized promises. Remembering how intimately he sent pleasant shivers through her that she didn't want to be feeling, but had missed more than she realized. "I'm not asking if you have someone in mind. I won't walk into that trap."

The corner of his mouth twitched in an unformed smile. "Trap? So cruel. It implies unwillingness on your part."

She didn't want to be enjoying this, but the banter made her pulse race more than anything had in a long time. "We're still talking about sex, right?"

"Until you slap me and walk out, or change the subject."

She hadn't considered doing either. Was she slipping? "This isn't all on me. We've both got the same things at stake, unless you know something I don't. You're not that single-minded."

Under the table, his foot nudged her toes, and his gaze never left her face. "I prefer the term focused. Right now, you're the center of that focus. Why are you so afraid of your own desires?"

"Excuse me?" The rapid change in subject, the way he'd avoided her accusation, and the not-very-well veiled insult knocked her off balance. It jarred her out of the moment and gave her a chance to pull her head back into line. What was he doing, taking the conversation here, knowing what they stood to lose if they crossed that line? Then again, crossing the line wasn't an issue if no one else found out "Maybe you don't know me as well as you think. I've grown up, and I've learned a lot about myself along the way."

"Or forgotten."

The witty back and forth was one thing, but she didn't want to play mind games right now. She wanted to cut to the truth. "You're toying with me, Damon. What's going on? What do you want?"

"I'm being honest. I want the same thing I almost always want. You."

If her thoughts and pulse had been going haywire before, it was nothing compared to the way they raced now. The words she didn't want to hear sounded so right. "I'm flattered, but you keep dancing around the heart of the issue. We can't."

"That doesn't sound like *I'm not interested.*"

The words hit closer to home than she'd like, gnawing at kinks she normally kept tucked deep, deep down. Her body reacted, betraying her determination not to fall into old habits. Anticipation skated over her skin, heightening her senses. She struggled to push the growing lust aside, and failed, but she wouldn't let him see that. Couldn't. No matter how much a part of her wanted to cave. "It is what it is. I'm going to be more direct this time and hope you don't brush me off with pretty words. What do you know that I don't? Why is it okay for us to cross the line now?"

His smug expression cracked, and he let out a shaky breath. "There are days I wish I'd turned down the college money and gone into teaching instead. You want me to be blunt. That's as honest as I know how to be. I want to put everything—our identities, our jobs, our hang-ups—on the shelf for the night. Shove them in a back corner, as if they don't exist. Because fuck if I can't stop thinking about who we were without all that hanging over our heads."

The force behind his words tingled in her toes and fingers and everywhere in between. Her brain hammered and knocked on her skull, warning her to put a stop to this before it went any further. The rest of her body insisted on hearing him out. "You make it sound easy."

He traced a line up her shin with his foot, and tingles of desire raced through her. "That bit is." His voice was low but firm.

Walk away or see this through? Back then, she'd walked away, to make sure she didn't lose herself in him. It had been too tempting to give him the same control outside the bedroom that she surrendered in it. But she'd grown since then. "Prove it." She knew herself, she knew what she wanted, and damn it, she missed the way he knew her body.

"I'd be happy to." He stood and extended his hand.

She slipped her fingers into his, and allowed herself to be led. Her hammering pulse beat in time to the back and forth in her skull, arguing against the part of her she usually suppressed, which wanted to take things further.

They stepped outside, and he nudged her toward an empty alley, out of the light and line of sight. When he pressed her against a nearby wall, her world shifted, and anticipation seared her veins. His warm breath caressed her ear, his voice low enough only she would hear it. "Three ground rules before we cross this line. First, when we walk into my hotel room, we leave our names and lives at the door. This is *not* related to work or anything outside of that room. We left those people at the office."

"All right." At least every part of her agreed with that. She buried the twinge that ached from behind her ribcage at her own dismissal.

He tightened his grip on her fingers, but despite how close he stood, he made no other contact. "Second, I'm in control, and you trust me."

Her mouth went dry, and agreement lodged in her throat. She knew that would be a requirement, and she did trust him. Then why was it so difficult to agree?

He stepped back. The air rushed in around them, but it didn't cool her fiery skin. His reply bled into the background noise. "Or we call it a night now, and forget this conversation ever happened."

"I trust you." The words slid out with far more certainty than she felt.

His smile wasn't lighthearted this time. It sank into her bones and left her feeling like she'd sold her soul in exchange for the most delicious punishment that existed. "Third, you stop me the moment you stop trusting me. You know the word. It's seared in my brain, too." Currents of heat lined his voice.

It sounded like a simple request, but something told her it wouldn't be nearly that easy. "Agreed."

NINE

Vivian requested one more concession, as they left the restaurant—that they go back to her place instead of his hotel room. There was a far smaller chance of anyone they knew seeing them, and her condo had amazing soundproofing. The half-hour drive, in separate cars, gnawed at every part of her. She squirmed in her seat, she second-guessed her decision, and she craved his touch like she hadn't in over a decade.

Now, with him standing behind her, just inside the front door, her pulse threatened to tear away. She kicked her sandals aside, and for the first time in ages, hesitation robbed her of any inkling of what to do next.

"Don't stop now." Damon rested his hands on her hips, and his breath fell across the back of her neck. "Love your place, by the way."

"I'll give you a tour later, if you'd like." What was she saying? This wasn't a social visit.

He nudged her forward. "I think we should start by checking out that spot over there, between the back of the sofa and the balcony." She let him guide her, stopping when he tugged her belt loops. "Don't move." He pressed his chest against her back and glided his palms under her shirt, to settle on her stomach. Each new touch—soft, gentle, and without hesitation—flitted across her skin in a teasing dance.

He swept her hair over her shoulder, and she tilted her head to the side, to expose her neck. He trailed his mouth up the slope, barely making contact, drawing her anticipation closer to the surface. "You need to be naked." As he spoke, he yanked her shirt over her head and tossed it aside. His suit and its buttons dug into her bare back. He trailed his fingers over her shoulders, hooked them in her bra straps, and dragged them down her arms, before unsnapping the clasp and throwing the lingerie aside as well.

Her nipples were already hard and eager. The warm air brushed her torso and a new wave of desire unfurled in her belly. He dropped his hands to her jeans and undid the button and zipper in an instant, and then scraped the remainder of her clothes down her legs. She stepped out when prompted. An ache spread between her thighs, reminding her how exposed she was.

Damon moved in front of her, still completely dressed, and raked his gaze over her. "So beautiful." His voice was strained. He shed his jacket and draped it over the back of a nearby chair. The fire of his attention lit along her arms, her stomach, her breasts—everywhere he looked. A small portion of her mind told her she shouldn't be on display like this. The wrongness increased her desire. She wanted to be, but only for him. She resisted the urge to draw an arm over her chest or cover herself.

"I never forgot how gorgeous you are naked." He rolled up his shirt sleeves. When he loosened his tie, instinct and memories cranked her pulse higher, until it pounded against her throat and ears. "I'm tempted to shove you up against the couch right now, and fuck you until you scream."

She bit the inside of her cheek, tempted to argue. Fast and frantic was fine sometimes, but it wasn't what she wanted tonight, and she wouldn't be impressed if that was his intention. "Whatever you think is best."

He smirked and shook his head. "At least say it like you mean it."

She shrugged. "Make me mean it."

"I will." When he removed his tie, the breath caught in her throat.

He relocated behind her, not touching her. She started to turn her head, to see where he'd gone, and his palm collided with her ass. The slap sent a pleasant sting through her, and she sucked in sharply through her teeth.

"I said, don't move." His voice was closer than she expected. He fitted something over her eyes, blocking the world from view. Given the width and the way it tightened around her head, she assumed it was his necktie. Her heart hammered at the loss of one sense, and the rest of her kicked into high alert. She heard nothing but her own breathing, the blood rushing in her ears, and the city outside.

She could smell him, though. The faint aftershave. The same scent she remembered, all these years later, that promised more.

"Top floor condo." His voice was distinct, but she couldn't feel him. "Living above most of the other buildings in the city, with a gorgeous view through that picture window. The one with the blinds open. I'm curious what you do out on that balcony."

A lot of things.

He spanked her again, the loud slap echoing through the room. The sting lingered longer on her skin this time. "I'm not asking me. I'm asking you. What do you do out there?"

"Watch the city. Get some sun. Enjoy being removed from all the insanity, even though I'm right in the middle of it."

"That's it?"

She thought about holding back the answer, but telling him about it was as enticing as being spanked. "Sometimes, I'll go out there to sunbathe in a two-piece. I'll strip my top off, to avoid tan lines, of course."

"Of course." He didn't sound as if he believed her for a second.

She didn't know what made her wetter, remembering the moment, or telling him aloud. "I'll rub the lotion over my breasts, spending longer than I need to, then slide my fingers between my legs. I stroke myself, wondering if anyone can see me. If anyone is watching, until I come."

He glided his palm over her butt, barely making contact with the still-tender skin, and slipped a finger between her legs. "So you're turned on by the idea someone might look over here and see you naked, blindfolded, and helpless."

"Maybe."

He slapped her—the other cheek this time. "Yes or no?"

"Yes."

He pressed his chest to her back again and kissed along her shoulder. "I feel your heart pounding. Slamming inside you like a jackhammer. Did you miss this?"

"Desperately." As the word flowed over her lips, she realized how true it was. She'd tried this with a few other guys. Nothing this intense, just being tied up, and a little spanking. Something about the way Damon knew her, though…

He pulled away again, leaving her body alone and begging for another touch. Any touch. "Naughty, raunchy girl. What would your colleagues think if they knew what you really liked, Viv?"

"You said we'd leave work out of this." The nickname and mention of reality did more to freeze her veins than all of her logic and rationale combined. It summoned a part of her she'd locked away and refused to admit existed, except on those nights where she was alone and drunk. Tonight she was neither, and didn't need those ideas in her head. She couldn't keep the edge from her voice. "And don't call me that."

"Why shouldn't I call you…? Holy shit. That's what Tippins calls you. You two? Really?"

She swallowed all thoughts of Jared, shoving them deep inside. Her palms ached, and she realized she was clenching her fists hard enough for her nails to dig into the skin. "Of course not."

"Don't lie to me." He spanked her again, hard and fast, pulling away before the sound finished reverberating in the room. There was no anger or jealousy in his voice. The gesture and words were all part of the game. "You were fucking Tippins."

"It wasn't like that, and it was years ago."

His breath danced over her skin. "What did you see in a guy like that?"

Kinship. She swallowed the answer. "He made me laugh."

Another slap, another tremor of pleasure and pain. "Clever. And bullshit." Damon's voice was cool. "Before or after Karen?"

Karen had been Jared's first love. The woman who used him, to get inside information on Skriddie, and sold it back to NSS. "How did you—?"

The palm of his hand meeting her ass at high speed cut her off. "My questions, my game. And Hayden talks. Before or after?"

"After."

"So his gorgeous blonde coworker helped him pick up the pieces of a shattered heart and build a wall around them until… Foster, too?"

As if. Until recently, she and Tate were rarely even on the same page, let alone fuck buddies. "I'm not some sort of vicious corporate ice queen, screwing any man who gets in my path. Jared and I had that kind of connection, Tate and I don't. Besides, he's never not had eyes for Alyssia."

Damon slapped her again. "That was just because."

The skin started to numb, but the sting sent endorphins racing through her. She wouldn't be able to keep up a conversation much longer. "Whatever you think is best, Sir."

He caressed her ass, then slipped two fingers between her legs. Inside her. She gasped at the tender penetration, wanting to beg for more. Instead, a whimper slipped out when he pulled away again.

And he was gone. Seconds ticked away into minutes and hours. Or that was her mind exaggerating time, because she couldn't see. When lips brushed her nipple, she groaned at the unexpected touch. He flicked his tongue over the hard nub, and then drew it into his mouth and scraped his teeth over it. Each time he sucked or nibbled, it tugged a cord that traveled straight to the insistent need between her legs, making her clit throb.

He alternated his attention between the two breasts, until her gasps grew so shallow, her head felt light. The lack of visual input made her tilt on her feet, and he dropped his hands to her hips to steady her. "Careful."

When he pulled away, it was only for a second. He kissed a lazy, meandering path down her chest and stomach, along her pelvis and over her thighs. He nudged her feet apart, and she complied. She thrust against his face—she couldn't help it—when he glided his tongue along her slit.

"You taste delicious." His voice was muffled. He plunged deeper, thrusting inside her, licking her opening. She had to tangle her fingers in his hair, to stay upright. When he drew a path to her clit and finally wrapped his mouth around it, her legs threatened to give out. He didn't suck hard, though. He flicked light patterns, teasing, taunting, coaxing her aching button out.

He hooked a finger inside her. When he hit her G-spot, her world tilted. The multiple points of contact tore an orgasm from her, and the light touch prolonged the exquisite agony. She screamed as she came, pushing against his face, not sure how much longer she could stand on her own.

He finally pulled away, and she wobbled on her feet. She didn't need to worry about stability, though. He crushed his mouth to hers, hungry and hard, tasting like her. She dove into the kiss, needing it as much as any of this.

He broke away with a growl and nudged her back, never removing her blindfold. His voice was breathless and deep. "Now I push you back against the couch and fuck you, until you scream so loud, you're hoarse."

"Yes, Sir." She let him half-push, half-lift her, until her butt rested on the sofa.

The sound of a zipper dragging down was the loudest thing in the room, and her senses flared to life again. The noise was followed by the tear of foil. A condom. She licked her lips. Her legs were forced apart, and she had less than a second's warning—the blunt head of his cock nudging her opening—before he thrust inside with a grunt.

She wrapped her legs around him, whimpering each time he slammed against her.

He bit into her shoulder. "You're so tight. I'd forgotten how incredible you feel." Something, his thumb probably, pressed against her still tender clit and ground in time with his pounding. The gentle teasing was gone. This was frantic and full of need, and she sank into the desperation. Part of her was aware of the familiar sound of him nearing climax. The punctuated groans. The staccato rhythm. She struggled to focus on anything but the orgasm rolling through her. Clenching around him. Making her thoughts fuzz. Stealing her breath and the last of her reason. She dug her nails into his back when she came again, holding him inside her with her legs. Squeezing him.

He hissed, gripping her waist tight and pumping until they were both breathless.

She leaned her forehead against his shoulder, unable to do anything but sigh and struggle for air. He kissed along the edge of her ear. "So fucking incredible." His voice was raw.

He loosened the tie and stripped it from her eyes. The dim lighting of the living room was harsh, and she blinked several times before her sight adjusted. He brushed his lips over hers, and then pulled back to study her. "You okay?"

"Better than." She tried to hop from the couch, but couldn't find her balance.

He wrapped an arm around her waist, to steady her. "Come on." He guided her toward the open door of her bedroom.

She hesitated at the edge of the bed, suddenly shy, as if she were twenty again. "You're staying, right?"

His expression relaxed. "Unless you kick me out."

"Good." She needed the ritual. After a session like that, her body ached for a different kind of comfort. She helped him strip out of his clothes, waited for him to get settled, then climbed into bed and curled up next to him.

Neither of them spoke for… she didn't know how long. He trailed his fingers through her hair, and she listened to his heart beat against her ear.

When the adrenaline faded, and the euphoria was nothing more than a sheen on her skin, she dragged up the words that had been sitting at the back of her mind since Damon brought it up. "It's not that I'm still hung up on him, you know."

She felt more than heard his sigh, and his hand paused for the briefest moment. "Tippins?"

"Mhm."

"Not the best pillow talk, Vi."

She smiled against his chest, even though he couldn't see. "I know. But I may not get another chance to say it, and it's important for some reason that you know it was completely physical."

He moved his palm to her shoulder. "Then why does the nickname bother you?"

"He was supposed to be like me. Single forever. He betrayed that. I don't blame him. She's good for him. Everyone should have someone like her." Why had she added the qualifier? Not everyone got their happily ever after.

Damon squeezed her arm and kissed her on the forehead. "We should sleep. We have work in the morning, and I need to get back to my hotel, to change, before I go into the office."

She wanted to ignore the regret in his voice. Tried desperately to shove aside that she'd heard it. Her mind refused to let it go, though. Were they going to be able to walk away from this? Did she even want to?

TEN

Damon rolled onto his back, letting the pleasant memories from last night spill through his head. He was disappointed to wake up alone in Vivian's bed, and tempted to join her in the shower when he realized the running water was what woke him. Before he could make up his mind, he heard the water shut off and the scrape of a shower curtain being pulled back.

Probably for the best. He needed to get back to his hotel. Let her get to the office. Work. The idea almost soured his lingering desire, but the scent of Vivian everywhere won out.

The bathroom door creaked open, and seconds later, she strolled across his line of sight, satin bathrobe knotted on, long legs on display. Watching her move made him instantly hard.

"You're up." She paused by his side of the bed. "You should probably go soon."

Up was right. "I'm thinking about it."

She gave a light laugh. "Don't think here. I need to get going, too."

He grabbed her wrist, to keep her from turning away, and pushed himself up on one elbow. "Last night was fantastic."

"It was. You were exactly what I needed."

He knew from the way she hesitated before snapping her mouth shut there was more to the thought. He was glad she didn't finish it. *Too bad it was only for last night.* "I get a goodbye kiss, right?"

When she leaned in, to oblige, the front of her robe fell open, treating him to an incredible view of the curve of her breasts, her flat stomach, and the tempting *V* hidden between her legs. His cock pulsed in response.

He wrapped an arm around her as she fell and landed against his chest. The impact stole his breath for a moment.

A light laugh escaped her. "What are you doing?"

He moved both hands to her waist, shifted his weight, and flipped both of them, so he was on top. He straddled her, her wrists pinned above her head. Her warm body beneath him pulled his already hard dick to a painful level of stiffness, as his erection dug into her stomach. He dipped his head in and trailed his nose along her slender neck, inhaling deeply. He kissed the edge of her ear, his voice barely a whisper. "You've got time for one more, before work."

She gazed back, eyes wide and breathing shallow. Pink dotted her cheeks. "I just got out of the shower."

He could have fragments of this with anyone. With certain lifestyles becoming more mainstream, it was never a problem to find a girl willing to give him total control. None of them were Vivian, though. Strong, aggressive, confident, intelligent, and gorgeous.

"If you want me to stop, you know what you have to say." He didn't like her being unwilling in the bedroom. Everyone had their own kinks, and that was fine, but non-consent wasn't his. Control and pain, yes. And only if she enjoyed receiving as much as he did giving.

She licked her lips, searching his face. He nudged her bathrobe open further and trailed a finger down her chest and over her breast, circling the hard nub of her nipple.

She sucked in a sharp breath between her teeth. He pinched and twisted. She arched her back, grinding against him with a moan.

"I bet you're wet." He glided his hand down her stomach and brushed her pussy. When he parted her folds, she gasped and jerked under him. "Mmm." He kissed along her neck and down to her collarbone. "It's a good start."

She gazed up at him, eyes wide. "We don't have a lot of time."

He trailed his mouth back to her ear, inhaling and memorizing the scent of her shampoo. He whispered, "I don't care." The problem was, he really didn't. He wanted to stay here with her all day. Marking her. Bruising her. Making her come. He'd respect *the schedule* though.

She twisted under him, pressing against his cock. Teasing. "You should." Her tone was playful. "I'm not blaming you; I'm just saying."

Holding her wrists in place, he relocated his hand to her breast. Her skin was soft and smooth against his fingertips. He didn't know if he had the patience to drag things out this morning, anyway. Maybe it was a good thing they didn't have much time. He scraped his thumb over a rigid nipple, and she pressed into his hand.

"Harder," she whimpered.

"One of my favorite words." He obliged, pinching and rolling the nub. Kneading the flesh beneath.

With each twist of his fingers, her hips shifted, digging into him. Nudging his erection. Her frantic thrusting became rhythmic, and her breathing grew shallow. She leaned her head back, lips slightly parted and cheeks flushed, her hair fanning out around her head on the pillow like a halo.

So beautiful. He drew his tongue along the edge of her ear, keeping his voice low. "I need to be inside you, Vi. Just me. I want you wrapped around my cock." He couldn't get her pregnant, and they were both smart enough to stay clean.

She opened her eyes, bright blue and boring right into him, and nodded.

He pushed her legs apart with his knee and hooked her legs over his shoulders. Her groan mingled with his when he pushed inside her, rough and fast. Feeling her spread open. Forcing his way inside. "Play with yourself, Vi. Finger your clit until you come. I want you tightening around my cock. I need to feel you."

She moved one hand between her legs and the other to her

breast. She pinched and stroked herself in time with his fast-paced thrusts. When her gasps became short cries, he knew she was right at the edge. He slammed into her harder, hitting something deep inside. She felt so amazing. So right. It took the last of his focus not to come yet. Pressure built in him, and his balls tightened until stars danced behind his eyes.

"Come for me, Vi." He spoke through heavy breaths.

She threw her head back, and a delicious sound tore from her throat. She clenched around him. Tight. Uncontrolled. Delicious. He couldn't wait any longer. He spilled inside her, pounding until he was spent, and even then, taking his time to slow.

When the desperate grind finally stopped, they untangled themselves, and he dipped his head in for a hungry kiss. She tasted like toothpaste and smelled like sex and body wash, and his senses devoured every bit of it. She scraped her nails along his neck, holding him, diving into him.

God, why couldn't they lie here all day?

FOURTEEN YEARS AGO

Damon dug through his apartment, searching frantically for the cordless phone before it stopped ringing. He found it on the coffee table, under a scattered pile of newspapers with office jobs circled. "Hello?"

"Hey." Vivian sounded faint, and the single word was strained.

That didn't stop him from grinning at the sound of her voice. "Hi yourself, gorgeous. I thought you were working tonight. Not that I'm complaining." In a few weeks, it wouldn't matter. Her lease would be up, she'd move in, and with any luck, she'd have a job with better hours that was less physically demanding.

"I called in." She sounded as if speaking took tremendous effort. "I don't think I can drive. I'm dizzy, Damon. I think I need to go to the hospital. I'm bleeding a lot."

He was already jerking on his shoes and grabbing his keys. His entire chest wrenched in on itself, until he thought his ribs might collapse. "Are you at home?"

"Yes."

"I'll be there in five minutes. Don't move, okay? I love you, Vi."

"Love you too."

He disconnected and tossed the phone across the room, not caring it missed the couch and clattered to the ground. He sprinted to his car. It'd be all right. She'd be all right. Please?

The next couple of hours were the longest of Damon's life—not that he remembered most of the details. Picking up Vivian. Wondering why he hadn't told her to call an ambulance. Asking himself if they'd have gotten there any faster than he did. And then the waiting. Sitting in the almost empty emergency room, unable to focus on anything but the clock and the fact he couldn't find anyone to give him answers.

Finally a nurse approached him. "Damon?"

He stopped pacing, but trapped his toes in his shoes. "That's me."

She nodded toward the door that had taunted him since they pushed Vivian through it in a wheelchair. "You can come back now."

"Is she okay?"

The nurse gave him a weak smile. "Well enough to tell me you were probably waiting out here. She can explain everything else."

He ground his teeth at the lack of an answer, but followed. Seconds later, she pointed him toward one of the small rooms at the back of a long hall. Vivian sat half-propped in the bed, face tired and pale, expression blank. She managed a weak smile when she saw him.

He crossed the room in a few long strides, and wrapped her in a hug. "I was so worried." They didn't have her hooked up to an IV or any other wires, except the monitor on her finger. That had to be a good sign. "Are you okay? They wouldn't tell me anything."

Her frame shuddered against his when she dragged in a breath. "They're very careful with the information they give out about pregnancies. They leave it up to the mother to share what she wants."

That made sense when he thought about it, which was a lot easier to do now he was holding her again. "You didn't answer my question."

She buried her head against his shoulder, and her voice came out muffled. "They can't tell for sure with the equipment they have here, but they think… I'm probably damaged. I have to see a specialist. They don't believe I should have been able to get pregnant to begin with. I lost the baby."

The moment he heard the words, he realized he'd expected them. It shocked his system anyway. His mind went blank, except for the repeated words, *it's gone, but she's still here.* He didn't know where to focus. "Christ. I'm so sorry." He heard his voice, but barely remembered saying the words.

She broke, her body shaking with sobs. "I didn't mean to. I'm so sorry." Her crying punctuated and blurred the words. "I know you wanted this, and I can't… I'm sorry."

"Shh…" He trailed his fingers through her hair. "It's okay. We're okay. We'll be okay." He held her until she was spent, neither of them saying much of anything. A couple hours later, the ER doctor cleared her to go home. She gave Vivian a list of instructions, made her promise to schedule a follow-up appointment, and handed her a prescription to help her sleep.

Damon helped Vivian slide into the passenger seat, before running around to the driver's side. He felt raw and numb at the same time, but she had to be doing worse. That didn't help him process the information any better. He didn't even know how much of it he had a right to worry about, beyond her health.

He watched her fumbled with her purse and the pack of cigarettes inside, as he stuck the keys in the ignition. Something else fluttered from her bag, catching his attention, and he grabbed for it at the same time she did. He reached it first, and as he processed the words, the last of the bottom fell out of his world.

"What's this?" He struggled to keep his voice calm but wasn't sure he succeeded.

"Nothing." She grabbed, and he jerked away. "A pamphlet. Nothing."

"About abortion?" The foul taste of bile coated his throat. "What the fuck?"

"I didn't know if I was going to do it. I was reading up on all my options." Her voice sounded as rough as his thoughts.

"I thought we'd already figured out our options. We had a plan. Is that what happened tonight? You went through with this, and it went bad?" He shouldn't have said that. The anger and hurt on her face confirmed it was a bad idea. He didn't know if he cared.

"No. God, no." She snatched the booklet from his hands and shoved it back in her purse. "I wouldn't have, without talking to you. I just… You were so sure, and I wasn't. I needed to know what else was out there. I didn't really want to do it."

"You couldn't have said something?" He was yelling, in a car in the middle of an almost empty emergency-room parking lot, at one in the morning. So what? "You know, when we talked this through. When we both decided it was what we wanted to do?"

"I couldn't say anything. *No* means nothing to you." The waver was gone from her voice, replaced with ice.

No. She wasn't throwing that back at him now. "That's not the same, and you know it. Besides, you didn't say *no*, you said *okay*."

"And you knew I was lying."

This wasn't happening. It couldn't be. He needed to be there for her, and now he couldn't be anything but furious. "That's not a valid argument. I wanted to take you at face value. Do you really not trust me enough to tell me the truth?"

She stared back, blue eyes as cold as her voice. "Do you trust me, when I say I would have told you before I made any decision like this?"

He jerked his attention away, staring out the windshield, hands gripping the wheel until his knuckles ached. "I don't know."

"That makes two of us."

ELEVEN

Vivian wiped the steam from the mirror and stared at her reflection. Her mother's face—eyes haunted by dark shadows, cheekbones too sharp to be attractive, and colorless skin—stared back, mocking her. Reminding her.

It had been three days since her miscarriage. Damon apologized for his outburst, but things were strained between them. That didn't stop him from doting on her every waking moment, though. It was sweet to the point she wanted to scream. He'd picked up some clothes for her and brought her back to his place, saying she shouldn't be alone. She had to force him to go to work, but he insisted she needed a little more time off.

The entire situation didn't sit right, deep down in her gut, but she let him lead, because she was terrified of losing him. Of scaring him away. Of being alone forever. The words bounced in her head, sang in her mother's voice.

She raked her fingers through her wet hair, hand shaking. This was why she left home. Ran, as soon as she was legally able. To avoid becoming this person. Instead, she'd tied herself to the first guy who came long and treated her better than dirt.

Her heart throbbed at the dismissal of what she and Damon had. It was more than that, the pain in her chest insisted. Rationalization would only make it worse, though. How many times had she seen it, growing up? Even when her mother's boyfriend broke Vivian's leg, her mother still said, *He's sorry, honey. He promises he won't do it again.*

"Are you all right?" Damon's voice shattered her out-of-control thoughts.

She met his gaze in the mirror. "No."

He reached for her, and she stepped away from his touch. His furrowed brow and the hurt in his eyes devoured her. She swallowed her own reaction.

"Talk to me." It wasn't a request.

And that was at the root of the problem. Not that he made demands like this, but that she let him. "I can't see you anymore." It hurt to force the words out, and once the decision hung between them, acid churned in her gut. This wasn't right. This was supposed to make her feel better.

He frowned. "Don't."

"I have to." She stepped around him, unable to look him in the eye any longer. "We're done, Damon." The proclamation ached.

"If this is about the other day, I'm sorry. I was stressed, but that doesn't excuse what I said. You know I didn't mean it."

"It is, and it isn't." She rubbed her face. The carefully rehearsed speech she had vanished, leaving impressions of what she wanted to say, but no structure to deliver the lines. Her thoughts jumbled and bounced, taunting her. "It's about the fact I told you *yes* when I didn't want to. And the fact I thought—even though I knew better—that I had to go behind your back to talk to someone at the clinic about my options. That I'm looking for a receptionist job, even though I love stripping, because you don't think it's respectable."

He grabbed her arm and spun her to face him. "You don't have to do anything you don't want to. You never have."

A bitter laugh slipped out, and she wrenched away. "You're not getting it. I *want* to make you happy. It's become an all-consuming thought. And it's not your fault. You never did anything but be wonderful, but I can't trust myself with you."

"*It's not me, it's you?* You know how weak that sounds, right?" He sucked in a deep breath. "I'm sorry. Look, I'll try to back off. To not push so hard."

"Except you can't." She hugged herself, to keep from falling back into him. "You wouldn't be you if you did that, and then we'd be at the same crossroads. I don't want to stand up to you, and I don't want to lose myself in you. And the only way I can see to get both is to leave."

"Vivian, you can't."

Her heart begged her to agree. He was right. If it hurt this bad now, how much worse would it be when she walked out the door?

And how much would she regret if she stayed? She closed the distance between them, kissed him on the cheek, and then backed away before he could respond. "I can. I don't have a choice."

Now

Damon dialed the home office the moment he walked through his hotel room door. While he listened to the phone ring, he stripped off his clothes. He could breathe again—at least mostly; Vivian's scent clung to him, taunting and seducing—he knew he was fucked if he didn't stop this now. Even though he said last night they'd check their real lives at the door, he didn't think he could do that.

And he wasn't going to jeopardize their careers over it.

"You know it's still ungodly o'clock here, right?" Camille's sharp question was punctuated by a yawn.

Right. Three hours earlier back home. "Sorry." He didn't care if he sounded less than sincere. "It can't wait." There were so many reasons why this had to happen now, and none of them were on a list he could give Camille. He'd sworn fourteen years ago he'd never let another woman get under his skin the way Vivian did, and he'd kept that promise to himself.

It hit him hard last night, in the restaurant; he never got over her. But this was more than the fact he still very much loved her. The problem—one of them at least—was that this time their careers would suffer if he acted. He'd face disbarment. She could lose her job. And he'd still let his dick coax him into her apartment. Let his heart convince him one last time this morning wouldn't hurt.

"Then… What's so important?" Camille asked.

"Take me off this case now." He was done asking, negotiating, pretending to bow. "Bring me back home. I'll clear up this mess with the GG Foundation and IasoChem. Life will go on." With each word, he convinced his brain more, and his heart clenched a little harder. *It would be so easy,* a voice whispered in the back of his thoughts. *Quit. You can do GG Foundation work as a consultant. You'd be done with this backstabbing bullshit.*

Great. Now he was trying to rationalize himself out of a career. No.

"Hayden's not going to let you go," Camille said.

"And why do we care? NSS isn't out biggest client, and yeah, we've got a lot of potential built up in this case, but they're not going to drop us. Not even if they could find someone else to take this last minute."

"That doesn't mean we can go out of our way, to piss them off." The drowsiness was gone from Camille's voice. "We want them as clients, now and once this case is over, especially if they keep doing things like this."

He ground his teeth at the implication—the glee she seemed to feel—that NSS wasn't done with the ethical and illegal fuck-ups. Not by a long shot. "Pull me, or I resign."

"You're not serious."

"As a videotaped confession, after someone refuses their Miranda rights."

"If you walk away from a senior partnership, you only hurt your career. People would line up, to lick my boots for your job."

"But how many of them will be as good at it as I am?" he asked. Her hesitation was the only confirmation he needed. "Bring me home. Assign someone else to this case. Fuck Hayden." He almost mentioned there was a conflict of interest, but everyone knew the basics of his past with Vivian, and if it hadn't been enough to keep him home before, there was no reason to draw attention to it.

"Are you going in this morning?" she asked.

"If I need to. But I prefer we start the transition sooner, rather than later. We're all in town anyway. We bill either way, right?" That would be the carrot she needed.

She laughed. "At least you're still you, Vicker."

He wasn't so sure of that. Or maybe the *him* he'd locked away in college was tired of being stowed. Too bad. "Is that a yes?"

"Sit tight, until I find someone to take your place. As long as you're there, you're on their clock. I'll have more details for you by this weekend. Call everyone else and tell them not to bother going in today. Leave Hayden until last."

That made him smile. He sank onto the edge of the bed after they disconnected. This was going to suck, but he saw no other way. Especially as long as his firm represented NSS. He'd known that from the start, but it was too easy to forget when Vivian was around. Removing himself from the equation was the only solution he could think of that kept them both employed.

⁂

THE MORNING with Damon played on a loop in Vivian's head, mingling with fragments of the past and their breakup, and taunting her. She pounded on the dashboard of her car in frustration. "*Fuck.*" She dragged the word out. She never should have let him back in this morning. Or last night. Or Monday. She might be a masochist, but this was fucking torture. Unlike fourteen years ago, she knew what she had to do to move on—put as much space as possible between them, and ignore every single urge until she believed she'd done the right thing.

She didn't care she left the house so late, she'd be stuck in traffic an extra half hour. It gave her time to think without interruption. The cars around hers inched forward, and she eased her foot off the brake enough to do the same.

The thing with Damon sent waves of terror through her, every time she thought about it. Not because of him. She didn't doubt for a moment he would have stopped at any moment if she wanted. It was a fear of her own response. She was supposed to stay in control of herself. She wasn't supposed to want to surrender everything to him, or to anyone. Last night was a one-time thing; they both agreed. Yet, so she gave in so easily again this morning. There was no part of her that wanted him to stop.

She'd already lost herself in him once. Forgotten who she was, and let him dictate her future, not because he demanded it, but because back then she hadn't been strong enough to insist otherwise. Last night was sex. Taking it further today was about her identity, and she wouldn't give that up. She was her own person.

Her phone rang from its mount on her dashboard, the jarring chime echoing through her stereo system. A glance showed her Tate's face on screen. "Answer," she said to the empty car. She waited for the telltale *click* of the line picking up. "What's up?"

Background noise on the other end of the line assaulted her. Indistinguishable chatter—and was that a PA system echoing through the receiver? "You busy?" Tate sounded out of breath and... excited?

"Stuck in traffic on 400. So, not really. Are you all right?"

"Yeah. Never better. Seriously. Um, look. So, we're at the hospital, and I know you don't want to, but I'm going to need you to take the NSS case back."

Concern spiked through her, but it was tempered by his upbeat tone. He sounded flustered but fine. "T? What's going on?"

He laughed. "Right. That. Lys went into labor two weeks early. I have to get back to her, so I don't have a lot of time, and I spent most of it telling her folks. NSS Legal already called the office. Apparently they're delaying until next week anyway, so you've got time to regroup. Sorry to dump this back on you, but..."

A rainbow of ambivalence spilled through Vivian. She kept her tone light. "It's okay. Best reason ever for passing me back something that was my job to begin with. Go be with Alyssia. And congratulations."

"Thanks. Talk soon." With that, the call ended.

She sank back in her seat, as music filled the car once again. She'd never heard Tate that excited about anything before. Except maybe when he announced his engagement to Alyssia. Vivian was genuinely happy for them both, though she was surprised to see Tate slide into this role so easily.

A new list of things to do ticked through her head. Send flowers. Make time to visit when they were ready. Split Tate's work up with Jared. Try to not dwell on spending the next couple of weeks in a conference room, with a man she couldn't control herself around.

She shook the selfish thought aside, and a new one slammed into the now empty place in her head. Tate said NSS delayed things the remainder of the week. Why?

TWELVE

"You take charge of server management with the crowdfunding stuff." Vivian ticked off the next item on the list of tasks she and Jared would split, with Tate out of the office. All three of them had discussed this vaguely over the past few months, but saved the details because they had time. Dealing with the depositions added to the list, because it would take Vivian away from the day-to-day as well. She saw a lot of long hours in her future, and she was okay with that.

Jared made another note on his phone. "As long as you deal with the community managers."

"Alan can do that, but I'll oversee." Diving into work like this made it easier to forget last night and this morning. Except, every time she paused and let her mind drift where it would, she was aware of the hum on her skin. The longing that hovered at the back of her thoughts, waiting to ask if she was sure she could move on. The trick was to not pause. Having Jared in the room also helped keep her distracted. "Are the two of you excited about being Uncle Jared and Aunt Mikki?"

He made another note. "I prefer Grand High Lord of Toys."

"*You* prefer? You didn't come up with that." Vivian didn't have to ask. The name had to be Mikki's idea.

"Nope. But you can't deny it's got a nice ring to it."

"You've changed a lot since you met her." Vivian wasn't sure where the comment had come from. It was like stating chocolate was different from vanilla. Now the words were out, her thoughts followed the path. "Does it ever bother you?"

"No. He's got a focus group to build use cases in a week, for site improvements. Marketing is supposed to be handling it, but can you keep an eye on it?"

"Sure." She added more notes. "Not at all?" She didn't know why she was pushing the issue. His refusal was pretty straightforward, and it was obvious to anyone how good he and Mikki were together. Vivian was looking for something though, and a simple *no* wasn't it. "You don't do the whole focus-to-the-point-of-obsession thing, the way you used to."

He glanced up from his phone, eyebrow raised, before turning back to his list again. "I do; it's just been redirected. I never stopped being myself with her, but I'm a more complete version of me."

That didn't make any sense. "It's not a complete you, if you needed someone else to fill in the blanks."

"It is to me. I've never felt like I had to give myself up, to be with her. Sure, we compromise, but I don't regret it. It's like"—he studied the ceiling for a moment, as if it might hold the answers—"she brings out sides of me I didn't want to admit were there before. Not bad bits, but pieces it was easier to shove aside when I only saw the world from my perspective."

His words tugged at something, but she couldn't grasp it. "What about all her impulsive ideas?" She sounded petty. "Not that I have any issues with Mikki. You know I don't. But the two of you are night and day."

"I know. And sometimes I'm in the mood for whatever she suggests, and sometimes I'm not, and it works both ways. That's where the compromise comes in, and I never love her any less because of it. What's with all the questions?"

"I don't know. My head's all over the place today. What's left on the list, besides audits?"

He set his phone down on the edge of her desk and leaned in, resting his arms on the wood. "I'm going to say something, and it might piss you off."

"I appreciate the warning." She winked at him. Jared was never known for his tact.

He laughed. "I know you and Tate think I miss a lot, when it comes to people." He held up a hand when she opened her mouth to object or apologize or something. "It's okay. I get it. You two have your living, breathing, thinking… things, and I personally think computers are a lot more predictable."

"Fair enough."

"But I'm going to give you the same advice you gave me after Karen, and I hope you don't use it the same way you intended me to."

Vivian looked at Jared, waiting.

He picked up his phone, but did nothing but turn it over in his hands. "I'm sure I'm not getting this exactly right, but the gist of it was, just because you take on one role behind closed doors, doesn't mean that's all you are. Sex is personal, work is business, and people are complicated and capable of wearing more than one mask, while still being true to themselves."

"I never said anything that wise. If I did, I was trying to make a point about staying detached in the bedroom." Which she hadn't done. Which was why her mind was so scattered.

"That was your point, yes. It's not mine. You're going to have to take the annual audit. I suck at that complicated-numbers shit."

She would have asked him what he meant, but she didn't want to know the answer. Instinct told her figuring it out had the potential to make an even bigger mess of her already muddled thoughts. "I'll start on the audits today. See how much I can get done before Monday."

Jared's phone buzzed, and as he swiped the screen, a silly smile spread over his face. "It's a girl. Holly Elizabeth Foster."

"You have pictures?"

He shared photos of the baby—a shock of dark hair like Alyssia, blue eyes like both the kid's parents, and a scrunched up infant face that said *enough pictures, let me sleep.* Vivian stowed the pang the images summoned. After that, the conversation mostly fell apart. They had to get back to work.

The problem was, without Jared there to keep her occupied, her mind was free to wander to places she didn't want it to go. She threw herself into her task list. There was plenty to do. The rumor was, NSS Legal delayed the questioning today and tomorrow because they were swapping out members of their staff. Damon wasn't supposed to be here originally, so with any luck, he'd be gone soon.

And I can miss him from the other side of the country instead of just halfway across the city.

She pushed the thought aside. It was as good a time as any to move on again.

As the hours ticked away, she managed to lose herself in the pre-audit paper trail. It was a nit-picky level of detail that required intense focus. When she reached the section about the crowdfunding group spending, something caught her eye. It was just an email newsletter. The kind of marketing crap so many companies sent to subscribers. It looked status-quo, besides the fact it was from NSS, and Tate still had it in the audit folder. But something about it felt wrong in her gut. What was she missing?

A knock on her office door dragged her from her work, and she looked up to see Jared standing there. She blinked and rubbed her eyes when she realized most of the lights were out in the hall behind him.

"You planning on spending the night?" he asked.

A glance at her computer told her it was after seven. How had she worked through lunch and everyone leaving for the evening? "No. Just lost track of time."

"We're heading to the hospital, and Alyssia wants me to make sure you come with us."

"Any particular reason?"

"I didn't ask. Because new baby, and you might as well be family?"

The words flicked on a spot of warmth inside. "You don't really see me that way."

"We do." He nodded into the hallway. "Come on."

If she was going to turn into an old maid, she'd do so with a surrogate family. The abrupt, bitter thought knocked her off-kilter. That wasn't her; she liked the direction her life was taking. The self-assurance felt genuine, but the thought continued to haunt her as they headed outside.

DAMON SPENT most of the day Thursday and Friday sifting through a backlog of GG Foundation paperwork and seeing if anything needed his attention. Officially, he was working on the NSS case for his firm, so he couldn't pick up any new law firm clients. Camille was smoothing things over, and new assignments were pending. He suspected they'd be pending until after the weekend, so they could keep him here and bill for his time.

And in the last forty-eight hours, he'd only thought about Vivian every ten minutes. Never once been tempted—not too much so—to call her.

He leaned back in the hotel chair and stared at the ceiling. He felt like a fucking junkie, itching for a fix. Best way to cure that was to cut off the source of his addiction. Part of him wanted to tell Vivian in person that he was leaving, but he knew that was about the worst way to move on. He'd ask to meet someplace private, she'd agree, they'd talk their way out of their clothes…

He pushed the flood of images aside, before they could become a vivid assault on his senses. The best solution was a clean break, in every way possible.

He sent her a quick email, and for the sake of professionalism, copied her colleagues on it. *I'm being assigned to a new case, and someone else will be taking my place Monday or Tuesday. I'm not sure who yet. It's been a pleasure working with you.*

Sending the message this way meant she couldn't reply with anything more incriminating. She wouldn't risk putting anything like that in writing. It wasn't a fair move, but it was the only way he could think of.

Next up, Step Two. He grabbed his wallet and his rental-car keys, and left the room. It wasn't quite five yet, so the strip club the front desk recommended would be relatively empty for the next couple of hours. By the time the weekend crowd spilled in, Damon would be well on his way through Step Three of getting over this disaster of a week. This intense, incredible, unforgettable disaster of a week.

THIRTEEN

One of the nice things about being in Atlanta was the great tittie bars—alcohol, gorgeous girls, and full nudity. Damon sank further in his seat and nursed his second beer. This place was all that, tied up in a pretty little bow, and two hours after arriving, he wondered what he was doing here.

One of the dancers pulled out a spare chair next to him, placed a bottle of Jack on his table, along with two shot glasses, and took a seat.

Damon raised an eyebrow but didn't say anything. He'd noticed her about twenty minutes ago, during her set on stage. She was attractive enough. Maybe five-foot-four, full hips and breasts, narrow waist, red hair pulled into pigtails. As far as he could tell, she was going for the girl-next-door look. Except the hair color was no more real than the exaggerated freckles on her cheeks.

"You look like a whiskey guy." She poured two shots. "But the trendy kind, who likes a name brand. Am I right?"

The assumption and bold delivery were enough to draw his attention, where nothing and no one else had that night. "Did the designer slacks give it away?"

She shook her head and nudged one glass toward him. "Nope.

It's the fact that Jack Daniels is giving us a bigger kickback this week, for moving their drinks."

He couldn't help but laugh. He pulled a bill from his wallet and slid it across the table. "I'll buy, but I'm not drinking."

"I noticed." She pocketed the money anyway. "You're tipping well, almost every single girl, but you don't actually look at any of them. The more clothing that comes off, the harder you study that half-finished, got-to-be-warm-by-now microbrew."

"I paid the cover charge; I met the minimum. It shouldn't be an issue." He didn't know why he was defending himself to her. Hell, at this point he didn't even know what he was doing here.

"It's not." Both drinks sat untouched on the table. "I was making an observation. And hoping that, since unlike so many of these guys here, you're both generous and head-over-heels for someone else, I might get a little extra money out of you and not have to put out. I'm Ginny, by the way."

"Damon." He still couldn't find the urge to pay for a table dance, let alone try to pick her up, but she was interesting to talk to. "What makes you think I'm head-over-heels for someone?"

"Attractive guy like you, surrounded by naked women, and you're not looking at any of them? You're in love, or you're gay. Or both. I don't judge. Now that I think about it, you making out with some other guy? That would be hot."

The suggestion wasn't doing anything for him. He leaned in and rested his arms on the table. "Nope, not gay."

"Lucky woman, then." She knocked back her whiskey. "I'm not drinking alone. It'll give you something to do besides tell me, *No, I'm the lucky one to have met such a gorgeous, delicate flower.*"

He took a drink. "I'm not nearly that poetic."

"So what's got you sitting here, instead of with her? You make too much money? You're too generous? You come from warring families, and your love is forbidden, and if you can't have her, you'll kill yourself in protest?"

He couldn't help but laugh at the description. "More like the last one, but without the Romeo and Juliet suicide-pact thing. Let's just say our jobs keep us apart."

She gave him a fake pout. "Big mean boss says you can't date his daughter?"

"What? God, no. Though I do like your imagination."

She adjusted herself and leaned in enough to give him a generous view of her cleavage. "Thanks. You know, a lot of guys say it's my best feature."

"I doubt that."

"Are you going to spill your guts willingly then, or do I have to keep making up stories, to amuse myself?"

"You're doing this for you?" He poured them both another drink. He didn't intend to get either of them drunk, but it would keep her boss happy and her at the table.

"I'm not doing it for you. You're hung up on a mysterious woman I know nothing about." She nudged her glass away and sat straight again. "Let's see. There's no tragic death pact, and she's not the boss's daughter. You really don't strike me as the cheating type, or the type who'd be interested in someone who is, so neither one of you is attached to someone else. Hmm…" Ginny twisted her face in exaggerated thought. "Maybe, you're a guy who really likes when things go his way—at home, in the office, anywhere you can get control—and it turns out adult life doesn't always work like that, so you dominate in the bedroom instead."

The words hit too close to home, for his taste. "Great. I'm being psycho-analyzed by a woman who takes her clothes off for money."

"Great." Her tone shifted to mocking. "I'm being condescended to by the guy paying me, who hasn't even asked me to take my top off yet. Everyone takes their clothes off for money. I just get my cash up front."

"At least you're not jaded."

She stuck her tongue out at him. "At least you're not sarcastic. Is she a stripper?"

This was more fun than it should be. It was nice to talk to a woman he wasn't trying to get into bed, and the conversation helped his unruly thoughts slide back into order. It wasn't getting rid of the desperate ache for Vivian, though. "What makes you ask that?"

"My psychic powers only get me so far before I need a guy to fess up. There's a reason you're here, but not looking. I figure nostalgia or masochism."

Or both. Vivian would kill him for spilling her secrets, but it wasn't as if he'd share her name. "She was. A long time ago."

"As in, months?"

"As in, more than a decade."

"No." Ginny tilted back in her chair and looked him over. "You're not that old."

"Thirty six." Why was he telling her all this? Because she was listening. Because he needed to sift some things through, and it wasn't working in his head. Because like Vivian, way back then, Ginny wasn't judging him.

"You look good, for an old man."

He ignored the dig, wanting something more substantial from her than another round of swapped insults. "You really like your job. Don't you?"

"I love it. It's paying for my doctorate in psychiatry. Did she love it?" She glanced at something behind him, before turning her attention back to Damon.

"I used to think so. Sometimes I wonder now."

"It gave me some of the best memories I have." Vivian's voice sliced into the conversation and sang through Damon's veins. She pulled out an extra chair and looked at Ginny. "Hey, hon. Can I get a glass too?" How much had she heard?

"Of course." Ginny was on her feet in an instant. "I'll be right back."

Damon shifted toward Vivian. He'd spent hours surrounded by girls taking their clothes off, but Vivian sat next to him in a simple button-down top and leather skirt, and his cock instantly perked to life. "What are you doing here?" he asked.

"I'm looking for you."

"Here?"

She gestured around her. "Middle-class club, cheap drinks, full nudity, and more than half an hour from the hotel."

That she second-guessed him so well was more of a blow to his ego than he'd like. Apparently getting distracted made him predictable. "So now everyone can read me?"

She furrowed her brow, studied him, and then glanced over his shoulder toward the bar. "She must be interesting. I've got to hear this. And I may have flirted with the hotel desk clerk, and slipped him a fifty to tell me he recommended you try The Glass Slipper."

Ginny set another glass in front of Vivian and filled it. "Is this her?"

Vivian rolled her eyes, but she was smiling. "I'm glad I'm not the only one distracted by us."

Ginny looked her over. "You're not as old as he said. I bet you still have wicked moves."

"I can't believe you told her how old I am."

Damon should have walked out of the club the moment he heard Vivian's voice. Instead, he watched her, letting her soft perfume bring his thoughts under control—and damn, if he wasn't fantasizing about her on stage. "You don't doubt it for a second. And she's right. You look better than any girl in here."

Ginny cleared her throat. "Not *any* girl, but I do see why he's moping. You two are cute together." She grabbed Vivian's hand and tugged. "You should dance for him. He's so infatuated with you, he hasn't looked at anyone else all night"—she adjusted her breasts—" not for lack of me trying."

Vivian looked back at him

He shrugged. "It's true. Also, I'd love to see you up there again."

"Come on." Ginny pulled again. "Teach a girl how it's done?"

"No." Vivian's protest was strong, but she didn't move to pull away. "Definitely not. Especially in public."

Ginny let go of Vivian's hand, dropped into her lap, and draped her arms around Vivian's neck. "I'll go up there with you. Please?" Ginny's smile turned sweet, and she widened her eyes. "I won't make more in tips the entire week."

Damon saw Vivian's hesitation. The waver in her eyes. The consideration. He didn't have to ask or guess. The temptation of being on stage again, along with helping out the girl, was winning her over.

"No one's going to let me up there." Vivian's tone was wavering. "Insurance issues, and all that bullshit."

Ginny nodded toward the bar. "See the bartender? He's best friends with the owner. Manages the place. We're fucking. He's not going to stop me if I make him money. You, my gorgeous dear—high class, blonde, thin—with little old innocent me? That'll make him money." She leaned in and whispered something in Vivian's ear.

Vivian laughed and shook her head. "That's happening anyway."

"Yeah, you're right. But don't let that stop you."

Damon knew why Vivian hesitated. As alluring as the idea was to her, if anyone recognized her, it could be disastrous for her career. He pulled out his wallet and slid his credit card to Ginny. "I want your most expensive bottle of champagne, and the room that goes with it."

It wasn't for drinking, it was to secure a VIP room for the next hour.

Ginny grabbed his card, and offered Vivian her free hand. "Don't make me look bad."

"Keep up, kiddo," Vivian said.

VIVIAN STEPPED into a second floor room with Damon and Ginny. There was enough space for a couch, an ice bucket with two bottles in it, and a small area to dance in. A curtain covered the far wall, and Vivian knew drawing it back would reveal the main stage down below. Something told her they wouldn't do that tonight.

Her entire day had been an exercise in futility when it came to focus, which worsened after she'd gotten that fucking cruel email of Damon's. She'd stewed on the message most of the day, hating herself for missing him, and struggling with the question of *what now*. By the time five rolled around, she decided there was really only one choice. She needed one more taste, before Damon went back home, and something told her he wouldn't complain. If all they had was this weekend, she was going to live it for all it was worth.

She hadn't expected that to include stripping, but the idea enticed her anyway. Of teasing Damon. Of flirting with this willing girl who made Vivian feel old and young at the same time. And with the promise of privacy, she couldn't to refuse the temptation.

Music filtered into the room through invisible speakers, and Ginny swayed with the beat. Damon wrapped an arm around Vivian's waist, and pulled her close. "Fuck, I'm glad to see you." His voice was low, meant only for her ears.

A simple phrase that filled her with a reassurance she hadn't realized she needed. She rested her hands on his chest, and pushed out of his reach with a laugh. "No touching the girls, Sir." She winked.

He shook his head, and sank onto the couch. "Of course not."

Ginny's exaggerated cough filled the room, as a new song kicked on and a pounding dance beat rolled through the floor. "Not that I'm complaining, but the drinks buy my time, not yours."

Vivian definitely liked this girl. She saw why Damon had been enjoying her company. She stepped up next to the redhead, instinct flowing back with the music, and driving her hips to sway.

Ginny moved fluidly along with her, sliding her back against Vivian's chest, then spinning. As long as Vivian didn't overthink her movements, they came easily—gliding her hands up Ginny's sides when the younger girl draped her arms around Vivian's neck. Grinding against her. Diving into the music.

As the first song wound down, and the next one took its place, Vivian trailed her fingers down Ginny's chest, undoing each button without hesitation, and finally pushing her top to the ground.

Each time Vivian caught Damon's eye, her pulse spiked. The contact from the dancer was pleasant. Soft fingers striping off Vivian's top. Manicured nails teasing over her skin. But her responses were simple and physical. It was the way Damon's gaze stayed on her, heated and intense, that made her heart hammer against her ribs, and her pulse speed through her veins.

As song two ended, both women wore only their underwear.

Vivian was impressed. Ginny knew her stuff. Song three started. In an onstage set, the remaining clothes would fall away quickly, to give any patient customer a glimpse of what they'd waited for.

Surprise tickled Vivian's senses, when Ginny draped her arms around Vivian's neck, pulled her close, and whispered, "I'm gonna grab a smoke. The room's yours, and I promise no one's asking any questions."

"Thanks." Vivian couldn't completely hide her smile.

Ginny scooped up her clothes, and pulled them on as she headed for the door.

Damon raised his brows, but quickly returned his attention to Vivian when they were the only two left the in the room.

"Remember the rules." Vivian danced closer. She was going to enjoy the hell out of this. "No touching."

Damon leaned back on the sofa, feet planted on the ground, and arms stretched to either side. "All right. I'll play."

Being alone with him dialed her arousal past one-hundred. It was the perfect blend of then and now. She never stopped swaying to the music, as she lifted her hair above her head and let it fall again in a curtain around her face. She swayed her hips and unhooked her bra. The garment dropped away and the cool air rushed into caress her bare breasts.

His attention trailed along her form, and her already hard nipples ached with memories of his touch. Part of her whispered something was wrong with this. No, she argued back. This was all so right.

She hooked her thumbs in her panties, shimmied the lace down her legs, and kicked the clothing aside. The air kissed the wetness between her thighs, and she bit her bottom lip at the rush of desire. The need to touch herself, or better yet, let him do it.

"I can help you out, if you'd like." Damon offered, as if reading her thoughts.

She shook her head. This was about the show. Whatever wicked things he had in store for her came later. "I said, no touching."

He shook his head, but he was smiling. "We'll do it your way, for now."

She straddled his legs, hips following the beat. It wasn't a proper lap dance unless she was in his lap. She saw his fists clench until his knuckles paled, but he kept his hands to himself. They'd only done this a few times when they dated. Doing something like buying a private room wasn't in the budget.

Even then, they'd followed the *no sex in the VIP room* rule, regardless of the fact most girls broke it occasionally. It wasn't about behaving, it was about the tension of keeping their hands to themselves until they were back home.

She draped her arms around his neck, and ground to the rhythm, never lowering herself completely into his lap. Everywhere his gaze traveled, scalding heat rose on her skin. She was close enough to feel his erection. Lowered just enough to brush but not press into it. Which one of them was turned on more?

She didn't think it mattered.

"You're fucking killing me, Vi."

She dipped her head next to his, and hovered her lips over his ear when she spoke. "I'm sure you can hold out. You're all about the self-control, Counselor."

"Not when it comes to you." His growl vibrated at a frequency she felt rumble through her entire body.

Before she could shift her weight, he grabbed her wrists and pinned them behind her back in one hand, and fisted her hair with the other. If she'd been turned on before, it was a dim light compared to the excitement that flared inside at his possessive grip. His familiar scent—warm, safe, dangerous—engulfed her and filled her head. He trailed his nose along her neck, until his mouth found hers, and he gave her a fast but desperate kiss. "I want new rules."

"Not here. My place."

"Did you just tell me no?"

She lowered herself into his lap, and pressed against his cock, shifting her weight enough to tease. "Don't worry. I don't plan on making a habit of it. I want you for more than just the next hour."

The closeness of his body, the heat, spiked her euphoria. He locked his gaze on hers. "Why are you here?"

She shook her head. "I'll tell you in the morning, because you'll be there for me to tell." She leaned forward and crushed her mouth to his. Hungry, needing to taste him.

He jerked her head back, and lay a row of nips down her neck, to her collarbone. He kissed back up to her shoulder, and sucked and bit the tender flesh. She dug her fingers into his arms and ground against him.

"What makes you so sure I'm going home with you?" Gravel lined his voice.

She shifted her weight until her hip met his hard cock, and then pressed against him. "Instinct."

He pulled her head back enough to look her in the eye. "I'm not going to be gentle when I finally get my chance."

Her pulse thrummed, and her chest tightened in anticipation. "I wouldn't want it any other way." She knew this was dangerous for her heart. Worse than it had been fourteen years ago. Worse than letting him in earlier this week. She didn't care. He'd become an all-consuming thought. A desire she couldn't sate with thoughts and memories alone.

FOURTEEN

THEY TOOK VIVIAN'S CAR, BUT SHE ASKED DAMON TO DRIVE. BY the time they reached her building, anticipation hummed through her veins, and his promise danced along her skin. He made minimum contact. A hand on her back, as he held the car door open. A brush on the arm, as they stepped into her place. Never more than a whisper of heat through her clothing.

She kicked the door closed, stepped out of her heels, and watched him set his shoes next to them. The two pairs looked so right together, next to her entryway. She shook the random thought aside.

He stepped behind her, pressing close, and gripped her hips. His breath caressed her cheek, taunting in its tenderness, when he said, "Go kneel on the edge of your bed, back to the door."

The show she'd put on earlier—stripping, dancing with Ginny, showing off for his private audience—heightened her arousal. Combined with Damon's slow build-up and promise without delivery, it sent her thoughts into a muddled spin. But drawing the moment out was as much a part of his gift as anything, and she knew the results would be worth it.

She heard him follow, his stockinged feet brushing the carpet, but he kept enough distance that she couldn't feel him. She did as she was told and knelt on the edge of the bed, ass resting on her heels, as she looked straight ahead at the wall.

"How many years has it been, since we broke up?" His voice was right next to her ear, closer than she expected. The calm words squeezed her already hammering heart.

"I don't know."

"You do." This wasn't like the other night. There was no teasing. No playful tone. Simply his low, balanced voice.

He knew as well as she did; she was certain. They'd both been twenty-two. The entire thing was burned in her memory, like most of their relationship. "Fourteen years."

"Fourteen. Sounds like a good number to me."

She tried to swallow, but her throat was dry. Wondering what he had in mind stole her reason and set her thoughts adrift. A familiar sound clinked behind her. A belt unbuckling. Her mind sharpened, honing in.

He pressed a palm to her back and pushed her forward. She caught herself on her wrists, and the new position left her rear in the air. Rough hands shoved her skirt over her hips. She whimpered at the friction and sudden exposure.

"You're not wearing anything under your skirt." His even tone was gone, replaced with the throaty voice that sent excited chills through her. "I know you were wearing panties before you stripped."

"I didn't want to put them back on. I like the cool air on my bare skin." She wiggled her ass to emphasize her point.

The first lash from the belt struck one cheek, and she whimpered at the shock of pain and adrenaline that sped through her.

"Count to fourteen. Take your time. That was one."

God, she'd missed this. "Two." She spoke clearly and was rewarded with the sharp sting of leather, marking her flesh. She sucked in a deep breath. "Three." Another lash. The vibration made her already wet pussy lips slide together. "Four." *Crack.* Her nipples pressed into her bra, begging for attention, and her clit sent daggers of want spiking through her. By the time they reached fourteen, her head spun. Her behind was numb in places, and euphoria sparkled through her vision, clouding it with stars.

Unlike the other night, when teasing added to the buildup, tonight Damon stayed mostly quiet. She barely had time to catch her breath, when she heard his zipper slide down. He grabbed her hips, and that was the only warning she had, before he pushed inside her, driving his cock in to the hilt. His rhythm was slow and steady, as he pulled almost all the way out, and then plunged back in again. He shoved a hand under her shirt and dragged the elastic of her bra over her nipples. The new rough touch jolted her senses alive again, and she ground back into him. When she tried to increase the pace, he spanked her.

"Not yet." His voice was jagged and raw. He kneaded her breast and scraped a thumb over the tender skin, pinching and rolling in time to his thrusts.

"Please, baby." For her, the anticipation had been mounting since she stepped into the private room at the strip club. She had a feeling it was the same for him.

He jerked her upright, pressing her back to his chest and thrusting at a maddeningly steady pace. Each pinch and squeeze and push deeper buzzed along her skin. It was all culminating, but it wouldn't push her over the edge.

He covered her hand with his free one, and moved her palm to her stomach. He nipped at her shoulder and then bit harder. "Not yet."

She whimpered and squirmed under the multiple stimuli. Her thoughts were fuzzed, and the room danced around her. She struggled to find her voice. "Please let me come. Dancing with that girl tonight… It only turned me on because you were watching. I knew I was going home with you. No one else fucks me the way you do."

He guided her hand lower, until it brushed her slit. He worked her fingers on both sides of her clit, held her hand in place, and applied pressure. When they stroked her swollen bud, orgasm ripped through her. She screamed his name when she came, bucking against his cock, trying to get closer to each touch and jerk away from it at the same time. He slammed against her harder, driving deep, striking inside, while his hips collided with her tender ass.

One climax blended into the next, and she lost track of her world. His familiar grunts reached her ears, and still the intense rhythm continued. He came hard, spilling inside her, and finally slowed and eased off.

He kissed the edge of her ear, his breath ragged. "And no one says my name the way you do."

She smiled and leaned back into him, letting him hold her upright.

He slipped out of her and made himself comfortable on the bed. She joined him and curled up by his side. Her ass would be tender and red, when the natural high wore off, and depending on how distinct the marks were, she might not be able to wear skirts at work for a few days. She didn't care.

Neither of them spoke, and that was fine with her. They'd want to take their clothes off before they fell asleep, but that could wait. What she needed most right now was to know he'd be there in the morning, holding her.

DAMON WAS SURPRISED the next morning, when he woke up and Vivian was nestled against him. In college, when there had been a *them*, she'd only ever lain in bed this long if she was basking in the glow from the night before. "You're awake," he said quietly.

"Mm-hmm."

"How're you feeling?"

"Sore. Comfortable. Wonderful."

The lilting calm of her voice made him smile. He kissed the top of her head. "I'll make breakfast, and we'll talk about why you tracked me down last night."

She nodded. "Do you have plans this weekend? Or are you flying out today?"

"I'm here until Monday, and I'm spending as much of my time as I can with you." Something occurred to him. "Except I probably need to grab my rental car, and a change of clothes or two from my hotel."

"After breakfast." She pressed back into him, butt grinding into his cock and dragging it the rest of the way to life. "And a shower."

He cooked, and she made coffee. There was no hesitation in the kitchen, and the familiarity both warmed and bothered Damon. She still kept her cabinets organized the same, and the dance they'd done back then, when they spent the night together, flowed through him as easily as any instinct.

When the dishes were in the dishwasher, she tugged him into the bathroom and turned on the water in the large shower. He eyed the removable massaging shower head, which had several settings. "Do you get a lot of use out of that?"

"Only when I fantasize about you." She stripped off her clothes and dragged a nail down his chest.

He knew it was an exaggeration, but he liked the flattery too much to call her on it. He shed his clothing as well, and nudged her toward the glass door. "Lucky you, the real thing's here now."

She leaned back into him, long enough to say, "Luckier than you know," before stepping under the hot jets of water.

It scalded his skin at first, but he adjusted quickly. They took turns soaping and cleaning each other, until he pulled her back into him, dipped his fingers between her legs, and fingered her till she came.

She returned the favor by dropping to her knees, and wrapping her full lips around his cock. When he couldn't take the teasing any more, he spurted against the back of her throat, she swallowed and licked him clean.

They only left the house long enough to grab his stuff, and he picked up Chinese takeout on the way back. He felt like they were in college again, fucking the weekend away, not caring about anything else. It was a lot easier than admitting, when Sunday rolled around, this all had to end. Neither of them mentioned their pending conclusion. That this was only temporary. Not through their John Cusak marathon—including the movies he did when teenage heart-throbs made formulaic eighties comedies. Not through cold leftovers they were too hungry to heat up, after Damon stripped Vivian down and fucked her with her back to the balcony window. And it never once came up when they finally collapsed in bed, sometime around one in the morning, talking about anything and everything under the sun...

Except work and the fact it would separate them again, when reality sank in.

Damon drew his fingers through Vivian's hair, as she drifted toward sleep. His opinion from Friday afternoon had shifted. He never once thought yesterday was a bad idea, and he no longer wondered if he was addicted to her. There was no question; he was hooked, and it would be a long time before the cravings stopped. If they ever did.

FIFTEEN

VIVIAN ROLLED ONTO HER SIDE AND PROPPED HERSELF UP ON ONE elbow, so she could see Damon. She didn't want to mention that he had to leave today, even though it was at the forefront of her thoughts. Something else gnawed at her though. Right now, with the sun filtering through the blinds and with no rush to be anywhere, it seemed like the safest time to ask. "We keep talking about us then versus now. Do you think what happened when we dated stunted us in some way?"

He brushed aside a strand of hair, tracing his thumb over her cheek as he tucked the stray hair behind her ear. It took him a moment to answer. "You mean a loving, passionate relationship, most people would give their right arm to have a taste of? Not at all."

She wanted answers, not sarcasm. "I'm serious."

His phone buzzed on the nightstand, and he ignored it, aside from a single glance. "So am I." He nudged her back, sat, and pulled her upright as well. "And no, I don't think dating scarred us. I think the way we broke up did."

The words stung, and breathed new life and vibrancy into memories of that day. How much it ached. How long it took her to shove the moment aside. How fiercely she swore it would never happen that way again, because she'd never put herself in a situation like that again. And yet, here she was. With the same person. Choosing between the career and surrogate family she'd built, and him. "How would you have preferred it go?"

"You already know that." His phone rang again, but he never stopped looking at her.

"Enlighten me."

He dragged his fingers through his hair, gaze on her face. "I would have preferred you tell me what you were thinking, before it became the kind of problem that tore us apart."

She clenched her jaw and glared back. She wouldn't act like a child about this, but she couldn't let it go. "So this is all on me?"

He shook his head. "I'm equally guilty. I knew you were holding back. I also knew you were happy with the decisions you made. It was me who didn't want to be heading in that direction. I let people tell me I should have been doing something else. I pushed it back on you, and I ignored that none of it felt right, hoping it would become right if we tried hard enough."

She climbed from the bed and grabbed her robe. Part of her wanted him to pull her back. Tell her they could figure it out. The reality was they couldn't. She nodded toward the nightstand and his phone. "It sounded pretty important." Because they had outside lives. Things that couldn't be put aside because the sex was good. *Is that really all this is?* No, it was so much more, but it didn't matter. Silence met her back, but she didn't dare look to see if he was already reaching for his phone or staring at her. "I'll make coffee."

DAMON SWUNG his legs over the edge of the bed, biting his tongue to keep from telling Vivian to come back. The conversation wasn't over. Every bit of him knew that. Yet, hashing it out wasn't going to change anything. Too much time had passed, too many things had changed, and in the next twenty-four hours or so, he'd be on a plane back home. Alone.

He reached for his phone, and snarled at the screen when he saw both missed calls were from Camille. No voice mail. Too bad that didn't mean he could ignore it. As if acknowledging the call summoned another, the device rang in his hand. He sighed and clicked *Answer.* "Yeah."

"Tell me"—a hard edge lined Camille's tone—"the reason no one's seen you in the hotel all weekend is because you're in your room, working on other things. Or you picked up a random girl. Or you drove to Savannah for the weekend, to see the sights. Promise me it's one of those things."

Tension clenched the muscles in his neck and sent irritation down his spine. There was no way anyone knew where he was. That would be ridiculous. Regardless of his doubts, his answer came without hesitation. "I'm working."

"Good." Despite the word, her tone didn't shift. "Because I hear a nasty, vicious rumor that this woman you knew ages ago isn't so much in your past as you claim."

Fucking Hayden. Damon drew in shallow breaths and tried to keep himself cool, the same way he would in a courtroom. Except it wasn't often he was on this side of the questions. The best lies frequently resembled truth. "Of course she's not. She's a Skriddie executive. We already talked about this."

"Don't jerk me around on this, Vicker. Are you fucking Vivian Graff or not?"

"Absolutely not." The denial tasted bitter, but he never hesitated.

"So these stories about flirting in the breakroom, about taking off from business dinners early together, that Vanya saw the two of you meet for dinner mid-week, that's all bullshit."

"Yes. Complete bullshit." He wouldn't mince words or protest or bring up fancy excuses. The less he said, the better. Especially since his chest clenched to the point his ribs ached, each time he denied it.

"I'm glad to hear it." Her tone slid halfway back to normal. "Because I don't have to tell you, something like that would cost you your job. Hers, if Skriddie doesn't like it. You could face disbarment, for sleeping with a witness. You already know all that."

"I do." But he didn't like hearing it vocalized. "Is there a point to any of this? You knew Hayden would balk at me being pulled off the case, but this goes beyond childish and unprofessional. I'm going to be real surprised if his name doesn't show up on our GG Foundation list next."

"Not smart, Vicker. Don't bring that stupid foundation up again. Your replacement is touching down in about three hours. Get your ass on a plane by tomorrow morning and swear to me none of this can ever be proven."

"There's nothing to prove. I'm booking a ticket the moment I hang up."

"Thanks." Sickly thick saccharine dripped from the word. "See you Tuesday."

He scrubbed his hand over his face and dropped the phone on the bed. Apparently, avoiding the inevitable hadn't stopped it from happening. Go figure. He focused on thinking about nothing, as he dressed, shouldered his bag, and padded into the kitchen.

Vivian stood with her back to the entryway, staring at the window, as the last of the coffee sputtered into the pot. Her robe hung off one shoulder and barely covered her ass. Her hair was tousled. And damn, if she didn't look more gorgeous than ever.

"Important call?" she asked, as she turned. Her expression was blank, except for the way the corners of her eyes tugged down.

"Work. Hayden's spreading rumors." He didn't want to tell her this way. He'd rather not tell her at all.

"About us." She closed her eyes and inhaled deeply before looking at him again. "We knew it was coming."

That didn't make it easier to accept. He dropped his bag on the floor and closed the distance between them. Her eyes grew wide—the first real emotion she'd shown since he walked in the room—but she didn't back away.

He cradled her face between his palms and slanted his mouth over hers. It was supposed to be a light kiss. A tender goodbye. When she dug her fingers into his chest, his restraint snapped. He dove into the moment, hard and hungry, tongue dancing with hers. She groaned against his mouth, sweet and desperate. Why wasn't there a way to make this work? Every time she shifted her weight, the sensations teased his need.

Hands at her hips, he lifted her to the counter and wedged between her legs. She hooked her ankles around him, deepening the kiss. He could fall into this moment forever and not want to leave. Her robe slid open, and he shifted his hands to her bare waist.

He wasn't sure where he summoned the strength from or why, but he finally broke the kiss. He pressed his forehead to hers. "I'm going to miss you." He struggled to catch his breath.

"Me too. But I'm glad we did this." She pulled back a few inches and looked him in the eye, without breaking contact. "What did you tell her?"

"Who?"

"Camille. What did you tell her, when she asked if it was true?"

The lie that came easily moments ago lodged in his throat now. He and Vivian both knew they had to be discreet, so why was he hesitating? "I denied it emphatically." He hated the way that sounded.

"That's the way it'll always be, isn't it?" Vivian's voice was so low, he had to strain to hear the question, even with her sitting so close. "As long as you work for the firm that represents our biggest competitor, we'll deny it."

"Vi, it's not..." What was he going to say? He'd given up the case, in order to walk away. He didn't see any solution that allowed them to keep doing this, let alone stop hiding it.

"It's okay." She nudged his body back with hers, as she hopped from the counter and draped her arms around his neck. Nothing on her face said it was okay, but her tone was almost convincing. "Just because we never really said it, it's no less true." She shifted her weight against him, teasing. Torturing. "I didn't expect you to tell her anything else, but it didn't stop me from hoping."

"I get it." He slid his hands to the small of her back, holding her captive. "I would go everywhere with you on my arm if it weren't career suicide."

Her laugh came out strangled. "I thought I'd never hear that again when I quit dancing."

"I—" The words stuck in his throat. He wanted to say them. Needed to tell her, for his own sanity. It wasn't fair to her though. He swallowed back the, *I love you.* "I know what I said back then, but I was never embarrassed about you dancing."

"Don't." She dropped her hands, stepped out of his grasp, and hugged her robe tight around her. "It's a nice sentiment. Don't ruin it."

He wanted to reach for her again, but the inches between them felt like a chasm. "I'm glad we did this too."

"If you ever—" She snapped her mouth shut. "Never mind. Have a safe flight."

He knew what she'd been about to say. It was the same thought running through his head, though he had no interest in vocalizing it. He never for a second considered it an option, because even though he knew it was the only solution, it wasn't one he'd ask for. *If you ever quit your job... You know, stop working for the competition... I'll be here.*

He wasn't completely aware of telling her *goodbye*, or walking to the car. He made it back to the hotel without too much trouble. Was it worth it to stay in town the rest of the day? He could fly out tonight. It was tempting, but if Camille told him to fly back tomorrow, he was expected to bill the hours in between.

Fortunately he wasn't expected to work, on top of that. He didn't think he had the mental capacity for it.

SIXTEEN

Vivian didn't know how long she stood near the counter, hands hooked over the edges, gripping until her fingertips were numb. The turmoil that raged in the back of her head over the past week surged to the forefront of her mind. All of it punctuated with a single statement.

I don't understand.

She shook the thoughts aside and made her way back to the bedroom. She showered. She dressed. She tugged at the sheet on the bed. Maybe she'd do laundry and wash Damon's scent from the blankets.

Despite the stakes being so much higher now than fourteen years ago, the decision didn't seem more clear cut. She wasn't simply proud of what she'd earned in her career, she actually loved her job. How many people could say that? Besides, quitting a job because of a man—no matter what man, or the fact she'd find new work quickly—meant giving up parts of her life for him. That thing she swore she'd never do. Women who ignored their friends for a guy needed to move on. But it wasn't love if she wasn't willing to make some sacrifices.

She sank onto the corner of the mattress and dropped her face into her hands. *Love.* Was it, actually? The hollow pit where her heart should beat said it was, but maybe she was fooling herself.

A voice she hadn't heard for years echoed in her head. Her mother's. *I love him sweetie… He says he's sorry… It won't happen again… He says it's for the best… I deserved it.*

But he's not like that. He's different. Vivian screamed in the empty room, as her own justification mingled with that voice from so long ago.

The last place she needed to be right now was in her own head, so time in the dance studio in the other room was out of the question. She might as well do some work. Tomorrow she'd be stuck in a conference room during office hours, and she had to finish making sure things were ready for the audit before then. *Focus on work.* The mantra repeated in her head. She shot down any follow--up thoughts about work being part of the problem, or suggesting she call Damon instead.

She set her laptop up on the desk at the far end of her bedroom and pulled up the information from Tate again. Where was she? Her mouse cursor hovered over a .pdf. It was the same one that caught her eye the other day, but she couldn't figure out why. She double clicked the file again and studied the contents. It was the NSS email newsletter, about their new crowdfunding website. The ad had gone out to their subscribers the day after Tate started having trouble with his pilot groups on similar software.

It had been irritating, but the site issues weren't exactly proprietary knowledge, so it made sense NSS would strike while Skriddie was recovering. Something about this email though…

Fuck me. She grabbed her cell phone and dialed Jared.

"Yeah?" Didn't matter how many years he worked as a top executive, he never answered the phone differently.

Vivian smiled at the familiarity. "Crowdfunding. Did you ever fix the security issues with the cloud-based apps?"

"You're working on a Sunday afternoon?"

She laughed. "Because you're playing video games with your girlfriend?"

"No. I got tired of being sniped and then tea-bagged. I'm catching up on some of Tate's work."

"See?" She had a feeling that would be the case. "Yes or no on the security?"

"No. Current technology makes the issue impossible to overcome. That's why we scrapped the features around it. Unless someone in operations wants to give me the budget and manpower to fix it."

Even though this was standard everyday business, talking to Jared helped her feel better. As long as she didn't think about why she needed to feel better. "NSS fixed it."

"No, they didn't." There was no hesitation or uncertainty in his response. "They're either lying, or they don't know the flaw is there."

That was what she thought. This was all circumstantial, but it made sense. "Who set up the crowdfunding servers?"

"Mikki. You know that."

"No. Not the patch job Tate pulled together. The original, the images—the stuff Marge Foster squeezed the bandwidth on."

"Dewson. He does all that stuff. You know that too."

She did, but she liked the confirmation. She also wanted to see if Jared reached the same conclusion she did, to confirm if she was on the right track or grasping at straws. "And who else was with us in Vegas? On the phone."

"Dewson."

"And who did all the server and network checks, when NSS started those rumors about holes in our security? And who else was up for the ethical hack job, when Mikki applied? The guy who wasn't quite qualified. Who threw a fit when he found out. Who just bought a car worth as much as Tate's Bentley on an IT salary."

Jared's exhale echoed over the line. "Fuck me."

"Exactly." She *was* right. Another piece slammed into place in her head and knocked her elation off-center. *Asshole.* "He knew, and he didn't tell me." The words came out more softly than she intended.

"Dewson?"

"Damon." The first night they came back here. She'd asked him twice what had changed. Why he was willing to cross that line. This was the answer. It might not be true, but something sinking in her gut told her she was right.

"Why would he tell you?" Jared asked.

It was a good question. They'd spent more than a day together, barely pausing to eat, and never really to put on clothes, but that didn't mean he would disclose that kind of information. It was part of what they'd agreed on. Why did it feel so much like a betrayal, then? Possibly because this was more than keeping a source's name secret. "I don't know. Thinking aloud."

"We've always known they had someone on the inside."

She was grateful to Jared for not pushing the out-of-place comment. "Do we think Dewson really did something like sell them our code?" Which was why it bothered her that Damon would keep this secret. It wasn't even questionable ethics at that point. It was more than the *is this okay?* of someone spilling what they'd heard in a business meeting. This was a contract violation. Possibly theft.

He doesn't owe you anything. He's still the lawyer for the competition. And it was still just sex. That was why it hurt so much. Because it meant Damon had as clinical an approach to the whole thing as she did, but without all the haunting doubt and second-guessing.

"If we prove this, NSS has to settle." Jared's comment yanked her back to the conversation.

"I'll call Legal and have them subpoena Dewson's bank records. Get Hayden and Dewson in line for questioning." Get back to business. That was what she needed to do. Ignore the acid devouring her gut.

"Let me know what I can do," Jared said. "And Viv?"

"Yeah?"

"I'm sorry."

She didn't have to ask. He meant the comment she'd made about Damon. "It's nothing. Talk to you tomorrow."

She fired off an email to their legal team and tried to dive back into work, but her focus was shot. She didn't have a right to be upset with Damon. If he knew, it wasn't something he could share. Before a single bit of skin was exposed, they both understood talking about this case was off limits. Betrayal and doubt taunted her anyway. Besides, he might not have any idea Dewson was selling Skriddie secrets to his clients. She drew a lot of abrupt conclusions, based on a simple conversation in a restaurant, and they could all be wrong.

Conflicting opinions raged in her head, each trying to convince her they were right, until she couldn't stand it anymore. She grabbed her phone and typed up a quick text to Damon.

You knew. Didn't you? Wow, way to sound accusatory. That wouldn't work.

Keeping something from me? This was a little too coy, obscure, and bordered on either flirty or psychotic ex.

She settled on, *Did you know about Dewson?*

Simple question. No accusation. A *yes* or *no* would suffice. He'd say *no*, and she'd turn this all back on NSS and go back to trying not to lose herself in the memories of the last few days.

The phone beeped with a reply. She reached for it, but hesitated, hand hovering over it. Waiting wouldn't change the answer. She forced herself to look.

Yes.

The single word knocked the bottom out of her stomach, and she dropped her phone. It clattered to the desk. Of course he knew. As much as she wanted to believe the passion was real, the connection was there, and everything that came with the shared moments meant something, it was simply business and sex. Maybe she was overreacting and being irrational, but experience told her she was finally acting sane. The last week had never been anything more that stolen moments frozen in time.

SEVENTEEN

Damon sat at his gate, waiting to board the plane. He'd lost count of the number of times he almost said *fuck it* that morning, turned the car away from airport traffic, and drove back to Vivian's.

It would only delay the inevitable for a few more hours. Instead, he'd fly back home, stuff this bullshit lawsuit toward the back of his thoughts, and focus on real cases. The attendant announced boarding would begin soon, and Damon shifted his laptop bag onto his shoulder. One perk of traveling so much for job was platinum status with almost every airline, so he'd board first. His phone chimed, and he moved to press ignore and set it to airplane mode. The name on the screen, Kyle Ridge, made him pause. At least they'd picked someone respectable, to take his place on the case. He clicked *Answer.* "This is Damon Vicker."

"Hey. You're probably boarding soon, but I need two minutes."

Fair enough. Damon expected a call earlier, maybe even last night, to go over any missing details of the case. It might have been a nice distraction from his own thoughts as well. "What's up?"

"Prosecution is talking about subpoenas on bank records. Camille didn't mention they knew about Dewson. Do they have enough information that I need to be worried?"

Damon furrowed his brow. First Vivian's brief, completely unsatisfactory text yesterday, and now this. Over a phone conversation in a Vegas hotel room? "What do bank records have to do with that?"

"Camille told me…" Silence spilled over the line. In the airport background, the attendant began boarding. "Never mind; I'll get the information from Vanya," Kyle said a moment later.

Concern built in Damon's thoughts, and he grasped for missing threads, struggling to stitch something together. "No, tell me. What does Dewson know that has to do with bank records?"

Kyle paused again, and the second dragged on. People lined up at the gate, to board the plane. "He's their guy on the inside."

"Obviousl—" Damon snapped off the sarcastic retort as everything tumbled together. Bank records meant money changing hands —either bribery or pay for work. Which meant Dewson was giving NSS more than just snippets of phone conversations here and there. How much, though? "Why did you know about this and I didn't?"

"Not a clue." Kyle's shrug was almost audible. "It's in the case notes I got."

"We'll now begin boarding our remaining passengers." A pleasant voice came over the loudspeaker.

"I've got to go." Damon let every foul word he knew scroll through his thoughts, but he kept them from his voice. "Good luck."

"Thanks, man."

As Kyle hung up, Damon glanced between his phone and the boarding line. This entire case had been an ethical gray area, but if money had changed hands, especially if it was enough for Skriddie to ask about bank records…

He should forget this. Not his case, not his problem. A year ago —hell, six months ago—he would have tucked away the misgivings and moved on. Except his mind wouldn't let him drop this, even if it didn't involve Vivian.

He was jumping to conclusions. Camille would clear things up. Five minutes tops, and he'd make his flight.

If I really want to.

Fucking voice. He brought up Camille's number, waited for her to answer, and exchanged strained pleasantries with her.

"I'm glad you called. I was going to wait until you landed, but now works." The false cheer vanished from her voice.

He tucked his own questions aside. They'd have more impact if she wasn't waiting her turn to talk. "Do tell," he said.

"Promise me again you didn't sleep with someone from the prosecution's witness list."

"We already had this conversation." A trepidation grew inside him. Did she know? Did he care?

"Damn it, Vicker. What are the odds anyone else knows about this?"

The right answer was, *There's nothing to know.* Something snapped inside, and apathy surged in. "Depends on how many people Hayden told."

"That's so much the very wrong answer." There was no snideness or fake cheer in her tone, or anything but irritation. "Bury this. You never even give a hint to anyone else that this happened. Get your ass back here and pretend last week was a dream."

"Final boarding call, Flight 728 to Salt Lake, continuing to Seattle."

He could hang up now, catch his flight, and do exactly what Camille said. Or he could push his luck, take a stab in the dark at how serious this was, and potentially ruin his career. Fuck it. "How about, instead, I tell Skriddie the details of this bullshit with their IT guy? That he's sold their software to the competition, he's planted viruses on their network, and he's drawn a healthy paycheck in the process? Even working for both companies at the same time is a contract violation." He might be way off the mark, and if so, this was about to blow up in his face.

"Is this extortion?" Camille asked.

Nope. He had it, all right. This was disappointing. How did he not see it sooner? "It's not. That would imply I have a price."

"So... what? You're going to violate client-attorney privilege, after already committing a very serious ethics violation, and you think you'll come out of this on top? You'll be disbarred. I'll file the complaint myself."

"That's fine." He turned and strode from the gate, toward baggage claim and the rental-car shuttles. This was insane. He was throwing away a career he'd worked over a decade to build. Flushing it all, when his only backup plan was to draw a small salary from a charity foundation as a consultant, handling arbitrations. It was possible he'd never be able to practice law again if he did this.

"I don't know what your bluff is, but you're not thinking this through." Panic crept into Camille's tone. "You tell them this, the case crumbles. NSS will have to reach a settlement now, the publicity on this could cause huge damage to our image. People here will lose their jobs."

He wasn't completely callous about the situation. He knew the last bit was thrown in as an exaggeration. "Do what you have to do. I quit. Not only the case, but all of it. I'm done."

"This comes down on Vivian Graff, too."

The threat made him pause, but he recovered quickly. "She wasn't involved."

"Really. It took two, to do what you did."

"I'm intimately aware of that. She wasn't involved."

"This conversation is over." The line went dead.

Damon shoved his phone back in his jacket pocket, already taking a mental inventory of next steps. Fax a formal resignation, shred his company credit cards, be prepared to pick up the bill himself for the last week—though if the firm could get away with charging NSS, they would.

Most important on the list was find Vivian, explain, and tell her he loved her.

And pray his impulsiveness didn't cost her.

Vivian almost managed to hide her smugness when their lawyers mentioned requesting Hayden's bank records and getting an early testimony from him and Dewson. Her smile grew a little more as the NSS legal team called for an immediate break and walked away in a small, chattering flock around Hayden.

Her victory vanished when they returned and said Hayden

would hand over the documentation willingly, and that he wanted to answer questions now.

The entire time, she squashed any thoughts of Damon. That he'd seen this coming. That the preceding days had meant nothing to him. Okay, so she did a shitty job of ignoring any of the thoughts. It would happen with time, though.

They asked the court reporter to start recording again, and the questions and answers flew. Vivian's mood soured the more time ticked away.

Hayden wasn't the villain here, he insisted. He'd been blackmailed. He made the mistake of asking Dewson for information once, after Vegas, and it was all downhill from there. Hayden painted a stunning picture of a guy backed into a corner for a mistake. After the lawsuit was filed, Dewson threatened to say Hayden had made him talk. Hayden didn't know what else to do, besides hand over the money.

Vivian wanted to scream what a bullshit story it was. Legal tried to poke holes in it and twist Hayden's replies back on him, but he had a counter each and every time.

Worse, when they called Dewson, he didn't hold up at all. His story sounded a lot more plausible—a guy turned down for a job he should have had, who made a little extra cash selling secrets to the competition. Even in the course of admitting guilt, he was such a wreck, he sounded like he was lying.

The conversation with Jared slammed back into her thoughts. She scribbled a note to Brian, the Skriddie head attorney. He gave her a brief nod, and seconds later said, "We're done talking to Mr. Dewson. We have a couple more questions for the previous witness."

If Hayden was shaken by the request, it didn't show. They dismissed Dewson and reminded Hayden he was still under oath.

Brian glanced at Vivian's scribbled note again, and asked, "How did you get around the security holes specific to your crowdfunding sites with the cloud based apps?"

Hayden's smug expression twitched, faltered, and then slid back into place. "There are no security holes in our software."

"That's fantastic." Brian didn't sound as if it were good or bad.

He might as well have been talking about someone mowing the lawn. "Then you wouldn't be opposed to us running a simple script against the site, to see how it responds."

He was referring to the same test the Skriddie quality assurance team had used, to find the issue in the first place. If the script found the same hole, it wasn't conclusive proof NSS used their code, but it was pretty damn close.

Hayden shook his head. "Absolutely not an option. Why would we let anything they wrote touch our network? Are you insane or just incompetent? Do you realize what the point of this case is?"

"We'd let your engineers review the code first." Vivian chimed in. "A joint venture, if you will." She locked her gaze on Hayden. "No one does or runs anything anywhere, without everyone's go ahead. And since your developers are skilled enough to have overcome this issue, I'm sure you trust them enough to okay a simple testing script."

Hayden narrowed his eyes and clenched his fist. "We need another break."

Half the room emptied, and the Skriddie legal team exchanged a round of smiles. Vivian glanced at her phone out of habit, and her gut sank when she saw the message from Damon.

We need to talk.

Déjà vu. And not in a good way. Her hedging sense of victory vanished, and she sent back a single word. *No.*

EIGHTEEN

It was almost two hours, before the NSS legal team returned to the conference room. Hayden wasn't with them.

"Our client's gone back to his hotel," Vanya said as she took her seat. "He's not feeling well."

Vivian kept her face an impassive mask. Despite the turmoil raging inside, about her personal life, something told her this was good news. "I'm sorry to hear it."

"Anyway"—Counselor Ridge nodded at the court reporter—"we're back on record." When she indicated she was ready, he continued. "We'd like to discuss settlement options."

Vivian heard a whispered *yes,* from Brian next to her, and couldn't completely hide her grin. In a louder voice, Brian said, "We're willing to discuss it. What did you have in mind?"

The next few hours passed in a blur around Vivian. They worked through lunch. A basic round of terms, *must-have*s, and *willing-to-bend*s were passed back and forth, and five o'clock rolled around faster than she'd expected. Everyone shook hands, said they'd continue tomorrow but wrap up and head home soon, and they were on their way.

Silence rang in her ears like a bell, threatening to dredge up things she'd rather not think about. Best option was keep busy. Besides, she had good news to share. She let the elation override anything else in her head, and made her way to Jared's office. He didn't look up when she paused in the doorway. Whatever he was doing had him furrowing his brow and glaring at his computer.

"Plans tonight?" she asked.

His head jerked up, eyes wide, and he blinked a few times before focusing on her. "Yeah." His voice was strained. "I had to let my head IT guy go. I'm seeing what kind of cleanup I have to do."

Right. That answered the question about Dewson's fate. "I'll help. Point me in a direction."

He waved a hand. "We've got it, but thank you. Did it at least pay off, or is it too soon to tell?"

She let out a light laugh. "NSS caved. It's still early, but it looks better than it has in a few years. I was thinking we'd all go celebrate when you were done."

"Tomorrow night?"

"Absolutely." Anything to fill her calendar and act as a temporary salve for the longing she refused to admit mocked her. "Do me a favor though—don't tell Tate."

"Your victory, your news to break. Just don't wait too long."

"Heading over there now." A call would work, but she wanted to see baby Holly now they were home from the hospital, check on Alyssia, and surround herself with people. Not a fair burden to place on them, but she'd be careful not to overstay her welcome. She bantered a bit longer with Jared, then told him goodnight, and asked him to let her know if he needed help after all.

As she headed to the parking garage and her car, she dialed Tate.

"Hey. I'm glad you called." He sounded tired, but happy. "How'd it go?"

"I'd rather say in person. Are you okay if I drop by?"

"That good or that bad?"

"Well…" She liked teasing and joking with him. It felt normal. "We still have a company."

"Very not helpful. I was going to ask if you were free tonight anyway. Come over. Lys wants to ask you something."

The way he phrased it and the shift in his tone drew Vivian's curiosity to the surface. "Like what?"

Tate laughed. "You have your secrets, I have mine. We'll share when you get here."

This was what she wanted. The thing she enjoyed about the life she'd built. Great friends, a good job with an honest company, and knowing her own decisions had led her here. The knowledge and reassurance didn't erase the ache behind her ribs, as she drove to Tate and Alyssia's house. The gnawing reminder of the text message from Damon that morning made her feel like her phone glared daggers at her, from its mount on the dashboard.

Apparently, it didn't matter how many times she told herself she'd made the right choice, it was going to be a while, before the sharp pain eased to a dull throb of longing.

Regardless of how many ways she rolled the situation over in her head, Damon really couldn't have told her about Dewson, but his keeping it secret might have cost her, Jared, Tate, and everyone she adored, everything they'd worked for.

And as much as she tried to reconcile all that, she failed.

DAMON SAT in the hotel coffee shop, staring at the wall, his drink cold and untouched. He could have sent Vivian text after text this morning, even after she told him she didn't want to talk. Explain what he knew about Dewson was nowhere near what there was to know. Plead with her to listen. Dump his entire thought process on her a sentence at a time over digital lines.

He wanted to do it in person. Needed to see her face when he told her, even if her answer was that she never again wanted anything to do with him. The problem he kept running into was how to approach her. Stopping by the office wasn't really an option. She'd been in those depositions all day, and something told him he wasn't welcome there. She didn't need the complications of explaining an out-of-place visit to her colleagues.

He could drive by her condo, see if she was home, and pray she'd buzz him up. He'd already done one loop, and her car wasn't parked there. Too many more passes by, and the stalker-ish feeling brewing inside would be amplified exponentially. Speaking of creepy stalker behavior, the fear she'd take it that way was the only thing keeping him from his last idea—seeing if she was with her friends. He had everyone's addresses, as part of the case files. If she hung with Jared and Mikki, she was probably out on the town, and he wouldn't find her tonight.

The odds were better Tate and Alyssia would be home. New baby and all that. Which was a situation he really didn't want to intrude on.

He had to talk to Vivian, though. Not to make a scene, but to ask for one more chance to be heard. That meant going with the stalker option—driving by Tate's house, looking for a familiar car, and hoping he didn't get bounced at the door.

It was after seven, so he needed to do this now, or go stir crazy for another night, sifting over more ideas. He tossed his coffee in the trash, programmed the address into the GPS, and took off. Forty-five minutes later, he turned down a street lined with lush lawns, huge yards, and houses to match. He was probably in the right place. Vivian's car parked in the driveway was another good indicator. Damon took the empty spot next to the familiar sedan and strode to the front door. He wasn't surprised when Tate answered, but the smile he received caught him off guard.

"You get lost on the way to the airport?" Tate asked.

"More or less." Damon wouldn't let himself think, because that would lead to *over*-thinking and second-guessing. He'd done too much of that recently. "Is Vivian here?"

When Tate opened the door and stepped aside, Damon's shock grew another notch. He hadn't expected a warm reception or anything short of a cold shoulder. Tate nodded toward a pair of glass doors leading to a patio. Vivian sat outside, holding an infant and chatting and laughing with a woman who looked a lot like

Jared, but attractive. The sight stole Damon's breath for a moment, and his mind went blank.

"If I were a different man, I'd give you the same advice V gave me a year ago." Tate's comment shattered the wall around Damon's thoughts.

Damon mentally shook himself back into the present but couldn't pull his gaze from the scene outside. "I'm intrigued. What kind of advice?"

"She told me not to mix business with pleasure."

That sounded like her. Damon smiled. "She's a smart woman. Way I understand it, that didn't stop you."

"How do you know that? Do the people at NSS talk about anything besides us? That's got to be the most boring fucking place on the planet."

"Vi told me…" Damon hid a wince at the slip. He hadn't meant to use the nickname, or mention they had that kind of conversation. Then again, he stood in someone else's foyer looking for her, when he was supposed to be back home, so one could draw a lot of conclusions. "Anyway, NSS isn't boring, necessarily. It's more like… a daycare, run by a kindergarten class."

"I like that."

For the most part, Damon's attention stayed outside. He watched Vivian play with the baby, smiling, looking very much at ease.

She couldn't have that for herself. The thought came out of nowhere and jabbed him. "You guys are more like the geeky high-school kids everyone is picking on, so you're going to destroy prom with your own weather-controlling machine."

"I'll accept that. I'm pretty sure one of us tried to do that, and my money is on Mikki."

"So, the advice… If it was so memorable and repeatable, why didn't you listen?"

"I've always loved Lys, and I've always wanted this. I stopped lying to myself, and let the past go."

Damon was caught off guard by the honesty. His past with Tate was relegated to tame insults and name calling. He always suspected the guy had depth, but he didn't figure he'd ever be in a situation to see it. "We're not close enough to be having this conversation. Besides, I'm not lying to myself."

"Never said you were. This is about me."

"Always is with you, kids."

Tate snorted with laugher. "Yeah, because you're so old and wise. Since I'm pushy and curious, are you here because the home office told you this was winding down?"

Winding down? Damon liked the implication. "There's no home office anymore."

"Love to hear that story sometime." Tate pushed away from the wall. "What are the odds I'll have the chance?"

"That's not up to me." Damon would respect Vivian's wishes, even if it meant leaving her to her life and never seeing her again. God, that would hurt like hell.

"I'll grab her." Tate stepped onto the patio and closed the door, cutting off all sound.

Vivian looked back at Damon and drew her lips into a thin line. She handed the baby to Alyssia and shook her head. Tate shrugged and turned back toward the house.

Damon's heart hammered against his ribs, and his entire frame clenched in anticipation of a *no*.

Vivian grabbed Tate's arm before he could open the door. She stood, and they exchanged a few words, before he squeezed her hand and stepped aside, to let her in.

She locked her gaze on Damon's, as she closed the distance between them, but she didn't speak until she stood less than a foot away. "So, now that NSS wants to settle, you can track me down?" Her tone was ice, and her expression matched. "Work out some kind of weekend agreement, where you get laid and we pretend there's no conflict of interest? Ignore that what you knew and kept to yourself could have cost Skriddie everything?"

No wonder she didn't want to talk to him, though the confirmation the case was ending in Skriddie's favor sent a wave of relief through him. "Do you really think this was just about sex?" Not what he wanted to say. He had to know before he told her anything else, though.

She clenched her jaw and bounced her leg, and took several seconds to answer. "No."

He let out a breath he didn't know he'd been holding. "Can we talk outside?"

She glanced over her shoulder, at the couple trying very hard to look like they were doing something besides watching them. "I should tell you *no.*"

"But you're already here…"

"Yes. We can."

He held the door for her, and she paused on the front porch, to wait for him, arms crossed.

She started talking before he could. "I can't do this, Damon. I can't walk this line with you. Seeing you sometimes. Pretending it doesn't have the potential to cost us our jobs. Watching you leave again. On top of that, for a while, I was terrified that, if you asked me to choose between my life and yours, I'd throw mine away. But I can't do that either. And just because you have control in the bedroom, doesn't mean I could ever give up me outside of it. And…" She dragged in a shaky breath. "Before I say any more I'm going to regret, why are you here?"

"I didn't know until I got here that you were in settlement discussions." He was shooting from the hip at this point, and that was as good a lead-in as anything. "Just like I didn't know everything about Dewson." She opened her mouth, and he held up a finger. "I knew he was their fallback witness for the conversation in Vegas. That was it. That's what I meant, when I told you I knew."

"But you know now." She uncrossed her arms, and shifted her body toward his. "Why do you know that and not that we were in settlement? Why are you even still in Atlanta?"

"I quit this morning." It felt good to say it. Better than it should, considering he needed to solidify his work future. "After I found out what they'd been hiding about the insider and realized I don't agree with the way they run their business. Besides I'd much rather be with you, if you're interested."

"I—" She worked her jaw up and down, and then bit her bottom lip. She furrowed her brow. "I can't ask you to do that. I wasn't willing to do it for you."

"Except you didn't ask, and I'd never want you to do that for me. You belong here. I don't belong there." He reached for her, and relief flooded him when she leaned into his touch instead of pulling away. He drew a thumb across her cheek. The simple contact quieted so much inside. "I love you, Vi. I always have. Since that very first day in the bar, when you challenged my fake ID. You need to know that."

She ducked her head, but not before he saw her frown. His pulse jammed to a stop when she didn't reply.

NINETEEN

Happy flutters spread through Vivian, and it was a struggle to keep the elation from her face. She hadn't realized how much she needed to hear this. How desperate she was for these words, from him. She felt guilty he'd quit his job, but he sounded certain, and she believed him when he said it was what he wanted. She finally met his gaze again, and asked in a quiet voice, "You're not just saying that?"

"What kind of sadistic fuck do you think I am?"

"Really?" She raised her brows, and her smile slipped out.

"Maybe wait to answer that until we get back to your place."

"I love you too." She closed the last few inches between them and brushed her lips across his.

He grabbed her wrists, gripping until it hurt, and held her close. "Tease."

"Yup." She didn't try to pull away. The possession in his grip tantalized and enticed, and heated her from the inside out. "But we're not doing this on their front porch."

He dipped his head, so his lips were next to her ear, and whispered, "Some of the neighbors might like that."

"Probably." She tugged, not to get away, but to urge him toward the driveway. "You're driving this time. I'll grab my car later."

"Tate's not going to ask questions if you leave it here?"

"He's not stupid. He knows what's going on, at least on a vague level." She slid into the passenger seat when Damon held the door for her. He closed her in and hurried to the driver's side. She continued, as he started the car. "I haven't told them everything, but they see a lot."

"I get that from them. And even though they're your best friends, they're not who I want to talk about right now." He backed the car onto the road, tossed it into drive, and headed toward her condo.

She leaned back in the seat, feeling relaxed inside her own head for the first time in ages, without the haze of alcohol or the rush of endorphins.

He rested a hand on her knee, palm searing her even through slacks. "I'm guessing it's my fault you're wearing slacks instead of a skirt?"

"It is."

"So you came here straight from work?"

She covered his hand and slid it higher on her thigh. "I haven't come anywhere since Saturday night."

He trailed his fingers along the inside of her leg, lightly enough to tease but with enough pressure to keep from tickling. "The thing that sucks about this is we're stuck in traffic. I'm glad you don't live too far away."

"I didn't mean to imply anything." This was amazing. They had time. They could play or be rough. Span every inch of the spectrum. "We're talking when we get home, not fucking."

"We're talking now. You're going to be too hoarse to say much of anything in a few hours."

"That's a big promise." She'd pay for the taunt. She was counting on it. "I'm going to be disappointed if you can't deliver." When he glanced sideways at her, she stuck out her lower lip in an exaggerated pout.

He moved his hand back to his side of the car. "That's a lot of pressure. I don't know if I *can* live up to it. Maybe talking is a better idea." His tone stayed firm and confident despite the words, and he kept his attention trained on the road.

Concession wasn't the kind of punishment she had in mind. She could yield now, or push her luck and his limits. Fuck it. She'd yield later, either way. She undid the first two buttons on her blouse. "I can show you how to start, if you like."

He grabbed her wrist, digging his fingers into the skin and sending spikes of temptation through her. His voice was rough. "I'd definitely like, but not now. Don't touch yourself until I say so."

"Or what?"

He shot her a smirk. "Or you won't like the consequences."

"Are you going to discipline me?" she asked, hope sliding into her voice.

"Nope. I won't lay a finger on you."

She laughed and settled back in her seat. "God, you're a cruel bastard."

"And you love it."

She did. Every minute of it. Every second spent with him. It almost felt as if fourteen years melted away over the last seven days. It wouldn't be quite that easy, but they'd make it work. She had no doubt.

"You know, I *would* rather talk about your friends. How are they? How's the baby?"

He was being facetious, but the question brought a new kind of joy to the surface. A reminder of the news she'd wanted to share with everyone, before he distracted her. "They asked me to be the baby's godmother."

"That's fantastic." Damon's joy sounded like it matched hers. "I can't think of anyone better to spoil a kid rotten."

"You'll have to help." She didn't know where the comment came from. A frantic confession of love on someone else's front porch wasn't quite a promise to always be there. Except she had a feeling, in their case, it was. They had time to talk all that through, too.

He rested a hand on her leg again and squeezed. "Damn straight, I'll help."

It was harder than Damon expected to keep from pulling the car over and finding them a quiet spot, to fuck the hell out of Vivian, rather than finishing the drive to her place. Especially when the conversation shifted back to flirting.

After what felt like an eternity but was really only twenty minutes, they arrived. He felt like a giddy kid, intertwining his fingers with hers and fidgeting on the elevator ride up. Temptation surged inside, to press her against the wall and kiss her until he could think again. Once he started though, he wouldn't want to stop.

They finally made it inside her place and set their shoes by the front door. His cock was painfully rigid, straining against his jeans. He had a feeling that would be status quo around Vivian for a while. He pointed her toward the room she'd turned into a dance studio, and she hesitated.

He kissed up her neck and murmured against her skin, "Trust me."

"I do." She didn't resist this time, when he nudged her into the room and stopped her in the center, so she faced a wall covered in mirrors.

He circled his arms around her waist. "I want you to watch. No closing your eyes. I want you to see what I see when you're aroused. How gorgeous you are when you come."

She met his gaze in the mirror, uncertainty in her eyes. "I don't think it's going to do the same thing for me it does for you."

"No?" As he spoke, he unbuttoned her shirt. "But you get a thrill from stripping."

"That's different."

"And I think you'll like doing something different." He peeled her blouse off and set it aside, before forcing her attention back to their reflections. "Don't look away." He settled his palms on her stomach, then glided up, barely touching her skin and skimming her bra. The slight parting of her lips indicated she was enjoying this as much as he was. It wasn't that he wanted to see himself. The flush that spread across Vivian's cheeks—darkening as she grew more aroused—the way she licked her lips unconsciously, and the squirm of her body against his were the most beautiful sights he could think of.

She inhaled sharply when he brushed her nipples. He continued moving, following the curve of her torso in a fluid motion, down her back and to her hips. He kept his gaze trained on the reflection of hers, as he undid her slacks and let them drop to the ground, to pool around her ankles. Every time she gasped or whimpered, his body reacted. Tightening. Wanting more of her.

He had to pull his attention from the glass, to inspect his handiwork from Saturday night. Red marks peeked out from the edges of lace panties and trailed down the back of her legs, lashes already fading but not so much he couldn't tell exactly what they were. He drew his finger under the edge of the elastic, along her ass. "So gorgeous." He kissed along her shoulder, inhaling her sweet, intoxicating scent.

She pressed back into his touch with a sigh. "Pleased with yourself?"

"Only when you're my canvas. Kick your pants out of the way."

She followed the command, leaning more of her weight against him in the process and not moving away when she had her balance again.

"Keep watching." He skated his hands back up to her breasts and caressed the full mounds through the fabric. The coarse lace teased his fingertips, and his nerve endings sprang to life.

When he increased the pressure, squeezing clothing and flesh, she gasped and leaned into his touch. Her gaze stayed on the mirror. She bit her bottom lip hard enough for her teeth to leave a pale impression. Her reactions increased his need. She ground her ass against his jeans, digging denim into his hard, desperate cock, and he groaned. Anticipation clawed through him, and he forced himself to slow down. To think.

Okay, not really think so much. All the blood had already drained from his head. But at least to make sure she enjoyed herself. He focused his attention on her breasts for several minutes, pinching until she whimpered and then easing off when she drew in short gasps for air.

"You make the most intoxicating sounds." He nipped at her neck.

"Only with you."

"You're not begging tonight."

"Not yet." She nodded at the mirror. "I'm enjoying the show."

Her resolve was stronger than his right now. He appreciated the image in front of them, but it had the opposite effect of curbing his desire. "Dip your fingers in your pussy"— his voice brooked no argument—"then taste yourself."

In the glass and in front of him, manicured nails scraped down her smooth skin, and vanished beneath the waist of her lingerie. She gasped and arced her back when she parted her folds, and she slid her hand up and down, stroking herself.

He grabbed her wrist and let out a strained chuckle. "Soon."

She pouted, brought her fingers to her lips, and licked each one methodically before moving to the next.

"Stop posing, and appreciate the moment," he warned.

"You told me it was like stripping."

"I told you it was different." He covered her hand with his and guided it down. "Watch. Enjoy." With both their fingers, he sought out her slit, pressing the fabric of her panties as they stroked.

She squirmed under his touch, and his pulse roared with need. He shoved their fingers to her clit, rubbing and stroking in time with her thrusting hips. If she bumped his cock much faster, he was going to come. He bit back the impulse, and massaged her button harder.

Her soft cries and the way she writhed under his touch told him she was close.

He kissed the edge of her ear and whispered, "Lose yourself in it."

She closed her eyes and leaned back her head, mouth open in a silent scream, as she came, bucking against their hands, her legs tightening and then wobbling.

He helped her turn to face him. The scents of sex, floor wax, and her shampoo dove into his mind and purged any remaining thoughts beyond instinct. He knotted his hand in her hair and crushed his mouth to hers. Her soft lips against his sparked his hunger. The need to be in her. A part of her.

Barely aware of their surroundings, he half-guided her back, half-stumbled along with her, to a waist-high cabinet against the wall. He was done with the mirror. He wanted to watch *her*. Experience as much of her as possible. He jerked his jeans open, possibly breaking the zipper. He didn't know, and he didn't care. His cock was swollen and purple with need. It jerked against his hand.

She scooted onto the cabinet and hooked her legs around his waist. "Fuck me hard, baby." Pleading filled her words.

Yes. Hard. Fast. Unrelenting. That was what he needed. He positioned the head of his dick at her opening and thrust inside her. The tight seal sucked him deeper, and his head swam. Only the most primitive noises made sense. Her moans of pleasure. His grunting. The creak of furniture, as he slammed against her again. And again.

Her face blossomed in that amazing expression again—the bliss of climax. Flushed. Breathing heavily. Lost in her own world. She clenched around him when she came, squeezing and coaxing. He tightened his fingers on her hips, not daring to let go. Not sure he could. *Thrust.* God she felt good. *Thrust.* He wouldn't last much longer. *Thrust.* Were those stars in his vision? *Thrust.* He growled as he came, spilling inside her. Still unable to stop. He pounded until he was spent, and she sank into him, breathless.

"I'm so glad you tracked me down this evening." Her voice wavered with exhaustion.

"Me too, Vi." He kissed the top of her head. "I'm so grateful you heard me out." And maybe once they fed this intense need to be a part of each other a few more times, they'd ease off and spend more time out doing things.

Though honestly, he hoped for many more weekends of fooling around in the shower, watching bad movies dressed in next to nothing, and ordering takeout. They had time, though. For the first time in over a decade, he felt like they had time.

TWENTY

As far as Vivian was concerned, declarations of love were great—wonderful and amazing even—but they didn't solve all the problems. She straightened her suit, using her reflection in the full-length mirror, on the back of her closet. Her gaze kept drifting back to the view of Damon's sleeping form. The simple reminder of the night before sent a new rush of heat through her.

Since he'd never been a fan of mornings, and he didn't have a schedule today, she let him sleep as long as possible. She'd wanted to wake up slowly. Spend the day lounging in bed. Finish the conversations that kept them up past midnight last night. Luxuriating wasn't something she could afford today, though; she slept too late as it was. However, there was one conversation that was best started now.

She fiddled with the key in her hand, looking between it and Damon. How could something so small feel weightless and as heavy as the universe at the same time?

As the time neared critical, she perched on the edge of the bed, careful not to wrinkle her work clothes. Her heart hammered in her chest so loudly, she was surprised he didn't stir. She reached for his shoulder, to nudge him awake, and he grabbed her wrist.

She grinned when he lazily opened his eyes. "You big faker," she said with a light laugh.

"Never with you." He sat and brushed a quick kiss over her lips. "Do you need me to leave, so you can get to work?"

Leave. She hated the sound of the word. She set the key on the nightstand, its imprint marring her palm where she'd gripped it. "Take your time. If you're still here when I get home—or here again—I won't complain."

He raised his brows. "I hate to say this, but I need you to define what you mean. Tell me what you're expecting." He met her gaze. "So I don't assume and overstay my welcome."

"I don't know." There was what she wanted, and then there were the obstacles reality placed in the way. She scooted closer, so her knee rested against his. "I keep thinking I don't want you to go, now that you're finally here. On the other hand, even if you don't currently have a job, you have a career and a life on the other side of the country."

"I've spent so much time on the road over the last few years, I don't know I'd call what I have in Seattle a life."

She slid her fingers under his. "Be that as it may, right now the key is an open invitation to come and go as you please." She hesitated on the next words. She rehearsed them infinite times in the shower, and if he were anyone else, she'd say what was on her mind without pause. But this thing between them, so old and new at the same time, scared her. Not for what it was, but because it was fresh enough, it might be a fluke. There was no foundation for her fear, other than she'd already lost out on this once, and she didn't want to again.

There was more to them than a handful of fleeting tumbles, but she worried anyway. She dragged the words past her doubt. "I don't know if you've got any irons in the fire, work-wise, but there are a lot of good firms here."

He searched her face. "Actually"—he dragged the word out—"the more I think about it, I know exactly where I want to be practicing, and the job is a pretty sure thing. I have an in with the decision makers."

Her heart paused, and even when it restarted, it limped at a tentative pace. It wasn't only his vague words; it was the hesitation in his delivery. Noticeable uncertainty wasn't supposed to be in Damon's wheelhouse, and she didn't know how to interpret it. He hadn't had time to interview here, unless he'd been thinking about it before he quit yesterday. "Where are you going?" she finally asked.

"The foundation's been looking for someone to bring on, full time. A person with actual legal experience, to always be available to consult, so people don't have to wait this long for us to find them an attorney. It's a remote position that can be done from anywhere, but we haven't been able to fill it because it doesn't pay what a lot of experienced lawyers are used to making."

He sucked in a deep breath, and exhaled slowly, as if cementing his next words before speaking. "How do you feel about dating a guy who's not even making half what you are?"

That was his hesitation? Relief flooded her. And he'd said *dating*. She liked the sound of this a lot. "As long as it's you, I don't care if you're flipping burgers. Though, I'll be honest. I think stripping would be a better use of your talents than working a grill."

He shook his head. "I'm going to leave that to you, but I do think I'll hook myself up with the foundation job."

"Do you have to run it by the other board members?" Her question was a teasing jab, since his brother, Ethan, and Ethan's girlfriend, Jaycie, had some serious pull when it came to decisions there.

"I may have to grovel a little, but I'll swallow my pride on this one."

Happiness danced inside her, twirling and pirouetting. "Does that mean you'll be coming and going regularly?"

"I hope to be coming a lot more than going, but if you're asking, my answer is yes." He pressed his mouth to hers, drawing out the kiss until she was breathless.

She was reluctant to stand. She had to be in the office on time but didn't want to go. "I'll see you after work, then."

He rose, tugged her to her feet, and slapped her ass. "I'll be here." He promised.

Four Months Later

Damon pulled the car into Tate's driveway, and Vivian held up her hand, so the garage light hit her fingers. The solitaire diamond against titanium sparkled in the fading evening. Damon slid his hand under hers, palm up, and intertwined their fingers. "You're staring at that ring more than you're paying attention to me."

She squeezed his hand. "Jealous?"

"Not for a second." He kissed the back of her hand. "But you're hesitating. Are you embarrassed of me?"

She glanced at Tate's front door and shook her head. "Absolutely not. Just still amazed this is real."

"Vividly and intensely." He stepped from the car and hurried to her side, to open the door. It only took him a few weeks after things settled down, to realize at least one evening a week, she and her friends hung out at someone's house. They'd quickly accepted him as part of the ritual, despite the occasional jabs about his poor taste in previous jobs. He'd never been part of such a close-knit group before.

He took her hand again, and they strode to the front door. The last few months had been hectic. Selling his place on the west coast. Finding a week Vivian was free to fly to Seattle with him, grab his things, and take their time driving home. Getting used to a new job. The time with her was worth it though, and the way she'd looked when he proposed was priceless. Next step was telling her friends.

They walked into the house without knocking. He'd had to get used to this custom on get-together nights as well. In his world, coworkers were people you said goodnight to and were happy to not see unless it was required. It was nice to be a part of something friendlier.

They were the last to arrive. Jared and Mikki sat on the sofa. Alyssia was on Tate's lap, in one of the easy chairs. Pretty standard sight.

Damon headed toward the baby in her playpen and picked her up. "Hey, genius."

Holly cooed and wriggled her fingers. Tate insisted each time she did that, she was waving. Alyssia argued four months wasn't old enough for that.

"Shiny," Mikki said. "Is that…?"

"Yeah." Vivian 's grin sounded in her voice. "Absolutely is."

"Let me see." Mikki insisted.

Damon set Holly back in her pen, as the adult version of *ooh*s and *ahh*s filled the room. Hugs, handshakes, and congratulations squished Damon and Vivian together. He couldn't take his gaze off her, though—the way her face lit up as she leaned into him, the flush on her cheeks, the happy sparkle in eyes far more beautiful than the diamond she wore.

He wrapped an arm around her waist and pulled her closer. It might have taken them almost two decades to get here, but it was worth it, to have this now, with her. He didn't regret anything he'd surrendered to be by her side. He finally made the right choices.

***

IF YOU'RE LOOKING for another sexy, angsty age gap romance, you want HARD FLIP. Ash is one paycheck from being homeless, and she just lost her job. She and her sister will be out on the street if she doesn't find a solution fast. Mischa's got the perfect proposal, but their fake engagement has more complications than either of them expected.

- Grab HARD FLIP today

***

FOR ANOTHER SEXY best friend's little sister romance, check out RESTRAINT. He's the CEO of one of the world's largest adult websites, she's his best friend's little sister… and a virgin. She should be off limits, but he can't stop fantasizing about unwrapping her under the Christmas tree.

- Start reading RESTRAINT today

IF YOU'RE LOOKING for another sexy, heart wrenching second chance romance, check out REGRET. Loss and grief bring Jonathan back to the small town where he spent his childhood summers. Baily, his best friend from back in the day, isn't happy to see him. When a hurricane strands them together, they have no choice but to confront their pasts.

- Click here to start REGRET today.

TO KEEP up to date on new releases and other news from Allyson Lindt, click here to subscribe to my newsletter.

PLEASE HELP this author's career by posting an honest review wherever you purchased this book.